Blood Curse

SHARON PAGE

APHRODISIA

KENSINGTON PUBLISHING CORP.
www.kensingtonbooks.com

Kensington Publishing Corp.
119 West 40th Street
New York, NY 10018

All Kensington titles, imprints, and distributed lines are available at special quantity discounts for bulk purchases for sales promotion, premiums, fund-raising, and educational or institutional use.

Special book excerpts or customized printings can also be created to fit specific needs. For details, write or phone the office of the Kensington Special Sales Manager: Kensington Publishing Corp., 119 West 40th Street, New York, NY 10018. Attn. Special Sales Department. Phone: 1-800-221-2647.

Aphrodisia and the A logo Reg. U. S. Pat. & TM Off.

ISBN-13: 978-0-7582-7831-9
ISBN-10: 0-7582-7831-4
First Kensington Trade Paperback Printing: November 2013

eISBN-13: 978-0-7582-7832-6
eISBN-10: 0-7582-7832-2
First Kensington Electronic Edition: November 2013

10 9 8 7 6 5 4 3 2 1

Printed in the United States of America

Praise for the "Blood Series" novels by Sharon Page

BLOOD FIRE

2013 Finalist for the WisRWA Write Touch Award for Erotic Romance
2013 Finalist for the Golden Quill Award for Erotic Romance

"An unusual allegiance of villains adds special interest to this love story. It's not your typical Regency romance, but is laced with the era's flair and imbued with the full flavor of a paranormal. Page's imaginative character development and an exciting plot are well worth the read."—*RT Book Reviews*

BLOOD SECRET

2013 Finalist for the WisRWA Write Touch Award for Erotic Romance
2013 Finalist for the Colorado Award of Excellent for Erotic Romance
2012 Finalist for the *RT Book Reviews* Reviewers' Choice Award for Erotic Paranormal

"[A] well-crafted page turner with intense sexual situations. It's a lovely take on the fairy-tale theme and a compelling story of lovers making sacrifices."—*RT Book Reviews*

BLOOD WICKED

2012 Colorado Award of Excellence Winner for Erotic Romance
2012 Finalist for the *RT Book Reviews* Reviewers' Choice Award for Erotic Paranormal

"Sexy vampires, damsels in distress, and lots of hot sex in Regency-era London—what's not to love? Page is a master at steamy scenes that leave the reader begging for more and this latest is sure to please. A thrilling, intrigue-filled plot and a hero worth dying for make this one a keeper." —*RT Book Reviews*

Books by Sharon Page

BLOOD CURSE

BLOOD FIRE

BLOOD SECRET

"Wicked for Christmas" in
SILENT NIGHT, SINFUL NIGHT

BLOOD WICKED

BLOOD DEEP

BLOOD RED

BLOOD ROSE

BLACK SILK

HOT SILK

SIN

"Midnight Man" in WILD NIGHTS

Acknowledgments

Some stories are fun to write from beginning to end, and *Blood Curse* was one of those stories. Thank you so much to the wonderful team at Kensington who make the process of creating a book so thrilling. I'd like to extend a special thanks to my wonderful editor, Audrey LaFehr, for her terrific support and encouragement, and for being so savvy, so talented, and so much fun to work with. I'd like to give a shout-out to Martin Biro, assistant extraordinaire, for taking care of so many things.

As always, a big thank you goes to my agent, Jessica Faust of BookEnds, LLC, who is always there to talk, help, share laughter, and give great advice. And I am forever grateful to my writing friends—writing a book involves a lot of solitary time with a computer, so it is wonderful to have people to talk to who understand.

Of course, this story wouldn't exist without the help and support of my family. I can't say thank you enough.

And to the readers—it is so wonderful to share stories with you all. An extra special thank you to you.

1

Kidnapped

"Dear heaven," Lady Ophelia Black murmured, as her fingers stroked the firm curve of the naked male bottom in front of her.

Even through her gloves she felt the smooth coolness of the Italian marble. The stone was spectacular. *Flawless.* Her fingers trembled a little more as they dipped into the shadowed indents of the statue's haunches, then followed the upper swell of the buttocks to the tight valley between.

Ophelia had never seen an actual man without clothes. But whoever had modeled for this statue was male perfection. Before she'd seen this incredible work of art, she'd had no idea how beautiful a naked man's bottom could be when it was made of firm muscle.

It was truly one of the most magnificent sculptures she'd ever seen.

She'd thought her own work was quite good—the dabbling she'd done with clay and more recently with stone. Faced with this homage to a ridiculously handsome man, she was humbled.

And nervous.

Ophelia flicked her tongue over her lower lip and looked

around. Except for her and two dozen statues of naked men, the gallery was empty.

Fires burned in twin fireplaces, one at each end of the room, and several candles cast a golden glow around her. Warm, bright, and inviting, the room should have filled her with a sense of welcome.

But where was her hostess, Lady Cresthaven?

Why did she have the creepy sensation she was being watched?

This room in Lady Cresthaven's home on Mount Street overlooked the rear of the house and a walled-in garden. The footman had referred to it as the gallery. He had told her Lady Cresthaven would be down momentarily.

But that had been at least a half hour ago.

Ophelia stopped stroking the beautiful marble piece in front of her. She paced between the pale, silent males. Resentment bubbled up. She was too nervous to really savor the remarkable . . . artwork surrounding her.

It had been a Herculean endeavor to sneak out of Mrs. Darkwell's house tonight. She had locked her bedroom door from the inside, but Mrs. Darkwell had a key, and if Darky decided to check if Ophelia was in her bed, the woman would learn the truth. Over the last few weeks, Ophelia had crafted a key to unlock the bars on her window—one of the advantages of having sculpting tools. Scooting out onto the window ledge, she had climbed down the side of the house, using ivy and window ledges. Since she'd been kept locked up for years, she'd barely had the strength to hold on. Twice she'd almost fallen.

But she'd made it safely down the ivy. She had taken a *huge* risk to come. Heaven only knew how she would be punished for her escape if she were caught. How dare Lady Cresthaven keep her waiting?

Ophelia walked around the statue whose bottom she had touched.

It was only to marvel at the stunning quality of the marble and the remarkably fine depiction of muscle.

Merely artistic appreciation of a sculptor's fine work.

That was all. Truly.

She was an innocent and she always would be. Touching *statues* of men was as close as she would ever be able to get to intimacy—

"Good evening."

It was a smooth, deep, seductive drawl—a voice dipped in chocolate—and it almost made her jump out of her half-boots. It was a *man's* voice.

One of the statues had come to life—

No, that was insane. They were marble. The voice had come from a real man. She was not alone after all . . . and her mysterious man had seen her grope a statue's bottom.

Her cheeks heated like bread put in a roaring oven. She was so embarrassed. She didn't want to face this man.

From somewhere in the middle of the sea of white marble people, the voice asked, "Do you like my friend's collection, Lady Ophelia?"

"I—I thought I was alone."

"You aren't. Though I have to admit, you do have a gentle touch."

Floor. Open. Now.

But the floor did not swallow her. A shadow moved between two white statues. No, not shadow. It was a gentleman with raven hair, large black eyes ringed with long, thick black lashes. As if he'd planned to disappear into the dark, the man wore a tailcoat of indigo, black trousers, and startlingly a shirt and waistcoat of black. From beneath a black beaver hat, a rugged face lit up with pleasure as he gazed at her, his lips quirking up in a hint of a smile.

Ophelia recognized him with shock, "Mr. Ravenhunt?"

"I hope you will forgive my ruse, my dear," he said softly.

"Ruse? The invitation from Lady Cresthaven, you mean?"

"Yes, my dear. I sent it."

She stared at his full, firm lips, mesmerized by the way his dimple winked and the lines at his mouth moved as he spoke. She felt strange inside—too hot, achy, as if she might be coming down with something. This happened every time she thought of Mr. Ravenhunt.

She'd met him on the very first afternoon she had escaped from Mrs. Darkwell's School for Young Ladies—the house that was Ophelia's prison, not a school. Swathed in a cloak with her hood pulled low to hide her face, she had crept into the museum just before it had closed.

It had been her dream to see the Elgin Marbles and the other Grecian statuary on display. She wasn't allowed to go out at all.

And she had to go when it was quiet—she couldn't risk accidentally touching an innocent museum-goer.

Then, just as the guard had informed her she only had a few minutes left, Mr. Ravenhunt had appeared. He'd struck up a conversation with her as they both studied a statue of an Olympian athlete crouched with a discus.

They had carefully avoided mentioning the athlete was naked.

Then Mr. Ravenhunt had walked her home—well, close to her home, so she could sneak through the mews, get in through the backyard, and climb up the back wall. It had been dark early, since it was still early spring.

It had been her first daring afternoon of freedom. She'd escaped more times, returning to the museum, and Mr. Ravenhunt had met her there almost each time.

Now, as she had to do each time she saw him, Ophelia took a step back. She could not let him get too close. She could hurt him—even kill him—if he touched her. She would do it even though she didn't want to hurt him.

That was what her awful power did.

His black eyebrows lifted as she retreated. Then she bumped something hard. Mr. Ravenhunt looked as if he was fighting to smother a laugh.

Ophelia jerked around.

Oh, it figured, didn't it? She had backed into a statue—into the front parts of a male statue, which had been depicted as aroused and erect. And very, very large.

Mr. Ravenhunt managed to quell his smile. "You are afraid of me?" he asked.

"No." She wasn't, actually. She was not afraid of what he would do to her. She was thoroughly terrified of what she might do to him.

A soft, kind look came to his eyes. They were absolutely black, so there was no difference between iris and pupil, which made them look striking and unusual. They glittered in the light. Framed by thick, long lashes, they were stunning.

She couldn't tell him the truth about her wretched, cursed power. She couldn't bear to watch him run away from her, too.

He bowed to her, an elegant bow that made her catch her breath.

"I shouldn't have used a lie to bring you here," he said. "I am sorry about that, but I had no choice. It was not as if I could send you a note inviting you to my home."

"No," she said again. He could not have sent a letter to her to ask to meet. It wasn't done—not letters from unmarried gentlemen to unmarried ladies. Especially not to ladies who weren't . . . normal and who were locked up to protect the world.

Ophelia wished she could think of more to say, other than parroting "no." But in her head, a voice warned: *Run, before you hurt him.*

"Lady Cresthaven was willing to play along with my game," he continued. "She met you at the museum per my instructions. Fortunately you came back as you had done every day."

He smiled once more. His lower lip was full and pouty. His mouth was more beautiful than those on any of the statues.

"I thought you would not be able to resist this collection, Lady Ophelia." He stepped toward her.

She tore her longing gaze away from his mouth. She *couldn't* kiss him. Or touch him. Or let him touch her.

"Thank you for thinking of me." Ophelia winced. The words sounded prim. Daft.

But what could she do? Since the first moment she'd seen this man, she'd been obsessed by him. At night, she made sculptures of him with clay. She had made one of his whole body, and in that one, she'd tried to guess what he looked like without any clothes.

She'd done them quickly and sloppily, driven by a mad passion to make something that looked so much like Mr. Ravenhunt that she could pretend she was caressing *him*, the actual man.

But she had to destroy her sculptures before morning, before Mrs. Darkwell could see them.

"You are very quiet." Ravenhunt's brows dipped in worry.

His face looked much younger than he behaved. From his relaxed manner of speaking with her, his lighthearted teasing, he showed obvious experience with women. She had guessed he must be almost thirty. But here, in the brilliant light of the chandelier, she thought his face looked like that of a young man in his early twenties.

"Are you so angry with me?" he asked.

"No. It's just—" Lying was so awkward, but it was all she could do. Why had he lured her here? What if he hoped for— for something like a kiss?

"I cannot . . . do anything," she said. How awkward she sounded. She would scare him away by sounding like such a ninny.

"I assure you I had no intentions of seduction, Lady Ophelia."

The day they'd met, she had given him her real name. It had been a very dangerous thing to do. But she had not spoken to a gentleman in years. Not since she had almost killed her fiancé just by kissing him. Not since she had been taken away to Mrs. Darkwell.

Mr. Ravenhunt took a step closer. He held out his hand, an invitation for touching.

"No!" she cried. She edged around the statue, no longer caring how embarrassed she should be to take cover behind a naked man with an enormous erect ... thing. "You mustn't touch me."

Ravenhunt dipped his handsome head in acknowledgment. "You will notice I am wearing gloves, Lady Ophelia. I believe you can't hurt me if I'm wearing gloves."

Ophelia almost toppled over. "You know about me? How could you know? That's impossible." Not even her family—all the family she had remaining—knew the whole truth about her power. Only Mrs. Darkwell did.

Gloves did nothing. She could hurt him no matter what he wore.

He grinned, a rakish smile of pure amusement. "I know everything about you. A kidnapper should know everything he can about his victim. Especially one as dangerous as you, Lady Ophelia."

Kidnapper? "What are you talking about?"

He surged forward, his long strides closing the short distance between them. Ophelia's heart seemed to take off in flight, pushing hard against her chest. But her legs tarried before they caught up.

Stupid, stupid legs.

She took two stumbling steps, and something grabbed her

from behind. It had to be his hand. She screamed. He jerked back, she almost fell, but he caught her and a white cloth clamped over her face.

His hand pressed it hard over her nose and mouth.

A scent like burned sugar filled her senses—a sickly, nauseating, sweet smell. Her legs wobbled beneath her. Desperate, she grasped Mr. Ravenhunt's forearm. She would have better luck pushing a carriage. His arm didn't budge.

She was touching him. She would kill him.

She shouldn't care!

She tried not to breathe, but of course, she had to draw in some air. Dizziness took command of her head. Ophelia tried to scream, but that only drew in more of the disgusting smell.

Blackness swept her up, thick and enveloping, and she realized with heart-stopping panic she was falling to the floor . . .

"Is it done?"

The voice came to him from behind a small grille placed within a heavy oak door. There was no light in the room, but as a vampire, the former Marquis of Ravenhunt could easily see in the dark.

His mysterious client had arranged that they meet here, in an abandoned church near the docks. The overwhelming scent of old spices and dust clogged his nose, and he could easily scent the fetid odor of river water and the ditches of sewage.

As with their other meetings, Ravenhunt—or Raven as he now called himself—stood in the dark, gloomy, long unused nave. His client would remain in the chancel, hidden by the rood screen that separated the spaces. Raven was forbidden to enter that other space. He had never seen the man who had paid him to kidnap Lady Ophelia Black.

The man claimed to be a vampire also. Raven did not know if that was true. Definitely his client was not human. Raven would have smelled that on him.

Raven had gone through numerous battles. As a mortal, he had fought in the war against Napoleon, then traveled to the exotic East, where he'd fought in uprisings in Ceylon. In Ceylon he had been turned. Returning to England as a vampire, he had allowed his family to believe him dead. His cousin had become the marquis, and Raven lived in isolation, acting as a kind of mercenary.

After all, when a gentleman was cursed to live forever, he had to do something to pass the time.

Approached by his mysterious client, he had become intrigued by the man's interest—and determination—to have Lady Ophelia. Raven had refused the commission, claiming he would not do it until he understood the man's motivation. To get him to take the job, his client had been forced to reveal the young woman's power.

The truth had annoyed Raven. She had the power to kill with a touch, and his "client" had at first refused to divulge it. So now he drawled lazily, "Yes, it's done. I have her."

"Good. Bring her—"

"I did not say I was going to give her up."

Silence from behind the door. Then the man barked, "What?"

"Now that I have her, I intend to keep her."

Raven turned abruptly and made his way through the dark, dank church. He passed pews coated with dust, and the various trappings of religious devotion, encrusted with dirt and hung with spider webs. His lip curled.

He had turned his back on his god a long time ago. When he had begun to be haunted by the faces of the men he'd killed. Every death had been justified. In the duels, he had defended his honor. In battle he had been fighting for king, country, God. So why was his soul ravaged by what he'd done? Why was he tearing himself apart over it?

He'd begun to understand that God did not reward a man

for obedient service. God only increased the level of punishment.

So he'd turned his back on God, lost his soul, become a vampire. Even in this deserted, long-abandoned church he felt pain. His skin sizzled, beginning to burn beneath his clothes.

Scrambling footsteps told him his client was following. Chasing him. Driven out of hiding by the fact his lowly hired assassin was in control now and had changed the rules of the game.

Chuckling, Raven ran through the church so quickly everything became a formless blur. If his client was in truth a vampire, the man could follow. But the footsteps receded quickly. Bursting out into a dingy, dark street, Raven shifted shape. His clothes dropped from him as his body changed, as his skin turned to something sleeker. He was naked when large wings erupted from his back.

Unlike other vampires, he did not turn into a bat. He became a creature like a gargoyle, with a distorted human-like body. Instead of feet and hands, he possessed talons. His skin became a silvery black. Flapping his wings, he soared into the night sky.

To return to his lovely prisoner, Lady Ophelia.

Her mouth was as dry as linen and her throat ached.

Dizzy, Ophelia opened her eyes. But wherever she was, there was very little light and she couldn't tell what surrounded her. Fear made her heart thunder. Her arms were stiff and sore, and she felt as if she'd rolled down a grassy hill—she ached all over. Softness was beneath her and silkiness touched the skin of her legs . . .

The *bare* skin of her legs.

Ophelia blinked, fighting to see in the dim light. A fire burned low in the grate—it was just coals—and the reddish glow barely illuminated anything. Hulking shapes loomed around her. It took minutes before she guessed one was a wardrobe, another was a vanity table, and two fluttering things that made her heart skip a beat were curtains.

Was she at home?

There was something wrong, but she couldn't quite remember what it was . . .

She couldn't remember coming back across town to Mrs. Darkwell's supposed school or sneaking back into her room. How could she have forgotten all of that—?

She hadn't come home! This wasn't her room at Mrs. Darkwell's.

The last thing she remembered was that sweet, horrible smell. The cloth pressed to her nose and the naked statues whirling in front of her eyes as she collapsed.

Mr. Ravenhunt must have brought her here. He had taken off her *gown*. She thought she was wearing only her shift. She couldn't be certain.

How dare that wretched man do this!

Heavens, *why* had he done this? What did he want with her?

She wanted to get up, but now she felt dizzy again. She knew why she felt lost and confused. It was the aftermath of whatever he'd given her to make her faint.

She fought the woozy sense in her head. Summoning her strength, Ophelia tried to move her arms.

She pulled with all the force she could muster, but her arms would not obey.

She now realized her hands were numb. There was something around her wrists. Furrowing her brow, she made her fingers explore. She touched rope, silky rope. It looped around her wrists and stretched her arms behind her head.

She was tied up. Tied to a *bed*.

The prisoner of Mr. Ravenhunt.

"Fool. Idiot. Twit." Enraged, she threw the words out. "You

silly, silly fool. You believed every word he said. You thought—"
She knew what she'd thought, but this she could not say aloud.

From the first moment they had met, she'd fancied he admired her. It had been so long since she had been near a man that the moment he had smiled at her, she had concocted a ludicrous fantasy about it.

Love, kindness, embraces, tenderness were not for her. She was a *monster*.

And she had allowed herself to be fooled by a monster worse than she.

What did he want from her? Was he a white slaver and she was to be shipped away to Arabia and put in a harem? Was he going to ransom her?

Her harsh, bitter laugh echoed in her quiet room.

Who would pay for her? No doubt Mrs. Darkwell would be happy to be rid of her.

Her family thought she was dead. Mrs. Darkwell had told her that. Her last living brother and her younger sister had been told that to protect them.

"Damnation!" Ophelia spat aloud. She pulled on the ropes, but all it did was drive the thick cord into her wrists. It hurt.

She knew there were men who assaulted women and forced sexual relations upon them. Was Ravenhunt a man like that?

If he was, he was an idiot. The minute he laid a hand on her, he was as good as dead.

He'd already touched her. He had done so to hold the cloth on her face and bring her here. He might be dead already.

With her weak fingers, she tried to find the knots at her wrists. Even though he would die if he touched her—might already be dead—she was afraid. He had worn gloves. So had others, who had then . . . died, but the touches had been longer. Some had just become very sick. What if he had not touched her long enough for her curse to work? What if he had not touched her very much to bring her here? He could have tossed her in a sack after all.

What if he just wanted to kill her?

He could do it safely with a pistol or a blade. He could hurt or murder her without touching her. After all, he knew what she was. What if he wanted to kill her because he thought she was evil?

Her power *was* evil. But she didn't mean to hurt people. It was something she could not control. To protect other people from her power, she kept away from them.

Closing her eyes, Ophelia made a solemn vow. If she made it back alive to Mrs. Darkwell's house, she would never leave it again. She would never break a rule again.

First she had to escape from Ravenhunt.

The fiend had tied her wrists and secured her bonds to the bedposts. She could reach the knots at her left wrist with her right hand, but no matter how much she tugged and clawed, she could not loosen the ropes.

Roaring in anger, Ophelia pulled wildly at them, but that only made them tighter. Her legs were free and she kicked and slammed the bed, but it didn't help.

Tears burned in her eyes, but she wouldn't cry. She had cried over so many people—people she had killed with her wretched power. She would not waste tears now. Exhausted from useless thrashing and fighting, she lay still.

A board creaked in the hallway.

She froze with fear. Was it Ravenhunt? Was he alive? Her heart galloped and she sucked in frantic breaths, her brain swamped by panic.

Think, Ophelia.

All she had to do was coerce Ravenhunt to touch her without his gloves and do it long enough for her curse to work on him.

Then what?

There might be other men here. Servants. She had to get past them, too—

The door creaked open.

"I assume you are awake now, Lady Ophelia?"

Deep, like the rumble of a lion, his masculine voice came to her. He was alive. He spoke mildly and softly, but in the tones of a gentleman who felt he was in charge. Smugness infused Mr. Ravenhunt's every word.

He would not be smug for long. If he touched her long enough, her cursed power would affect him, and then he would pay for kidnapping her.

That thought banished fear. Instead, anger blazed in her heart as how evilly pleased with himself he sounded.

"Yes, I am awake, you foul blackguard." She snapped the words at him, sounding utterly unlike herself. Usually her voice was so soft it could barely be heard. But her angry shout must have been heard by everyone in the house.

A dark shadow filled the doorway. With so little light, it was hard to distinguish him at first. It occurred to her he carried no candle or lamp and he had walked up a dark corridor to this room without trouble.

This must be his house. Apparently he knew it well.

He wore his dark clothing and his hair was black, so she could barely see him. "I demand that you untie me. Now!"

He shrugged. "I am considering it. I'm not sure which one I prefer."

"*What?*"

"I cannot decide if I prefer having you tied to the bed in that erotically fetching way, or having you free so I can see what you would attempt to do to me."

Nausea roiled in her belly. Erotically fetching?

She could make out a little more of him where he stood in

the doorway. It was not easy to see him. She had to rest her cheek against the pillow to do it.

Mr. Ravenhunt's shoulder was propped against the door frame, his arms folded over his chest. Relaxation exuded from him. Obviously, he wasn't afraid that anyone else in the house—servants, for example—would learn she was his captive. They all must know.

She wanted to spit on him. But years with Mrs. Darkwell had taught her to pretend to be a docile prisoner, to bide her time.

But she had never been in such a vulnerable position in her life.

"Please untie me." It took every ounce of control she possessed, but Ophelia spoke in the meekest voice she could.

"Not just yet, my dear. You look very appealing this way."

The softness of his voice sent a shiver of terror down her spine. What *did* he want from her?

"Please . . . my arms ache. I'm frightened. Do you mean . . . to kill me?" There, she'd asked it.

"No, Lady Ophelia, I do not mean you any harm. In fact, I might be the closest thing to a savior you have. Now wait there. There is something I must do—to ensure your safety. Then I will be back."

Ravenhunt drove his curricle into the stews that ran off Whitechapel High Street. He had no coachman, kept no servants.

He'd lived alone in his rented house on the outskirts of Mayfair ever since he'd returned to England. Lady Ophelia was the only other person who had been in it.

He slapped the reins sharply to set his two blacks galloping down the cobbled street. With expert touch, he veered around carts and slow carriages.

In London, none of the naïve and innocent mortals had any idea what monsters prowled their streets. Some vampires hunted the elegant, wider boulevards of Mayfair, or the dark streets surrounding the gentleman's clubs and gaming hells. For the purpose of feeding, Ravenhunt now came here, to the maze of intertwined, narrow lanes, and rickety buildings packed with unfortunates.

When he'd first been a vampire, he'd been driven by lust and hunger. Too many of his victims had been fair maidens or voluptuous courtesans. He tried to forget their faces now. Those pretty faces wild with lust as he'd drunk their blood, then white with fear as they understood he was taking their lives along with their blood.

The prettiest ones he had changed into vampires, then abandoned.

He alighted from his carriage and tied the reins to a post. With his gray coat swinging around him, he strode deeper into the stews, passing through a narrow passage onto a dark, stinking lane.

"Slumming, Ravenhunt?"

"Feeding," he answered brusquely. "I don't hunt fragile maidens anymore, wolf. I like my prey bigger and stronger. Unlike you, I like my food with fight."

The wolf was the Duke of Wolfcairn, prowling the stews in human form. As a human male, he was two inches taller than Ravenhunt. He was lean, with black hair and a shock of white-gray in it. The wolf's laugh held the undercurrent of a growl. "I don't prey on the weak or the fair either, Ravenhunt."

Wolfcairn wore a gentleman's attire and carried a gold-tipped walking stick. Ravenhunt dressed to disappear.

"I forgot. You aren't Ravenhunt anymore. Gave that up to your young cousin. Too cowardly to keep up the ruse of mortality?"

Damn, he hated encountering Wolfcairn. The wolf liked to

goad him—just as Wolfcairn liked to goad all the outcasts of the demon world who hunted here, in the depths of darkness, dirt, and poverty.

Raven was an outcast. He avoided all members of the demon world, like other vampires, wolf and dragon shifters, warlocks, satyrs.

There were many vampires in London. The vampire queens controlled different clans. There were even the "tamed" vampires who belonged to the Royal Society for the Investigation of Mysterious Phenomena.

Raven claimed no allegiance to any queen or any vampire clan.

In the shadows, Raven saw a warlock perform magic tricks with handkerchiefs and flowers to dazzle a large-bosomed lady-bird who had been waiting on the street corner in a low-cut velvet dress.

Raven came here for blood, as did the wolf. Others, like the warlocks, came for sex.

"I am not cowardly," he said coldly. "I gave up my life and title to protect someone I love. You are damned arrogant, Wolf-cairn, and bloody stupid to keep your title. Unlike you, I don't need a title to prove my power and superiority."

"Indeed? What about a wager? A thousand pounds' wager that, if we chase the same prey, I will catch it first."

"I don't have time tonight."

"No time? We have eternity, man," Wolfcairn pointed out.

"Someone is at my home, waiting for me."

He remembered what Lady Ophelia had looked like. Stretched out on the bed and tied up.

Lovely, slender limbs. Her shift had been soft, clinging muslin that draped damned fetchingly over her pert, pretty breasts. Her golden hair had fallen from her pins, and it flowed around her in a halo of shimmering waves. Innocence shone in her big blue eyes.

Hades, it was like handing a six-year-old boy a cream cake and warning him not to eat it.

His cock had been going mad in his trousers, throbbing, pulsing, and bucking against the placket.

And her neck—

Pure temptation. Ivory skin, soft and perfect.

He had to get control of his hunger. He couldn't bite her and feed from her. So he'd come here to do it instead.

"Why aren't with her, you fool?" Wolfcairn asked. "Why hunt for prey in here when you have a delectable treat at home?"

"Never mind, wolf," Raven growled. "I accept your wager."

A woman's sobs reached his ears. He saw the wolfman turn his head toward the sound and tip up his nose as if he was scenting.

"A female in distress?" Wolfcairn asked.

"Probably a dockyard brute abusing some poor, bedraggled street tart."

"The perfect appetizer," the duke said. "I will even give you a head start, vampire."

"I don't need favors from you," Raven snapped darkly. "On the count of three."

But by the time he'd reached two, Wolfcairn was already running for the dark alley. Screams now came from there.

Cursing, Raven ran, using his vampire strength to catch Wolfcairn. He couldn't lose this meal. Not when he had to return to Lady Ophelia.

How could he have just left her here?

She should be thankful he was gone and he hadn't hurt her. He was obviously mad. How could kidnapping her and tying her to a bed make him her *savior*?

Ophelia shut her eyes. Toad. Warty, smelly toad.

Calling him names did help to stave off fear.

Would he come back?

Her stomach rumbled. She had not eaten since her dinner at Mrs. Darkwell's and she had not eaten much. She had been too caught up in the excitement of planning her escape from the house. No one had noticed her lack of appetite since she ate alone, of course, so she would not accidentally touch someone.

A mouth-watering aroma reached her nose.

Her tummy clenched in sheer pain. Dinner now seemed like it had been a century ago. But if those delicious smells were for her, she was not going to feel *grateful*, for heaven's sake.

The only reason she was hungry was because some dangerous, villainous man was holding her prisoner. Out of pride and anger, she should refuse his food. But she had learned through her captivity with Mrs. Darkwell that she had to eat, even when her stomach was in knots with fear. Starving herself hardly helped in an escape.

Could she appeal to the servant bringing the food? Maybe convince whoever it was to free her?

Hope flared. Then the tiny flame of it went out as fast.

Ravenhunt strode into her room, carrying a tray laden with dishes. Sweet scents and savory aromas swirled around her.

Heavens, she *hated* this man.

It was a crime he was so handsome. That behind the high cheekbones, full lips, and dramatic black eyes lurked the heart of a madman.

He smiled. She stared up at him, mute with fury. How desperately she wanted to kick him. How could he smile kindly at her?

"Are you hungry?" he asked softly. He put the tray down on the vanity table.

"Yes," Ophelia said, keeping her voice shaky and weak. "I am starving. I'm faint with hunger. Can you untie me so I can eat?" She hated sounding like such a weak ninny. Ravenhunt made her want to roar like a tigress and slash at him with claws.

"Sorry, love," he answered gently, a rueful smile on his lips. "Then you would touch me, and we can't have that."

"You've already touched me," she pointed out dryly. "It didn't hurt you. And the gloves make no difference, usually, just so you know."

"I do know that. I made certain I did not touch you for long. I wouldn't want to risk what those pretty hands could do to me."

"You touched me for quite a while, though, bringing me here. Normally that would make someone seriously ill. But you are—you are stronger. I want to know who you are! And how you know what I am!"

"I was hired to kidnap you, love, and I had to be fully warned about what you are."

"Hired?" She squealed the word. "By whom? What madness is this? Who would want—?"

"Questions later," he interrupted. "First you must eat. Afterward we will amuse ourselves."

"For heaven's sake, let me go."

"I'm sorry, love, but I cannot. You will be here for a very long time. You can entertain yourself by asking questions. I have other ways of amusing myself."

"How are you going to do that?" She hated him and his smugness.

He grinned. "By pleasuring you."

2

Assassin

Pleasure her?

"You are completely mad!" Ophelia shouted. She *hated* this. Hated being bound to a bed, utterly at his mercy. She had read horrid novels at Mrs. Darkwell's about girls being taken captive. It wasn't thrilling in reality. It was terrifying.

With Darkwell, she knew why she had to be a prisoner. She'd accepted it. But she didn't deserve this. This she could fight.

She had begun hurting people with her horrible power when her monthly courses had started. Ever since then, she'd tried not to cause pain to anyone.

But she wanted to hurt Ravenhunt.

"You can't touch me," she threw at him. "You just said so. You can't pleasure me. You must keep *away* from me."

"So they say," he responded, in the typical jaded drawl of a London gentleman. "But Society also used to say I was completely mad. And you are hungry."

As if he'd summoned it by his words, her stomach growled again.

"Unfortunately, I assume you still consider me a foe, so I

cannot take the risk of untying you yet." Tossing that casually over his shoulder, he walked past with a small table, which he set beside her bed. On his next journey to her side, he brought the tray and set it on the table.

"I apologize for taking so long to prepare this."

Ophelia sputtered. "You should apologize for making me your prisoner."

"Considering I saved your life, pretty one, you should be thanking me."

"Saved my life? What rubbish—"

She broke off. Ravenhunt stood at the side of the bed, one elbow propped against the bed column. She had forgotten how tall he was—over six feet. Gracefully, he settled on the edge of her bed. She fought against the ropes, but couldn't get her hands close enough to touch him.

A moment ago, she would have happily slapped her hands all over him to hurt him. Now, she wasn't sure she wanted to kill him. Not until she found out the meaning behind his cryptic words.

What did he mean, he had saved her life?

She opened her mouth to form a question and a spoon slipped in. Something creamy touched her tongue. Hunger made her close her lips around the silver spoon and suck off something that tasted like sweetened chocolate. It startled her. It was dark and lush and wonderful. She had never tasted anything so good.

She released the spoon. Stared up at him. "Who begins a meal with the dessert?"

Shadows clung to his high cheekbones and full lips. His smile was gone, his mouth turned down at the corners. "Someone who is trying to make amends."

Firelight reflected on his dark, dark eyes, making them gleam like the eyes of a predator. She flinched.

He looked away and pressed another spoonful of the creamy chocolate to her lips. "I forgot you need light."

He put the spoon down. The bed creaked, the mattress lifting as he stood up, long legs straightening. Firelight limned him with a reddish-gold glow as he moved across the room. A light flared, then another and another. He left two candles on the vanity, and returned, carrying one to the bedside table.

Strangely, the fact she could see him made her hope that seeing her might touch some decency in him. The way he had fed her was surprisingly gentle. And he had spoken of wanting to make amends.

"Why are you doing this? No one would pay a ransom for me, if that's what you desire."

Her brother and sister thought she was dead, after all. Her younger brother, Harold, known as Harry, was now the earl and head of her family. Harry would dismiss a demand for ransom as the work of a madman. "Can you not just let me go?"

Ravenhunt studied her. His rubbed his fingers against his temple as if his head ached. "If I cut the ropes securing your arms," he said finally, "can I have your word you won't touch me and attempt to kill me?"

She hesitated.

"It would not serve you to try to kill me, my dear. There are men who want to make you their prisoner and experiment on you. Do you understand of what I am speaking?"

"No, I have no idea." Experiments? Like men of science? Fear clawed at her again—he had to be mad.

She had to play along. The only weapon she had right now was making him believe she was going to be obedient and docile.

"You will have to trust me for now," he said.

She nodded, biting back her real desire to scream at him, to tell him he was insane.

Her arms were numb. To have them free, to not feel so vulnerable, she would agree to anything. "I promise I will not touch you," she whispered.

Silver flashed in front of the candle's flame. A knife blade.

He stretched over her, his large chest moving close to her face. Grasping the rope, he sliced one, then the other. Her arms fell limply against the bed.

She wriggled her fingers. "Oh, that hurts," she gasped as feeling returned.

His hand came close to hers, then he drew it back. "I wanted to massage your hands. They must be sore."

"They are beyond sore!"

He sighed. "I am an assassin, Lady Ophelia. You have seen an inordinate amount of kindness from me. More than I've shown anyone in a long time."

"A-an assassin," she parroted numbly. Strangely, she didn't feel any deeper fear at the word. It was as if she had reached the limit of horror she could comprehend and nothing more could go in.

"Can you sit up?" he continued, as if she had not spoken. She struggled to do so. He moved around her, careful not to brush against her. She pushed up, the covers falling away. Her hair was a mess, half-falling from her pins, hanging around her in a tangle of gold.

Her assassin dutifully tucked two pillows behind her back.

This was madness.

"After I've eaten, are you planning to kill me?" Ophelia truly didn't know how she could speak so coolly. Exhaustion had settled on her. She'd been on a bed for hours, unable to sleep, starving, and the drug she'd inhaled still made her feel a bit dizzy. She was almost too tired to care if he tried to kill her.

"I do not intend to kill you. But you have to know I did not take you of my own volition. This is an assignment for me, and I was paid handsomely to do it."

"Who paid you?" she whispered.

"I have no idea."

She made a sound of frustration. "That makes no sense. How could you not know?"

He didn't answer, and realization dawned. "You're going to give me to this person," she gasped.

"No, I am not."

"What do you mean, you are not?"

"I've changed my mind."

Should she be relieved? "Then what are you going to do?"

He shrugged in that languorous way of gentlemen. "I don't yet know."

He was a madman. "What will this unknown person do, since you are double-crossing him?"

"I assume he will attempt to destroy me," Ravenhunt answered, as if he were speaking of the weather. "He would also come after you—or send someone else to do what I did not. That is the reason you have to stay with me. You will be safe with me."

"No," she said. Then stronger, for her head was clearing, "No, I am not going to stay with you. You are insane."

He sighed, turning away from her and back to the tray. "You rescue a woman," he muttered to himself. "The first woman you have ever bothered to save. Do you see any appreciation for your trouble?"

"Rescue me?" she sputtered. "Stop saying that! You took me prisoner—"

A plate thrust at her, the food almost toppling onto her chest. Surprise broke off her words. Her stomach ached at the anticipation of digging into ham, eggs, and potatoes. Abruptly he set it down on her lap, forcing her to grab the plate to prevent it spilling.

A slightly bitter, brewed scent filled the air. She glanced over. A silver urn flashed as he poured coffee in a cup. He downed half of it without any sweetening. Black. Then he grimaced. "Cannot drink this stuff," he muttered. He spat it back into the cup and set the cup aside.

"I deserve to know what you are going to do to me!" she demanded.

A sardonic laugh left his lips. "I would tell you if I had any idea." Then he sighed. He poured coffee into another delicate cup and held it out to her.

With her hands still a bit numb, she wrapped both around the warm china.

"This is the entire tale, Lady Ophelia. I agreed to kidnap you, an innocent young woman, which was unusual for me. Normally I am paid to destroy beings. But I was promised a fortune as payment, and I could not resist. As I said, I was to hand you over to my client."

He paused, rubbing his chin.

The hot coffee was making her head wake up. Frowning, she said, "You promised me the entire tale. I think I deserve that."

Broad shoulders moved in another languorous shrug. "The man knows about your power. I believe he wanted you to experiment on you—find out how your power works, how it can be controlled, if someone else could obtain your power."

"No one could do that."

Matter-of-factly, he said, "There are ways."

"Who would want it? It's a curse—"

"Not for someone who would want to be indestructible. I was to give you to him after I acquired you. Tonight I went and told him he's not going to get you. Now, eat."

Ophelia took a bite of her ham. "You speak as though you *do* know who paid you to capture me."

When Ravenhunt said nothing, and she'd swallowed more bites of his delicious food, she added, "Can you give me any hints?"

"This is not a parlor guessing game, Lady Ophelia. This is

serious. The only place I can be certain you will be safe is with me."

"Why should *you* care to keep me safe?"

"You are young and you don't deserve to die. Nor do you deserve to be cut open and studied."

Her stomach rebelled. She turned and suddenly a chamber pot was in front of her and she lost every morsel of food she'd just eaten into its depths. Facing it, she whispered, "C-cut open?"

"It is what men of science do to try to understand people like you."

Oh God. Her insides heaved again. Ophelia lurched over the pot he held. It hurt terribly for there was nothing left in her to come up.

She hated to be sick in front of him. She wanted to be alone. She wanted to be . . . home.

At least back at Mrs. Darkwell's, which was as close to a home as she possessed. Never would she have dreamed that Darkwell's prison would feel like a safe home.

Ravenhunt's gloved hand moved toward her head. He stopped before he touched her and withdrew his hand. "Do you want a glass of water?" he asked.

She ignored the question. "Am I really supposed to believe the man who kidnapped me is actually my rescuer?"

"Yes."

"I can't. I don't trust you. And remember, I do have the power to kill you." She tried to look menacing. She lifted her hand toward him in a blatant threat.

Instead of retreating, he reached out. His hand gripped hers.

"What are you doing?" she cried. She tried to pull free. She could spare him if she broke the touch in time.

He would not release her. He moved his hand so he was holding hers. He threaded his fingers between hers.

Heat burned between their hands. This had never happened

before. Her hand screamed with pain, but smoke rose from his fingers. His hand appeared to be *burning*. Terror grabbed her, strangling her voice.

Lifting their joined hands, Ravenhunt watched the smoke with detached fascination. How could he bear the pain? It was as if it were happening to another man, not him.

Finally he drew her hand toward his chest.

"No." She fought to pull back. "That *will* kill you and I won't do it."

"I'm interested to discover if it will. There's only one way to find out." Prying her fingers open, he pressed her hand to the skin of his throat, above his collar points.

"It will kill you," she said desperately. "Perhaps not right now, but it will. Why would you be so foolish if you know about my power?"

Smoke—or steam—poured out from under her palm on his neck. Fine powder, like dust motes, floated into the air.

"It appears your hand burns me," he observed.

She could not do it . . . she could not knowingly kill him. "Yes, it is burning you. How can you stand such pain? Please, let us stop this."

Thank heavens, the madman listened. Slowly he removed her hand. He tipped his head to expose his throat to candle-light.

Her hand went to her mouth, but it did not smother her cry of horror.

A large, red burn in the shape of her hand curled around his neck. Smoke still rose from it, and blood and fluid oozed out.

"Why did you do that? Why did you force me to hurt you?"

"It will heal. In minutes it will be gone. But at least we have answered an important question." Ravenhunt sighed. "I hoped I would have a great degree of immunity to your powers. It's unfortunate—I was looking forward to kissing you."

Pushing back his thick black hair, he got up from the bed.

She blinked. Already the burn on his neck was healing. The skin had grown over the wound, new and pale. It was astonishing.

"It will have to wait until later. I have to go out now, my dear."

But she refused to be abandoned again, not when she had so many questions. "What did it mean that you healed so quickly?" Ophelia demanded. "And just because that happened, it does not mean you are not going to die."

An amused smile lifted Ravenhunt's lips. Fathomless and black, his eyes glinted at her. Candlelight shone along his irises as if they were mirrors. "I can assure you I won't die. But kissing you will have to wait until later. I have to go out."

"I am never going to kiss you—"

But in the blink of an eye, he had left. He veritably disappeared from the room, he'd gone so quickly.

She was no longer tied to the bed. She could escape.

He would never forget what it was like to kiss Lord Simon Black's hot, hard mouth.

Valde, son of the woman who called herself Mrs. Darkwell, pulled open the door of the crypt that bore the name Black, the family name of the Earls of Darlington.

"Simon," he whispered as he walked down the steps into the cool, dark depths of the tomb. His voice came out hoarse. His heart ached with great pain.

Stone coffins lay in neat rows within. The air was not dank or musty, for he came here many nights—at least once each week. Valde ducked his head to miss the low threshold, for he stood seven feet tall. Slowly he walked to the coffin he wanted. Unlike those for the earls, this one was simple. There was no effigy of his beloved Simon on the lid.

He touched the lid, running his hand over the marble.

Closing his eyes, he remembered the first time he had

stripped off his clothes with the handsome, blond young man he'd loved . . .

It had been after a ritualistic ceremony. He was a demigod, or at least was one quarter god, and he had been determined to learn the secrets of black magic. Simon, an earl's son, had been drawn to the warlock world, and was also trying to learn the dark arts.

After the ceremony, they had been alone in the field where the chanting and spell-casting had taken place. It was mid-summer, the air sultry and moist. He wore a robe of black silk with nothing beneath. The soft summer breeze was like a naughty caress when it slipped up his robe.

Simon had worn a gentleman's attire. White shirt, waistcoat, tailcoat, breeches, and boots.

The air had felt charged—as if it might burst into storm. But there was no storm threatening. It had been mutual awareness, mutual desire.

He had known the invitation to touch was there when he'd gazed into Simon's blue eyes. He cupped the lad's cheek. Ran his thumb over those full, tempting lips. Velvety and more fascinating than any woman's, for they were as plump as a female's but firm and slightly rough because they belonged to a man.

He'd slid his hand around Simon's strong neck. Drew the lad close to him.

Breathless moment. God, so arousing and breathless.

His mouth had touched Simon's lips.

It had been like coming to life. Hot desire ran through his body. His staff had gone stiff as a brick, pushing hungrily at his trousers.

Kissing Simon like an eager swain, Valde had recognized the young man of twenty-two was a virgin when it came to the matter of two men making love.

Slowly, he had undone the cravat that held Simon's shirt

points against the golden stubble of his throat and jaw. He'd kissed the exposed neck, loving the scratch of stubble, the scent of cologne on the young man's dewy skin.

He caressed Lord Simon's broad chest. One mere pass of his hand had the lad's nipples pointy and erect. Then he'd undone Simon's trousers. There had been one murmur of protest from the innocent young man, but he'd silenced that with a passionate kiss.

Then his hand had slid into Simon's small clothes and had wrapped around a thick, straining, vein-covered cock . . .

Valde touched the coffin, closing his eyes to fight grief.

He could not open the coffin. Simon was not undead. There was no beautiful, un-aged face for him to caress. No perfect vampire or demon lips to kiss.

They had taken the man he had loved and had killed him before he had immortal life.

The damned vampire assassin who had taken Simon, who had been working for one of the evil vampire queens, had left him with a decaying corpse.

He hated them—the vampires and the queens.

Hated the Royal Society, even though that group of vampire slayers believed he was one of them.

He knew what he wanted. He was the bastard son of a demigoddess, and he was denied the power of a god. For a short time, as a child, he had been possessed of the magical powers of a god, with the ability to change weather, to move things with mere thought, and to make mere mortals fall in love with him and do whatever he asked. But as punishment for being the bastard son of a mortal, all of his power vanished when he reached the age of eight. When he had finally become just old enough to understand that his power could let him rule the mortal world, it was taken away from him.

Then he was taken from his beautiful mother, Mrs. Darkwell, who was the daughter of the goddess Aphrodite.

He knew the gods and goddesses of old legends did exist—but they could interact no longer with the human world. The only time they could intervene was when one of their own came into the mortal world.

Aphrodite's daughter had done that. She had fallen in love with a mortal.

And he, as her son, had paid the price.

He had been forced to live as a mortal boy, working like a servant on the farm of an angry and brutal mortal man.

What he wanted was power.

He wanted his chance to rule.

Valde wanted revenge.

And he knew there was a woman who had the power to kill with just her touch. If he had that power, he could have all the vengeance he wanted.

He knew where she was—with that damned vampire assassin. The one who had taken Simon from him.

It was going to be a pleasure to begin his reign of terror—starting with the destruction of the vampire Ravenhunt.

3

Jade

Twilight had settled on London, blanketing the town with a purple-gray gloom. Raven walked through the streets, using his preternatural powers to move so quickly he was invisible to mortals. He walked in the center of the road, dodging carriages. Horses whinnied and reared as they sensed him pass. Nervous coachmen steadied them, and when these men saw nothing in the road, they crossed themselves.

Raven reached the house that had once been his: a huge home of golden stone on Grosvenor Square that spanned half the block. His cousin lived here now. His cousin was mortal. When Raven had left the world to believe him dead, his cousin Anthony had inherited the title of Marquis of Ravenhunt.

Some vampires who were peers attempted to live normal lives. They kept their titles, lived in their mansions, and tried to act like humans. He knew of many. The Earl of Brookshire was a vampire earl who also worked for the Royal Society. So was the Earl of Blackmoor. The Duke of Greystone was a vampire and a dragon hunter.

There was only one thing Raven missed of the mortal world. Tonight he was going to go and see her. His heart ached already at the anticipation of laying eyes on her for the first time in a week.

With lightning speed, he crossed the lawns, strode over the flagstones of the terrace, and reached the side of the house. He needed to remain clothed so he could not shift shape and fly.

His heart rate, normally so slow as to be almost unde-tectable, sped to a thunder.

It was these moments that made an eternity of hell bearable. This was the only reason he did not walk out into the light and destroy himself.

He did not destroy himself because he had a girl to protect. His sister, Frederica. Even though he could never let her see him, he could watch over her and keep her safe.

At first, given his black-hearted disposition and his natural enjoyment of violence, he had enjoyed being a vampire. He'd reveled in the power. But having so much power quickly be-came boring. His prey was too easily hunted.

At least, when he'd been a mortal solider, he had stood a good chance of getting blown off the face of the earth with a well-placed pistol shot or a cannon ball. The risk of death made it more fun.

He'd gone looking for death.

Unfortunately the moment it had almost been handed to him, it had been snatched from his grasp by a vampire queen who had wanted him to be her lover for eternity.

As he approached the house, Raven took a breath. The sooty smell of hundreds of burning candles touched his nos-trils. He detected hundreds of blends of perfume, along with the heady smells of bouquets of flowers and a lavish supper.

Over all those smells, he was flooded by an overwhelming coppery-smelling wave—the aroma of blood given off by hun-dreds of mortals.

His fangs shot out.

Hades, they were more unruly than his cock—always lengthening at the wrong time.

"Calm yourself," he muttered to them. "You will not be feeding here tonight. We are here for another purpose entirely."

Likely he should feel something—some anger, some regret, some bitterness—to be reduced to climbing the wall of his former home instead of walking in the front door.

The stone blocks of the house wall cut into his bare hands, but each wound healed instantly. Hoisting himself over a railing, he landed lightly on the terrace on the upper floor. Below was the ballroom, but he entered the window of his sister Frederica's bedchamber.

Her scent lingered. Light, lavender, sweet as a meadow of flowers.

Her bed was turned down, ready for her to slide into it at dawn, exhausted after a night of dancing. His portrait hung across from her bed. That gave him a good dose of guilt. His sister missed him. She wanted his picture where she could see him every day.

Frederica thought him dead.

This was her second London Season. His cousin Anthony, the marquis, was her guardian and overseeing her introduction to Society now that she was eighteen. She would soon find a husband.

Raven wanted to ensure the gentleman she accepted was worthy of her. He could do that by standing in the shadows, learning whom she became engaged to, then hunting down the truth about the man.

Frederica's silken pillow, her folded nightdress, her brush and perfumes on the vanity—all the signs of her happy mortal existence—brought up too much guilt and pain.

Raven stalked out of the room.

The house was filled with servants, but he moved so quickly

no one saw him. He slipped through the crowd, to the receiving line, where his cousin stood and his sister glowed. Her honey brown curls were threaded with a white satin ribbon, decorated with emeralds. Pink shone on her cheeks, her green eyes sparkled for every guest.

Folding his arms over his chest, Raven could tell which callow young men were already in love with her.

Then he saw a gentleman he did not know by name, but he recognized the type. The kind of man he'd used to be before he had fallen in love.

Three words described the handsome man smiling at his sister.

Scoundrel. Libertine. Rogue.

Frederica blushed. Her lashes fluttered. Suddenly she appeared awkward. The damned seducer—a fair-haired bastard in impeccable dress—lifted her hand to his lips and gave a slow, sensuous kiss to her fingers that was intended to make her melt.

Raven knew what the rogue was doing. Picturing her naked.

He wanted to step out of the shadows, drag the bastard into an empty room, and drink his blood dry.

He couldn't do it—it would break his sister's heart if the man just disappeared. Frederica had sense. And if she did not see through the blackguard's intentions, then he would kill the man and get rid of him.

He watched her through the ballroom windows, from the darkness of the terrace.

Frederica danced twice with the rogue. In fact, she danced every dance with an admiring gentleman.

Raven wanted to lock her up in her room where men could not get at her.

Of course he couldn't do that. He couldn't even go near her. What would he say? That he had never died, he had been turned into a vampire?

He watched until the guests began to leave. Dawn was close and he had no choice but to go. He couldn't stay out long in daylight—meeting Lady Ophelia that late afternoon at the museum had almost turned him to dust, for example. Frederica's beau had left, so he felt it was safe for him to go.

He walked out across the terrace, into darkness, striding with vampiric speed.

"So here you are," said a sultry voice. "Why do you come here, you foolish boy? There is nothing for you here."

Raven stopped. He turned. He knew the voice, and it made him curl his lip with hatred.

It was a testament to the vampire queen's power that she had been able to approach him from behind and he had not heard or sensed her.

Ever since he'd left her, since he'd refused to be her sexual plaything, she had left him alone.

Why in hell had she come after him now?

Queen Jade smiled at him, flashing marble-white teeth and two long, curved fangs. She was adorned in a fur-trimmed pelisse. Her pale skin appeared to sparkle in the moonlight, as though she were dusted with diamonds. Long and black, her hair spilled down and almost touched her ankles.

"I come here because there is only one woman I love on this earth," he muttered. "And that is my sister."

For years, he'd been Jade's pet. She had turned him into an assassin of vampires—commanding him to kill the demons she wanted rid of.

Jade cocked her head. Her face was exquisitely lovely—her eyes large and silvery-green, her features smooth and perfect. But she not only had no soul, she was cruel and vicious.

She gave him a loving smile. It made him want to vomit.

"I have allowed you to have your independence for long enough." She held out her hand to him. "You belong in my services. I have allowed you to help other vampires and the Royal Society—and kill for them—because it suited me. Now, you have something that I want very much."

He did not move toward her. He snarled. "What is that?"

She came to him. Her long-fingered, beautiful hand stroked the side of his face. When he had first been turned, he had craved her every touch. He'd lusted for her every moment of the night. Now he felt nothing but revulsion and hatred.

"The girl. Lady Ophelia. I need to take her power away from her."

How did she know he had Lady Ophelia? She could not read his thoughts. Raven grimaced. She probably had spies watching him. "Why?"

He used his jaded, unconcerned tone. But he was worried.

He didn't understand why he felt that reaction. Why should he care about Lady Ophelia? Was the girl not just a nuisance to him? Yet, he pitied her, while he hadn't felt anything but disgust for mortals and their weaknesses for a long time.

He had teased her with his threats to pass the time by pleasuring her. It was entertaining to make her angry.

Maybe that was a sign he spent too much time alone.

"Does the power kill our kind?" he asked Jade. "Why the hell do you want it?"

"Yes, it does kill vampires." Jade floated around him, her hair fluttering on the cool breeze. "It kills us very slowly. At least, it would kill you slowly for now, but her power will become stronger. If she keeps her power, it will become so strong she will be able to kill a mortal without touching him. And she will kill against her will. I mean, she will not want to hurt anyone, but she will not be able to control it. You, Ravenhunt, can take her power away from her. You would be doing something kind for her, freeing her of her curse."

Poor kid. He knew what it was to be a monster—to kill against his control. But he did not trust Jade. "How would I take this power?"

"By making love to her." The queen laughed. "Is that not always the way? By giving her pleasure, by touching her heart, you will cause her power to become stronger. Then you will have the ability to take it from her."

"What does that do to her?"

Jade shrugged. "It might kill her. Such strong power could not be taken without a great cost."

"I'm not interested."

"You will be. For if you do not do it, your sister will be destroyed."

He lunged for her, but Jade lifted her hand and he found he could not move. She was extremely powerful for a vampiress. "Remember, dear boy, if you kill me, you die. And I have acquired insurance. Other vampires are instructed to kill your precious sister if you do anything to me."

Hades, he hated Jade. When he retreated, she gave peals of high-pitched laughter.

"If you are an obedient boy and bring me her power, nothing will happen to your sister." Jade wagged an ivory white finger at him. "You will be tempted to drink Lady Ophelia's blood," she went on. "Insanely tempted. It will lure you. In truth, if you were to drink her blood, it would be the most pleasurable experience you've ever had."

"I've had many pleasurable experiences," he said coldly. "But I know I can't drink her blood. That would kill her, and I can't do that if I have to take her power to protect my sister."

"No, you cannot drink from her," Jade warned, her gaze haughty, "because it would not only kill her, it would also destroy you. I will give you a week to acquire her power. You must do it by making love to her."

"How can I do that when I can't touch her?"

"As I said—her power will kill you slowly. As you grow closer to the point where you can take her power, you will have developed immunity. But first, you must start giving her orgasms—without touching her. Unless you give her pleasure, unless you can make her climax, you cannot take her power. I will come to you again to tell you more."

"Damn you, Queen, I need to know more now. How do I take her power? Is it by a spell? What in Hades am I supposed to do?"

"You begin by making her come. That is all you need to know for now." She lifted her arms and rose into the dark sky.

Over the roof over his former home, he saw enormous bats circling.

If you hurt Frederica, Queen Jade, I will destroy you. He sent the threat through thought to Jade.

I will not touch her if you do as I say, Jade answered in his head. *But the bats stay—they will not hurt her, but they will prevent you from double-crossing me.*

Raven spat at the grass. There were dozens of bats. He could try to fight them, but he would lose. Then Frederica would be hurt.

He had no choice. To protect his sister, he had to do as Jade asked.

He had to seduce his captive.

It had been a long time since he had touched anyone without the intent to kill.

Arms folded over his chest, Raven leaned against the door frame and watched Lady Ophelia rattle the glass doors that led to the terrace. Ornate metalwork crossed each door, acting as bars. They covered all the windows and doors in the house, making an effective prison.

"Worked your way through the rest of the house, did you?" he asked.

A sharp gasp escaped her. She whirled around. Moonlight poured in, touching her pale oval face with a silver-white light. "How long have you been standing there, watching me?"

She amazed him. Most women would be swooning and weeping at being held prisoner. But fury radiated from Lady Ophelia.

"Not long," he said.

Even when she was angry, her voice was husky and beautiful.

"I take it you've kept many prisoners here," she said. Again, when she should show fear, she snapped at him. Her large indigo-blue eyes burned with condemnation.

"No, my dear. You are the first."

"Then why is your house like a prison?"

"Look at it from the outside, Lady Ophelia."

"What on earth do you mean?"

"From the outside it's not a prison. It's a fortress. I am tempted to let you leave this house, just so you can learn what awaits you out there. You will come scurrying back."

"I would not."

Ravenhunt grasped her chin, forcing her blazing gaze to meet his frustrated one. "There are men out there waiting for the chance to drag you into a laboratory, strap you down, and cut you open to examine you. You wouldn't survive it, and your death would be slow, lingering, painful."

Smoke rose from his fingers, from the contact of his skin with hers.

"Don't touch me," she cried, shoving his hand away.

Her chest rose on fast breaths. Her face was white. So many emotions were written on her face he could not read them all. But one stood out—pain. He saw deep pain in her eyes. He knew what raw pain looked like. He'd seen it in his own eyes after the first time he'd killed. He'd seen it in the eyes of men on the battlefield. He'd seen it in Frederica's eyes, after she'd been told of his "death."

"You never touch anyone, do you?" he asked softly.

"Of course not. *I can't.*"

"No kisses?"

"N—no." She hesitated. She winced. So there was a tale there. She had kissed, so what had happened? The mortal must have died.

"No embraces. No holding hands. No dances?"

She wrapped her arms around her chest. "I cannot touch anyone at all. Even gloves don't help if the touch is prolonged, like a dance."

"Do you like to dance?"

Wistfulness replaced pain. "Yes."

Raven stroked his chin. "There is something I want to do. It will hurt eventually, but not for a while."

Before Ophelia could move away, he came to her, pulled her into his embrace. His head bent to hers, and as she reeled back, realizing what he meant to do, his mouth touched hers. Softly. Then he pressed more. His mouth opened, coaxing hers to open, too.

His tongue touched hers.

He was kissing her. An intimate, passionate kiss.

Her lips sizzled. A burning sensation washed over them. Smoke rose between her and Ravenhunt.

She fought to push him away. Her lips did not hurt, yet there was no question her kiss was burning him. Hurting him.

But he was not going to let the kiss end.

4

Rescued

Ravenhunt drew back from her sizzling lips. "Stop worrying and enjoy the kiss," he urged. "I'm not going to die."

"I wish you w—" Ophelia began, but his mouth covered hers again, capturing her words, as he drew her tight to his hard body and kissed her deeply.

She couldn't say she wished he would die. It wasn't true. But she wished he would just . . . leave. So that she could get away.

This kiss was . . .

Oh, she was terrified of kissing.

Her first kiss had ended in horror. She had watched the man she loved fall to his knees, clutching his throat. David's face had turned purple, his tongue had protruded, and his eyes had bulged out.

The horrible attack had stopped and he had lived. But she had never let herself see him again.

Ravenhunt kept kissing her. She held her lips so hard and tight they began to ache. She was going to kill him, and even though this was his fault, she was sick with guilt.

His hand cupped her jaw and slowly stroked. His fingertips

massaged her skin beside her ear, making it tingle. His gentle touch soothed her. She found her spine was no longer ramrod straight with fear. Her legs began to melt.

Slowly, ever so slowly, her lips softened against his. The pressure of his mouth on hers made shivers of pleasure race down her spine. His lips were so firm but velvety. She ached inside—a strange, empty, throbbing feeling.

She pressed close to him, hard against his body—

What was she doing? He was her *captor*.

This was awful. The wonderful kiss she finally had was from a man she despised. It was *wrong*.

Ophelia shoved hard against his chest.

This time Ravenhunt let her go.

Raven's mouth was hot with pain—pain that shot from his sensitive lips through his entire body. Jade had told him Lady Ophelia's power would kill him slowly. She hadn't mentioned it would hurt like hell.

That kiss had felt like his lips had been sliced by razors.

He touched his stinging lips tenderly. The pain was easing.

It had been hell while he'd been kissing Ophelia, but at least it hadn't hurt her. Just him.

He could bear it for his sister's sake.

Lady Ophelia grasped up her hems and scurried away like a frightened animal. She had pulled her gown on, and it hung around her, for she hadn't bothered with her undergarments.

Many times he'd seen his sister run away from him in such a pose—biting her lip to fight tears, her heart filled with black fury toward him. When he'd become head of the family at twenty, he had seemed to spend most of his time leveling his sister's dreams, breaking her heart, and, as she would describe it, ruining her life.

How was he going to coax Lady Ophelia into his bed? She could not see him as anything other than her captor. Raven had hoped her simmering anger might ignite into passion. Perhaps it would, in time. But he needed a way to cut to the chase.

He had to give Ophelia orgasms. How was he supposed to do that with a woman who ran away from him?

Ophelia would be searching for escape. There was no way out of his house. It gave him time to think.

How badly was it going to hurt him to seduce her? Hell, he couldn't begin to guess. And it didn't matter—he had to do it.

Raven stood absolutely still for several minutes.

Then he knew what to do.

From the battlefield, he knew the fear of imminent death made a man turn to anyone for help and rescue. Even an enemy.

There must be a way out.

But with each room she ran into and searched, Ophelia was losing hope.

No wonder Ravenhunt had left her room unlocked and had let her run around his house. No wonder he had not pursued her when she ran from him.

This house was indeed a prison. Except for the two of them, it was utterly devoid of life. No cook resided in the kitchen, no maids tended to the rooms. Ophelia hadn't encountered another human soul.

The house showed its neglect. Cobwebs were strung from ceiling to bedposts and furniture in every room but hers. She had found no other bedroom that appeared occupied by her captor.

Every door to the outside was locked. He must carry the keys with him.

If she'd had her sculpting tools, she might have been able to spring open a lock. But she had nothing. Even if she broke a window, each one was covered with bars spaced too tightly for her to squeeze through.

If she could get hold of the keys . . .

If she let him kiss her again, could she search him for the keys? She shivered as she imagined running her hands over his body, pretending to be filled with desire but actually trying to find her escape.

She didn't want to touch him. But she had to.

Now she had to find him. Or let him find her. She must ensure he did not guess her plan.

Where could she let him find her? She was on the upper floor, a few doors down from her bedroom. Ophelia pushed a door open. This bedchamber, too, was festooned with dust and spider-webs. But the bed was made.

This had to be Ravenhunt's room. But why in heaven's name was it not cleaned? How could he stand sleeping in there?

"Ophelia."

Ravenhunt's voice made her jump.

He had found her, and now she must make this convincing. She had run away from him once—it would be artificial and suspicious if she suddenly threw herself into his arms.

She couldn't rouse his suspicion.

Weakness. She hated to act like a ninny, but weakness would be believed. Mrs. Darkwell had bought in to it on the times she'd escaped from the woman's house. If she was docile, meek, and frightened, no one thought she had any courage at all. No one thought she was using her wits.

She made her shoulders shake. "Are you going to force a kiss on me again? Are you going to attack me?"

"You liked the kiss," he answered softly. He stayed put, studying her. Not moving, as if she were a deer he didn't want to frighten.

"I—" How to play this? "I didn't want to like it." That was honest. But she knew it also was not a denial that she wanted him to kiss her again.

"Maybe I always wanted to know what a real kiss was like,"

she continued, hurriedly. She had to sound genuine. "But I can't."

"Think of it as just that. A chance to see what a kiss is. Forget who I am. Imagine the man of your fantasies kissing you."

His words made her want to mentally kick herself in the bottom. He had been the man of her fantasies for two weeks. "You're going to do it again, aren't you?"

"Yes," he said simply.

Then he was there in front of her, and she supposed she was so nervous she hadn't focused on him coming to her. He'd seemed to move in a heartbeat.

Let him touch you. Don't panic. It's not that you want this. It's that you have *to do it.* His scents filled her head. Sandalwood, witch hazel, wool, and leather. She looked up at him, her lips parted invitingly. Hoping he didn't need any more encouragement than just her standing docilely, waiting for him to master her again.

Anything else—any faked enthusiasm—would look strange.

He tipped up her chin, kept his finger there, as gentle as if she were fine porcelain.

His mouth lowered to hers. So slowly, her heart was pounding when their lips touched. It was like a burst of thunder after waiting and waiting for it.

She gasped into his mouth.

A plot . . . just a ploy . . . that was all it was supposed to be. She kissed him as passionately as she could. Everything he did to her—the play of his mouth on hers, the touch of his tongue to hers, the way his tongue teased hers—she tried to do it back to him.

Deep inside, she throbbed and ached. She was responding.

Stop *feeling* things, she warned herself. The *keys*. Find them!

Kissing him back, she put her arms around him. Awkwardly. She let her palms skim down his back.

She was searching for pockets.

Ravenhunt wrapped his arm around her back, clamped her close, and gave her such a long, intense kiss she almost fell dazedly to the ground.

She clung to his coat, knowing now he had no pockets in them.

He picked her up, his hands at her waist, and then pulled her forward. He supported her on his right thigh, with his leg thrust between hers. It made the most shocking pressure against her private place.

It made her want to wriggle against him to ease the yearning she felt there.

He was kissing her breathless, making it hard for her to explore him, to get her hands to the waistband of his trousers to search for pockets.

Did he know what she was doing?

And how could she be so . . . aroused for her captor?

Raven knew exactly what she was doing. Kissing him in the most tempting way she could as a distraction. While she ran her hands all over his body.

She was searching for the keys to the doors.

Clever lass.

She had found the perfect solution to his problem of building her trust. He needed her to escape. He needed her to find the keys.

Groaning, Raven slid the lapels of his tailcoat from under her hands. He jerked it back, shook his coat off his shoulders, let it slide down his arms.

He sensed her sudden tension as his coat came off. He also pulled off his waistcoat. Neither made a *thunk* as they hit the floor, which she must understand meant there were no keys in the pockets.

His keys were hidden in a place she would easily find.

He should hasten her to her objective, but Hades, he didn't want to. Her touch hurt, but it aroused him. Blood flowed down to his cock, making it as hard as a cricket bat.

It felt bigger than one.

How long since he had last had sex?

Two years. Since he had left Jade. He got aroused—randy, aggressive, irritated—but he didn't want to have sex anymore. After Jade, he never wanted to touch another female vampire again. As for mortals—once they caressed him, they got more than they bargained for. His hunger was unleashed along with his lust. He couldn't help but feed from them.

He couldn't feed from Lady Ophelia.

Fighting his nature made his every muscle shake. He had to—for Frederica.

Softly, Lady Ophelia explored the skin at his neck. Damn, he'd forgotten how sensitive the skin of *his* throat could be.

How erotic it was to feel a woman's gentle fingers stroking the muscles of his neck.

His heart started to pump faster.

Her hands skimmed along his shirt at his shoulders. Up behind his ears, which made his breath hitch.

As a vampire, his skin felt more alive. When she touched him, with her power, it was like having lightning crackle over him.

Painful, but hot.

But where did she think he'd hidden the keys? In his hair?

Her hands went down his back. At least she was getting closer. Raven smothered a grin as he kept kissing her. He wanted to go for her neck, kiss her there, but that would be—

Too much temptation.

He would bite her if he tried it.

She moaned. He knew she was faking every fluttering sigh

and soft groan. But she had a lovely, throaty voice, and her moans were so sensual . . .

His cock was so filled with his blood it was getting harder to keep control.

He had to.

He couldn't do what he wanted, which was to rip off her dress, and kiss, lick, and suck her all over. What he had to do was let her go.

At least, let her run a certain distance, far enough to get into trouble. Then he would fly to the rescue.

And his seduction could begin.

Raven's lips and his skin burned with heat and pain—it was the pain from her power. If he wasn't a vampire, with superhuman strength, the burning of his lips would be agony.

Lady Ophelia's hands went lower. Down his back to below his waist. His cock pulsed with a shot of arousal and bucked against his belly. His prick had shifted shape from limp to rock-hard faster than he could grow his wings.

She groped his back. He would have to help her as the key was not trapped within the linen folds of his shirt. It was somewhere quite different.

Raven pulled off his cravat, opened the throat of his shirt, and yanked it off as quickly as he could.

Strange. Normally his naked chest was a bluish-white, as though he'd been frozen in ice. Even when he fed, he didn't gain a more normal color. He looked more like a marble statue than other vampires did. Many of them easily passed for mortal.

But right now his skin was lightly flushed. It looked almost human.

He gazed down at her beneath his lashes. Ophelia was the most fetching human he'd ever seen. Pink glowed on her cheeks. She possessed the dewy skin of a lady who protected her face with bonnets and parasols. Amber lashes swept over eyes that glittered and sparkled.

She was so human, so alive; it was like taking a blow to the chest.

Stupidly, he broke their kiss and put his lips to her throat. It lured him like iron to a magnet. Pulled him there as if he were a dumb chunk of metal.

Her skin tasted of warmth, lightly of salt, possessed a lovely, unique flavor.

Her heartbeat pulsed under his lips.

Drinking from her would be the most pleasurable experience he'd ever known. So Jade had said. His instincts were screaming that it would be.

All he had to do was plunge in his fangs—

No. If he did, he would sacrifice his sister.

But, hell, he was going to kill pretty Ophelia, wasn't he, when he took her power?

Remember, idiot, she has to escape. He had to move this along. Before he bit her. Or fucked her.

Raven gripped her wrists. He moved her hands so they were on his trousers. On his arse.

Ack. Ophelia jerked her hands back up. She'd wanted to search for pockets, but she was not ready to cup his . . . his derriere.

Her palms touched smooth skin. The skin of his bare back.

He shifted his position, lowering his leg, pulling her hard against him.

Against her tummy, there was a bulge in his trousers. Ravenhunt believed she desired him. Just as she'd wanted him to.

But now she felt awful. It stung her pride, churned up fear, made her want to be sick. She didn't want to think she was embracing, kissing, exploring a man who was half-unclothed and whom she hated.

At least the fact he was naked above the waist meant she had fewer places to search for the key.

What if the key was in one of his boots? How would she explain sticking her hand down in one of those skintight leather things?

Worse, what if it was down *inside* his trousers?

He must have a pocket of some sort. And if she couldn't find it there, she would make up some reason for him to take off his boots. She could say she was afraid he would step on her toes while kissing her.

She had gotten good at lying since she'd had to keep her power secret.

Wait? What was he *doing*?

His hand was sliding between their stomachs. Ophelia took a quick look down.

He opened the placket of his trousers. He was pushing them *down*.

She could not let this continue.

Even for the key.

Ophelia tried to pull her hands away but he grasped her wrists and drew her arms around him. Behind his back, he planted her hands on the edge of some soft material. His linen *drawers*.

He had put her hands on his underclothing.

This wasn't what she wanted. Panicked, she started to move her hands away—

Her fingers brushed a rigid lump.

Shutting her eyes, tense as a drawn bow, she explored. The shape in his drawers was long, slender, and hard. A shape very like a key.

In his arousal, he must have forgotten he had put her hands right beside the key.

She gathered her courage. Then she thrust her tongue into his mouth to play with his, kissing him with desperate abandon.

To distract him while she eased her hand down the back of his drawers.

Firm, hard contours met her fingertips. It was the warm skin of—*gah!*—the globes of his bottom. Then she brushed cool metal.

She was breathing hard into his mouth, half-paralyzed with fear. She was terrified he would feel what she was doing.

Sliding her other hand down, Ophelia cupped the curve of his derriere on the outside of his underclothes. Her fingers felt stiff. But she managed to squeeze his rump. He jumped, apparently startled by her boldness. In that moment, with him distracted, she slid out the key. It was cold and hard against her palm, and she curled her fingers around it.

With her object hidden in her hand, she didn't need to endure the kiss any longer. What she needed was to get away from him.

She tore her lips away from his. "Stop! I don't want this."

His lips curved up. "This is sudden. You seemed to be enjoying it up to now."

"I was not!"

"You liked it and that bothered you. I understand, Ophelia. I'll leave you alone." He took a step back.

She couldn't believe he would surrender so easily. But her heart soared with relief. She had the key squeezed so tight against her palm it was cutting her skin.

Shrugging, he picked up his shirt, then buttoned his trousers. "Until next time." With that and a quick bow, he strolled away from her, still half-naked. Humming, for heaven's sake.

There would not be a next time.

That made her smile. Smugly.

*　　*　　*

Ophelia pushed open one of the front doors. It creaked as it opened. She winced, then remembered she didn't have to. There was no one to hear it.

After she had taken the key, she had hurried up to her bed-chamber to hide it. She knew she could never escape with him in the house.

He had come up to her room at dark, had shouted through the closed door that he was going out and he had laid out a supper for her in the dining room.

She hadn't planned to waste time eating, but once she was racing down the stairs, she'd smelled the delicious aromas and she'd run to the table to grab some food before making her escape.

Where the food came from, she had no idea. There were no cooks or maids after all. She'd stuffed a slice of roast beef in her mouth in the most unladylike way, swallowed it fast, and thrown down a glass of wine for courage.

Now she stepped out onto the front step, her heart thunder-ing.

She was *outside*. She'd done it.

She quickly drew the door closed behind her and locked it from the outside. There was a slim chance Ravenhunt had no other key and would find *he* was locked out of his prison of a house. At the very least, a closed and locked door might give her time to get away before he discovered she was gone. It would be what he would expect to find.

She was out, but she had no idea where she was. On the out-skirts of Mayfair, she would guess. Ravenhunt's house was old—but across the street there marched a line of new townhomes. The street appeared to have some affluence, but was not of the best address. Perhaps it was a street where city merchants lived. It was quiet—only two carriages rumbled down it. But having at least some people around her gave her confidence. She must be safe now. If Ravenhunt pursued, she would scream. On a street such as this, which was not the stews, surely a cry for help would actually bring assistance.

But she was not about to wait about and be caught again. Ophelia lifted her hems and ran down the street. At the corner, she saw the name. Hope soared—she knew where she was. Only a few blocks from Mrs. Darkwell's house.

One of the carriages slowed in the street at her side. A young man leaned out and called, "Can I help you, miss?"

She was about to shout, "Yes!" Then she stopped. Beneath his beaver hat and mop of brown curls, the young gentleman stared at her. What if this man was helping Ravenhunt? What if he meant to take her back to that prison?

She kept running. It took only two more blocks and she was panting. Her chest heaved. Pressing close to the edge of a fence that surrounded a house, she sucked in deep breaths. A narrow and shadowy lane led off from the street—she stood at the corner of it.

What on earth was she doing? She didn't want to return to Mrs. Darkwell's, but where else could she go?

She had escaped Ravenhunt's prison. Why should she rush back to Mrs. Darkwell's house, which was also a prison to her?

She was free. She could finally, for once in her life, make a choice. Eight years ago, she had been taken away from her family to protect them. Willingly, obediently, she had gone, because she had been so afraid of hurting people.

She did not have to live in a prison anymore.

She could go anywhere in the world—well, she could if she had some money, and if she stayed away from people so she did not hurt them—

"Lady Ophelia. How clever of you to have escaped that fiend."

The clipped baritone voice startled her. It certainly didn't belong to Ravenhunt—it wasn't as drawling, jaded, or gravelly.

Ophelia spun around and found a gentleman standing behind her. Beneath his tall beaver hat, gray hair fell across his lined brow. A gray beard adorned his long, thin chin. Spectacles reflected street flares. Two younger, thin men in dark tailcoats accompanied him, flanking him. They carried . . . pistols.

"Who are you?" She had never seen this man before. How could he know she'd been a prisoner?

"I am Cartwell of the Royal Society."

She frowned. "Why in heaven's name is the Royal Geographical Society interested in me?"

Cartwell smiled, his manner paternal and condescending. "Not that Royal Society, my dear. Now you must come with me."

"No. I have no idea who you are, so I have no intention of going with you." She was tired of being forced to do things. She wanted her choice.

The men advanced and she backed away.

"I am here to protect you," Cartwell said.

"I've escaped. I am going to protect myself."

"I cannot allow that, Lady Ophelia." He spoke calmly, but with an implied authority.

"I do not give a fig what you want," she retorted.

"Do not force the issue, Lady Ophelia," Cartwell snapped. "It is the best for you if you quietly come with us. Given you were taken captive by a dangerous man, I should think you would be appreciative—"

"Appreciative?" she snorted. "I am tired of people telling me I should be thankful that they've locked me in a room and won't let me out."

"This is madness." It was one of the young men who spoke. He had tangled red hair beneath his hat, as if he never combed it. He pointed the pistol at her, bringing it level with her bosom. "You are to come with us."

"Or you will shoot me?"

Ravenhunt's words came back to her. He had warned her that people wanted to hurt her and that she should depend on him for protection.

She should be afraid.

But Ophelia was tired of people wanting to hurt her. She didn't want to hurt anyone. She wanted to be normal.

Suddenly, she realized they had backed her into the shadows in an alley between houses. Where people from the street would not see her.

She held out her hands and lunged toward the redheaded man with the gun. He jerked back, obviously terrified of her touch. "Boo!" she cried. "If you shoot me, I'll still touch you first."

The other young man was moving toward her, and he trained his weapon at her head. "I'll grab her—"

"Stop," barked Cartwell. "Do not lay a hand on her. It will kill you."

"I should shoot her now," snarled the redhead, his voice filled with arrogance and bravado. "She is a monster. This idea of studying her is madness. She should be destroyed." His finger was on the trigger.

The shot fired, smoke rushing from the pistol. The explosion roared in her ears. Darkness rippled in front of her eyes, as if a curtain had been drawn. Her hands went to her chest.

She expected to feel pain, to feel her body be ripped apart.

But there was nothing.

Dazed, she looked up. Ravenhunt stood there, between her and the pistol.

Ravenhunt. Naked.

How had he—? How could he have moved there so quickly?

He half-turned to her. Blood poured from a wound in his chest. "Are you all right?" he shouted at her.

"You've been shot."

Her eyes widened as she drank in the muscles of his chest— which she had seen before, but which looked all the more impressive under the glow of the streetlight. Her gaze went lower. Yes, utterly naked. Not a stitch on him.

"Ravenhunt, for heaven's sake, you don't have clothing," she cried.

"This you notice, when one of these idiots shot at you?"

"You are wounded." He had been shot in the chest, and blood was rushing out of the wound like a river.

Her legs wobbled, but she stumbled toward him. She had to use something to stop the flow of blood.

She shouldn't touch him—

He would die if she didn't.

"It's all right, Lady Ophelia."

"Stand down, Ravenhunt." The gray-haired man held a strange weapon pointing at him. She recognized it from pictures in books. A medieval crossbow.

In front of her, Ravenhunt seemed to disappear. But he didn't. There was a blur of movement, like ripples in the air on a hot day. Next thing she knew, the arrogant young man who had fired the pistol was lying unconscious on the ground, Cartwell was disarmed, and nude Ravenhunt held the crossbow pointed at both men.

The other young man fired. The pistol exploded with a roar, a flash of powder. The ball slammed into Ravenhunt.

She screamed.

Blood blossomed on his side. There was an enormous, bloody, black-rimmed hole in the side of his chest. It should have felled him, just as the first shot should have, but he just frowned at it.

Ravenhunt stalked to the man, grasped his arm, and twisted it sharply. A loud *crack* filled the air, as the man cried out. The pistol fell.

"Run, you Royal Society bastard," he snapped at Cartwell. "Run before I shoot you with your own damned crossbow."

Cartwell ran, stumbling on the cobbles.

Ravenhunt turned to her and crooked his finger. "Come, Lady Ophelia. We must get you to safety. There are likely more of them—Cartwell's flight will send them in pursuit of us."

She knew she was being a meek and cowardly fool. But she walked toward Ravenhunt. Even though he was naked. Even though he must be insane. Even though he had kept her as a prisoner.

He had taken two pistol shots for her. She was dazed and unable to think.

Ravenhunt stepped toward her, and she realized the blood was no longer flowing from his wounds. With shaky fingers, she touched the first wound. The blood was dry. The hole was smaller.

She looked at the wound on his side. He said nothing. Just stood and let her look.

When she straightened, the hole in his chest was gone.

"You've healed," she gasped. "That's impossible!"

Ravenhunt inclined his head. "I have a power, too, Lady Ophelia. The power to heal myself." He smiled. "Do you believe me now, Ophelia? Do you accept that you are in danger and you can trust me?"

"I—I don't know. Those men were going to kill me. But you took me prisoner. Was it for them?"

"No. But you have to understand now why I kept you and would not let you go."

"Why are you not wearing any clothes?"

"I was undressing for bed when I realized you had escaped."

"And you ran out naked?" *Naked* was not a word she was supposed to say to a man. Suddenly she thought of something. "You must have known I took your keys when you left. You would have tried to lock the door. You knew all along."

He began to shake his head, but he looked guilty.

"You let me escape. You let me take the key, you followed me. When I thought I was so clever and I had defeated you, I hadn't at all!" Somehow that made her the angriest. That he must have been laughing at her at every step.

"I had to let you understand the dangers out here," he said.

"You let me escape because you knew they would attack me."

"I had to make you appreciate the danger is real."

"Why? Why would you care? What do you want from me? I have nothing to give. All I do is hurt people."

Ophelia threw the words at him and tried to run from him.

But Raven caught her wrist and pulled her hard against his chest. He cradled her. Raven knew this touch was not for seduction. He heard the self-loathing in her frantic tones. She had a power she could not control, and he knew what hell that was like.

He hugged her.

"You shouldn't do this," she said bitterly. "You might die."

"Then give me a kiss. If I'm going to die for it, I want to make it worth it."

"We cannot kiss here. You are not wearing any clothes."

He laughed at that. "True." He released her and bowed. "Come back to my home with me. Let me keep you safe."

"But what am I going to do? I mean, from now on. I cannot live like this."

He kissed the top of her head. He was naked because he had changed into bat form and had flown to her rescue. It had been a closer shave than he'd planned.

"There is a solution, Lady Ophelia," he said softly. "You can give up your power. You can give it to me. But—"

"But?"

"You will have to come with me, where you will be safe. Then I will explain. Are you willing, Lady Ophelia?"

"Do I have a choice?"

"Yes, you do. You can run away from me now."

"And risk getting shot by more of those lunatic men. Or I can trust you. I choose you. I will go home with you."

5

The Bookstore

The door closed behind her, Ravenhunt turned the key in the lock, and Ophelia faced him, knowing she had willingly stepped into her prison. Now she would find out if she had been wrong to believe him.

"How do I give you my power? Why in heaven's name would you want it?"

He led her to the dining room. The forgotten supper was cold, but he handed her a crystal goblet brimming with white wine. She sipped, for he seemed to be waiting for her to drink. When she paused, he motioned with his hand for her to drink more.

She frowned. "Why do you want me to be tipsy before you tell me?"

"You are remarkable. You were just attacked by men of the Royal Society, and yet you are flinty-eyed and calm with me."

"You are avoiding the question."

"You are a worthy adversary, Lady Ophelia. But I want you to understand we aren't fighting anymore." He pointed to the door. "You are free to go whenever you wish."

"I don't wish to right now."

He plucked her glass from her hand and filled it again.

"Why do you want my power, Ravenhunt? Is it because you are an assassin?"

"I don't want to use it, love. It is my plan to destroy the power so no one can use it. Only I can do that, and I have to take it from you to do it."

She took another sip of the wine. It was dry and tart and delectable. His words did make sense. She could be free of the power. And it would never hurt anyone else—

He lifted her hand to his lips as she drank a little more of the tempting wine. He brushed her fingers with a gentle kiss, then turned her hand and gave a long, lingering kiss in her palm.

Tendrils of smoke rose, and she snatched her hand back.

"To take your power, Lady Ophelia, I have to make love to you."

"You have to do *what?*"

Ravenhunt dropped to his knees before her. He pushed up her skirts, exposing her stocking-clad legs, then the silk of her garters, the bare skin of her thighs.

In her shock, the wineglass tipped in her hand, the golden liquid splattering on his head. He just shook his hair. With her skirts bunched up and captured in place by his hands, he pulled her toward his face.

"What are you doing?" she cried.

He pressed his lips to her belly, just above her private place. His eyes were closed, his thick lashes touching his cheeks. He groaned with pleasure. She still had her shift covering her, but what he was doing was scandalous.

She tried to push him away. "Stop it. You are making this up. How could I give you my curse—my power, as you call it—by making love to you?"

This must be a ploy to fool her into surrendering her innocence, to get her into his bed. Why he would want to do such a thing, she couldn't imagine. She had burned his mouth, and smoke had risen from his lips when he kissed her hand. What was wrong with this madman that he would want to kill himself just to get her into his bed?

Beneath arched brows, his dark eyes reflected candlelight at her. "I can't explain exactly how it works, but I was assured by experts that it would."

She had to admit he looked innocently at her, as if speaking the truth. "Good heavens, what sort of experts would tell you how to take an evil power from a woman through . . . through those sorts of things?"

His lips lifted in a gentle smile. "You are adorable, Lady Ophelia. You have to trust me. I just saved your life, did I not? I am trying to protect you, exactly as I promised I would. Would you not want to be free of the power to take human lives just by touch?"

Of course she would! It was what she dreamed of . . . that one day she would wake up and discover she no longer hurt people. Then she could leave Mrs. Darkwell, and she could have a life like other women. But there was one problem . . .

"I can't make love with you." Ophelia put her hands over her face. "How could I do such a thing? It is what husbands and wives do. I am not *married* to you."

"You are astoundingly innocent." He sighed. "You do not believe me, do you?"

"I don't know. It sounds . . . impossible. You saved my life and everything you warned me about seems to be true, so I do trust you. But this sounds utterly insane."

"Isn't your power impossible? How could you destroy people just by touching them? But you do. Ophelia, you have to believe I want to free you. If you require marriage to come to my bed, then I am willing to do it."

"Heavens, you can't mean you would marry me?"

"Yes. If necessary, I would."

He must be joking, yet Ravenhunt's level, steady gaze showed no hint of amusement. He looked completely serious. "No! I would never marry you."

"Then let me pleasure you."

Abruptly, he pulled her forward again so her tummy bumped against his mouth. She could hear deep, harsh breaths. He put his lips against the juncture of her thighs, through her shift. He kissed her there.

Her eyes were so wide with shock, it hurt. "Stop that!"

"I can't," he growled. "I have to do this. I have to take your power from you, to free you."

"Why? Why must you?" She jerked away from him, her heart pounding. She managed to drag herself free. Her crumpled skirts fell down to cover her legs.

Ravenhunt looked . . . wild. His eyes were narrowed and seemed to be burning fiercely. His mouth was a slash of agony. He raked his hands through his hair, turning it into tangled waves that fell to his shoulders.

"I need to because—" He frowned and ran his hand through his hair again. "It doesn't matter. If I take it, Lady Ophelia, you'll be free. I'm going to free you from this power, whether you like it or not. So, tonight, we are going into town. There are people who will prove to you that what I am saying is true." His dark brow lifted. "By the time I am finished with you tonight, Lady Ophelia, you will be begging me to make love to you."

He'd gone too far with those last words, damn it.

By making such a bold statement, he had scared her away. Even now, in the hackney carriage, Lady Ophelia was huddled in the shadowy corner, as far from him as she could possibly sit.

Raven wanted to kick himself.

But he hadn't been thinking. He'd been driven by hunger

and lust. Right now, he was fighting like Wellington to avoid the scent of her blood. Sweet, enticing, it promised delicious warmth on his tongue—and a rich flavor that would stay with him for days.

When he'd been on his knees in front of her, he'd scented her blood and the musky aroma of her cunny. He'd almost lost control.

Jade had been right. The smell of Ophelia's blood was the most intoxicating scent he'd ever known.

He wanted it. Even just a drop—just one incredible drop.

He knew damn well he would not stop at one drop.

"I apologize for my crude words earlier," he said softly. He had to seduce her. She had to be a very willing partner in this, or he could not get her power.

"Harumph," she muttered. "I would not marry you."

"Remember the prize at the end of this. You would be free of your power."

"And married to *you*."

"You don't have to marry me. Just be my lover, and then you can be free."

She bit her lip. In the gesture, he saw how uncertain she was. She wanted freedom, but for a gently bred maiden, the price was frightening and high.

He had to take it slower. *Seduction, damn it. Remember?*

He should sit beside her, and slowly, carefully, make her more receptive to him. But it would be damned impossible to be so close to her and hang on to his control. He was fighting hard inside to not drink from her. In the small confines of his carriage, he couldn't escape her alluring smell. He could hear the thunder of her blood. Her heart had been pumping hard ever since he'd said those ill-chosen words to her about making love to her. It was like an echoing drumbeat in his head. On its rhythm, his head filled in words: *Drink. You are so hungry. Take her.*

Raven managed to give her a seductive smile. When what he wanted was to jump across the carriage to her, sink his fangs into her neck, and pleasure her lovely breasts and her creamy, hot cunny while he savored her blood.

Can't do that. Get command of yourself.

"This is a fool's errand," she said coldly. "Even if you convince me this crazy tale is true, I won't—"

"Freedom always comes at a price." He bit off the words so he softened his voice. "I promise you'll also enjoy it."

"But how could it work? It makes no sense. Anyway, how do you know all of these things?" Her gaze narrowed. "Who are you?"

He was astounded she hadn't yet guessed he was a vampire. Given how much he wanted her beautiful blood, he was amazed he'd hidden it so well. "I know about the preternatural beings that live in London."

"How? Do you know Mrs. Darkwell? Is that how you know about me?"

"It doesn't matter how I know about you. All that matters is that I can change you. I can free you, if you let me. Now, no more questions. I will lead you tonight. Then you can make your decision."

Watching her turn to the window and stare out, he felt a strange pang in his chest. The light from street flares caressed her face as they passed them. She had a sweet face. An upturned nose, plump lips. Large, guileless indigo-blue eyes.

She wore a cloak he had loaned her. The night was cool. The hood engulfed her, the hems trailed below her feet. He never bothered with a coach, and he kept no servants. He had needed the hackney to bring her. He knew the Royal Society would have spies watching the house—it had been easy to enter the minds of their weak sentry, to make those young, stupid men believe they were seeing nothing, then he had walked Lady Ophelia out, right under their noses.

She had a core of strength, but she was vulnerable. He could sense it about her. Normally, as a vampire, he would prey on weaknesses in mortals. But because he admired her courage and strength, her susceptibility provoked his sympathy.

He didn't want to hurt her. He couldn't understand why the thought of taking her power and taking her life was hurting him so much. He'd had to kill as a soldier and as a vampire. He had to do this to protect his sister. Why did the thought of taking her life fill him with so much guilt?

It hurt in his gut. That was something he'd never experienced before.

"A bookshop in Charing Cross? This is where your experts reside?" Ophelia held on to the hood of Ravenhunt's cloak as she surveyed the front of the shop. The cloak trailed behind her, and the hood dipped over her eyes.

The store looked well weathered. Paint on the once-elegant sign was faded. The glass in the front was dusty.

"This is one," he answered. "The others, whom you will meet soon, reside in far more interesting places."

She couldn't understand him. He had come up with this strange tale that she had to make love to him, yet in the hackney he had sat back in the shadow and had acted as if he wanted to avoid her. On the other hand, she had done the same, determined to avoid him.

He had saved her life.

She kept remembering that. He had come to her rescue, and he was offering to give her the one thing she wanted in the world—freedom from her wretched power. The freedom to be among people. To go home. What did she have to lose, really, by believing in him? She couldn't go on living alone.

But could she be *intimate* with him? A small voice inside whispered this might be her only chance to ever know what it was like to hold a man. To make love . . .

Ravenhunt held the door open to the shop, waiting for her. Books were stacked up against the bow window, hinting that there were so many inside it would be impossible to move between them.

She stood at the door but didn't go in. "I really do not see how a bookseller can prove I will be 'cured' of my cursed power by—by doing things with you."

"Come in, Lady Ophelia," was all he said.

She didn't. "Who are these experts? I think I have the right to know. Where are these interesting places? I'm not going to take one more step until you tell me."

"Trust me."

Gah. It was an impasse, yet he was in control, and she knew he knew it.

She hated to give in, but she would learn more if she went inside. She would learn nothing if she stayed on the threshold. Glaring at Ravenhunt, she let him win this round, and she went in.

The dust on some of the books tickled her nose. Ophelia sneezed. But she didn't care about the slightly musty smell. She liked it. She had always *dreamed* of being able to walk into a bookstore again. After she had come into her power, she was never allowed to go out. She'd dreamed of going to places—to stores, Hyde Park, museums and galleries, Gunter's for treats, to balls and parties. And to bookstores. She had so longed to go to a bookstore again.

Then she realized something strange. "It is late at night. Why is the store open?"

"The owner works late. He is a historian as well as a merchant."

She was surprised. For once Ravenhunt gave her an answer. She couldn't resist examining the books on the shelves. Moonlight spilled in through the window and illuminated them. A glow of candlelight came from the back of the shop.

She ran her gloved fingers over the row right in front of her eyes. Gilt lettering on the spines gleamed at her. "I could spend a lifetime in here," she mused.

"A bluestocking?"

She blushed. That was a term for bookish ladies, but *ordinary* ladies. "I've always wanted to come to a bookshop. And go to a modiste, a milliner's, a confectionary . . . I've never been able to do any of those things."

"I am sure Guidon would be happy to part with as many books as you desire."

Ophelia assumed Mr. Guidon owned the shop. "I have no money."

"They will be a gift from me," Ravenhunt said. "After all, I've kidnapped you. Buying books is one more way to make amends, I hope."

Ophelia saw one in front of her. *The Elgin Marbles*, it was titled, and she tugged it out and opened it. Pen-and-ink drawings greeted her eyes, rich with detail. Oh, she was almost willing to say yes to his offer, just to hug this book to her chest and never let it go.

But she didn't want to take gifts from him.

Though he saw the longing in her eyes as she gazed at the pictures, Raven knew it was going to take much more than books to make amends. A lot more than that to seduce her. "Let's go to the back of the shop and you can meet Guidon."

The narrow space forced her to bump against his chest. Blood. Sweet skin. Beautiful feminine smells.

A shock of desire went through him. Pain ran through his jaw, and he felt the bones of it grind and shift.

His fangs erupted.

He had to keep his face turned away, his lips covering them. Ophelia's scent was even more dominant to him here than it had been in the carriage.

Her scent was a temptation that made his jaws ache with hunger and desire. She was walking in front of him to the back of the shop. She'd pushed back her hood. Her pale hair was twirled and pinned in a chignon that bared her neck. Her skin was dewy, soft, tempting. It would be like biting into an iced cake—delicious, decadent, sheer damned pleasure.

Damn. Jade hadn't told him his hunger for her would get worse.

He hung back and let her walk ahead. The sight of her neck left his jaw aching with the pressure of his elongated fangs, and had given him the hardest, heaviest erection he'd had in years.

Making love to her was going to be easy. Hurting her was not.

Ophelia had expected a bookish-looking sort of man. A bit plump, with spectacles and little hair, or very thin and hawkish looking. She hadn't expected Mr. Guidon would be so tiny he looked like a gnome, with wild tufts of yellowish hair. He wasn't sitting on his stool, he was perched on it, the way a hawk would wait on a branch before flying in pursuit of prey.

Before she or Ravenhunt spoke, the small bookseller leapt off his seat and made a decorous bow in front of her. "My lady, I am at your service."

"How do you know who I am?"

"His—I mean, Mr. Ravenhunt told me."

Ravenhunt cleared his throat and said, "I told him days ago, when you first came back with me, Lady Ophelia."

"Came back with you? I take it he does not know you kidnapped me?" she asked sardonically.

"I do know that, my lady." Guidon took her hand and led her into a small parlor at the back of the store, one that looked out over a tiny, dark yard. She pulled her hand away, her cheeks flaming. Smoke rose from the bookseller's palm.

"I'm so sorry," she gasped. "I should not have let you touch me. I might have hurt you. I probably have hurt you."

His strange little face studied her with a grave expression. "No, my lady, I assure you, you did not. You cannot harm me with just a small touch like that." He held out his hand. Ink stained his fingers, but there was no sign of a burn. Even though there had been smoke. "Now please take a seat and be comfortable. I shall make tea."

Ravenhunt remained standing as she sat. "One moment," he said stiffly. Then he followed Guidon out.

What was he up to? Telling Guidon to agree with his ridiculous story? Well, she was not going to accept anything just on this strange man's assurance. She wanted proof.

Her face went hot. Heavens, how could she even discuss this with this odd, little bookseller?

What madness had she tumbled into?

Raven followed the vampire Guidon into the small kitchen. He spoke in Guidon's thoughts while the vampire poured water into his kettle. *Somehow she hasn't figured out that I am a vampire. She cannot find out. I have to seduce her, and she is not going to let that happen if she thinks I'm an undead demon who wants to suck her blood.*

Guidon scuttled to a crockery jar and put biscuits on a gilt-rimmed plate. He made a sound of disapproval. *My lord, she will find out. You think she is naïve and unknowledgeable, but she is not. I think, under other circumstances, she would have put clues together quickly and have determined you are not mortal.*

Raven leaned against the door frame, stepping back to allow the troll-like vampire to move swiftly around his tiny space, assembling the accoutrements for tea on a silver tray. *How do you know that, Guidon?*

I know of her from my studies of the history and genealogy of the metaphysical beings of England. I know Mrs. Darkwell. Lady Ophelia has had many shocks in her young life, and I am sure that being taken prisoner was most troubling for her. She has endured a great deal. She is by nature a very clever young woman, yet given the grave weight weighing upon her, I suspect her mind is not working as well as it should. She is distressed, and that has slowed her wits where you are concerned. What reason did you give her for appearing naked to rescue her?

He had told Guidon about that by thought. *My reasoning was meager and transparent. She should have been more suspicious. I think, because she was frightened and I had saved her life, she was accepting.*

He could see the vampire's point. Ophelia had endured a lot, and she was probably too overwhelmed to take in any more—to really try to guess what he was.

Guidon spun around. His large, protruding eyes were wild with anger. *I will not allow you to do this to this innocent young woman. To take her power will kill her.*

That's why I came to you, damn it. I don't want to hurt her. But the vampire queen Jade will destroy my sister if I refuse. Is there any way I can take her power without hurting her?

You truly do not want to kill her. You? You are an assassin—

Damn it, I know what I am. Even through thought, the words came out as an angry shout. *I shouldn't care, but I do. She doesn't deserve to die. But I can't sacrifice Frederica to protect her. There has to be a way to save them both.*

There is. Steam poured out of the kettle's spout, and its lid rattled under the pressure. Guidon plucked it off the heat and poured it into his teapot. *She must fall in love with you.*

Hades, how would her falling in love with me save her? He sounded like Ophelia. She hadn't believed his story; he didn't believe Guidon's. *How am I going to make her do that anyway? I'm the vampire who kidnapped her.*

I do not know exactly why it works, but I know her antecedents, and I know from where she came. I know that love, both given and received, will protect her.

So where does she come from?

That you do not need to know. But mark my words, she also needs your true love to protect her.

Raven shrugged. *I think I can do that. She's quite sweet and lovely. She possesses an ingenious mind and a strong character.*

Guidon set the teapot on the tray. He wagged his finger. *You must understand this. If she does not die when you take her power, you probably will.*

It didn't surprise him. He kept his face expressionless and remarked carelessly, "There's always a catch."

Guidon considered him. "Is it a price you are willing to pay?"

"To save two innocent women? Hell, as a soldier I was willing to give my life for our mad king, our fat regent, and my wretched country. Yes, I am willing to die."

"Let me give you something, my lord—"

"I am not 'my lord' any longer," Raven growled quietly. "To that world, I am dead, and there is another marquis."

Guidon nodded, then he disappeared, leaving the tea tray on a small table. Raven followed. The small gnome-like man had gone to the very back of the shop. He unlocked a door with a large, iron key. Inside was a closet, with shelves of books. "The rarest volumes. The only old ones to survive. This one will explain to you what you must do."

As he drew it out and blew dust from it, Guidon was blushing.

The librarian pressed it into his hands. "There are steps you must take in this seduction, or it will not work. It explains how you can protect her, and how the power will destroy you."

What had they been discussing in secret? Ophelia watched both Ravenhunt and Mr. Guidon with suspicion. Carrying a tea tray, the small bookseller was actually blushing. Ravenhunt stroked his jaw, obviously worried about something, and he carried a leather-bound book beneath his arm. The book was closed with a tarnished hasp.

Guidon set down the tray and Ravenhunt said quickly, "So you see, Lady Ophelia has been kept a prisoner for years, Guidon. She has never had the chance to visit a bookshop and buy books. I've offered to buy her whatever her heart desires. But I don't think she wants to accept a gift from me."

She jerked her head up, startled. "No, I don't want—"

"Would you accept a gift from me, my lady?" Guidon asked. "I am so troubled by what you have had to endure. I would like to give you several books."

"Oh, I shouldn't. This is your livelihood."

"Not my sole one. I am also a historian of the metaphysical world of England. And I wish to give you this gift. It would break my heart if you do not accept."

"Then I shall." She smiled at him, but frowned at Ravenhunt. He was up to something. She did not think he had been discussing gifts in the back of the shop.

Mr. Guidon poured her a cup of tea and handed it to her. "Now, I shall explain to you how you can be free of your power." He had been blushing—now he turned flaming red.

"It—it is true that in-intimacy does it," he stuttered. "I mean, it takes your power away. You must—he must—it is about making—"

The poor man ran his finger around his collar. Finally, a flood of words exploded from him. "Making love allows the power to be taken from you. It takes time, though. It cannot be done quickly. There must be a seduction. And love will protect you."

He poured tea and literally threw it down his throat.

"But why do I have this power? Where did it come from?" How could he know about it? Was any of this really the truth?

"It is a power you inherited, my dear, from your mother. She did not have the same power, you see, but in you, this is how it was manifested."

"I don't understand. My mother was quite normal."

"It is hard to explain, my dear. But I believe your mother would want you to be free of your power now, Lady Ophelia."

"How could you know that? What do you know of my mother?"

Ravenhunt got to his feet, grasped her arm, and forced her to stand. "We should go now," Ravenhunt said. "The sooner we leave, the sooner you will be free, my dear."

She tried to protest, but Ravenhunt hurried her out of the shop. In the back, in Guidon's cluttered parlor, a clock chimed twelve. The hackney had waited, black horses whinnying and pawing restlessly. Ravenhunt had paid the man several shillings to keep him there. Street flares lit up the street, and the smoke of fires wafted across the moon like ghostly fingers.

Ophelia stood just outside the shop, feeling lost inside. Even though Guidon had told her that it was true that intimacy with Ravenhunt would free her, it had felt unreal.

But now was the time for reality. She was supposed to return to Ravenhunt's home. Allow him those intimacies. It didn't matter about love and desire. This was a mechanical thing she was supposed to do, a series of impersonal steps that would free her forever.

Except it wasn't impersonal. She couldn't look at it that way.

"Let us go," he said coolly. "It's only midnight. It's not late yet."

"Are we going to your house? Are we going to—to do things?"

He came up to her, his expression gentle. Softly, he stroked the back of his gloved hand along her cheek. Just for a moment. She willed herself not to draw away. If she wanted freedom, she had to accept his every touch—at least the small, quick touches that she could permit before she feared hurting him.

"Not yet," he said.

"Then where are we going? To see more experts? I—I am willing to believe you." *But am I willing to do it? I don't know. I'm scared.*

Gently, he put thumb and forefinger to her chin and tipped up her face. She caught her breath. The heat and sizzle began where the pad of his thumb touched her skin. His lips came close to hers. Her lips tingled in anticipation.

But he didn't kiss her.

"Seduction should be a slow and enticing thing, Ophelia. I am not going to force myself on you. I know exactly how to make you want to make love. Just trust me."

She had already accepted she would have to. At the lack of a kiss, she felt a pang of disappointment. She'd begun to enjoy them. "Let us go, then. I do not want to do things slowly. I need to be free. I cannot live like this anymore. I will do it—"

"With your teeth gritted and your eyes shut," he broke in. "No, we do it my way. Understand?"

She nodded, knowing she had no choice. "Do you not have to touch me much more than you've done already to make love? Will it not hurt you?"

He grinned—a wicked combination of curved lips, dimples, and a quick flash of white teeth. The sheer handsome beauty in that naughty smile stole her breath. Then she frowned. Something had been wrong in that smile. But she wasn't sure what.

Before Ophelia could grasp the thought that nagged her, Ravenhunt lifted her hand to his mouth. He gave a slow, lingering, hot, teasing kiss to the center of her palm. She felt hot everywhere.

Then he let her hand go. "There are many ways to give you pleasure, little one, without my touch. Let me show you."

6

Spanked

Their hackney carriage lurched away from the curb, and Ravenhunt joined her on the seat. Ophelia peppered him with questions.

"Where are we going? To more experts? What is it you want to show me—really what is it? Because I can't see how you can show me about what you . . . said. About not touching! I don't think that is even *possible*."

She knew she was acting unlike her normal self. Usually she was quiet. A "fade into the wallpaper" girl. A girl whose duty it was to be isolated and alone, and one of the easiest ways to accomplish that was to keep one's mouth closed. All those questions she threw at him surprised even her. They rushed out with such speed she had to gasp for breath.

"It is possible." Through the carriage window, the glow of a street flare reflected on Ravenhunt's dark eyes, making them bright and silvery.

"Of course you choose the most unhelpful answer to share with me. Then my questions must be—how?"

"You'll see."

"Not good enough," she shot back. Ravenhunt was tall,

well-built, strong—and insanely courageous, for who else would stand in front of a pistol shot to protect someone? She should be intimidated by him. But she no longer felt that way.

"Tell me how," she demanded.

He shrugged. "First we build anticipation."

With the jingle of traces, the creak of wheels on cobbles, the hackney stopped. "Here we are," Ravenhunt informed her, his eyes masked by shadow, his voice as smooth as sin.

She folded her arms over her chest. She was willing to sit for hours—a prisoner is accustomed to long stretches of utter silence, immobility, and boredom. "Where is here?"

"I take it you won't move until I tell you."

"I am more than willing to bankrupt you in hackney fares by sitting here for weeks. Years, even."

He laughed in the gloom. "All right. This is a club where couples come to engage in sexual adventure."

"*What?* I am not leaving this carriage."

"You are."

How unconcerned he sounded, as though her disobedience was of no consequence.

Squirming with frustration, she knew she was going to lose this round. She guessed he intended to carry her inside. He didn't seem to worry about touching her.

Then she spotted it. He held the small, thick, leather-bound book in his hand. Mr. Guidon had given it to him, and she had watched him flip through the pages while the bookseller had spoken with her. She had seen Ravenhunt's dark brows shoot up while he read.

She thought he'd left the book at Guidon's. Obviously he hadn't. While they had been in Mr. Guidon's parlor, he had not let her take even a glance at it. No matter how much she had asked and begged, he wouldn't tell her what it was. She couldn't try to pull it free of him—it was an old book, likely very rare.

But her argument had distracted him. She caught her breath. And lunged.

One instant the book was there, temptingly close to her hand. The next it was over his head.

"You move so quickly sometimes I cannot even see you."

Ravenhunt did not say a word. He tucked the book into an inner breast pocket of his coat.

"What are you?" Ophelia asked. "You know everything about me. Please tell me more about you. I want to know."

Raven could not tell her the truth. But he had to give her some kind of plausible story. "I'm like you. Mostly normal, but with a few unusual powers that ordinary people do not possess. It's those powers that make me a . . . vampire hunter, an assassin of vampires." It was partly the truth, partly a damned audacious lie.

Needing to bring an end to the discussion, Raven jumped down from the hackney to the cobbled street, then handed Lady Ophelia down.

As he had her hand she bit her lip. "You touch me so much. Are you not afraid of what it will eventually do?"

"I enjoy touching you, and I enjoy knowing that my touches are some of the very few you've enjoyed." He gazed directly into her deep blue eyes. "I'm not afraid of you, Lady Ophelia. Now you aren't afraid of me anymore. I think this new state of affairs between us will mean an enjoyable evening."

"Enjoyable? I don't think so." From beneath the oversized hood of her borrowed cloak, she cast a nervous glance toward the house. Her tongue flicked over her lips, leaving a gleam of moisture that sent one more jolt of arousal to his already hard cock. Another thing to fight while fighting his hunger.

He lifted her hand and kissed it until she gave soft, breathy moans. "It will," he promised.

"All right. I believe you," she whispered.

He offered his arm. She laid her hand lightly on his fore-arm and let him lead her up the steps. He felt pain but didn't show it.

He wasn't as confident as he let her believe. How would she react to the club? Lady Ophelia was innocent, extremely so. As a prisoner, she had been more cloistered than a nun.

Would she be frightened by bold sexual displays?

Hell, he would have to deal with it if it happened. He wanted her to recognize that sexual pleasure was natural and normal, and that she didn't need to fear it. Playing voyeur might arouse her, giving him the chance to start his mission to take her power.

He'd selected this club for a reason. It was a house on the edge of Mayfair, and since it served both ladies and gentlemen of the *ton*, it was the epitome of elegant erotic fun.

He detected Lady Ophelia's quick breaths before he rapped on the door. "Don't be frightened."

She jerked nervously with each thump of his fist on the door. "Easy for you to say," she muttered. "I suppose you come here all the time."

"No, I have never been here." Couples came here, and he had never been part of a couple—this was not the kind of place he would have taken his fiancée. He'd never had a regular mistress. "It will be an adventure for both of us. You will see that sex is enjoyable without the problems of love and marriage."

He slid his arm around her waist, but she jumped away so quickly he never even felt the pain. "*Problems* of love?"

"It's fraught with problems—" He broke off. Damn, he was supposed to make her fall in love with him for her own protection. On the other hand, maybe this was a role that could work in his favor. When he'd been engaged, his wife-to-be had endeavored to change him. She had told him women always viewed husbands as projects of improvement. Maybe he needed to pretend to be jaded about love—hell, not really pretend—

then let Ophelia convince him of how precious it was. Nothing would be more guaranteed to win her heart.

As long as she didn't find out he was a vampire.

"Love is a complicated thing, and leads to much unhappiness." He put on his best Byronic brood. "This is about pleasure. Here, you have to let me touch you. We have to appear to be an amorous couple in search of adventure. Mr. and Mrs. Ravenhunt."

"Oh heavens, really?"

She seemed more horrified to pretend to be his wife than to enter the sex club.

"Yes," he growled. "It will ensure you are protected. Stay close to me. That way no man can whisk you away and try to seduce you more forcefully."

"Forcefully!" she squeaked. "I do not want to go in here."

"There's nothing to fear. They will be too afraid of me to do anything to you. I promise." He lifted her gloved hand and kissed it. Pain singed his lips but he refused to stop.

She jerked her hand away. "I don't want you to *hurt* yourself. I'll do this—but I think it's hopeless."

It couldn't be. Not if he wanted to save both her and Frederica. But he had to lead her slowly. He knocked quick and hard. The doorman eyed him through the grille, then opened the door.

In moments, they were inside. Red silk covered the walls, along with prints of tattooed and bejeweled men and women in a multitude of sexual positions. Lady Ophelia's cheeks turned as red as the walls. Above them, strips of white silk flowed from the chandelier to the walls, giving a tent-like look to the room. He handed her cloak, along with his coat and hat, to the beefy doorman, and they were strolling from the large foyer, with its exotic décor to a hallway painted and decorated to look like an exotic oriental garden, though the statues were of Greek gods and goddesses. Like a terrified animal, Lady Ophelia slid her gaze hurriedly around, as if seeking danger. Would she run if she saw something that frightened her? Propelling her along the paneled hall, he kept watch on her and not everything around them.

"These statues are magnificent," she exclaimed. She ran away from him, and planted herself in front of a muscular Atlas, bent beneath the weight of the earth. Her fingertips were pressed to her full lower lip as she made soft sighs of pure admiration.

"You enjoy art—or just his admirable proportions?" Raven asked it teasingly, but he admired the glow of vivid pleasure in her eyes. When Ophelia was happy, she sparkled like a star.

"I love such classic statues. I have—" She hesitated.

"What?" he coaxed.

"I have done my own sculptures. Trapped with Mrs. Darkwell, I had to do something or go mad."

"That was why you were savoring the Elgin Marbles at the museum."

She nodded, but he saw the light fading in her eyes, as if it were extinguished by the memory of the early evenings they had spent together there. Probably because it reminded her she had been duped and kidnapped.

"You can touch," he told her. "Given the scandalous things done here, I don't believe anyone will mind."

She shook her head fiercely. "I shouldn't. You are like the serpent in Eden, tempting me to do so many things I shouldn't."

"There are no 'shouldn'ts' for you anymore. You are special and unique, and the normal rules of Society do not apply to you."

Her face looked grim. "*That* is true."

"It does not have to be all cursed." He led her hand to the bicep of the muscular marble arm. "You love sculpture, you want to touch it. Indulge yourself."

She was as stiff as a board as he moved her fingers over the

smooth contours of the stone. He forced her to trace the sinu-
ous lines up to the shoulder. Then her lips parted to exhale
quick breaths, and Raven knew he was breaking though the
cold shield of unhappiness that had quickly enveloped her.

"It is remarkable work," she whispered, as if they were in
church and she was afraid to shatter the reverent atmosphere.
Her eyes shone, glowing with more than admiration. She loved
this.

"So you are a female sculptress? That's unusual."

"I—I suppose." She glanced at him, but she didn't stop
touching the marble Atlas in front of them.

It had been more than a hobby, he realized. She couldn't
touch anyone, yet like any human she had yearned to do it. Not
just feel someone's touch and savor those expressions of affection and love, but give them herself.

He had assumed he had become heartless when he'd been
changed into a vampire and had been made soulless. But he
knew he had a heart—it cracked for her with a considerable
shot of pain.

"I would like to see your work someday," he said softly, by
her ear.

"Oh. Oh, you wouldn't be able to. Everything is at Mrs.
Darkwell's and I can never go back there—"

"That's true," he said darkly. "I would never let you go
back. You are going to be free, Ophelia. I vow it."

She looked down the hall. "There are more statues—" She
broke off. A blush ran down her face like a stage curtain drop-
ping. "Oh my goodness," she whispered, her voice strangled.

Turning, he saw the reason for her flushed cheeks and shock.
Many other statues lined the ample hallway, but they depicted
sex. Muscular men mounted dainty Grecian goddesses from on
top, underneath, from behind. One group showed a woman in
savage ecstasy being penetrated by two figures—each half-bull,
half-man, with cocks the size of cricket bats.

"You aren't going to expect . . . any of that, are you?" she asked.

She was frightened. But it was his duty to transform her from a woman who had learned not to touch into a wanton lover. "Only the fun things. It will just be between the two of us."

For one moment, he toyed with removing choice from the equation. As a vampire, he had the power to compel a woman to offer her throat. He could control a mortal's thoughts; he could make her do anything he wanted. That was the kind of undead being he was. But here, now, that wasn't what he was allowed to do. Guidon told him he needed her consent; he needed her to be willing. He could not manipulate her mind, or he would not be able to take her power.

"Why do you hunt and kill vampires?" she asked quietly, surprising him. He thought he'd distracted her from that. "There were vampires at Mrs. Darkwell's. They didn't hurt anyone."

"Some do. We shouldn't speak of this here. People wouldn't understand."

She glanced around. Laughter came from down the hall, but they were currently alone in the statue-filled corridor, with its watered silk walls and gleaming floor. "I should not be here. What if I touch someone or someone touches me? It doesn't take much for me to hurt someone . . . normal."

"I will keep you by me and ensure no one touches you." He put his hands on her shoulders and placed her in front of him. Behind her, Raven gritted his teeth as pain shot through his arms. At least she didn't appear to feel it. He propelled her toward the laughter and noise at the end of the hall. On the way, he lifted his right hand from her shoulder, whisked a glass of champagne from a footman's silver tray, and pressed it into her hand.

She wrinkled her nose and peered at the slender flute, the golden liquid, the popping bubbles, as if he'd given her a witch's brew. "I've never had champagne."

"Try it. If you want to be free of your power, you are going to have to spread your wings a little and fly into adventure."

He watched her slim, gloved fingers pinch the stem. Her lower lip plumped as she rested the gilt rim of the glass on it, then sipped. Her eyes widened, large and blue. A soft giggle escaped. "It tickles," she whispered.

He bent close to her small, delicate ear. Her golden curls brushed his lips. "See. Pleasures await when you are adventurous."

He let his breath whisper over her ear. But getting so close he breathed her scent, and it was a damned mistake. Fang eruption occurred, and he had to hide them. At least he stood at her back, where she could not see.

The drawing room doors were open, and he directed her inside. He kept his attention on people around them—to ensure no one collided with Ophelia. His glower made men step back and women retreat to give them space. Gentlemen near the door wore tailcoats, waistcoats, trousers, cravats. Fully dressed, they wouldn't shock Ophelia. Most of the women wore just shifts, corsets, petticoats. Or filmy nightdresses of silk. Though in the middle of the room there was probably an energetic orgy taking place, with eager males penetrating every orifice of bounteous and willing women.

"Oh, he's tied up!" Ophelia cried.

Raven looked up. His jaw dropped down.

He was staring at a muscular, naked arse. The crowd had gathered in a circle around the display in the center of the room. A riding crop whistled through the air and landed with a sharp *thwak* on the tight, rounded rump. Broad shoulders jerked, muscles twitched, and a black scarf tied at the back of his head showed he was blindfolded. He looked about two-and-twenty, with curly blond hair. His arms stretched above his head, his wrists tied together. Ropes ran from his bound hands to hooks in the ceiling.

Hades, Raven had thought this was a club where, if there was play of this sort, the males were dominant, the women submissive. Apparently, he'd chosen the wrong one.

Another woman stepped forward—the dominant females wore corsets dyed black with their large bosoms jiggling on top of the boning. She spanked the young man with a wooden paddle. A third attended to his rump with the flat of her hand.

Ophelia twisted to face him, her eyes as large as saucers. "You wish me to tie you up and smack you with things?"

"No. Wrong club," he muttered. "Come, this is enough for tonight." Between visiting Guidon and coming here, they had spent enough time out. He should get her home before dawn.

"Was this your idea of what we would do instead of touching? Spanking?" she asked, her eyes wide and guileless.

The image of spanking her voluptuous bottom speared him. But he was not going to have her do it to him. He should have known Lady Ophelia would not be so easily quelled.

"It can be erotic," he said. "But I—"

"Well, if it's what you wanted to do," she said briskly, "I'll start on you."

A bark of a laugh left his lips. That was not going to happen. He could not deal with being struck, not by a woman. Not after his years with Queen Jade.

"No, you will not. We are going to return to the house."

"You want to go home already? We just arrived."

"I did not expect the men would be submissive," he growled. "I don't want to give you too many ideas. We need to go. It's almost dawn."

Damnation, he was rattled. He should not have said that.

* * *

"You do not really want me to spank you, do you, Raven-hunt?"

"Indeed, I do not." But he gave her a smile filled with devilment, thoroughly mischievous. They had stepped into the foyer of his house. Using the key she had swiped earlier, he locked the door, then slid four bolts across to secure it.

Yes, he had definitely allowed her to escape earlier, for those heavy, awkward bolts had been left open. Now he was making sure his house was completely secure.

She couldn't bear to think of men who wanted to kill her. She was too tired.

Spanking. Ophelia never would have dreamed she would think about spanking a man so she did not have to think about assassins and mad scientists.

He turned to her. Moonlight spilled in through small windows flanking the door, sending blue streaks through his hair, casting blue shadows across his crisply sculpted features.

His was a beautiful face. Her fingers tingled. Suddenly she was compelled to sculpt it. To remember every detail so she could slowly coax marble to flow in those magnificent lines.

"To be honest," he said, "I was planning to spank you."

She quirked a brow. "I wouldn't like that. It would hurt."

"I would never hurt you." His voice was smooth as chocolate, deep and husky. "Think of the way it would tease your skin."

"A blow would not tease me!"

"A soft blow. Just enough to ignite your nerve endings. Enough to make your skin sensitive and your nerves sizzle. To send a rush of electric sensation through your body. To make your quim ache and pulse. To make you feel, my dear. I could make you come, just by spanking you."

"Come? Come where?" she asked, confused.

"Coming means the orgasm you will have."

She looked at him, lost. "What is that?"

"When your body feels pleasure—when it feels sexual stim-ulation—tension builds inside you. Your body works toward a climax, with the pleasure building and building until you want to scream. Then it explodes inside you, on a wave of pleasure that melts your soul, my love."

She shivered. His husky voice was like a magic spell. She al-most said yes. "Spanking is a punishment."

"In this case, it would be erotic foreplay."

Ophelia shook her head. His mouth hardened, forming harsh lines to bracket his firm, bronze-pink lips. "A deal," he offered, gruffly. "You spank me first, then I do it to you."

She frowned.

"Come, love. I'm allowing you to do it first."

"All right." But her agreement was a lie. She was not going to be struck on her bottom—no matter what he thought she'd agreed to. "Do we go up to the bedroom? What about your room? I haven't seen any other bedchamber that looks like it is used."

She had almost forgotten about that. It was another mystery about him.

He shrugged. For a man who had got what he wanted, he looked troubled. "My line of work—killing vampires—keeps me awake at nights. That's when I hunt them. So I don't need to use a bedchamber." A sharp tug of his gloved hand and he'd un-done his cravat. He let it drop to the floor of the foyer.

Ravenhunt was undressing right here.

It startled her and he smiled. "Your mouth is a huge O, Ophelia. You shouldn't be shocked. You've seen my naked body before."

Yes, all muscle and lean sinewy strength, and it had been shocking. "Why do you hunt vampires at night? They sleep in the day—I learned that at Mrs. Darkwell's. They are dormant and vulnerable. Isn't that the best time to go after them?"

There was a pause while he took off his tailcoat, then his waistcoat, and he let those fall carelessly, too. "You have to know where their lairs are. It is easier to protect the populace by hunting at night, so you can assassinate a vampire before it takes a victim."

That made sense, but she felt there was something not quite right. "You'd still need somewhere to sleep. You would just do it in the day."

"Since I have no servants, I just use a daybed in the study. It's easier than having to tend to more unnecessary rooms myself."

"Why do you have no servants? Is it because you keep kidnapping women and that's hard to explain?"

"The hunting and killing of vampires is an odd profession. We're supposed to keep people from learning vampires do exist. Along with other beings with special powers, like us."

One quick whisk of his arms and he pulled his shirt off, baring his perfect torso. "It's too cold and impersonal in here for a spanking to be any fun."

He started off, his clothes over his arm, and Ophelia followed. In for a penny, in for a pound. She had come back with him to his house, knowing full well what she had agreed to. In that club, she'd glimpsed other things happening in the corners of the room, when she'd quickly averted her eyes from the naked stranger who was tied up.

There was one woman on a man's lap, the skirts of her shift pushed up and her naked legs spread over his. She was leaning back with her back against his chest, and his hands were between her legs. Her bottom rose and fell on him with a rhythmic motion. They were doing something private and intimate in front of so many people, and they were doing it so they could both watch the man in the middle of the room.

Shocking, yes. But she'd felt a wave of hot . . . awareness.

Ravenhunt led her to a door at the other end of the hallway from hers. "The master's apartments," he said, pushing it open. "If I used a bedchamber, this would be the one."

It was the room she'd looked in earlier. In the center was the enormous bed—it stood at the height of her waist, with a dusty canopy soaring above. The counterpane was smooth and clean, but she suspected if she struck it, a cloud of motes would fly into the air. Balls of dust gathered like tiny kittens here and there on the floor.

He strode in and opened a chest that sat at the foot of the bed. "Ah, here it is. Thought it was here." Straightening, he had a much smaller wooden chest tucked under his arm.

It wasn't until they reached her room that he satisfied her curiosity. He set the small trunk on the vanity table and flipped open the lid. Out of it, he took a long thing that looked like a small whip, with a black leather-wrapped handle, and a long leather strap that dangled. Next he withdrew a wooden object, with a smooth, rounded paddle and a wood handle.

"What are those?"

"Accoutrements for spanking."

"You have a chest filled with things to use for hitting someone's bottom?"

"Not only that. They are all kinds of devices for enhancing sexual play. All gentlemen keep them. We spend much of our time when we aren't using them dreaming of how we will."

She was sure Ravenhunt was teasing her.

He led her back to her bedroom, where he tossed the wooden paddle onto the bed. "We should get started." His shoulders shook as he undid his trousers. His long lashes shielded his eyes, but she thought he looked . . . not aroused, but troubled.

One swift motion of his hand shoved his trousers down. Underneath, he wore nothing. His muscled, taut bottom was bared to her.

He planted his hands on the bed, spread his legs with his trousers bunched around the top of his boots. He hung his head, his straight black hair falling around his face.

She was supposed to smack him. With the paddle.

She couldn't use her hand without really hurting him.

All right. He wanted it. It was like a dare—and she'd never had the chance to do daring things. She'd been locked up for so long.

Curling her fingers around the smooth, varnished handle, she lifted the paddle. Held it above his bottom.

Oh heavens, she didn't want to hit anything so perfect. Pale, firm, and defined by the muscles beneath his smooth skin, his rump was a work of art.

Wouldn't smacking it be like a desecration?

"Come on, Ophelia," he groaned. "Do it."

She closed her eyes. Swung. But lost her courage at the end of the arc and arrested it, so the paddle only lightly tapped him.

Ravenhunt's breath came out in a fast, harsh stream. She couldn't see his face, but his back was tense and he made a growling sound. Then he groaned, "Excellent. But you can do it harder next time."

"It doesn't hurt?"

"It hurts in a good way. That's part of the—of the pleasure."

She tried again, being more firm. A quick slap to his hard right cheek. It barely jiggled, since his bottom was so taut.

His head bucked, his long, lean body braced on arms locked straight. So straight, the muscles bulged and his veins were like cords looped around his forearms. "God, that was good."

"You liked that?" Was there something to this she didn't quite understand? She would assume it wasn't pleasurable at all. But he twisted to face her, and there was such an intense expression on his face. Harsh lines ringed his mouth. His eyes were bright and intense. "Spank me again. You can't leave me hanging now."

She obliged, trying with a bit more force.

His deep, throaty moan vibrated through her. Goodness, he did like this. A thrill ran down her spine, a sensation that shot down between her legs and throbbed there, aching and demanding.

Instead of hitting him, she ran the flat of the paddle over the curve of his rump. If only it could be her hand touching him. Feeling how soft his skin was, even over that hard, solid muscle. She noticed the dusting of dark hair. She longed to coast her hand all over him, even down between his legs from the back and touch the fascinating large ballocks that dangled there.

She couldn't touch him. Certainly not there. Smoke rose when they touched. Contact with her obviously burned him, and she couldn't inflict that on tender places.

Oh, but she wished she could touch him.

"You do?" he asked softly.

Had she said it out loud? She must have. "Yes," she cried. "I want to grope your backside, and fondle the muscles on your arms, and put my arms around you, and—and—"

"Then do it," he said.

She smacked his bottom lightly with the paddle. "I can't. I'd hurt you."

"You know, love, I really don't care. It would be worth it to be touched by you."

Crazily, madly, she put the palm of her hand against his rump. Against the red mark the paddle had made.

But Ravenhunt flinched and smoke rose, and she snatched her hand away.

"Spank me," he urged, and she heard the note of laughter in

his voice. Turning, he winked at her, his long lashes flashing over his dark eye. She giggled.

When had she last giggled? She couldn't remember. Never had she thought it would be over a bare bottom and a session of spanking. This was utterly surprising. It was fun.

"Come on, love, you're killing me with suspense. I'm on the brink of a colossal erotic explosion. It hurts."

Goodness, she was not doing her duty here. She lifted the paddle and swacked him. She paddled his bottom lightly, then firmly, then gave one daring, hard smack.

"God," he muttered. His hips moved back and forth rhythmically, in time to her spanking.

"I had no idea," he growled, "it could feel so good—"

He broke off and shifted, so he was sideways across the bed. Her eyes went huge. From here, she could see his private parts. Huge and straight and thick and sticking straight out.

He wrapped his hand around the enormous shaft. Between moans, he gasped, "You are amazing. The most erotic woman with a paddle I could dream of."

Ophelia giggled shyly, then gasped herself. His hand ran along the length of his erection. He gripped tight, pulling at it.

How stunning. How marvelous. How strange. He was so rough with it. Surely those strokes, in that fearsome grip, must hurt.

And his moans . . . so loud, so intense, they made shivers go down her spine.

She spanked him again, and suddenly his head jerked, his body bucked, and he let out a cry of agony. His shaft seemed to swell to incredible proportions before her eyes. He jerked his hips up at the same moment a white fluid shot forth from his erection and spattered over his hand.

She gaped at him, the paddle dangling from her hand.

He straightened, and he cleaned his hand on a corner of the disordered bedsheet.

"Spectacular," he murmured.

Before she could think of a thing to say, he moved with his amazing speed. Next thing she knew he had the paddle in his hand and he grinned rakishly at her.

"Your turn," he said.

7

Coming

Beneath her skirts, her bottom was round, plump, and quivering.

Raven had swiftly changed positions, tossing her gently on the bed so she lay on her tummy, and he stood beside the bed with his trousers hanging off his hips and the paddle in his hand.

He brought it down, stopping just before the flat of the paddle struck her rump. Coming that close, anticipating the way her generous arse would jiggle when he struck, he was rockhard again. Even though he'd just climaxed so hard he'd thought his brains would melt.

"No," she cried. "I can't do this."

"You can," he murmured. He gave her a light tap with the paddle.

Hell, if he could do it, she could. With Jade, he had been whipped regularly, flayed all over his body. The idea of being hit again had made him darkly angry. But having Ophelia spank him had surprised him.

It had been playful. Fun. Erotic.

But she was tense with fear, and he had to make her melt.

He gently caressed her curves with the paddle. Having her spank his rear had kept him from going mad for the scent of her blood. It had also given him a reason to keep his face away from her curious gaze, so Lady Ophelia couldn't see how his fangs had launched out when he got aroused again.

With her, now, he was more than just sexually excited, more than hot and aching to pummel her sweet little ass. The tempting aroma was stronger than ever.

"You aren't spanking me," she whispered. She was twisting to see behind.

"I'm touching you without my hands. Fondling your lovely arse with the paddle."

She quivered at his words.

"Like it?" he murmured. He gave the lightest tap with the wood, making her bottom tremble under her gown.

"It—it tickles." She giggled.

He tried a firmer spank. This was what he enjoyed. Being in charge.

"No, I'm not ready to be spanked yet. I'm not. I'm just not. Please, please don't?"

He needed to command her, but not frighten her. "More caresses," he promised, and he ran the paddle over the globes of her bottom.

She giggled. The sound of her delight rang in his ears. If he closed his eyes, he could remember the sweetly desperate way she had protested that she was not ready to be spanked yet. It touched his heart, brought a smile to his lips.

Savoring the soft, silvery sound of her laughter, he set down the paddle. He laughed, too, and that made hers go on, until she hugged herself, smiling beautifully.

He was a man who no longer had any reason to smile, yet it was impossible not to laugh with Ophelia.

Their game had to end for the night. Dawn was close and

she was tired. As much as he hungered for the chance to apply the paddle to her luscious derriere, he had to wait. He had to let her sleep. And he had a pressing reason to stop now.

Hunger.

He had to satisfy it. Now.

Lifting the paddle from her bottom, he said softly, "That's enough for tonight. You need to sleep." Grasping her wrist, he quickly helped her sit up, then released her. Shirtless, he had his trousers pushed to his thighs, revealing his enormous erection. He saw how she tried to look away from his cock, but her gaze always riveted back to it.

He ruthlessly pushed his hard prick down and struggled with his trousers until he fastened them over the bulge. "Let me take you to your bedroom and tuck you into your bed."

She erupted into giggles again. "How can you say that—offer to tuck me into bed so sweetly—after you were going to spank my bottom?" But she finished her laughter with a yawn, which set her giggling again.

He held out the paddle for her, so she could grasp the handle. Pulling on it, he whisked her to her feet. She swayed on her slender legs, obviously exhausted. Yawning again, she put her hand over her mouth.

Not caring about the pain that went through him, Raven lifted her into his arms and carried sleepy Lady Ophelia to her bed. There he helped her undo her dress, and gave her privacy to slip on a nightgown he had acquired for her. He had gotten it from a madam who ran a brothel for vampires.

As he drew the covers over Ophelia, she gave him a smile that speared his heart. Her smile was so adorable it touched him. She glowed like a woman in love.

He was supposed to win her love. Why should it feel like he'd been kicked in the gut?

Returning to his room, Raven noticed the cobwebs at the

ceiling, the coldness of the room since he never needed a fire, and the sense of emptiness in it even though it was filled with furniture. It was as if the room had no soul either.

He pulled on his shirt, swiftly fastened it at the collar, and shoved its tails into the waistband of his trousers. He had no time to worry about the lonely feeling of his room. He could not go back to Ophelia and watch her sleep. He couldn't stay with her.

Another wave of hunger hit him, so fast and hard he had to grab the bedpost. His fingers gouged into the wood. Inside, he seethed with hunger and lust.

He wanted her neck. Wanted to sink his fangs into it. Wanted it now.

Cursing, Raven ran down the corridor, passing the door to Ophelia's room. He forced his legs to keep moving. Launching over the banister, he jumped off the stairs and landed on the tiled ground floor at the foot of the staircase.

Raven pulled on a cape, grasped a silver-tipped walking stick, and headed out the door, locking it behind him. His destination was the docks. He would reach them just before the first glow of daylight touched the sky. Many people would be out, beginning their working day. He had little time until full daylight came, and he ran the risk of being burned to ash by the sun's rays.

He had to satisfy his hunger as quickly as he could.

Ophelia couldn't sleep. Snuggled beneath her soft sheets and warm counterpane, in a new silk nightgown that Ravenhunt had given her, she felt utterly exhausted. Truly, she couldn't even keep her eyes open. But even when her lids dropped and shut tight, she couldn't fall into sleep. Her wits whirled.

She had *spanked* Ravenhunt's bare bottom. She could still hear the soft *thwacks* in her head and the hoarse, rough rasp of his groans. His aroused groans would stay with her forever. She'd never heard a man sound like that—

Well, she had, at that naughty club or brothel, or whatever it was.

She had never *made* a man sound like that. Moaning, groaning, with excitement. She had never made a man feel pleasure. When Raven had climaxed, with his face showing such agony and his hand gripping his erection hard as his hips jerked . . .

Oooh. It had been a stunning sight.

She had made this beautiful, strong, sensual man come, as he had called it. She had made him laugh with delight, and when he'd done so, he was breathtakingly handsome. Deep lines had ringed his wide mouth, and crinkles appeared at the corners of his eyes, and his laugh had been throaty and masculine.

She'd giggled in earnest, soft helpless giggles, until she was consumed with mirth, with a warm happiness in her heart.

She was laughing with joy. Those moments of sexual play had given her true joy. She'd forgotten that he'd kidnapped her; forgotten she was required to do something against her upbringing and her breeding: give up her innocence to a man she would not marry.

Though, in a way, she already had given up her innocence. She still had her maidenhead—but she was hardly naïve and unknowing anymore.

As he'd tucked her into bed—such a sweet thing to do—she'd asked, "How can I make love to you without killing you?"

"You don't have to worry," he'd answered. "You will be free."

But how could she not worry when she hurt him each time she touched him—?

Ophelia's eyes suddenly opened wide in her shadowy bedchamber. She sat up, her covers tumbling down. Ravenhunt didn't say *he* wouldn't die. Heavens, surely he wasn't willing to sacrifice his *life* to save her?

That would be insane. He barely knew her. It wasn't as if he could actually care about her. How could he? Love was something that built. That took time to grow.

Why would Ravenhunt be willing to give his life for hers, when he barely knew her? What sort of man did that?

A hero. A noble knight of old.

He had saved her life once already. He had been struck with two pistol balls for her. As amazing and strange and improbable as it sounded, the man who had kidnapped her had become a hero to her. More of a champion for her than anyone had ever been.

The glowing coals in her fireplace gave the room a soft glow. Ophelia was groggy with the need to sleep, but her mind would not stop. Why could she not stop questioning him and simply give her body to him and believe him when he said she would be freed?

But could she do it if the price was to kill him?

She had to know—

The door creaked softly. That must have been responsible for the breeze, for her windows were shut tight.

A shadow moved, filling the doorway with darkness. Just as on the first night, it was Ravenhunt. He leaned against the frame with his arms crossed. His broad shoulders stretched across the opening's expanse, his eyes lost to the shadow. Only the prominent lines of his face were revealed by the fire's glow—his high cheekbones, his blade of a nose. But this time instead of being filled with fear, she sat up. She pushed off the covers. The instant after she did, she knew what she was doing. She was welcoming him.

She wasn't afraid of him. Not anymore. But she was afraid *for* him. "Is taking my power going to kill you?"

"Always blunt and direct, aren't you?" he countered from the shadows.

"Why do you never answer my questions?"

A deep laugh came out. "We both throw questions at each other and never answer them."

"Are you risking your life to save me? Why?"

"I'm not. Neither of us will die." There was the soft creak of the door frame as he straightened. He prowled into the room. "You should be sleeping. I came to make sure you were."

"Shouldn't you be asleep? Aren't you tired, too?"

"Not yet. As I told you, I often stay up all night, and go to sleep at dawn, then I sleep away the day, and wake at twilight."

He sat on the edge of the bed.

Questions collided in her head, and she was definitely dazed with tiredness. Why did he want to take away her power? What would he do with it?

Oh God, did he want to use it?

Why hadn't she pushed him for answers? It seemed, since he had captured her, her brain had ceased to function. When she'd been a prisoner at Mrs. Darkwell's, all she'd had was time to think, but with Ravenhunt it was as if she were finally pulling cobwebs off her brain.

She wanted to put questions into words, but he came to the edge of the bed. "Sleep," he said softly.

Deep and soft, his voice flowed into her thoughts. She wanted to obey. Ophelia fell back, her head landing on the pillow. Her hair fanned out around her—she'd forgotten to braid it for sleep. It would be tangled, but she was too tired to care.

So tired. But something nagged at her thoughts. Something she couldn't quite grasp but that wouldn't let her sleep. "I still don't think I can sleep."

"What you need is to be exhausted—to have your body worn out and your mind thoroughly tired, too. Too tired to think but satiated and happy."

Heavens, she had never felt more exhausted in her life, but

that did not help her sleep. "How could I do that? My head is spinning. I'm so tired, yet I cannot sleep."

"I have the perfect solution."

Ravenhunt came to the bed, and brought his hand forward. He reached into a pocket, drew something else out. A snap of his wrist made it uncoil. It was a length of black rope.

"Close your eyes," he murmured. "Concentrate only on what you feel."

"A—are you going to tie me up?"

"Not yet. I want to show you how enticing a rope can feel." His voice flowed like rich, amber honey. "Think of nothing else but what you feel."

She did as he asked. She fought to think only of the soft touch of one end of the rope over her cheeks. He drew soft circles that tickled. The rope was not scratchy and rough, but soft, as if made from velvet.

The end of the rope slid across her upper lip.

Ophelia gasped. Little bolts of lightning seemed to sizzle on her lip. He traced the shape of her mouth slowly with the dangling rope.

He was just touching her lip with the velvet length, but it made her throb and ache between her thighs. Heat flared there. Moisture pooled. She wriggled her hips.

"Lift your nightdress."

She couldn't resist the hoarse, dark command of his voice. Almost as if they were acting on their own, her hands clutched the skirt of her nightgown and she tugged it up. Her eyes were still closed, but cooler air brushed her thighs. The curls at her pubis were exposed.

The rope touched her inner right thigh. Up it went, and she sighed, almost sobbed, as she felt the caress on her skin.

She felt like marble coming to life—as if she'd been cold stone for her whole existence, and finally she was beginning to feel.

He possessed a master's touch. Smooth and soft, the rope stroked around the intense, tingling place between her legs, first in agonizingly slow caresses that made her shiver, then in faster slaps that made sensation streak though every inch of her. Ravenhunt tapped the top of the aching nub and she cried out. Her achy, throaty squeal flew up to the dark ceiling.

Something built in her. Her hips jerked with the sensations. She arched up, trying to lift her hips to tease her throbbing, demanding nub with the rope.

Ophelia opened her eyes. Between his large hands, Ravenhunt had drawn the rope tight. He sawed it gently over her throbbing, yearning quim and that magical place that felt such pleasure when it was touched.

Heavens, yes.

He lightened the caress, so it barely touched her, and she whimpered. "More . . . please," she whispered.

"Of course."

But Ravenhunt played a maddening game with her. He stroked harder until she moaned with agony, then slowed the passes of the rope until she rocked and bucked desperately for stimulation.

"Please," she begged, when the pressure and ache and tension built hard once more, yet he took the rope away. "Please don't stop." She felt as if she would go mad. She felt like a half-formed statue, ready to take shape only to have the artist put down his tools and walk away.

Ravenhunt gave a slow smile that seemed to say he had a secret she could not begin to guess. How handsome he became when he smiled. He lost the hard, grizzled look to his face, the cold austerity that made him look like an assassin. His eyes softened, and appealing lines bracketed his mouth. He became . . . beautiful.

"I wish I could touch you." Deep and growling, his voice

echoed in her thoughts, as if he could speak directly to them. "I'd love to do this with my tongue."

That brought an immediate, shocking picture in her head.

She imagined having her legs spread wide, her private parts bared. His body would lie between her legs, his head at her most intimate place, and his tongue would slick over her throbbing nub—

All her tension coiled and snapped, like a cracked whip. "Ravenhunt!" she cried, in desperate agony.

But this wasn't pain. It was as if a cold, unbreakable shell around her had cracked, and pure fire was pouring out. Her body arched as all her muscles tightened in exquisite glory.

It was so good. Pleasure swamped her, pleasure like she had never known. She cried, laughed, sobbed, knowing nothing but pleasure.

He watched her though the journey, through each happy, lovely twitch of her body. It eased, and she relaxed, limp and boneless, into the bed.

"Now, you'll sleep. I promise," he said.

Just as she was about to fall hazily into sleep, she whispered, "I didn't know a rope could do that—could feel so wonderful rubbed against me."

"You have to trust me, Ophelia. In this type of sexual game, I'm an expert. I always use ropes in sex. No matter how I do it, I want to build your excitement. I want you to dream of me stroking you with ropes. Or spanking you. I want you to anticipate each teasing touch against your round, voluptuous bottom. Each stroke will make your cunny clench, and will send throbbing pleasure right to your clitoris, my dear. I believe I can make you come just by spanking your bottom."

Heavens, heavens. Her heart thudded, even as she floated in delicious pleasure, even as her lashes drifted shut.

The bed creaked as he stood. Softly he said, "I will return to you when I wake, but it will be late in the day. You should rest until then. Go to sleep."

Satiated and tired, Ophelia knew she would finally sleep, but she could not wait until tomorrow.

I told you having an orgasm would give you a good sleep. I've left something for you in the kitchens. I'll be up when it is evening. Remember, you haven't been spanked yet.
—Ravenhunt

Sitting on the edge of her bed, in the robe Ravenhunt had left for her, Ophelia shivered—that was nerves. Then quivered. *That* was desire.

Heavens, what was she thinking? She didn't want a spanking. But then she imagined him standing in front of her, almost naked, sporting a huge erection and carrying a paddle.

She squirmed on the bed. Actually, she did rather want a spanking. She wasn't afraid of it anymore.

Ravenhunt's strong, slanted handwriting flowed over beautiful notepaper, which was the color of thick cream and just as smooth. Why did he want her to go to the kitchens? They were in the basement.

Basements in ancient houses held dungeons. And those had iron shackles—

Ridiculous. Ravenhunt had specifically written *kitchens*, not *dungeons*.

She knew it was already afternoon. The mantel clock and sunlight peeking around the drapes told her. She had slept for hours.

It had been years since she'd spent a whole night in wonderful, undisturbed slumber. It never happened at Mrs. Darkwell's. She'd always woken in the grip of a nightmare.

Ravenhunt had acquired slippers for her, too. Delicate satin ones and they sat on the floor by the bed. She slipped her feet into them, then padded downstairs.

Curtains had been drawn back throughout his house to let in light. Last night, when they had come back in from the brothel, everything had been closed up, dark and forlorn.

That was how he lived—cut off from the world in a darkened fortress.

He behaved like a prisoner. Just like she had been.

The house was brighter with daylight coming in, but it was still quiet, so eerily so that it made her shiver. A house of this size was never silent. There was always noise, even just the patter of footsteps or the hushed chatter of family or servants. The sense of being almost completely alone gave her a creepy feeling, as if she were the only person alive in London.

She wasn't, of course. Ravenhunt was sleeping upstairs.

Ophelia made her way down stone steps to the basement. The ceiling was low, the walls formed of large, thick stones. Large wood beams crossed over her head, and she made her way to an open door through which light spilled. Wonderful smells poured out from there—a sweet aroma that must be the fresh fruit, along with the rich scent of roasted meat, and a yeasty tickle to her nose that promised bread.

She hurried into the preparation area of the kitchen.

An enormous feast waited for her, spread out on a wood worktable.

She found baskets of fresh breads, pastry on plates, a cold roast beef sliced for her, and bowls filled with grapes, oranges, and one incongruous-looking pineapple, complete with its spiky skin and leaves. A piece of paper was held in place with an uncut, exotic yellow lemon.

My apologies. The meals today will have to be cold. I hope it is adequate.

Adequate? It smelled spectacular, and with all the color, it was like a lush painting. There were no servants; Ravenhunt had prepared all of this himself. For her.

Sex made a woman hungry, too. She was thoroughly ravenous. Planting her bottom on a stool with a worn seat, Ophelia drew a plate toward her. She took one of the buns, tore it, and ate it in great chunks. Gooey, delicious fresh bread was her absolute favorite.

For days, she had been too nervous, apprehensive, and afraid to do more than nibble when he brought her food. With a feast in front of her now, she ate like a madwoman.

Then she frowned. When had she ever seen him eat?

Not once, actually. She'd just assumed he ate food before bringing it to her.

What if he didn't? There were beings—creatures or demons— who did not eat. She knew that from Mrs. Darkwell's house. Some demons survived on blood. Some survived on souls.

He had told her he had special powers to heal. He was not normal, just as she wasn't.

Squirt. She'd pushed through the peel of an exotic, delicious orange, and shot herself in the eye with juice.

She'd been incredibly dense. Not about the orange—about Ravenhunt.

He was going to take her power by making love to her. He had to know witchcraft, or he was a wizard, or a demon with magical powers. From her time at Mrs. Darkwell's she knew such creatures existed.

Could she make love to him without knowing who he really was?

Men could make love to a lady without any questions. They could do it without love, affection, or thought. But she wasn't like that.

Or was she?

Last night, when Ravenhunt had stroked her with the velvet surface of the rope until she . . . um . . . came, she hadn't cared about questions or who he was. She had lived for each sizzling moment.

Sex with him made her feel *alive.*

And she wanted *more*.

Except right now she had to wait for Ravenhunt.

Ophelia finished her meal, then she went back up to the ground floor and wandered through the house. It was so still and quiet and shadowed it was like walking through a tomb.

She discovered a piano beneath white Holland covers, but didn't dare uncover it. Every room was shut up, never used. Ravenhunt stayed in his room all afternoon—she didn't hear any sound from it, though she didn't open the door or even knock. As he'd told her, he wasn't going to come out until it was night.

Finally, she went back to the kitchen, where she ate more and drank the rest of the wine.

She twirled her empty glass in her fingers. Wine made her feel more lighthearted. She decided she wanted more of it, too.

Ophelia found a supply of dusty wine bottles in the basement. Daringly she uncorked one and poured a glass. It was a rich, hearty, heady red wine.

She was just biding her time until she would have sex. That made her feel naughty. And wild.

Ophelia took the bottle to his dining room. It was not swathed in covers, and it had been dusted and tidied, but it was obvious it had not been used for ages, except for when she had eaten in it. Why didn't he eat here? Why did he live so alone?

"I no longer feel like a prisoner," she whispered.

As if to celebrate, she filled the glass, and sipped. Sipped and sipped until it was gone, then refilled her goblet and had more.

Two-thirds of the bottle had disappeared when an amused, deep baritone asked, "Having fun?"

A bit poddled, she met Ravenhunt's dark eyes. "Yes." Already, the anticipation made her feel hot and tight inside. "What are we going to do tonight? Are you going to spank me?" She felt wanton and giddy to even ask such a thing, and she twirled in a circle.

"You are foxed," he observed.

"No, I am free." The old Ophelia, prisoner of Mrs. Dark-well, would have never asked such a thing as casually as she had done. She was no longer quiet, retiring Ophelia. "So what are you going to do to me?"

"I have a few ideas," Ravenhunt said.

She was more than just a little foxed. Lady Ophelia was drunk. A strange feeling welled up in Raven. Disapproval and the need to give her a lecture on being more careful.

His reaction was what it would have been for Frederica, his sister. He shook off the feeling. Ophelia drunk was good for him. It would make her seduction easier.

But he couldn't completely lose the sense of feeling protective of her.

Ophelia was naïve but she had strength, too. He admired it. Her strength and courage made her more than just a pretty young woman—it made her beautiful.

He wasn't in love with her. He had been in love with his fiancée. He knew what the emotion felt like—an obsession to have and possess a woman.

Even as a marquis' heir with the courtesy title of earl, he'd lived in fear he wasn't good enough for the beautiful Lady Margaret, daughter of a powerful duke. He'd been afraid she would flit away to someone else—a duke, for example. To prove himself to her, he had fought a duel for her, pummeled her other suitors in Gentleman Jackson's ring, and pursued her like a madman. His love for her had turned him from a confident, carefree young buck into a man haunted by doubt, aware of every misspoken word or unfulfilled opportunity to win her heart.

Love had leveled him. It had eroded his strength.

But once he had won beautiful Margaret's heart, he'd felt like a king.

Then he had lost her. She'd died.

What he felt for Ophelia was just a man's need to protect a woman. It wasn't tempestuous or all-consuming. It wasn't love.

But according to that blasted book of Guidon's, it had to be if he wanted to save her. He had to fall in love with her, and he had to make her love him.

How in hell was he going to fall in love? Losing his fiancée, and then becoming a vampire, had sucked all the capacity for love out of him.

Now Ophelia stared at him boldly with bright, drunk eyes. Swaying a bit, she undid her robe, and she let it fall to the ground. A gruff laugh rose from his chest.

Ophelia was a sweet thing, and it was going to be fun to pleasure her tonight.

And somehow he had to find a way to fall in love with her, seduce her into loving him. Then he had to die while loving her.

Damn, how did a vampire who had no soul, who had a heart like ice, do that? He had to hope the answer was in Guidon's book. He'd read it until dawn and hadn't found any answers.

There had to be something in that damned book. Somewhere there had to be a guideline for vampire assassins on falling in love.

"You're frowning." Ophelia sashayed unsteadily toward him. She ran her finger around her lips. Wine had stained her lips the dark red of blood.

He fought not to think about that. He'd fed before coming to her. A quick bite, as it were.

In her pale ivory nightdress she looked almost angelic.

He had to fall in love with her so she wouldn't be destroyed. Fall in love with her, then lose her forever. She would be free. In a way, so would he—making love to her meant he was going to finally die. He laughed, the sound sharp and bitter.

Her swaying body suddenly stilled. She frowned at him. "Do you not want to do this?"

"Yes, of course I do." He was going to die—it was his destiny. He wanted to make love to her as much as he could before he did.

Not caring what it would mean for him, he caught her in his arms and kissed her. Wine was tart on her lips. A jolt of agony shot through him, so strong and so unexpected, he reeled back with it, pulling away from the kiss.

The pain inflicted on him by her power was stronger.

So what was he going to do to her?

There was a lot he wanted to do. Watching her come last night, he'd wanted to slide his cock inside her, feel how creamy she was, feel her walls clutch around him. He liked to watch her come, but he wanted to make her come with his prick.

Or his mouth.

Instead Raven held up an ivory wand. The closest he could be to her was sliding the wand inside her hot, wet cunny.

"What is that?" Ophelia found it hard to speak—her words were slurred together.

"Lean over the table, love," Ravenhunt commanded.

Doing so made her bare bottom stick out, just as his had done. "I don't want to be spanked now." Though actually, she felt light and airy enough that she didn't mind the idea. "No, changed my mind. You can if you want."

He tapped the wand against her bottom. "Oooh," she whispered, and she wriggled her hips. She swayed her rump back and forth, then tauntingly up and down. At his laugh, she blushed, certain she must look silly, but she wanted him too much to care. "Please," she whispered.

The cool firmness of the rod stroked over the curve of her bottom, then slid between her thighs. The length brushed her nether lips from behind. His strong hand thrust it forward so the length of it grazed along her cunny. She gasped. The cool, smooth ivory was thrillingly teasing. He worked it back and forth, until it eased her sticky lips apart.

"It's not as large as I am," he said.

It's not? It seemed rather large. But even with her wits fogged by wine, she remembered seeing Ravenhunt without his trousers and his erection had seemed startlingly enormous.

"I'm going to put it inside you, beautiful one," he murmured. "If it hurts you, tell me."

She nodded. But with all the wine sloshing about inside her, she couldn't feel pain at all. Gently, he slid the thickness of the ivory wand between her lips. The tip touched her entrance. She should be shocked. But she ached to be filled.

"Please," she whispered.

She was so tense, so filled with anticipation. Aching and throbbing inside. The wand went inside her, and she felt a twinge of pain. She winced, but it vanished swiftly.

Then there was nothing but pleasure, silky pleasure sliding through her whole body.

He stroked the wand in and out. She rocked against the table, eyes closed, thinking only of sheer delight. Deeper and deeper, he went. Ophelia moaned. Gasped. Then she squealed when the wand went so deep that shocks raced through her everywhere.

His finger slipped between her nether lips, and pressed against her nub. "You can't touch me—"

"I can't resist." He rubbed her there. A few firm caresses in perfect unison with the thrusts inside her.

Oh heavens. Oh goodness. Oh—!

Pleasure burst in her like fireworks. Glittering, brilliant delight raced through her every nerve. Her body thrashed against the table, as it danced to sheer ecstasy. The climax ravaged her. She wailed in glorious agony. He quickly moved his fingers away from her, and she didn't need his touch there anymore. But the climax was so intense . . .

Her sex was clutching at the wand inside her, pulsing around it. Ravenhunt kept thrusting it, and the pleasure went on and on. Her legs were weakening—

She couldn't help it. She grasped his arm. She needed to touch him. Ached for contact. A huge jolt of sheer agony shot through her where her fingers gripped his forearm. Ophelia screamed with it.

He roared with pain. Ophelia fought to let him go, but her fingers wouldn't obey. He grasped her hand and pulled his arm free.

She jerked her hand away from his. "I'm sorry," she whispered. Tears burned in her eyes, dripped to her cheeks.

He draped her robe around her. "It was not your fault."

In front of her eyes, he licked the ivory wand and her jaw dropped.

"This way I can taste you," he murmured. "Don't worry. Tomorrow night, we are going to have to ensure you don't touch me. It hurt you this time, as well as me. Tomorrow we have to tie you up."

8

All Tied Up

Tonight was about sex, just as if he were still a mortal man.

Raven strode down his hallway, dressed in a robe he never wore anymore. He wasn't aware of cold, and with his house mostly unused, it was usually as cold as a tomb. He'd lit fires and made it warmer only for Ophelia.

Years ago, he used to enjoy playing bondage games, when he had been an ordinary British marquis, and not a blood-drinking demon. He did what any peer did—indulged in all the sexual games on offer in London's brothels. That had been before his engagement to Lady Margaret, when he was a randy youth eager for experience. He'd been eager to learn sexual technique so he wouldn't be callow and unskilled in his marriage bed.

He'd learned what every young gentleman did: there were things you did with a courtesan you would never do with a gently bred wife.

So he walked toward Ophelia's bedchamber, preparing to tie her up, but he didn't know exactly how to go about it. Doing this with a woman of Ophelia's breeding was foreign to him. A wanton who saw ropes would know what the game would be.

Ophelia was going to have to be guided step by step.

An arousing thought.

And it would distract him from thinking about her sweet blood.

Raven reached her bedroom door. Shock fixed his feet to the threshold. His jaw all but dropped to the floor and slammed into the wooden boards.

Ophelia awaited him.

Naked.

She sat on the edge of her bed by the bedpost. Her loose hair tumbled in pale curls over her shoulders and down to the curve of her bottom. Her arms were pressed to her sides, which pushed her full, round breasts together and pointed dainty pink nipples straight at him.

He almost staggered back.

How sweet she looked. Framed by long pale lashes, her huge indigo eyes sparkled with anticipation, until her gaze riveted on the ropes. Her hand went delicately to her chest, but her nipples tightened and lengthened, a sure sign she was intrigued and aroused.

Beneath his heavy robe, his cock swelled with a rush of blood and bucked up to smartly smack his stomach.

He was in a damned strange situation. To save Lady Ophelia, he had to condemn himself to destruction. The only way to save her was to coax her to fall in love with him, which meant she could never know the truth about him.

He'd read through Guidon's book—a book that managed to make sex sound pedantic and dull. But the gist was: he took her power through sex and he saved her by winning her heart and by giving her his.

Nothing could save him.

Hell, it was fair enough. He didn't deserve to be saved.

The sex he was to enjoy with her was to fill his last days on earth.

Slowly, Ophelia stood, naked, all that golden hair gleaming

in the firelight, making a halo of gold around her. Definitely she was growing to trust him.

Hades, she was beautiful. Raven felt a deep tug of sympathy. She should have been able to use her beauty to flirt and tease and enjoy love. She should have been able to marry and be happy. But it wasn't just her power that was hurting her. He was betraying her. He was coaxing her to open her heart, and in the end he was going to hurt her when she gave her power to him and he died.

He knew how devastating that was. How crippling and agonizing that pain and grief was.

"Will it hurt to be tied up?" she asked.

"No, I promise it won't." He kept his voice soft and coaxing. "Does the idea entice you?"

A pink flush raced over her cheeks while she considered. Blushing fiercely, she nodded. "I have to admit it does. Doesn't that make me very naughty? Or bad?"

"It makes you delightful," he said. It was true. The wicked one in this was him.

Her gold-amber brows lifted. Apparently she was surprised by his answer. "Delightful?"

Half-turned from her, Raven let a wicked grin play on his lips. "Many women find it freeing to be bound. You can't be improper if you have no choice, after all."

"So how do we begin?" She put her wrists together and held them out daringly. "Like this?"

Raven could immediately picture the black velvet ropes around her slim wrists. In that moment, he didn't care she was a lady at her core and he had no right to be playing bondage games with her. He wanted it. In his trousers, his cock hardened at once, heavy and pushing hard against the fabric.

Gruffly, he said, "I tie you to the bed. Lie down."

"You are terse and commanding, aren't you? You could ask nicely."

Her voice wobbled a bit, betraying her nerves, but also her displeasure at his curt order. She fascinated him—she was demure and ladylike, but inside she was strong. She'd had to be strong, he supposed, to survive. But to win her heart, he had to be stronger. Ophelia had to learn to let herself trust him, to give herself to him body and soul.

"I never ask nicely," he growled. "Not in games like this." Holding the ropes, he scooped her up, put her over his shoulder for a second, and tossed her lightly on the bed.

She bounced and scrambled to sit up, but he wrapped the rope around her wrist. Fast, but not with a vampire's speed. Black velvet slid smoothly around her slender pale wrist. Raven knotted it firmly, making a loop that she could not slip her hand through.

His cock bucked again at the thought of what would come next.

"That's tight," she gasped.

His throat was damned tight. "Too loose and you won't have the fun of feeling bound and beyond your control. It's tight enough to make you my sexual prisoner, but not enough to hurt."

"Maybe you made a mistake."

"I never do."

He knew she was wrestling between her upbringing to be a good and proper young lady and her natural erotic, sensual nature. The way to encourage her to play, to free her to enjoy this, was to take control.

He drew the rope to the bedpost and the sudden tug made her fall on her back. Her breasts jiggled, her flushed nipples bobbing temptingly. It took him only moments to wrap the rope around the post and tie a secure knot. While she pulled hesitatingly at the rope, testing its strength, he caught her other wrist, and attached her to the post with smooth ease.

He did it without touching her skin and without hurting her.

Raven stepped back. The sight of Ophelia like that, with her arms raised behind her head, black rope in a band at her wrists, struck him like a blow. Her breasts wobbled softly with her every quick breath. Her pink nipples were distended, as plump as thimbles, revealing she was enjoying it.

He'd never been so aroused. But damn, he couldn't touch her.

Panting, she met his gaze. She blushed again sweetly.

"You are beautiful, Ophelia," he said. "Even though you're the one in ropes, I feel bound right now. Bound by you."

She blew at a strand of hair that dangled over her face. "I don't understand."

He whisked the hair away. "Watching you is so enthralling. Every time you tug at the rope, the way you turn your head to peek at how it's tied to the bed, the way your breasts sway as you move. I feel like your captive, Ophelia."

Ophelia would not quite believe Ravenhunt, except that he spoke slowly as if he were trying to understand himself what he felt. He sounded sincere.

She remembered waking here as his prisoner. Now, being his prisoner in fun, for carnal games, didn't feel frightening.

True, she felt unsure and awkward, just as she always felt. But she was caught up in erotic excitement, too. It made her cunny throb.

Even with nothing touching her but the ropes at her wrists, she was becoming aroused. Ophelia could smell the lush scent of her juices. She felt wet and slick between her legs.

What was he going to do to her? He couldn't touch her. He couldn't go inside her, as much as she ached for it.

She didn't know what he planned. For once, not knowing was driving her mad in a delicious way. The anticipation allowed her thoughts to run riot. What could he do without touching her to make her "come"?

"You look very thoughtful. Have you ever fantasized about this?" Ravenhunt sat on the edge of the bed. The blue velvet robe he wore highlighted the paleness of his skin. His cheekbones and strong jaw looked to be carved of marble. But his eyes were dark, so black they were unfathomable.

"I—" She couldn't reveal the *truth*.

After reading the gothic novels, sometimes she had thought about being taken captive and ravished. When she had been a prisoner at Mrs. Darkwell's and she'd had nothing to do but sculpt and read. Locked away in a room, she had not only sculpted, she had also spun wild, erotic fantasies. She'd dreamed of a dark, mysterious man taking her prisoner, seducing her, and falling madly in love with her . . .

She'd ended up in that very situation.

But she could never admit it.

"Of course I haven't," she said firmly. "What are you—" She broke off. Ravenhunt held another rope. The length of it dangled from his strong hand.

"I know you have thought of this." His voice was a deep, husky growl. It slid over her as decadent as hot, dark chocolate.

But she could never reveal those fantasies to anyone. They were her most shocking secret, and she would keep them buried forever. "No."

Smooth velvet teased her bare ankle and, startled by it, she jerked her leg away. But Ravenhunt captured her foot, and had her ankle tied and bound to the column at the foot of the bed in moments.

He crossed his arms over his chest. His robe gave a glimpse of white skin and sculpted muscle. More ropes lay over his hand. She was his prisoner again, and he was watching her with a shiver-worthy heat in his gaze.

He watched her with such intensity, her heart hammered. She had to say something. "You are very quick at tying knots."

"Practice."

When her other foot was equally bound to the bedpost, he paced slowly at the end of the bed.

"W-what do you do to me now?"

"Whatever I desire."

The rough way he said it made her heart thunder, made her wetter, hotter, and made her cunny clench in a slow, intense way.

"Imagine what I can do to you now," he said.

He moved away from the bed, and she strained against the ropes to see what he was doing. But her bindings were too tight, and she couldn't lift up enough to watch. She was tied spread-eagle to the bed, her legs parted and ready for him— well, ready if he could make love to her. She was served up for him, unable to refuse to do anything he wanted.

She should be afraid. But she wasn't. She trusted him. Perhaps more than she had done with anyone but her family. She'd never had anyone else she could trust.

She was ready to do anything he wanted—

He turned, the leather-bound handle of a whip in his hand, the long tail trailing to the floor.

"No," she gasped. "That I won't do! I cannot take that."

"I will be the judge." He approached the bed. His robe was open, giving glimpses of his muscles as he moved, prowling with confidence. The light played on the ridges of his abdomen, the strong lines of his chest.

Tension raced over her—her muscles tightening.

"I won't hurt you." He lifted the whip and let the leather tip trail up her right leg, skimming over her naked thigh.

She hadn't expected that—a tickling tease over her bare skin instead of a swift, sharp flick of the leather. "Are you going to whip me?"

"This is about teasing you. I want you to delight in what you can feel. I would never hurt you. Trust me."

The lash of the whip danced up her naked inner thigh. Oh heavens, she shut her eyes and savored.

The whip moved closer to her sex, to her curls already damp with her juices and her plump nether lips. She wriggled on the bed. To feel so much, yet not be able to move—it was thrilling.

He flicked the whip lightly and the leather tail lightly slapped her. There was no force behind it and it didn't hurt. It made her cunny wetter.

With his lashes low over his eyes, his mouth tense, Raven stroked the end of the whip's handle over her nether curls. The leather barely grazed them, and tickled her so she giggled and gasped at the same time.

"You see you can trust me," he said, his voice rich as sin. "All I want is for you to know pleasure—the pleasure you've never been able to have."

He slid the whip's firm handle between her curls and across her aching clit.

She screamed in surprise. Hot sensation streaked through her.

Heavens, it felt good.

She arched her hips up, seeking to press her clit against the handle again. He let her pump against it, pleasuring herself for a mere moment, then he moved it away. She moaned and he smiled. The smile of a man who knew he was in control.

Teasing her, he traced the damp tip over her tummy. She trembled, wriggling on the bed. His robe was partly open, un-belted. Giving teasing, thrilling glimpses of his gorgeous naked form—his taut stomach, his broad chest, his thick, enormous erection.

Amusement glittered in his eyes. Slowly, the end traced her navel. The whip coasted so lightly over her belly, it was as if a flame teased her skin. Focused on her beneath thick lashes, he reached her breasts with the whip. He traced them in a slow, light spiral.

A flick of his wrist and he brought the handle of the whip against the underside of her right breast in a quick, abbreviated tap. Her breast bounced. Goodness, the rise and fall, the bounce of their weight was as hot, as pleasurable as being caressed.

He tapped her breasts, playing with them, making them jiggle heavily. Ophelia closed her eyes, whimpering with delight. It felt so good.

She wished he could do this with his hands—

He couldn't. She must stop wishing for what she could not have.

Her lids lifted, her eyes opened to his smile. Roguish. A tease of dimples, beautiful curved lips. "Nipples now," he said.

She gasped before he even touched them.

Flicking the whip's handle, he strummed it over her nipples.

"Oh goodness!" She arched off the bed. Goodness was meaningless. It was glorious. Pleasure shot to her cunny, almost exploding there.

He tapped harder, right atop her nipples.

Too much!

She'd been on the brink, but the shock of the taps pulled her back. She let him do more, then begged him to stop, for after a few gentle strikes with the whip, her nipples were large, engorged, so sensitive she was sobbing. "I think I want to stop," she began.

"But I've only just started," he said. But he did stop.

He leaned to whisper in her ear, "What would you fantasize about, Ophelia? Close your eyes. Would you like to be in a harem, where the handsome Turkish prince uses you for his decadent pleasure? While he ties you up with silks on plump cushions, blindfolds you, then drives his cock deeply into you?"

"I don't have such dreams—"

"I know you do," he said, and she squirmed. How could he know? Was it so obvious on her face?

"Perhaps you fantasize about a castle, where you are chained in a dungeon by a handsome duke who is determined to ravish you." The very tip of the whip brushed her nipples again, barely a touch, but so wonderful. "How would you want to be ravished, Ophelia? By more than one man? Your duke and your Turkish prince could take you together."

She had to keep her eyes shut. Wild images played in her head. She couldn't look at him while she was thinking these things.

Something smooth and thick pressed to her nether lips. She opened her eyes. He held the ivory wand he'd used on her. Slowly he plied it between her wet nether lips.

The thick ivory slid in. "I wish it was you," she whispered. "I want your cock—" She couldn't believe she was saying such things, but she couldn't bear wanting him and not having him. "It's so long and so beautiful and I want it inside me so much."

"Shh. Let me make you come."

With long, slow strokes, he slid the wand deeply inside her. Filling her. He tapped her clit with the whip handle as he did.

"Three men making love to you," he murmured. "One thick cock deep in your cunny, thrust inside by a man eager to make you come. Another man suckling your beautiful breasts. A third man to slide his prick inside your sweet, voluptuous bottom—"

"Oh goodness!" she cried.

Everything came together at once—his wicked stories, his naughty games with her clit, the thrusts of the wand. Ophelia pulled hard at the velvet ropes as the orgasm swelled inside her. She tore at them as she exploded.

Pleasure commanded her now, and she surrendered to it.

Her rump bucked up, the bindings at her wrists and ankles strained, and she cried out to the heavens.

His lips touched hers, and it seemed so right that their mouths sizzled together.

The restraint of her arms vanished—he'd cut the ropes—and her arms flew free. She wrapped them around him. She shouldn't, but she wanted one precious second to hold him tight.

While she came and came and came.

She let him go.

Breathing hard, Ravenhunt moved to her feet. He held a small dagger and he sliced the velvet ropes. Her legs relaxed bonelessly into the soft bed. With swift, spare motions, he untied her ankles, tossing the cut ropes away. Then he undid the bonds at her wrists.

She looked at him shyly, shut her eyes, looked around the room, and awkwardly met his steady gaze once more.

It had been thrilling. He'd fed her the wickedest fantasies. Just imagining what he'd said had been thrilling. Though in truth, she wasn't really picturing three men. She was thinking of Ravenhunt doing all those things to her.

"What are you thinking, my dear?" he asked. Crinkles touched the corners of his eyes, lines bracketed his lips as he smiled.

That he was the only man she ever wanted to dream about. But she couldn't say that. This was about sex, not about love. She was perilously close to saying she loved him—but how could she yet, when she barely knew him? How could she when she knew all of this was only to take her power?

He helped her sit up, then released her hand, of course. "I guess I do like being tied up," she whispered.

Her words almost crippled him with arousal.

Raven yearned to touch her. He'd never wanted to caress,

stroke, and fondle a woman more. She gazed up at him with sweet innocence, and wild carnal thoughts ripped through him.

He wanted to take her now, while she was slick with her pleasure. Give her climax after climax, until she almost fainted in ecstasy.

Not yet.

She rubbed her wrist. The ropes had been soft velvet but had left pinkish rings around her wrists. He lifted her right wrist to his lips, ready to kiss the place where her skin was marred—

Pain shot through him—he expected it—but she gasped in shock. Her face contorted in pain. At once, he released her. If it would only hurt him, he would have kissed those marks tenderly, as if to make them better.

But his touch hurt her.

Guidon's book had talked about that. As Raven began to attack her power—as he began to prepare her body to surrender it through sex—she would experience the pain of her power.

Damn, he couldn't hurt her. The book had said the pain would eventually stop. If they took their sexual games far enough, they would both escape the pain.

But for now, she looked so stunned he let her go.

"Sorry, my dear. According to Guidon's book this is what must happen for me to take your power—you will start to feel the same pain when we touch." He related what that chapter had said. "But it will stop."

"Why shouldn't I know what it feels like? It is my curse, after all. Why should I be immune?"

"It isn't your fault, and you should not have to suffer."

Damn, Raven hated the thought of being destroyed now. Before meeting Ophelia, he would have welcomed it. But now . . .

He would love to spend eternity playing bondage games with Ophelia.

"I am pleased to know you like to be tied up." He kept his

voice soft to disguise the rawness of it. He had to fall in love with her, then die brokenhearted.

She shivered, and her breasts swayed. Tempting him.

After he took her power, she could be touched. But he wasn't going to be the man to do it—he would be dead. A stab of jealousy hit his heart at the thought of the lucky man who would eventually have her.

It was irrational to be jealous.

Ophelia studied him, her head cocked to the side. "You are so gentle with me. It makes me forget what you said about yourself. That you said you were an assassin. My goodness, I can even trust you around me with a whip in your hand . . . trust you to give me pleasure and not hurt me." She nervously licked her lips. "I've never had anyone I could trust—I've never been able to feel close to anyone, since I was so afraid of hurting people. I can't imagine you as an assassin now, even though I've seen how dangerous you can be. I want to understand you. Why did you become an assassin? Why would you kill—you are a gentleman, aren't you? I know gentlemen fight duels, but they don't . . . do whatever assassins do." She lifted her hands, as if to touch his shoulders, but she froze.

She looked so hurt that she couldn't touch him.

To build her trust, he had to explain something. Give her something. "I was a soldier. For a long time. Killing was what I learned to do well."

"You fought against Napoleon?"

"I fought against everyone. I fought Napoleon, I fought in India, I fought in the uprising in Ceylon. When there were no battles, I went in search of them."

"Why?" Her eyes revealed how perplexed she was. "I should think battles are awful. I would be relieved when one was over. To be safe and—and normal again."

He jerked his head up. She had spent her life wanted to be

normal; he had spent his life looking for death and conflict. Two more opposite people he could not imagine. How could he capture her heart? She was looking at him like he was a dangerous beast or a strange creature she'd never encountered before. She couldn't understand him.

"Did you find it exciting?" she whispered.

"No, it wasn't that." Or was it? "There was excitement, I suppose," he said, considering. "Being in battle meant you spent a lot of time doing things like fighting, marching, setting up camps, cleaning your rifle. The basic job of survival took much of your time. It meant I didn't have to think."

Her indigo eyes widened. "That sounds terrible. How could you have wanted to be in the midst of battle simply so you didn't have to think? What did you not want to think about?"

"Lady Ophelia, you've had graver troubles than I."

"But I've hurt people, too, and it haunts me. I suspect it haunts you, too."

He stared at her. "It does." That made it a greater wrong that he had continued to do it as a soldier. Then he'd done it as a vampire, using mortals as his prey. There couldn't be any man less deserving of a woman's love.

"After you were a soldier, did you become an assassin of vampires to do good?"

Raven laughed at that. "No, it wasn't that." Damn, why had he said that? It was a statement that demanded an explanation. "I did it to pursue and destroy vicious vampires."

"Are all vampires vicious? I knew some female vampires, and they seemed like ordinary girls to me."

"Vampires claim they are not vicious."

"I suppose I could be called vicious," she said, her brow furrowed. "They are no different from me—forced to do something against their will."

"You are not vicious, and you are nothing like the vampires

I hunt," he said. "That's enough questions." He had a long way to go—many more bouts of pleasure before they would be ready for him to try to take her power.

Ophelia watched Ravenhunt stand and stretch. His bare back was beautiful—a play of candlelight and shadow on a broad vee of muscle. She ached to reach out and stroke his magnificent back, let her hands follow the broad shoulders and run all the way down to his lean hips and muscled bottom.

Of course she couldn't.

She also wished he would not shut her out when she asked him questions. But it seemed as impossible a wish as the one to caress him.

His expression was one of dark, brooding gloom. He lived alone, in the darkness, and it was obvious the violence in his past troubled him greatly.

"Who are you, really?" she asked softly. "You put yourself in exile the way I was told I must. What are you that you had to do this?"

"Just a soldier."

"I know that's not true. When soldiers return from battle, they are happy to be away from war. They want peace and they—"

"No, love. On that you are wrong," he said. "Many soldiers find they can't live with peace. As I said, surviving keeps a man busy. Soldiers are used to the excitement and fear of fighting for their lives and for other men. They are used to making instant decisions and throwing courage or madness at a hopeless situation. Peace does not sit well after that."

"How could you prefer that? I don't understand."

"Men have their reasons."

"Yes, the things you don't want to think about and that you will not tell me about."

Of course he said nothing in answer. He lifted his hand, almost touched her bare shoulder. His hand stayed there, not quite making contact, but it felt as if little bolts of sizzling power jumped between her skin and his.

"Did you become an assassin to live as you did in war?"

"I—Hades, it's complicated."

Ophelia folded her arms at her chest. "I am going to find out what you are—"

"Love, I hunt and destroy vampires. The undead would want me dead. For my own protection, I have to live like this." Raven stopped talking. Some of that was actually the truth, but the last thing he could let her do was learn his whole truth.

"Can you stop hunting vampires?"

"No." He had to bring a halt to this conversation. He braced his arm against the bedpost. In this position he towered over her, and she gazed up at him. Their lips were close, and he took the whip and used its tip to caress her nipples. He drew them to full, erect points.

"You—oh." Her sentence dropped to a moan as he lightly strummed her right nipple. "But you look so unhappy—oooh!"

He slid the whip down, rubbing it between her thighs, rubbing her clit.

"Goodness—the only time—"

She was still fighting to talk. The way to silence her would be to dive between her legs and lick her senseless. Or thrust his aching cock in her to the hilt. He'd been sporting an erection for hours, and his ballocks were in pain.

"The only time I've seen you smile is when we do . . . love-making things," she gasped.

So demure and sweet. He owed her something, but not enough that he frightened her away. Stroking her clit, he murmured, "I cannot stop hunting vampires, love. It's too late for me. But yes, carnal games with you make me very happy."

He'd found her erotic triggers when he'd painted images for her of sex slaves and multiple partners. Raven withdrew the whip handle from the soft, damp cleft between her legs. "Get on your knees on the bed."

Ophelia did so obediently.

"Bend forward and rest your cheek on the bed. Keep your bottom up in the air."

"Oh yes. Tie me up again," she said boldly. "I want more."

9

A Delectable Neck

"Put your hands behind you, crossed at the wrists."

Ravenhunt's dark voice sent a tumble of shivers down her spine. On her knees on the bed, Ophelia stuck her naked derriere up in the air. Vulnerable, true, but she felt so erotic.

She squirmed. She'd never ached so much between her legs. Desperately, she wanted to touch herself there. It was an insistent hunger, a screaming need to be stroked.

Ravenhunt eased the whip between her legs. She sighed in relief as the leather-wrapped rod ran along her nether lips. "Oh yes," she whispered.

But relief was short-lived. He took the whip handle away, and something scratchy ran around her ankles. She squeaked in surprise, sat up, and turned to look, which meant she was no longer in the scandalous, naughty position that had thrilled her so much.

Rough, hemp rope was wrapped around her ankles. Humming casually, Ravenhunt tied a knot, securing her legs together at her feet.

She loved the pressure of the rope. Even the scratchiness— such a contrast to the silkiness of the sheets beneath her.

"Hands behind you," he instructed. Clipped. Curt. Demanding.

She returned to the position he had commanded, her hands clasped and resting against the swell of her bottom.

He slid the rope around her wrists. Her hips wriggled, which worked the rope at her ankles. Excitement spiked through her, rushing from her tied-up ankles, up her legs. Exploding between her legs.

"Oh!" she cried out. Not quite a climax, but she felt a rush of wetness.

Ravenhunt pulled the rope encircling her wrist tight. "Being tied up makes you free," he murmured. "For I am doing this to you, and you have to do as I want. *Whatever* I want."

"Yes," she whispered. Panting so hard she could barely speak.

"Now this." He took a strip of black silk and twisted it, turning it into a column of wound silk. He pressed it to her lips, and when she lifted her head, gasping in surprise, he gagged her. It took him moments.

"Not too tight." His deep, smooth tones were filled with satisfaction.

Ophelia let her cheek sink back against the bed. Another strip of silk was quickly fastened around her eyes.

She was gagged, blindfolded, and bound for him. But this was a game, and she wasn't scared. She liked it. She remembered the sort of fantasies she used to have—about being taken by a forceful, dark man, one who was immune to her power, and who would haul her roughly into his embrace and press his hard, strong body against hers.

She shouldn't want such things in reality. But this—

"This is fun, harmless pleasure, Ophelia."

She couldn't see him, but his voice was soft and close. Her nape tingled—she was sure he whispered by her ear. "Many women dream of this. You did so because you wanted to be taken by a strong man. It's natural, my angel, because you believed you couldn't accept a man's touch. Many women who know they cannot be naughty dream of having pleasure forced on them. It's exciting to be out of control and subjected to enticing, erotic acts."

The whip stroked along her spine and she quivered. It caressed the cheeks of her bottom.

Was she really quite ready to be utterly out of control? Would he whip her there? She couldn't ask, for she had the gag between her lips.

Then shockingly he slid the firm, long handle between her cheeks, so it glided horizontally in the valley of her rear. He left it there, stuck between the globes of her bottom.

"Now for your clit, angel."

Rough rope sawed between her thighs. She squawked in protest, but the gag muffled it. His hands firmly rubbed it until it seated beneath her nether lips, lightly abrading them with each fierce breath she took. When she moved, the rope did, too, sliding over her clit.

Oh! She saw sparks shooting in front of her closed eyes.

"There's more. Would you like more?"

He was tempting her to take a bite of wanton pleasure and she couldn't resist. She couldn't speak for the gag. She nodded and she accidentally jiggled the rope against her oh-so-sensitive clit. She cried out into the silk strip.

"Warmed oil," Ravenhunt said softly. A soft drizzle hit the base of her spine and she jolted. Something massaged it gently downward, coating the valley of her rump. Pain stabbed her quickly and the soft stroking stopped.

"I won't hurt you. I'll use a wand instead. Coated in oil."

There was a pause and then something warm and firm tapped her bottom.

For one thrilling moment she thought: It must be his erection. Then she felt the rigidness of it, pressed against her bottom.

No, the wand he'd used on her before. Gently, he traced along the valley of her derriere. Until he reached the entrance there.

She tried to jerk away, but he slid a rope around her waist and held it so she could not roll or wriggle in escape.

Lightly he traced around that place, that forbidden place.

"You are sensitive in there, too."

Ophelia shook her head. How could she be? This wasn't . . . well, proper.

"I will show you."

The wand, slick with oil, penetrated her bottom. Just a bit. Her muscles clenched in refusal. He eased it back, but when she took a deep breath, relaxing, he pushed it forward again. Over and over he did this, and it stopped hurting, stopped making her tense. Her bottom was slick with oil. Her muscles no longer clenched.

She actually—

Wanted it inside.

Now, when he put it in just a bit, she moaned. She began to rock backward. Each light push on the wand seemed to make her clit tighten. She was tense everywhere—the tension before pleasure burst.

Oh God. It went in deeply, and she gasped. It felt good. She'd had no idea her bottom could be aroused.

Slowly, he began to thrust it. "It's all the way in now." His voice was gruff, strained. "Right to the hilt."

Oh yes.

"Now we know how much your sweet, plump ass can take. All of it."

He withdrew it all the way and she thrust back, wanting it in again. He obliged, the thickness of it pressing against the ring of her entrance. It went in with a pop and a sweet sense of fullness. He took his time, slowly pushing it in, withdrawing, then pushing more. Goodness, it filled her so much.

"It is stuffed deep up your arse," he growled.

Naughty words, and she almost melted in boneless splendor as he began pumping the wand into her. She moaned into the gag. Her rump was completely stuffed. She played with that word in her head. Stuffed. So scandalous, yet so delicious.

His thrusts were long, slow, gentle, but taking her to the brink.

"Rub your clit against the rope," he commanded. "Come for me."

She twitched and moved until she made the rope saw against her. Three swift jerks of her body and—

Oh God!

The orgasm took her swiftly, claiming her. Goodness, it was so good. Her body seemed to coil up, then stretch out, her every muscle twitching with the fierce sensation.

Fireworks streaked before her blindfolded eyes, and she screamed with delight into the gag. When it was over, he swiftly cut the ropes at her hands and feet. His capable hands undid the blindfold and gag, and she was free. She blinked, still dazed.

He stood at the end of the bed, his cock straight, thick, engorged. It looked so large she was certain her hand could not encompass it. Like a cutlass, it curved upward, tilting toward his rock-hard stomach.

His hand wrapped around it, and her eyes went wide as saucers. A large, strong male hand gripping an even larger cock. Heavens.

The way he held his shaft surprised her. Almost without mercy. His grip was hard, his face contorted in agony.

Then he stroked, his hand drawing along the thick shaft until he reached the underside of the acorn-shaped end. Beautiful and intriguing, his straight, thick cock seemed to grow out of a nest of black curls. His ballocks hung beneath the curve of that marvelous sceptre, though they seemed to have tightened up and pulled close to his body.

The top of his erection was adorable. Smooth and rounded, like a head looking upward.

His strokes went faster and Ophelia caught her breath. He jerked his cock harshly. Roughly. Almost beating it.

His eyes shut and he drew in a sharp breath. His hand fastened around the rigid length, just below the head. His other hand gripped his balls.

A jet of white fluid spurted out of the top of his cock. It arced like a fountain, spattering his hand, his leg.

He ducked his head, breathing hard.

Then Ravenhunt lifted his head, and the candlelight seemed to glow at her where it reflected on his eyes. He made a sound like an animal's growl.

His muscles still jerked with his climax, and his hand was sticky with his semen, but all Raven could think about was blood. The rich, teasing scent of it filled his nostrils. He jerked his head to the side as pain shot through his jaw. His fangs lengthened, scraping his lip, but Lady Ophelia had not seen it happen.

He heard her blood rush through her veins. Each pump of her heart pounded in his ears like a drumbeat.

She was so beautiful. And she would taste so good.

He released his cock and lunged for the bed. Startled, Ophelia fell back, sprawling on the white sheets. Her skin was flushed pink with her blood. So much blood—

The curve of her slender neck gleamed like pearl in the light. His fangs brushed her skin. Incredible pleasure shot through him, more powerful than any orgasm. His throbbing cock jerked and went hard instantly.

He wanted more. Needed more. Her blood. All of it.

His fangs scraped, easily gouging tiny holes in her delicate flesh. Two droplets of crimson blood—perfect, round, shining—dribbled out.

"Ow," she gasped.

The blood drop ran down and touched his lower lip.

Her blood was ambrosia to a vampire like him.

Another welling drop released the luscious scent of her blood to him. He stuck out his tongue and lapped it up.

"What are you doing?" Ophelia protested, and she pushed at his shoulders. Then she squealed and jerked her hands from him. Pain shot through him, but Raven didn't give a damn. His jaw ached and throbbed, and his head was filled with her smell.

More.

No.

But he couldn't stop. God, he wanted her blood. She tried to wriggle out from beneath him. He gripped her arms, and dimly he heard her cry out, beg him to let her go. He bent to her neck. His teeth hovered over her skin. One quick plunge, and he could have it all—

He shoved her away from him. She fell to the bed, and her pale, white hand clamped to the wound on her neck.

This was what he was. A killer.

His muscles shook and screamed as he fought the yearning to leap on her and drain her dry. He roared with the agony.

No longer did he care about hiding the truth. She was going to find out he was a vampire. He leaned over her, and she stared up, her pretty mouth open in shock, her blue eyes wide and confused.

"Ravenhunt?"

It was all over.

His mouth was an inch from her neck and he was shaking so hard he thought his body would rip apart.

Damn it, no.

"Sorry," he whispered in her ear. His muscles cramped, then

extended, and pain shot through him. His clothes dropped off. His body changed, twisting and pulsing, as his bones reshaped, his muscles pulled and lengthened, and his back began to spread, until his wings grew and expanded. He rose in the air, spread his wings, and spiraled over her bed. With a harsh beat of his wings, Raven flew out through her door opening, seeking the place in the roof where he could quickly fly out.

He had to feed.

10

From Frying Pan to Fire

*H*e'd *bitten her.*

Shocked, Ophelia pushed herself up on the bed on arms that still burned with the pain of touching him. Her heart pounded in her chest, loud as the hooves of a frightened horse. Her wits spun, and she couldn't quite believe what she'd seen.

She shut her eyes and opened them again, but there was no Ravenhunt. Only his clothing lay in a pile on the floor.

It had truly happened. She wasn't losing her mind.

A minute ago, Ravenhunt had lunged over her and pinned her to the bed. He truly did have sharp, curved fangs instead of teeth—fangs he had pushed into the skin of her neck. Pain had hit her, and she'd felt blood spill from the wound. Horror had gripped her. She'd tried to push him off, but he was too strong—

He'd pulled back from her, roaring like a beast. In front of her, he had jerked and thrashed as if in a seizure. Then he'd disappeared and his clothes had dropped to the floor in a disordered puddle, after which an enormous creature, like a bat or a gargoyle, had flown out of the bedroom.

Ravenhunt had been that gargoyle. He had transformed into a winged creature.

Ophelia jumped off the bed, landing on unsteady legs—legs that propelled her to the bedchamber doorway faster than she could think. She should not be chasing him. It was insane to do it. But she had to know what was going on. Gathering her courage, she leaned out the doorway and peered down the hall.

After having firelight in the room, she couldn't see a thing. The hall was a stretch of dark, but she heard movement, then her eyes registered the faintest glow of moonlight spilling into the hall from another room.

The small shaft of silvery light reflected on Ravenhunt's wings.

Her heart skipped a dozen beats as she drew back into the room.

He was flying away from her, leaving her, and it didn't appear he was going to come back and attack again. Though she couldn't be sure.

Her fingers went to her neck. Sticky droplets of drying blood perched on top of the wound.

She stared at the red smear on her fingers. Rubbed them together, but that did not make the blood disappear. He had fangs, he had tried to drink her blood, and he could change into a bat.

She had even *wondered* if he could be a vampire and she'd dismissed the idea. She had been so trusting, so naïve, so utterly foolish. Why had she not listened to her instincts? He'd offered freedom and she had grasped at it, desperately and pitiably, trusting everything he'd told her.

For most of her life, she had been held prisoner by people who had lied to her. Even her parents had done so. They had tried to make her believe she would change and would one day be free. Even Mrs. Darkwell had lied—pretending that there was no way Ophelia could escape her power.

Ravenhunt had lied by omission. He certainly had not told the truth and revealed he was a vampire.

It was time she took charge of her life. But what exactly was she going to do? She was trapped in a vampire's house.

Ophelia leaned on the door frame, trying to think. Why had he spared her? Why had he changed into a bat and flown away?

That she could answer. He couldn't kill her yet. He wanted her power. That was all she was worth to him—her horrible power that she'd been cursed with. He must have planned, after he'd taken her power away, to feast on her blood for his dinner.

The warty, evil wretch. The slimy, scummy vulture. The— the *monster.*

Cold fury rushed through her, filling her with determination. Every horrible word she called him gave her strength.

He had gone upstairs. He'd told her the house was a fortress that she could not escape, so where was he going?

Sorry, he had whispered. Could it be an apology? Could it mean he hadn't wanted to hurt her? He was flying away—a vampire's version of fleeing—to protect her. She knew it was because he couldn't feed from her yet, but it meant he was flying *to* somewhere. Where?

Fired by anger, by the determination to beat him and get away, Ophelia stepped out into the eerie darkness. Running her hand along the wall to guide her, she made her way down the wide corridor.

Perhaps she was heading into danger, but logic told her he intended to fly to somewhere that wasn't in his house. If he was escaping her, it meant he was leaving her.

When he had gone to rescue her, he'd done it without any clothes. Now she knew why—when he changed shape, his clothes fell off him. That meant he had flown out of his house to find her.

There must be a way out of his house. She had to find it.

At the end of the corridor, the door to the servants' stairs stood open. The narrow steps disappeared into darkness.

She would go up.

The stairs creaked beneath Ophelia's feet. When she reached the top, a cold draft leaked out of a doorway, brushing her bare arms. Something was open to let the outside night air inside.

Here, grayish moonlight streamed in through a few dirty windows. It gave enough light to reveal there was no winged Ravenhunt above her. Unless he could perch, curled up, the way ordinary bats did, and he could hide in the rafters.

In the dim light, she saw the attic was divided into two spaces. Cold air wafted through one doorway, which must mean a window was open and that was how he'd escaped the house.

It might be a way out for her.

Except she was four stories above the street.

Following nippy air that made her shiver and hug her arms, she made her way into the quiet room. It was a large space, and she saw at once he hadn't gone out a window. There were only two and both were shut, encrusted with dust. Beds stood in rows in the dim space, obviously intended for servants, but the brass frames were bare of mattresses. No one had used this room for years.

Something cold and slippery hit her cheek and slid down.

Her scream filled the room. She wanted to run but couldn't see where to go. She forced her legs to stay put. She couldn't be a coward now.

Another slippery, horrible thing dropped to her lips—

Water. It was water dripping down on her.

There had been a light patter of rain earlier, when they'd been in the bedroom. She had barely noticed it. Flushing, she felt stupid remembering how excited she'd been, how aroused and thrilled and happy.

She really had been an *idiot.*

No, she wasn't a fool. She had been trusting, but was that so bad?

Ophelia looked up. The ceiling was slats of board, aged and dark, against a midnight sky. One more drop fell and she stood under it and saw a change in the blackness above her—a place where she glimpsed gray clouds. A slight grinding sound came from the ceiling, and then the small rectangle of cloudy sky was gone, leaving inky, uniform darkness in its place. No more rain fell.

There had been an opening. Now it was gone.

And so was Ravenhunt.

The key.

Ophelia had stood, staring up at the ceiling for minutes before she remembered Ravenhunt's robe tumbling to the floor when he'd shifted shape. His clothes must be in his bedchamber. His key was either with his robe or his clothes. He couldn't have taken one with him when he shifted shape.

It was her way out of this house—out of the nightmare of being a vampire's prisoner. He wasn't the hero she thought he was. Instead, he was a monster, an undead demon who fed on blood.

It changed *everything*.

Yes, he had rescued her from those men—though she had only his word for it they were from the Royal Society and wanted to dissect her to study her power. Yes, he had flown away tonight rather than hurt her, but he had wanted to bite her. His fangs had actually cut her flesh.

Fighting his hunger for her blood had been a tremendous struggle for him. How vividly she'd seen it. It was part of his nature and it was something he could not control. That was something she understood. She knew what it was like to have a power you could not stop, no matter how hard you tried. What if he gave in next time?

Ravenhunt would kill her.

The key. She had to find it. Hiking up the trailing ends of the robe, she ran out of the attic room and raced down the stairs.

Panting, she reached his room. His clothes had been just

tossed on the bed, and she slid her hands through them to find the key. His shirt and trousers carried his scent—sandalwood, and a spicy smell that was unique to his skin. Smelling it made her throat tighten. So did remembering his beautiful, almost-naked body standing at the foot of the bed. She thought of his dark eyes, bright with desire, as he watched her, admiring the way he'd tied her up.

Tears burned in her eyes. Why? Why should her silly eyes be filling with tears? She hadn't lost him; she'd never actually had him in the first place. He wasn't mortal, and he didn't care about her.

Her fingers brushed cold metal. With a soft cry of triumph, she grabbed the key—

She couldn't escape anywhere while wearing nothing but a velvet robe. Key in hand, she took two steps toward the door to go to her own room, when inspiration struck. His lush skin-smell was still in her head. His clothes were imbued with it.

His *clothes.*

Female clothes were hopeless—long, tangling skirts, heavy fabric, corsets. No one could escape anywhere dressed like that.

She would wear his clothes. It meant drenching herself in his smell, and she wanted so much to forget him, but she had no choice.

Cool air swirled around Ophelia as she stepped out onto the front step. It was madness, but she couldn't just run away and leave his door unlocked. She turned the key in the massive iron lock, hearing it engage with a *clank.*

For a moment, she stood there, taking deep breaths. Raven-hunt's house was on the outskirts of Mayfair. The entire world seemed to be in the street. Carriages were packed in the street and could barely move. Many people filled the sidewalk after disembarking from their carriages. There was a party going on just two houses from Ravenhunt's, which meant many people were alighting from their vehicles.

Surely she was safe. Surely no one from the Royal Society would attack in front of all these people.

She had weapons, too. In a drawer in his bedchamber she'd found a box containing two pistols, along with shot and powder. Two loaded pistols weighed down the pockets of the great coat she had found, swinging and hitting her legs as she moved.

Though she prayed she didn't have to use them. She didn't want to have to hurt anyone, even villains who wanted to hurt her. She'd done enough killing and hurting through her life.

She was not just escaping Ravenhunt; she was going to escape from her life. She would go away, somewhere far away, where she could hide from other people.

It would mean she would be a prisoner, but at least she would be her own prisoner, instead of being kept hidden and locked up by someone else.

She was going to take charge of her own life. Finally.

Ophelia began to walk down the steps, then stopped. How could she blend into this crowd of people? She would have to walk along the sidewalk with them. She would bump against them, be jostled by them, perhaps she would have to grasp someone to steady herself.

She couldn't risk hurting anyone, but she had to get away. There was no way now to get to the mews without going back through the house.

At the bottom of the steps, Ophelia held her breath, made her body as slender as possible, and tried to slip between people. But from behind, something struck her and she jerked around in blind panic. A desperate apology sat on her lips—but how could she say sorry for killing someone, not now, but hours or days from now? Whoever had hit her would sicken and die—

It was a walking stick. A gentleman's stick had hit the back of her leg. Something utterly safe, but it meant the gentleman, who walked with his wife, arms linked, was nearing her.

She stumbled back, clearing the path, as the elderly couple passed her. Then she jumped to the side as a group of foxed young men staggered together toward the party.

"Out of the way," one of them shouted at her, a short, portly buck. His gaze went over her, taking in her borrowed breeches, shirt, and oversized great coat. "You are no lad. That's a plump derriere squeezed into those breeches." His leering and sneering tone made all the others laugh.

Another of the group, skinny with spotty pimples on his cheeks, barked, "She's a useless, grubby urchin, that's what she is. She's blocking the sidewalk."

She sensed something move beside her. It was the first gentleman, and he'd lifted his hand to grab her.

"Don't," she gasped. "Dear God, I could kill you." She took a quick step to the street, and tripped in Ravenhunt's too large boots. She fell toward the third of the young, drunk men.

His hand struck her shoulder, but only for a brief second, because he gave her a hard shove out of the way. She fell to her knees, wincing as they struck the ground. "Here," the man shouted. "Mind your manners with your betters. You don't walk into gentlemen, you little piece of rubbish." His hand lifted, as if preparing to deliver a slap.

"Do not touch me," she cried. She scrambled to her feet and rushed toward the busy street, stumbling off the sidewalk. Horses whinnied, a coachman shouted vile curses at her, and she turned to see hooves clawing at the air above her head. The metal shoes flashed, the horses seemed to be screaming in her ears, her legs felt caught in treacle.

She forced her numb limbs to work and jumped out of the way.

Hard cobblestones struck her hip and her shoulder. She

landed on her side, and seemed to bounce off the cold, hard street. Pain screamed through her body, but dazedly, Ophelia got to her feet.

Then she ran like a rabbit, weaving around horses and carriages. Men shouted at her, a riding whip struck her shoulder, which made her cry out. At least the thick fabric of Ravenhunt's coat absorbed the crack of the lash.

Men chased her. Men in dark coats, some with tall, black beaver hats, who were well dressed, and some who wore rough clothes and gray wool caps.

She ran. She ran in between the carriages, trying to keep close to the vehicles so she could hide, yet avoid hooves, wheels, and whips. Somehow she reached the end of the street without being trampled. She stumbled through the intersection. Sound was everywhere, filling her head with raucous confusion. Her lungs burned with exertion.

She raced across the road to the opposite sidewalk. Sucking in breaths, she stopped against a wrought-iron fence at the front of a house. Her insides felt as if they would heave up. But she didn't want to stop long. Holding the fence, she dragged herself onward, until she reached a narrow gap between two rows of houses—a small, dark alley. She threw herself into the stinking space, and plastered her back against the damp brick wall.

"What in Hades do you think you're doing?"

Deep and soft, the masculine voice came out of the shadows. She almost jumped out of her loose boots.

Ravenhunt. He was standing beside her in the shadows, where there had been nothing before. He gripped her wrist. She fought to get free, even as the pain began where his fingertips pressed hard into her flesh.

"Let me go. I'm not going to die as your dinner—"

"You aren't going to be my dinner." He released her wrist, but he moved so his body was in front of hers, mere inches away. His large hands braced against the brick on either side of her head. Rough brick bit into her back. He was naked; she couldn't see him because he loomed over her, but she knew he must not have a stitch of clothing on. His muscular neck was bare. Faint light gleamed on the naked expanse of his wide, straight shoulders and his broad chest. His body stood in front of her like a wall. "I've fed on blood and I've gained control of my hunger, Ophelia."

"None of that reassures me in any way," she protested. "You are telling me you went out and killed someone and drank their blood." She couldn't stop staring at his teeth. They looked normal now. No fangs. They must disappear when he was not feeding. When they came out, it must mean he was ready to bite. She watched them nervously.

His lips cranked down in a frown. "I did not kill anyone. Now, listen to me. There are a dozen armed men coming after you. I am the only hope you have—"

"Hope for what?" she threw at him. "Hope that I survive a little longer, until you can no longer resist and you plunge your fangs into my neck? Or do you mean, hope to survive until you take my power so you can then kill me?"

"Love, this is not the place to argue."

"It will have to do. I am not returning to your house. And I am *not* your 'love'."

He stiffened and twisted to look at the mouth of the narrow alley, while his arms and body kept her trapped. "They're coming, damn it. I can smell them."

"We have to run," she whispered, her voice hoarse.

"It's too damned late—"

Twang.

A sharp, strange sound filled the air—the sound of something snapping. Ravenhunt howled and his body fell forward, pressing her against the wall. She tried to push him back, but she couldn't move him. Then he slid down, his hands pulling along her arms.

Good heavens, he was collapsing. She froze, because pain was shooting through her arms where he touched her. She couldn't help him. She could barely move. He fell heavily to the ground, landing on his side.

Oh God. A long shaft stuck out of his back. It was an arrow of some kind. Despite the sheer agony in her body, Ophelia dropped to his side. "Ravenhunt!" She felt along his strong back. Her fingers slipped in his blood.

"Should I pull it out?" she whispered. God, could she? "I don't know what to do. Will I hurt you more if I try to pull it out?"

"No, love." His eyes were black as pitch. His hand clutched hers, but then the pain came and he had to let her go. "Pull it out. Then I can heal."

She gripped it and tugged, hoping to ease it out. But it wouldn't go. He gave a cry of pain.

"I can't do it."

"You have to." His voice was harsh. "Pull hard, don't think about hurting me. Yank as hard as you can and rip it out."

She pulled, wincing as he fought to smother a roar between his gritted teeth. It should be easy to hurt him—he was a vampire, and he had wanted to bite her. But it was not easy. She could not stand to inflict pain on him.

Then, with a horrible sucking sensation, the arrow came out.

Hands gripped her shoulders and jerked her backward. She was dragged along the cobbles in the alley. She could see legs all around her, male legs with boots.

She struggled—

A cloth was clamped over her face, and Ophelia breathed the same sweet, sickly scent she had when Ravenhunt had kidnapped her. Wildly, she struck out, trying to fight, but whoever gripped her face wasn't afraid of her.

Her arms flailed weakly.

She saw Ravenhunt jerk to his feet. But a man in a black cloak stepped in front of her, lifted a crossbow. The arrow flew. It slammed into Ravenhunt's chest and he fell back.

No! She screamed it in her head, for she could make no sound.

Was he destroyed? Could even a vampire endure such a thing? Desperately, she reached out toward him, but she was too dizzy and weak to move. He had been right, right about everything, and now she was going to die.

She couldn't let him be destroyed for her—

She tried to fight free of her captors. Somehow she got to her feet, but then the brick walls whirled around her and her legs seemed to disappear beneath her.

Ophelia blacked out.

11

Prisoner

Ravenhunt!

Ophelia opened her eyes in a panic. She remembered every-thing. The horrifying *twang* of the crossbow's string, the way his body had jerked as the arrow slammed into his broad, bare back . . . the look of agony in his dark eyes as he'd collapsed on the ground.

Dear heaven, she couldn't see. Even with her eyes wide open, she stared into unfathomable blackness.

Fabric scratched her cheeks and the bridge of her nose. Something pressed against her eyes and the back of her head.

She was blindfolded.

Ophelia felt herself move through the air—she wasn't fly-ing, someone carried her in strong arms, but not with any care. Her legs struck something; her shoulder bumped an unyielding surface that could be a wall. Ropes bound her arms to her body and secured her wrists—too tightly. She couldn't move her legs. Far too slowly, her senses came back. Pungent mustiness of old, damp wool flooded her nose and made her gag. It was a scent wafting up from just below her nose, so she knew they had bundled her in a blanket.

Panic made her heart thunder, her breaths sounded like hissing steam. If she could calm down, she might be able to *hear*. She fought to focus.

Whoever carried her breathed heavily, and his breath stank of beer and onions. Scraping sounds came to her ears, which she guessed were shuffling footsteps on a hard floor. There were other footsteps, too, crisper ones, which meant boots striking the ground in a refined gait.

Voices reached her ears, indistinct, as if through a thick, muffling fog.

"Bring her in here," growled one voice—a deep and harsh male voice.

"No one can speak of this. If the rest of the Society learns of it . . . damnation, they have vampires within the Society. They've allowed the enemy to breach the walls." This was a second voice, and it was low and filled with righteous anger. "If they knew about this, they would stop us. It's the poison within. They want us to stop hunting monsters. They talk about acceptance. All of it is lies. They are trying to convince us to stop hunting them so they can take over the world."

Hunting monsters. To these men, she must be a monster. Her heartbeat galloped, but her heart had nowhere to go, and she felt the pounding against her rib cage, even up in her throat.

There was a sharp, sour smell, as if someone had spilled brandy on the floor.

More footsteps sounded on the floor behind her, and her heart jolted with increased fear. There were more than just the two men. How many, she couldn't distinguish. But with so many people surrounding her, she couldn't hope to escape. She had to stay still, pretend to be unconscious. And wait.

Ravenhunt couldn't come for her. He'd been shot just before she'd passed out.

It was sheer agony to think of it. Was he . . . heavens, was he dead? Could a vampire, who was undead, actually die? She didn't know.

What if he had been destroyed? Her teeth sank into her lip, tears leaked under the blindfold.

She had to get away to go to him. Only hours ago—was it even that long?—she had fled, believing she must run for her life from Ravenhunt. Now, she was determined to help him.

Perhaps she was crazy to want to do it and insane to feel anything but fear for a vampire.

But Ophelia didn't care anymore. Ravenhunt was the only person who had ever really protected her. She owed him so much.

How was she going to accomplish an escape when she was wrapped in a blanket and held in the strong arms of a man who thought her a monster that deserved to be killed?

Her breathing sped up, and she sucked in musty air. The blanket and the rock-hard arms were squeezing her lungs and she could barely breathe.

Don't panic. If she could confront the fact Ravenhunt was a vampire without fainting or collapsing, she could cope with this. What she needed was courage. Ravenhunt had told her how brave she was. Perhaps she had better believe him.

With black cloth tied over her eyes, she couldn't see a thing. Ophelia strained to hear sound, but it was quiet. She was in a place that smelled of spirits—a wine cellar? The basement of a tavern? There was only the dull echo of footsteps.

A clattering sound, following by a soft creak—a door opening?

"We must succeed in our mission." The second man spoke again. Anger punctuated his every word. "We can never have peace with monsters like these. It is our sworn duty to slay them, and slay them we must."

Ophelia fought to not tremble. Her captors must think her unconscious, oblivious to everything they said.

"The foolish old men of the Society called them 'tamed' vampires," snarled a new voice, one she had not heard before. "Bloody hell, a vampire is a soulless beast. It cannot be tamed."

"We have to make the Royal Society pure again," whined another man, who had not spoken before. "But we were told to wait—"

"We had the opportunity to capture her and we took it," growled the first voice. "She had escaped Ravenhunt, we had to act."

"I agree," said the second man.

"With her power, we could destroy them all," said the first man. "It was senseless to wait."

The lust in his voice made bile rise in her throat.

"Agreed," the second man repeated. "We need time to study her for our purposes and our purposes alone. We will give the doctor the chance to try to understand where her power comes from," the second man said, authority in his tone.

"Then he takes her?"

"Possibly," snapped the second man. "Or we kill her. I do not believe anyone should possess her power."

She shuddered, even as the whiny man spoke again. "Double-cross him? That is madness."

"Not when we have the upper hand." The second man's voice was cold as an iceberg.

Whom were they speaking of? Could the man who wanted to take her be Ravenhunt's client?

The men remained silent. The scent of alcohol grew stronger. There was mustiness—it stank like a damp basement. Another door groaned on old hinges. Ophelia was brought into light. She could see it at the edges of the blindfold and feel it on her face.

Strong arms juggled her, and then a cold flat surface pressed against her back, her bottom, her legs. She had been laid on what felt like a table.

"Get the doctor in. Let's be done with this." The speaker was the second man.

Doctor? Was the table for operating—?

"Wait," cried the first man. His voice was higher-pitched now. "How is the surgeon going to cut her up without touching her? I never asked. Will it not kill him?"

"It can be done with a minimum amount of contact." That was the low-timbered tones of the second man. "He will be gloved—"

"That isn't enough with her," broke in the first man.

They wanted to dissect her, just as Ravenhunt had warned her. Nausea cramped in her belly. Everything Ravenhunt had told her was true. He was in truth the only person she could trust, even though he was a vampire.

But she knew it too late, far too late, for he had probably been destroyed for her.

Ravenhunt had suffered in his past. Even though he'd refused to speak of it, she seen the hint of his pain raw in his eyes, and she'd watched his body stiffen. He'd retreated from her, and she knew he was deeply troubled. She did not know how he had become a vampire, but whatever had happened to him pained him greatly.

She'd been a fool to run away from him.

The second man gave a mocking chuckle. An awful sound, filled with evil delight, and it crawled over her like rats on her skin. "She will be strapped down."

God, no.

There was a sound, like a snap of metal. Strips of cold, hard iron pressed against her—she knew that pressure must come from the straps the man had spoken about. The flat surface of them compressed her skin, pushing down across her shoulders and her thighs.

She couldn't pretend she was unconscious. She must fight before she was helpless.

Caught in the blanket, she thrashed and threw her body from side to side, trying to roll free.

"The monster's awake."

"Stop her."

"Don't touch her—"

But that warning came too late. Strong hands gripped her and shoved her onto her back. The man gave a howl of panic and jerked his hands away. Ophelia tried to move but the straps came across her again and were immediately cinched tight, sucking her down against the hard surface. She was bound to the table.

"The doctor will be here soon."

Footsteps moved away from her. The door shut with a mournful creak, then she heard another sound. The *clink* of a key turning in a lock.

He couldn't heal with a crossbow bolt sticking into his chest, damn it.

Raven gripped the bolt. He was weakening. It was strange—normally a crossbow bolt would bring him down, but it would not kill him. The shot had to go right through his heart to do that. This arrow had driven into his chest just below his heart, and the tip was protruding out of his side. But his hand was feeble. He could barely keep it wrapped around the shaft.

There was no way he would be destroyed before he could save Ophelia.

Growling like a wounded dog, Raven hauled on the shaft with all his waning strength. The arrow's points tore through his flesh. Blood ran down his stomach, his crotch, his legs. All the blood from his feeding was pouring out of him. His skin was turning white. He held the arrow in his hand, but his body was not yet healing.

What in Hades was wrong?

Raven gripped the brick wall behind him, dragged himself off the blood-slicked cobbles. Now he saw the precious red fluid no longer flowed out of him like a river. The wound began to heal, more slowly than ever.

Was it something about the crossbow bolt?

Then he understood. Taking Ophelia's power was supposed to destroy him. He'd assumed it would happen quickly, maybe in a blinding flash of flame, or a big agonizing *poof* where he turned into dust.

He'd never thought to ask what exactly would happen. Not that he would have trusted the vampire queen Jade to give him the truth.

Dredging up the rest of his strength, he shifted shape. How was he going to find Ophelia?

He tried to glimpse into her thoughts. Vampires could do it with their prey. Get into the thoughts of the mortal they wanted. But he couldn't with Ophelia.

She was not prey, after all.

He tried to connect with her thoughts, speak to her that way. He knew of vampires who could do that with a lover.

Ophelia, he shouted, through his thoughts. *Where are you? It's Ravenhunt. Speak to me through your thoughts. Lead me to you.*

"Ravenhunt?" Ophelia whispered.

She was rubbing her head against the table, twisting it, and trying to move up and down. The surface was wood, and the blindfold had snagged on splinters. She could work it free. "Ravenhunt, are you here?" she whispered.

Love, I'm speaking in your thoughts.

He'd said that before. It hadn't made any sense. "You cannot do that," she whispered.

Vampires can. All you have to do is think but do so as if you are talking to me, and I will hear your thoughts, too.

Could she? She shut her eyes, with the blindfold still covering them, but looser, and she thought very hard. *Ravenhunt, can you hear me? I'm trying to send my thoughts.*

In her head, she heard a gentle deep laugh. *You don't have to work so hard. Let your thoughts flow naturally, but think of me, as well, and we can speak this way. Now tell me where you are.*

I don't know. Even in her thoughts, it came out as a desperate and frustrated wail. Then she realized the true miracle in all this. *You are alive? I saw the bolt hit you and the awful way you collapsed. I thought you were dead.*

For some reason I was weakened and it was harder for me to pull out the arrow and heal. Love, I have to get to you. Can you see anything?

They blindfolded me, the wretches. They wrapped me in a blanket. To protect themselves from touching me, I guess. Then they put me on a table, which is really just a slab of wood, and they clamped metal straps over me so I can barely move. But I've almost got the blindfold off, which is no easy task, let me tell you, when I cannot move my hands—

You've almost got it off. Ophelia, how?

The fabric of the blindfold snagged on the rough table, and I've been wiggling around as much as I can to work it free.

You are amazing.

Even in her thoughts, he sounded awed. *It will only take me a few seconds more, I think.* Wincing, she pushed her head hard against the table and forced her body to move a little, up and down, by forcing out all her breath in her lungs so she was slim enough to wriggle under the strap.

The blindfold pulled up, along with her hair. Her teeth sank into her lip to smother a cry of pain. The fabric knot wasn't pressing into her head anymore—the blindfold was loose. She shook her head back and forth. The blindfold fell down, lying over her nose. She could see!

Euphoria lasted seconds.

She could see and now she knew what sort of room she was in and what surrounded her. Sickening. Horrible. She lay on a table in the center of a dark room. Faint light came in high, small windows. She was in a basement and those windows let in the glow cast by street flares outside.

Her eyes grew accustomed to the faint light. It was still hard to understand everything she was looking at. Some things were too shrouded in shadow. Rows of wooden shelves lined the walls, and the light reflected on dozens of glass jars. It looked like a basement filled with preserves—

A hand floated in a jar.

Ophelia jerked her head to the side, fighting the urge to vomit. Gathering courage, she looked again. Was that an *eye?* It was round and white and could have been a pickled egg, except for the round blue spot that must be an iris. She gagged and forced herself not to look away.

The body parts must be in alcohol. That explained the strong odor.

Was *she* supposed to end up that way? In pieces in jars?

Ophelia, can you see yet? It was Ravenhunt's silky, reassuring baritone, speaking softly in her head. *Where are you?*

It was as if he was with her. Her panic eased. All she had to do was bring him to her and she would be safe. She believed in him.

In her thoughts, she told him about the body parts. Even in her mind, she could hear how she fought not to cry. She quickly described the rest of the basement room: the damp stone walls and the table that stood along the wall; stacks of dusty books, measuring rulers, paintbrushes, quills, and bottles of ink. But nothing she could see helped to reveal where she was.

Can you see anything outside? he asked.

She peered at the windows. They were above her and to her left, since she was flat on her back. She could see the sky, and the tops of buildings.

Off-key singing came from outside. A couple stumbled past the window. She could see the torn hem at the bottom of the woman's skirts and her black buttoned boots and the man's shiny boots, his breeches, the bottom of his tailcoat. Both staggered.

There had to be a public house here.

But really, there was a public house at every corner.

In her thoughts, Ravenhunt coaxed her. Could she see buildings. People? Signs?

She twisted her head to look out the window that was behind her. It was the direction the drunken couple had come from.

There is a sign for an inn, she told Ravenhunt. *It's the Eight Bells. I'm in the basement of the building that is opposite it and up one, I think.*

Good. That's all I need, Ophelia.

Footsteps sounded outside her door, and there was a rattle at the lock. Someone was opening her door.

They are coming back, she thought desperately. *It's too late. A doctor is going to cut me open. You'll never get here in time—*

I will be there in seconds, angel. I promise you.

Ravenhunt?

There was no answer. Ophelia couldn't explain it, but she had a cold, empty sensation in her mind for seconds. It went away, but she was sure it was because their connection had broken.

The door opened.

A short, plump man leaned over her. His white shirtsleeves were rolled up. He wore thick, round spectacles and a waistcoat of gray with dark spatters on it. Ophelia saw red stains on his rolled-up sleeves and realized it was blood.

He threw a bundle down on the table and unrolled it. It was a sheath of leather and as it opened, the light gleamed on blades.

This was the doctor and with those things he would cut her open.

"No," she cried. "You cannot do this. This is inhuman—"

A gag was pulled between her lips, and it jerked painfully at the corners of the mouth. "Take care not to touch her."

She recognized the voice as that of the second man. He was tall and muscular, and wore a gentleman's clothes. His hair was jet-black, slicked back, and receding at the corners. It gave him a devilish look, along with his dark eyes. They looked as pure black as Ravenhunt's.

But much more cruel.

Another man watched, at the edge of the shelves, his fingers stroking his chin. Clear blue eyes peered at her. His features were perfect, like a Greek statue. His hair was gold. At his side stood the man who had attacked her the first time she escaped. The grey-haired man called Cartwell.

"This blanket has to be removed," the doctor barked. "How can I get to her to begin with a wool blanket wrapped around her?"

"We had to ensure she did not touch us." Now she knew, from his voice, the blond man was the first man.

He stepped forward with scissors from the bench and hacked at the blanket. She flinched and tried to pull away as much as she could. When he had it cut to pieces, he ripped some of it back, but not enough to let her hands free.

She fought to break the rest of the blanket, lifting her arms. The straps bound her across the upper arms. Her hands were now free.

"Damnation," yelled the blond. He came at her—he carried a dagger. He plunged it at her wrist and she screamed more shrilly than she ever had.

The tip went through the sleeve of her dress, securing it to the table.

The other man did the same to her other arm, and she was pinned, like an insect secured to a board.

"Now I begin." The doctor nodded with satisfaction.

A blade cut through her shirt, and the doctor tore it open. He looked up and met her eyes. She couldn't speak; she could only make fierce sounds around the gag.

"One day," he said, "I will determine how magic resides in the bodies of demons like you."

"We need to know," said the second man, "so we can destroy her power."

"Or take it," said the first man.

"That you may not be able to do." The doctor sliced through her shift. He was going to start cutting into her abdomen. To do that would kill her.

"There are stories that such powers like hers can be taken by magic, but that only works for other demons," the first man said. "Mortals cannot take it."

"The damned vampires who have infiltrated the society refuse to try," the second man snarled.

"No, they cannot do it," interjected Cartwell. "If they do, it is said it will destroy them. It would destroy a vampire to do it just as easily as it would destroy a human being."

Ophelia jerked, forgetting for one moment the doctor, who

had returned to his row of instruments. It would destroy a vampire to take her power?

That meant it would destroy Ravenhunt. He was going to free her from her power—but he would die to do it.

The doctor returned holding a thin instrument with a long, evil-looking blade. Standing over her, he lowered it to her stomach.

12

Touch Me

No! Ophelia struggled under the straps that clamped her to the table. She couldn't break free. She shut her eyes and gritted her teeth as the blade touched her belly.

A loud scream filled her ears, and she opened her eyes wide. A dark shadow stood between her and the doctor. Before she could see what it was, the doctor rose off his feet still screaming. The knife fell from his hand. He was thrown across the room. His short, portly body crashed against the wall of shelves. Jars flew out from the impact and smashed to the floor. His high-pitched shriek overwhelmed the shattering of glass, and he landed, sprawled on his stomach, amidst the wreckage.

She could see what the shadow was. A huge winged creature. It swooped at the other men, who scrambled to retreat, almost tripping over each other. Like terrified rabbits, they scampered toward the door and Ravenhunt chased them. At least, she thought it was Ravenhunt. Who else could it be?

She fought the straps holding her down, straining to see what was happening. But it was impossible. She couldn't lift off the table far enough.

Seconds later a naked Ravenhunt stood in the doorway.

Ophelia was no longer shocked to see him that way.

"I'm bound by the straps—" she began, but he ripped the ones off her legs with his bare hands. The metal creaked, twisted, snapped.

This display of strength and power didn't frighten her. But seeing Ravenhunt safe made her long to touch him.

"You are alive." Her voice was a choked whisper. "I feared they had killed you."

"I'm the undead. I don't die."

"But you can be destroyed," she gasped. How could he sound so unconcerned about it? She was so relieved, so grateful to him. She yearned to hug him to show it, to wrap her arms around him and press her head against his strong chest. Then she hungered to kiss him. Kiss him all over with joy because he was alive and he had come for her.

She wanted to kiss every single inch of him. Even naughty places.

She couldn't do any of those things. Even if she were free she couldn't.

As the band clamping over the top of her chest came off, Ophelia drew in a deep, grateful breath. She almost choked— the stench of blood and alcohol was thick in the air. Ravenhunt came to her, bending over her, concern stark in his eyes. Once she stopped sputtering, she managed to whisper, "I'm all right. It's just the awful smell." She met his intense black gaze, and the anger there made her lose her breath.

"Are you hurt, Ophelia? If you are, I will rip them all apart. Tear them limb from limb."

She laid her hand on his arm. "No, don't. I am all right." Then she remembered and pulled her hand away. Startled by his dark rage, she'd forgotten. "You came in time—just before the doctor was going to cut into me. You saved me." It seemed so inadequate, but she could only express all the emotion roiling in her—the relief, the happiness, the shock, the fear—in words. "Thank you."

Never had she believed she would thank a vampire. Yet he was kinder to her than anyone had ever been. She supposed it was because he was like she was—a killer who was feared by the world.

His lips kicked up in a smile, and she caught a glimpse of the sharp points of his fangs. He turned from her abruptly, watching the door and the high windows. "Wait until we are sure we are safe before you thank me, love. I believe they've run. But they might have only retreated to get sufficient weapons and they intend to come back."

His strong arms went around her and he lifted her, his large hands supporting her bottom and her back, but she struggled in his cradling arms. "Don't do this," she begged. "It will hurt you."

"I don't care."

"I do," she said.

Making a growling sound of frustration, he set her on her feet. He left her and prowled over to the fallen doctor. Three cavalier words, thrown out with a devil-may-care confidence, and with a certain amount of bitterness, ate in her heart.

Did he really not care? After all, he was willing to be destroyed to take her power. Of course, it would make sense that he didn't care if she hurt him now. He knew he was going to die. Why was he doing all this for her?

It gave her the strangest feeling, as if her heart was swollen and no longer fit in her chest. But she didn't want to win her freedom at the cost of his . . . well, his life. She couldn't live with taking that away from him. Didn't he understand that?

She stalked toward him, where he was crouched on his haunches at the side of the unconscious doctor.

"Raven—" Her voice died as he roughly rolled the doctor onto his back.

From this view, the doctor's rotund stomach looked like a hill. Blood smeared the neck, his waistcoat. Grimacing, Ravenhunt pushed the man's head to the side, then bent toward his neck—

"No!"

It had come out without thought. He looked up at her from beneath the fringe of his coal-black hair. "I need to feed, and this would let me finish him off. He deserves this for what he was going to do to you."

He said it so matter-of-factly. But Ophelia felt the blood draining out of her head as she imagined his teeth sinking into the man's neck, as she thought of him drinking blood. She grabbed the shelves as her legs almost melted beneath her.

She managed to hold her body up, but the horror made her dizzy. Ravenhunt needed blood now—he needed to feed, he said. Yet he had gone to feed after almost biting her. That had not even been a full day. How many victims had he taken since becoming a vampire?

At once he was beside her, his hands on her waist, and he supported her.

She pulled away from him. "No, I don't want this. I don't want you to—to drink his blood out of revenge." Warily, she faced him. Agony was etched on his handsome features. "What happens if you don't feed when you want to?"

He turned away, resting his hand on the shelves. "The craving becomes stronger."

"What happens after that?"

"I always have to feed eventually," he said, over his shoulder. "It will happen even against my physical will, if it must. But I understand how you feel. I won't do it in front of you."

He went to the door, looked out, then he took a few strides

down the hallway. Now she saw there was a corridor formed of stone walls beyond this room, and it led to a heavy oak door. At the end of that corridor was yet another door, which stood partly open. That was where her captors had run.

"I have to get you out of here, but we cannot go that way," he muttered.

"There are the windows." She pointed to the low windows that gave a view of the sidewalk and street.

"Good idea." He gave her an approving smile.

"How do we break them?"

"That is easy." From the large table, he took a dusty book, flung it, and the glass shattered. It was formed of small panes held with putty and wood, but Ravenhunt threw with such force, the entire thing exploded into pieces.

"Climb up," he said. "I will help you out the window." He motioned to the table. It astounded her how it didn't bother him to be naked. Her shirt was cut into tatters at the waist, but Ophelia had to admit she didn't care. She just wanted them to escape this horrible place.

She hesitated. "You'll have to touch me."

"It's all right. It won't hurt for long." He held out his hands to lift her onto the table.

"Wait. I know we don't have long and that we must escape. But I have to tell you what I learned. Those men said that a vampire who takes my power will be destroyed. You have to—"

"I know, Ophelia. I've known it all along."

"You know and you—you are willing to die to free me?"

This time he hesitated. He threw a glance back toward the door. "It's complicated. There is a way out for both of us. Guidon told me how it can be done. But that is for later."

He grasped her hips and lifted her. With his amazing strength, he easily lifted her up on the table.

Impulsively, she swiveled and bent down. Her hands cupped

his jaw, which was soft to her touch, but rough and scratchy, too, because it was shadowed with black stubble.

She had never cradled a man's face.

She had to stop touching him. But as she tried to move her hands, he grasped them and held them against her face. His eyes widened, his dark brows shot up and disappeared beneath his mussed hair. His full, beautiful lips parted. "Ophelia, there's no pain. I don't feel any pain."

How could it be possible? He cupped the back of her neck with his hand and drew her to him, so their mouths were only an inch apart.

Ophelia surged forward and hastily, clumsily, pressed lips against his. Her heart thundered. They could be caught and killed any moment. But she wanted to know if she could do this without pain. Just one quick, wild kiss.

Heavens, his lips were so warm and velvety soft. When her mouth touched his, there was a sizzle—but a glorious, thrilling, exciting one. The gentle contact of their mouths stole her breath. It made her hot and achy inside.

He drew back. "There was no pain."

"Does it mean you took my power?" Reality hit her. There was no joy, no happiness now—just horror. If he had taken her power, she'd killed him.

"I don't know. But it means I can get you out of that window. Come, Felie, let us hurry."

Felie. A pet name. She'd never had one.

Ravenhunt jumped onto the table beside her, then he wrapped his arm around her hips and lifted her so she could grasp the ledge of the window. She gripped it—a small piece of glass bit into her hand, but she didn't care about pain. Pulling on the ledge, she tried to scramble up, but he gently pushed her, so she was out the opening in moments. Ophelia scrambled to her feet—the window was just above the level of the cobblestone street. She turned to help him, but he leaped up from the table, soared cleanly out of the window, and landed on his feet beside her.

They were alone in the street, which was good as Ravenhunt was naked.

"We have to run, but you're—"

"We don't have to run," he insisted. "Since you can touch me now, I can transform into a larger bat, and you can ride on me."

"Ride on you? You mean—in the air?"

He nodded, and then his body jerked and writhed as he went through his transformation. She had seen it in his bedroom, but she'd been too shocked to really understand what had happened to him. His skin stretched in ways that must be impossible. Beneath his pale skin, his muscle and bone reshaped. His back widened, then in the blink of an eye, huge wings formed out of his back. His body had barely changed in size. He still possessed legs, a man's torso and hips and—and all the other parts. He looked more like a gargoyle than a man and in this form he was covered in sable-smooth black fur.

He turned, so his broad back and his wings faced her. Smoothly, he dipped down on one knee. She climbed on his back, lying along the lean, hard planes. So strange that instead of skin, she was pressed to velvety fur. She wrapped her arms around his neck, and her legs around his waist.

Then his wings flapped, raising up dirt from the street, and sending a soft breeze to ripple over her.

Together, they rose into the air. His wings beat slowly, with a languorous, graceful smoothness, but they lifted swiftly. By the second building they passed, they had reached such a height that they flew past the upper windows of two-story buildings. A heartbeat later, she could look down upon the roofs of Whitechapel High Street. Ahead were open fields beyond the London Hospital, a stretch of gray-tinted blue with moonlight. Shadows clung to the buildings, and Ravenhunt flew within them. She supposed it meant they disappeared from view when they were in the dark.

She held her breath. They climbed higher and higher. She felt as if she could reach out and touch the moon. For one moment, she felt a twinge of fear—they were dizzyingly high—but it disappeared. She had nothing to be afraid of when she was with Ravenhunt.

Ophelia drew in a deep breath. Up here the air felt and smelled different—cooler, crisp, clean. Her arms were securely wrapped around his neck. His powerful muscles flexed and moved beneath her slim arms.

As they'd risen into the sky, she'd heard shouting down below them. Her captors must have discovered she had escaped.

She could not believe she was flying. And if he'd taken her power, why was he not dead? What had he meant that Guidon had told him there was a way out?

Beneath her, she saw the streets of London laid out, following the curves of the Thames. Powerful wingbeats took them closer to the buildings below them.

Her heart dipped and then soared downward, and beat frantically when he climbed again.

Now she knew what it was like to fly. Exhilarating. Amazing. Somehow it seemed even more miraculous to fly close to the buildings below, to just graze over them, to whirl around them. Below them were narrow, elegant buildings with bow windows and painted signs that shone with gilt.

Charing Cross. They were going to Guidon's.

Ravenhunt slowly descended to the sidewalk outside the bookstore. He landed lightly on his feet, then crouched so she could safely slip off his back. It was dark—no light glowed in Guidon's shop. She looked back to Ravenhunt and in the seconds she'd peered into the shop, he had transformed back to a man.

"Is he asleep?"

"He's a vampire."

A vampire? She'd never dreamed of that, though it explained why he had been working in his shop at night. "What about you?" she asked Ravenhunt. "It is cold and you have no clothing. You cannot go in to see Guidon this way. We must get you clothes so you do not catch pneumonia."

"Love, vampires do not become sick. The Royal Society will have armed men watching my house, so we cannot return there. Guidon will help me acquire clothing. This is the safest place for you." He touched her cheek. The warmth of his hand on her skin was enthralling. But she couldn't do this yet.

"We must find out from Guidon if I've lost my power—" She could not make herself say, "and if you are going to be destroyed."

Ravenhunt hauled open the door. It was unlocked, and they stepped into darkness. Ravenhunt slid a bolt in place to secure the door behind them, then he took her hand. He threaded his fingers through hers—she hadn't held hands like this in forever. She had last done it with her sister Lydia—she hadn't seen her sister in years, nor her younger brother, Harry. Not since her family understood her power and kept her away from them. She had not started her life by killing people—it had begun when she was thirteen. She had hurt servants by accident; she had made her family ill, she had almost killed the man she loved. Then she had been locked away.

Holding someone's hand felt reassuring.

But it reminded her of what she'd done. Probably destroyed Ravenhunt.

"Guidon?" he called.

There was no answer, only silence, but Ravenhunt murmured. "He is in his garden."

"His garden? It is the middle of the night. How do you know?"

"He told me by thought."

She let him lead her through the crowded bookshop, in the narrow aisle between shelves, skirting stacks of books. At the back, they passed through Guidon's kitchen, its kettle on a table. Ravenhunt opened a rear door, and Ophelia walked out first into a tiny, walled garden.

The gnome-like man—vampire, she now knew—was crouched in front of a hedge of flowers. It was late at night, the sky velvety black, yet the garden was alive with color. She gasped, surprised.

Guidon jumped up and faced her, a beaming smile on his strange-looking face. He looked very happy and proud, and she smiled at him, despite her fears.

"Lady Ophelia, it is delightful to see you." He bowed.

"It is lovely to see you, Mr. Guidon," she answered. He did not appear shocked that Ravenhunt had no clothing.

He waved toward his house. "My—Mr. Ravenhunt, you will find a robe upstairs, if you wish. While you dress, I will show Lady Ophelia my garden. Then we can speak of what has happened."

"Do you know what has happened?" she asked, startled.

"I can imagine."

Ravenhunt left for the house and she could not help but blurt, "I am able to touch him now. It means he has taken my power, doesn't it? Does that not mean he is going to die?"

"Are you afraid of that?" Guidon asked.

She gaped, perplexed. "Of course. I don't want him to sacrifice himself for me."

"That is a good start." He almost skipped over to a bevy of huge white flowers. They were the size of saucers. "This is a moon flower. They bloom in moonlight."

"They are lovely. What do you mean by it is a good start?"

"What will save Ravenhunt is your love, Lady Ophelia. He is worthy of it, even if he believes he is not. However, it must be true love, deep and powerful, to save him. I do not know if you care for him quite enough yet. In my garden, though, you will see how beautiful things can be that live for the night. That bloom only in the night."

"I know Ravenhunt is beautiful, and I believe I do love him."

"You cannot completely love him, my lady. Not yet." Guidon pointed out other flowers with a gnarled, ink-stained finger. He spoke like a proud father about his children. There were lance-shaped white flowers with a pinkish tint and hairy leaves that he called Nottingham catchfly. He had borders of pink and purple four o'clocks. A beautiful yellow flower that was as tall as her he called evening primrose, creamy yellow night gladiolus, and elegant Casablanca lilies, which were very exotic.

"One would think a vampire would be denied the pleasures of a garden, but it is not so," he declared happily.

"It is one of the most beautiful gardens I've seen," she said, honestly. "The flowers show how much you love it."

Guidon waved toward the back door of his house. "We should go back inside."

They stepped inside as Ravenhunt came downstairs in a robe that reached his knees. He had it belted at his waist, wrapped around him to hide his naked body.

Guidon insisted they sit and he made tea. She poured it for them all. Guidon addressed Ravenhunt, "Do you have the book, my lord?"

"No, it is at my home. I had to leave my house in a hurry."

She swallowed. He'd had to run because he was going to bite her, and then because he had chased her outside. Then she realized what Guidon had said. "You called him 'my lord.' But he is not—"

"There are still secrets between you. That is why you have not entirely saved him yet, my lady."

Guidon stood and took Ravenhunt's cup. He held it so she could see in the bottom. There were leaves there, and they had filled one half of the cup, making a perfect straight line through the center.

"You have given some of your power to him. Right now you are both sharing the strength of your power. It is half with you and half with him, which is why you do not hurt him when you touch him. But once he takes all your power, unless he wins your love, he will be destroyed. Ravenhunt, she cannot love you without knowing the truth."

"I thought love saved her," Ravenhunt said.

"It saves you both," Guidon answered.

"What more can I tell her?" Ravenhunt's full lower lip thrust out. "She already knows the worst of me. My brutal past and the fact I am a vampire."

"She needs to know everything." Guidon turned to her. "What do you wish to ask him?"

There was so much. So much, she couldn't think of one thing. Then a question popped out, even though she hadn't really thought of it as the one to ask. "Why would you risk your very life to save me?"

Ophelia licked her lips, waiting for his answer, and when he fell back against his seat and groaned, her heart pounded with worry. There was something he did not want to tell her.

Raven had no idea what in hell Guidon was talking about. Ophelia knew the bad things about him and still cared for him. It should be enough. But, damn it, if Guidon insisted it was not enough, he knew the vampire had to be correct.

Guidon touched Raven's shoulder but looked to Ophelia. Now Raven thought of her as Felie—his special, sweet, and incredibly courageous Felie. "You love him now, do you not?" Guidon asked.

A fetching blush raced over her soft cheeks. "He was willing to die for me. No one has cared for me so much. Yes, I know I do. So how can that not be enough?"

Raven grimaced. He'd done this for his sister—Felie did not know that. Without knowing all the truth, she must have thought he'd done this solely for her. That was why she cared about him. If she knew the truth, she'd probably feel betrayed. And fall out of love. Women tended to do that. With Margaret, his fiancée, he always had to prove his love. Margaret was always emotional and upset, accusing him of betraying her, of not really being in love with her. She had always threatened to stop loving him if he did not reassure her with one grandiose gesture after another.

Was that what Guidon meant?

"You must understand that she cannot truly love you until she knows everything about you. You have been given a reprieve—a short chance to win her love once and for all. If you are not honest or if she does not fall in love with you, you will be destroyed."

He poured more tea in Ophelia's cup and pushed it into her hands. "Love is a most powerful emotion," Guidon said to her. "It can literally save lives and souls. But if it is built upon a foundation of deceit, it can never be real. To have magical properties, love must be real."

Raven knew Guidon might be talking to Felie, but the words were meant for him.

"I will leave you now," Guidon continued. "Here, in my parlor. You will be safe here in my home, and you will have privacy."

As Guidon left, he stopped in the doorway. He picked up a bowl and sprinkled the contents in the doorway—flower petals, and bits of dried leaves. There was a sweet, pungent smell.

"That will protect you from others who might intrude," he said. "I will sprinkle these around the doors and windows. No men of the Royal Society could cross these. They would lose consciousness at once."

Once the librarian left them alone in his parlor, Raven raked his hand through his hair. "Guidon is correct—I haven't told you everything, Ophelia. I haven't told you why I must take your power."

She was perched on the edge of the chair opposite him. She bit her lip, then said, "It is not to save me, is it?"

He was sprawled over the settee. "I always wanted to save you. I thought I was going to kill you by taking your power and I refused to do that. I was only willing to try to do it when Guidon told me that love would save you."

He had to tell her everything. He sat up, took her hand, and lifted it to his lips, giving a gentle kiss to her fingertips. Threading his fingers with her slender ones, he held her hand. He liked touching her. But when she knew the truth, would she let him touch her again?

He told her about the vampire queens—what they were and how they ruled the vampire world. "One of them turned me. I was bleeding to death in the mud after a battle, with my stomach ripped open by a sword and my throat cut. I probably had a musket ball lodged in my leg, as well—it's hard to remember the details."

"And you wanted to be a soldier?" She stared at him as if he were insane.

"Yes." He kissed her hand once more. "I was tempting fate, waiting to get killed, and fate had finally delivered. But Jade, one of the vampire queens, had decided she wanted me for a mate."

"To be with her for eternity?"

"Jade was never that faithful. A plaything for a few years was what she wanted. She created me and I had to serve her, acting as her assassin, destroying vampires who did not follow her rules. At first she kept me with her at all times, like a pet. She kept me in her house on the fringe of Mayfair. No one guessed Jade was feeding on residents and servants along the exclusive street."

He grimaced, but he knew he had to go on. "Jade wanted your power and she commanded I take it, even though it would risk your life. I refused, but then she threatened someone I love."

Surprise widened Ophelia's enormous blue eyes. "But you are so alone. I thought you had no one. No family."

Hades, he saw it in her face. Confusion.

"I am alone now, Ophelia, that is true. But I wasn't always alone. I have a much younger sister. She is only seventeen. She believes I am dead and I have not spoken to her since I was turned. That was while I was fighting in Ceylon in 1817—when I toured the world looking for wars to fight in."

"Do you have parents? Does your sister live with them?" Her brows drew together. "And she thinks you are dead—she hasn't seen you since you returned from Ceylon? You let her believe you were gone? She must be heartbroken."

Her gentle heart was wounded. Now he knew why Felie claimed to love him. It wasn't that he was worthy; it was that she had a soft heart and she felt emotions deeply.

"I couldn't go to her and tell her I had become a vampire. She would think me insane—or she would have been terrified. It was for her sake that I let her believe I was dead. Before my supposed death, I was the Marquis of Ravenhunt. My sister, Frederica, lives with my cousin, who is her guardian. When I lived with Jade in her Mayfair house, I was only blocks from my sister, but I couldn't go to her."

Her eyes went even wider. "You are a marquis?"

He shook his head. "Not anymore. I can't live in the mortal world. How could I explain that I don't age? That I eat and drink nothing and need blood to survive?"

"I suppose you couldn't. It is so terribly sad, though."

Raven didn't want to think about that. He had no choice.

"Jade threatened my sister's life if I did not take your power. I lied to you, telling you I was doing it for you. I was doing it to save Frederica."

"I understand why, if you had to save her," Ophelia said softly. But she knew what it meant—he did not love her.

Yet she did love him—perhaps even more—now that she knew he had been willing to give his life for his sister.

Impetuously, she launched across to the settee and threw her arms around his neck. "That is the noblest thing I've ever heard," she whispered.

"You aren't angry?" He cupped her face. "I did it for my sister at first, but now that I know you, I would have done it to free you."

"Do you really think it is enough—if we have love?"

"It has to be enough. It is supposed to be enough to save you, Felie. That is what I care about."

"But I'm afraid for you—"

"Don't be."

"What should we do?" she whispered.

"I am going to take you home, love. I want to make love to you. I can touch you in every way I've dreamed."

"You've dreamed of touching me?"

He drew her to him, pulled her against his broad chest, cloaked in the robe. "With my hands," he murmured against her ear. His lips grazed her lobe and she shivered in intense pleasure. "With my tongue. With my cock."

Oh heavens. Wild images leapt into her head. Her hands trembled, not with nerves or fear, but with yearning. With a lifetime of wanting to hold someone—

She only wanted to hold him.

"You've never been able to touch anyone, Ophelia. I want to be the first." Raven lifted her hand to his lips and suckled her wrist. She giggled, then squirmed in front of him. "Ooh, that feels lovely."

He wanted to ease her back onto the settee and—

No, my lord Ravenhunt, you cannot seduce Lady Ophelia in my parlor. Guidon projected the words into Raven's thoughts, sounding prim and shocked, even in thoughts.

Tonight will be the night, Lord Ravenhunt.

Raven nibbled the soft, silky skin of Ophelia's wrist, then quickly kissed his way up to her shoulder, where he ran his tongue over her ear. *Indeed it will be.*

I mean tonight will be the chance to take her power, Guidon said. *You must study the last chapters of that book exceedingly well. You must commit it to memory. Leave the poor young lady alone. You are not yet ready to seduce her.*

Damnation, Guidon, he muttered in his thoughts, *you know how to ruin the mood.*

13

Five

Before he even changed back to human form, Raven was hard. He had transformed and flown from Guidon's back here—to his dark home—with Ophelia riding on his back. She'd grown used to flying. Instead of clinging to him, his brave temptress rode him like a goddess on a magical steed.

He had landed on the roof, on a steep pitch, his claw-like bat feet gripped the slippery tiles, curling around the edges.

"Hold me tight," he told her. With a flick of his wing, he triggered the lever. His secret door slid open. It worked with pulleys and gears, making a soft, grinding noise. He lowered through the square opening.

When he had set her on her feet on his attic floor, he transformed back. As fast as his muscles and bones had shifted shape, more blood rushed down to his cock.

"Doesn't it hurt?"

He glanced down at his prick, thick and straight as an iron rod. "Actually, it does—"

"Not that, Ravenhunt. I mean when you shift shape."

"Yes." He shrugged. "But not as much as I hurt desiring you."

She lifted her brow. Apparently that wasn't a romantic state-ment. Then he saw how her hands ran along the cuts in her clothing. Hell. Moving with a vampire's speed, he came up be-hind her and tore the fastenings of her shirt open.

"What are you doing?" She jerked away.

"Taking it off. I will burn it, so you never have to think of that damned place again."

She wrinkled her nose, looking so sweet his heart lurched. "It's too cold to undress here." Her hand strayed up and stroked her tangled hair. Pulled out of her pins, it fell around her in disordered waves.

His cock bucked and smacked his gut—with her untamed hair, she looked like a woman who had just been fucked to an earth-shattering orgasm. But she was not disheveled because of pleasure, she had been through hell. "Come, I will take you to bed."

Her fingers touched the slices in her clothing. "First, I won-dered if I could bathe?"

"Of course. I will prepare it at once. You must relax in your room."

What he wanted to do was hurry her to bed. He wanted to caress her, kiss her, lick her all over, make love to her. But he could understand those damned Royal Society men had made her feel unclean. Raven bowed, in the nude, and he headed for the kitchens, to heat the water for her bath. Since she knew he was a vampire, he had nothing to hide. Using his preternatural speed, he tore upstairs with heavy buckets of water, filling the deep tub to the brim.

On a seat, he placed a stack of soft, folded towels—they were his, as he had no spare for guests—and set out a bar of his sandalwood soap. Then he gave her privacy, closing the door as she walked into the steam-filled room.

Returning to his room, he dressed carelessly in trousers, a shirt, a hastily tied cravat and coat. This would allow him to blend in with passersby, while he observed who was watching his house. Raven left by the kitchen entrance into complete darkness, locking the door behind him.

Men surrounded the house. Well hidden, but he could easily see them. For him it was like seeing them in daylight.

These were Royal Society men watching the house. From what Ophelia had told him, he knew there was a splinter group of the Royal Society—men who objected to having vampires in their midst, and who wanted to destroy all monsters, who believed "demons" could never walk among the mortals.

Whether the men watching this house were part of that group, or were men loyal to the Society, Raven didn't know. Now he knew the situation, he went back inside, moving so quickly the world blurred around him. But he couldn't go to Ophelia in her bath.

He had to read that book.

Ophelia was in the bath, naked, while he was stuck in his dark and dusty study, reading Guidon's mouldering book.

Raven could picture her in the bath. Steam rising around her, shielding her lovely body like a veil, giving him only tantalizing glances of pearlescent skin. Her hair would be wet, sticking to her damp skin. Her nipples would be hard, with diamond-like drops of water dripping from the sweet, pink tips—

He was as hard as a brick, and he couldn't take the pain anymore. But he had no choice. He had to deal with the book.

He had read it over and over, and knew the four lines of the spell that would free her from her power and send it to him.

The more he read, the more Raven wondered why she had this power. If she had been born with it, how could he remove it by using a spell? Had she been cursed with it? Why? It would have to have been when she was very young, before her menstrual courses began. Who would have done such a thing to a child?

Guidon had told him to read the part that explained how her power could be taken from her. He was to read it until he found the truth in the words.

Hell, he'd read them for an hour while she soaked sensually in a bathtub. He could smell the sandalwood soap—it was his soap and the thought of that normally masculine aroma on her feminine curves was driving him mad. His ears detected the faint splash of water. That brought to mind images of the lucky water hugging her curves, lapping at her breasts.

The book told him what Guidon had said—the only way for Ophelia to give up power and survive was through love. A shared love opened a conduit that allowed magical power to flow back and forth. It had to be true, deep romantic love.

The book was written in Latin, and while he'd studied Latin at Eton, he could not have cared less about languages and hadn't paid much attention. His translation to English was clumsy, he knew, but he hoped it was good enough. He'd scrawled it over a bunch of sheets of notepaper.

Translated, the book's title read: *The Demonica, volume XI.*

Raven read the passage about love again.

A special love is needed to break this curse. A love with the strength to endure for all time. It must be built upon complete honesty. It must be proven that this love can withstand the great blows that would destroy any lesser love. It must be able to survive the storms of betrayal and heartbreak.

How in Hades were you supposed to know if you loved someone that strongly? How could Ophelia know if she felt that way about him? Wasn't the only way to prove love could withstand those things to have it last a lifetime? Wouldn't they only know when one of them died?

The spell that released her from her power looked innocent enough, but spells and incantations were evil things. There was always a catch. This one had to be spoken after he'd given her several orgasms. He had to admit he liked the sound of that.

Raven leaned back in the chair—dust flew up when he did. *Guidon,* he called in his thoughts, *I've read the passage. How do I prove Ophelia's love can endure betrayal and heartbreak? I do not intend to do any of those things to her.*

He waited, cursing the time it took Guidon to answer. He would miss Ophelia's bath time. And he wanted to join her.

There is one great blow that you could give her—finally, Guidon answered. *It would shake her love to the very core. It would make it almost impossible for her to love you. If her love for you were to survive that, it would be proof your love is true.*

What in hell are you talking about? Raven snapped. *What great blow? Never would I hurt her.*

Another damned long pause, then Guidon spoke primly in his head, *You don't know, do you? I thought you knew, my lord. Think of the men you hunted for Jade and you will have your answer.*

Don't be so damned cryptic. I don't have time for this.

You have to solve it for yourself, Ravenhunt. There is nothing I can do.

He sensed his connection with the vampire librarian disappearing. *Damn it, Guidon, answer this. If she loves me so deeply, what happens after I take her power? Do I survive, or do I break her heart then? If I survive, what can I do? I can't accept her love—I'm a vampire. Without her power, she will have the chance for a normal life—to have love and children.*

You can provide those for her.

I cannot go out in daylight. I drink blood. I have to skulk through London, hiding in shadows. She deserves better.

You could transform her, Guidon answered. *Give her eternal life. Then you would be together forever.*

No, I couldn't do that to her—condemn her to be like me—when all she has wanted is to be free of her cursed power.

That proves you are falling in love with her, Ravenhunt.

Raven felt the connection vanish in his head—it was as if a

door had closed. Damn, he had more questions and no answers. Was the only answer to their love heartbreak? Even if they both survived this, he would have to let her go forever. He would never curse her to be a vampire.

How could he take her power unless he could fulfill the requirements of the book—that their love had to be strong and enduring?

Guidon, listen to me. He yelled it through his thoughts. *If I can't prove it, what happens to her?*

The vampire librarian responded. *I believe she will survive, Ravenhunt, because she loves you and I believe her love is strong. As the one who could cause her pain, the full price for taking her power will land on you.*

So I don't survive.

You may not.

Raven growled in his head, *If I knew for certain she would be all right, it is a risk I could take. I don't care about me, as long as she will be safe.*

Ophelia opened her eyes, dozy from the heat of the bath, and gasped in surprise. Ravenhunt sat by the tub, on a stool. Fully dressed, he held a towel for her.

"I've soaked in this tub for hours, and I never thought you might want to bathe, too," she said.

"I washed off with a basin and cold water."

"That doesn't sound pleasant."

A grin tweaked his sensuous lips. "It was that or go mad while waiting for you, imagining what you must look like, naked in here."

"You could have joined me."

"I couldn't. I had to read that book of Guidon's. It gave me the incantation to use to draw out the rest of your power." He stood, holding out the towel like a curtain, waiting for her. "I am supposed to repeat it after your fifth orgasm."

"My fifth?" She could not believe it. He had given her many orgasms in a row, but she hadn't ever had five.

"That's when all your defenses will be down and your body will be able to release the power to me."

"I don't think I could have five." Really, just two usually exhausted her. Ophelia stepped out and he clasped her hand to help her—the tub was deep, filled almost to the rim with warm water.

"You can have five," he said.

She didn't believe him, but loved the burning glow in his eyes as he said it.

"If you are planning to give me five climaxes, why are you dressed?" Inexplicably she was nervous, even though she trusted him. She was about to give up her power, and she didn't know what would happen to either of them.

His strong arms wrapped the thick towel around her, surrounding her with warmth as he embraced her, too. But still she shivered.

He kissed her neck. That made her go stiff with shock.

Ravenhunt drew back. "I don't want to frighten you. You know I won't bite you. I can resist my hunger."

He must have fed, but she didn't want to think about that. He had asked her to touch him, and she yearned to do it.

Awkwardly, she turned in his embrace. She hadn't touched in so long, and she'd never caressed a man she wanted to entice. How did she begin?

His hands slid around her, cradling her bottom and he drew her to him. Lost in wondering how to touch him, she lost her balance and fell against his chest. Her cheek pressed against his shirt. She closed her eyes. Tentatively, she laid her hands against the firm, strong muscles against which her cheek was pressed. Even through the linen of his shirt, she could feel the defined shape of his pectorals. Her palms savored the strength of him, unyielding beneath her touch.

She slid her hands higher, toward his neck. Earlier, she had wrapped her arms around his neck to hang on tight while they flew over London. Now she let her fingers caress him, stroking the column of muscle. She ran her fingers up and down, for his skin was like velvet beneath her fingers.

He groaned softly. His eyes were closed, his lashes lush crescents of black on his cheeks. His lips parted on quick breaths.

He looked this way before he would climax. She was making him look so sexually agonized with just her touch.

Mmm, she slid her fingers into his silky tresses. She'd always dreamed of running her fingers through a man's hair. Now she could do it and do it to Ravenhunt, the only man she wanted to touch.

A giggle escaped. His hair tickled. It was so thick and beautiful. Ophelia pressed her fingers to his scalp, gently massaging.

His eyes opened. "That's lovely," he murmured. His head dipped back and he gave a guttural moan. "So good. No one's ever done that to me."

"It's like stroking a cat." She giggled again. "You are practically purring."

"Don't ever stop," he muttered in a low, throaty growl.

"I'm afraid I have to. I want to explore all of you."

He let his head drop back again and this time he made a soft howling sound. She couldn't help but laugh. "I need to get your clothes off," she said.

"Take them off then. I want to feel your hands all over me. But I'll help by taking off my coat." Ravenhunt pulled it off, tossed it to the floor of the bathing room. She had been so touched by how he had prepared the room for her, laying a fire for warmth, stacking soft towels, and setting many candles around the room so she bathed in a bright, gold glow.

It had been so sweet the way he had rushed, at his preternatural speed, to do it.

Her fingers fumbled on his quickly tied cravat. She had to

stand on tiptoe to do it. She was too eager to touch his skin to deal with his clothes. But he wanted her to undress him.

He helped her tug his cravat open, and he slid it out from around his neck and threw it aside. His collar points dropped away, revealing his strong neck, down to the hollow at the base of his throat.

She caught her breath. Warmth exuded from the linen of his shirt, tempting her. Strange, but he felt warmer than he had when she had first been brought here as a prisoner.

All she had to do was get beneath his shirt and she could feel more of his beautiful skin. Her palms tingled. Her fingers itched to begin.

Holding her breath, Ophelia opened the ties of his shirt at his throat. Ravenhunt stepped back, pulled it over his head, and lowered his arms. She loved the way his biceps bulged, the way his chest muscles rippled then settled as he let his arms rest by his hips. He dropped his shirt.

This magnificent chest was hers to touch. She planted her hands over the hard curves of his pectoral muscles. He made them twitch under her palms. She giggled. Looked up to him and saw his smile.

His nipples had tightened until they were two hard points that tickled her palm. She rubbed them and he groaned with desire. His nipples grew harder. She wanted to explore. To see what her touch could do to him.

With her thumbs, she lightly strummed his nipples. Awkwardly at first, then she found a better rhythm. His head fell back. "God, yes, Ophelia. Your touch is beautiful."

"Thank you." She'd sculpted male bodies, but she'd never touched one. Even though he was formed of solid muscle, his skin was so soft. She slipped her hands up to his shoulders, ran along them exploring their marvelous breadth. Then down to explore his biceps. His forearms were like iron.

She touched his hands, loving that she could thoroughly explore them. Veins were raised in the back, his fingers long and elegant. She giggled even when she stroked his knuckles. It was so wonderful to feel the wrinkles there and the crisp edges of his fingernails.

Then she lifted his hand to her mouth and kissed it, the way a gentleman kissed a lady's hand.

Under thick lashes, Ravenhunt watched her. "No one's done that for me."

Smiling, Ophelia turned his right hand over and kissed the palm. His skin was slightly rougher there, and she playfully brushed her lower lips sensually against him. He responded with a shiver. "That sent a shock right down to my cock, love."

There was a place she could not wait to touch. But she wanted to please him, too. Watching him saucily, she kissed his fingertips. She ran her tongue down his index finger. She sucked it.

His eyes widened in astonishment as she playfully suckled him. Her wanton thoughts went to his cock—she'd seen it, but had never been able to touch it.

She was panting now. She had her hands on his back, stroking the broad, smooth muscle there. Her hands went lower, to his low back, tracing the curve of his spine.

Her fingers brushed the waistband of his trousers. Think of how naughty, how wonderful to slip her hands down lower . . .

She did. Warm, smooth skin met her touch, as firm and sculpted as marble, but so much more arousing to feel. Her fingers dipped into a hot area . . . heavens, the valley between the cheeks of his derriere. She explored there, then touched one cheek, running her fingers over it. Being wildly daring, she squeezed his firm bottom.

"Like my arse, do you?"

A hot blush raced over her cheeks.

He grinned. "There's no reason to be embarrassed or shy. I appreciate your interest."

"I like all of you," she said honestly.

His dark hair fell around his face. "I love being touched by you. No other woman's hands have felt so exciting on me." He reached to unbutton his trousers but she stopped him.

"Let me. It's a dream come true to do that to you," she said.

He laughed. It was harder than she expected, for his trousers were strained by his erection, and it took a great deal of strength to undo the buttons. She had to fight to slip them through the holes. The placket fell open, and his erection, straight as a rod, sprang forward.

Its musky scent teased her. She could touch it, but she still approached warily, reaching out her hand with caution, as if it could bite. Her fingers bumped the head, making it sway.

"The head likes to be stroked. It's very sensitive," he said softly.

Tentatively, she caressed it, with her fingertips. She followed the contours, from the rounded top, with the tiny hole in the center, to the sweep of velvety skin to the crown that ringed it, before the long, thick shaft began. Clear, silvery fluid leaked out, making her fingers sticky.

He moaned in pleasure. Then she moaned in surprise and delight: as she fondled him, he cupped her left breast. Beneath his hand, her heart thundered. His thumb played the same lovely games on her nipple as she'd done to his.

She almost melted to the floor. She gripped his erection to stay upright. Then let him go. "I was squeezing you! I'm so sorry."

"I liked it." He put his hand over hers and guided her to slide her palm along the shaft. "Stroke me."

Her hand slid to the hilt, slickened by his moisture. Her fingers did not reach all the way around, at the base of his enormous cock. Such amazing textures. Veins ringed his thickened shaft, her palm felt each ripple. At the base, crisp hairs tickled her skin. She even let her fingers graze his sensitive ballocks.

"Lovely, my dear. But since I can touch you freely, I want to do something I've always dreamed of."

She gazed at him, wondering, knowing she looked terribly innocent. "What?"

"My mouth on your cunny. My tongue licking you to heavenly ecstasy."

"Your mouth?" she gasped and in her shock, she gave a rather ruthless tug on his cock. He merely laughed, gathered her in his arms, and with his trousers drooping around his thighs, he set her down on a soft rug on the floor close to the warming fire.

He parted her legs and got on his knees between them.

"You aren't really going to—"

Her words died. Ravenhunt bent and took her nether lips into his mouth, gently sucking them. Then his tongue flicked them apart, and his slightly raspy, warm wet tongue ran over her clit.

14

Tasting Her

Her hips jolted up and she almost smacked him hard in the mouth. Ophelia reached down to him in apology, but his tongue flicked over her sensitive, throbbing nub, and she screamed.

All she could see of Ravenhunt was his dark, glittering eyes, his arched brows, his thick, untamed black hair.

Her hands flailed in desperation. It was so good. It must be more amazing than seeing heaven. She made fists and banged them against the rug. Her hips worked wildly, she couldn't control them.

Touch was the most wonderful thing in the world.

Gently, slowly, something slid inside her wet . . . cunny. Ravenhunt's fingers filled her. He thrust them in and out while he gave her clit so much glorious attention she was sobbing.

Tension coiled in her. Tighter, tighter, so stunningly tight . . .

She burst in a fierce, intense orgasm. Her screams could have been heard at Mrs. Darkwell's. Delicious pleasure claimed her. She was beyond control, her body moving at the command of her climax. She shut her eyes tight, opened them wide.

"Oh Ravenhunt," she gasped.

"Raven," said his deep, hoarse voice.

He moved over her, so his legs were between her spread ones, and his arms bracketed her shoulders. "I used to be called Raven. It was always my nickname. Call me Raven—it was the name the people closest to me always used. I would love to hear you say it."

"Raven," she whispered. "What is your real name?"

"It doesn't matter," he rasped.

The weight pressed against her belly. It was his cock, trapped between them by the weight of his hips. She knew he was supporting much of his weight.

Even though she'd come, her body moved instinctively. Her hips moved, to seek to put his erect cock right against her clit.

Underneath him, her breasts pressed against his chest. Soft dark hairs tickled. Her nipples were squashed a bit by him, but it was a sensual feeling.

"I want to make love to you. I want to be deep inside you. Buried to the hilt. Do you want it, Felie?"

The harshly spoken words set her aflame. "Oooh, yes."

"There shouldn't be pain. I want to join with you, Felie."

She'd almost forgotten she could touch him, she could use her hands. She ran them down his broad back, coasting over planes of firm muscle. Her inquisitive hands reached his naked bottom. He no longer wore trousers—he had quickly pulled off them and his boots. She touched bare skin. Cupped his taut rump. Felt the hard muscles flex as he lifted his hips.

Heavens, the tip of his huge cock touched her slick cunny. Her nether lips parted, letting him slide in just a bit.

"Oh!"

He captured her mouth in a sizzling kiss, tangled her tongue with his. Lots of luxurious play with his tongue. A kiss that made her heat like molten wax.

He thrust his hips forward, and his cock impaled her, sliding deep, filling her. She clutched his shoulder. It felt wonderful.

She felt so full, so full of his hot, thick cock. He drew back, and she gasped as she felt the pull of his shaft inside her. Gracefully, he pushed forward again, and his cock went so deep his groin collided with her clit.

Her eyes rolled back in ecstasy. She moaned fiercely.

He went so deep, his skin sliding and teasing her skin. Each thrust teased a secret place inside that sent waves of delight over her. Each thrust banged her clit.

Ophelia gripped his shoulders. They moved together. She thrust, trying to match his strokes, seeking release.

She wrapped her legs around him. Touching him all over. Loving him—

Oh heavens!

Raven drew in a controlling breath. He bowed his head over her, fighting for control. Her cunny held him tight, squeezing him with slick heat. Her pussy pulsed around him. Her eyes were closed, her mouth strained as she moaned and cried out through her orgasm.

"Raven!" she cried. He thrust into her, driving into her climaxing quim.

"I love this . . . love you. Oh!"

Never had he heard those words gasped so desperately on a woman's lips. His fiancée had never said it like that.

He slanted his mouth over her. Kissed her full, soft lips. Nuzzled her jaw as she sobbed and rocked against him. Her climax seemed endless.

He kissed her throat—

Suddenly, her scents overwhelmed him. The scent of her pussy, the sweetness of her skin, the richness of her blood, pumping like mad beneath her skin.

He pulled back.

"Your fangs are out."

He ducked his head. Focused to make them retract. He'd already fed, damn it, while he was outside. There was no hunger in him.

His cock was still hard. She'd only come twice.

"It's all right. I can control them." He withdrew his cock, which ached as it left her hot cunny. "Three more, love. Let's have them in bed."

Four orgasms and she had drifted off to sleep.

Raven got up from the bed and lifted the sheet and counterpane, gently covering Ophelia with it. She lay on her side, curled up. He should wake her and give her one more orgasm and take her power—then turn her power over to Queen Jade to protect his sister.

Then he would die.

Or so Guidon said. There was something in his past that would destroy Ophelia's love for him, and he couldn't escape his fate of destruction unless she knew the truth and loved him in spite of it.

He had no idea what in hell it was.

Raven was tired of the world of demons, with its curses and spells and the fact every hope for escape and happiness came with either a destructive price or a devious catch.

He didn't want to wake Ophelia, either. She'd endured hell earlier and survived. In one day she had learned he was a vampire, she had been taken prisoner and almost dissected. He was thankful she was able to sleep.

There was time—time for him to make her climax again. He could try taking her power tomorrow. It meant giving her five more orgasms tomorrow, but he was ready for the delicious challenge.

Outside, stars glittered against the black sky. It was night again, a whole day since Ophelia's blood scent had tempted him beyond sanity and he'd had to run. Tonight, after he had gone out to see who watched his house, he'd hunted quickly in the stews for prey. In mere minutes, he'd found a brute of a man to feed on. It had taken away the ferocity of his hunger, allowing him to return to her.

But watching her sleep, Raven could picture her blood thrumming through her veins. He had to get out and feed again.

How could he ever dream of a future between them? He couldn't make her into a vampire, and he couldn't stay with her because he feared he would lose control and take her blood.

It didn't matter if she loved him or if there was a reason in his past for her to hate him. He had to die, damn it.

Destruction was his only future.

Raven left her bedroom and dressed. He had to go and find prey—and while he was doing it, he was going to ensure his sister, Frederica, was still safe.

He left the house, locking it carefully, and passed through the streets fully dressed. He walked, but moving at such speed he was a blur. Mortal London moved past him with no clue he was there. Animals sensed him. Dogs barked and howled, horses shied, but their human masters chastised them with no idea the animals had better senses.

It took mere minutes to come to Mount Street, to find his old house. Candlelight blazed from the window, but there was no ball here tonight. His sister must be out.

Then his hearing picked up a soft, feminine sigh, the delicate sound of a girl being pleasurably caressed.

Hades.

Was that his sister? If the scoundrel from the ballroom was taking liberties, he would drink the blackguard's blood and tear him limb from limb.

Vampires could move almost silently. Or they should be able to. Raven stepped on a fallen branch as he made his way around the shrubbery in the dark. It broke with a snap and a young woman gasped, "Someone's there. Someone has followed me."

"Wait here." The masculine voice was filled with determination, but sounded young also.

Raven retreated into the shadows by the lilacs. Worry for his sister had made him clumsy.

"Hello?" The young man stepped out. Beneath his hat, his golden hair gleamed in the moonlight. The lad moved slowly, his eyes scanning around him. He looked like he expected danger, a battle. But he should suspect someone like her cousin, the new marquis, or a governess might have stumbled on them.

Raven saw what the young man held in his hand. The lad's fingers gripped tight around the end of a wooden stake, and he held it at shoulder height, ready to plunge.

Raven reeled back on his heels, stunned.

A vampire hunter? What in Hades was Frederica doing with a young vampire slayer? And why did the man believe that whoever Frederica thought was following her was the undead?

Guilt and horror hit Raven. Had she somehow learned he had been turned into a vampire?

It broke his heart. He would never hurt his sister, yet what else could she believe but that he was a monster? Even as a mortal man, he'd been a killer, though that had been sanctioned by war. But if she now knew what he was, she must know he was violent and vicious and she must be terrified of him.

Raven wanted to know exactly what was going on. He could not have the boyish vampire slayer catch him. Using his powers, he entered the young man's mind. *There was nothing here. It was an animal that broke a branch. You found nothing. Now return to her.*

The young man stopped and stepped back from the lilacs, a dazed look on his face. Raven studied the young man. Golden hair beneath his hat. A handsome face, but a young one. The face looked suspiciously clean-shaven, as if the lad had barely begun to sport facial hair. Moonlight illuminated large blue eyes that looked blank for several seconds. Then the lad shook his head and lowered his stake. He dropped it into the pocket of his greatcoat.

The young slayer's clothes were those of a gentleman, Raven noted, as the boy crept back to Frederica. "There was nothing there. I couldn't find anything. It must have been an animal that broke a branch. That must be what we heard."

It was easy to plant suggestions in the lad's mind. However, it did not please Raven that Frederica had moved into the boy's embrace. Couldn't she see how daft the lad had to be? Raven had felt no resistance in the boy's mind to his suggestions.

"I'm so afraid," Frederica whispered, though Raven could easily hear her muted voice.

"The vampire came to my room last night," she continued, clutching the young man's arm. "He was a giant bat! It was horrible. Terrifying! He tried to get in through my window."

Raven's blood ran cold. That vampire had not been him. One of his brethren was trying to attack his sister?

It had to be a minion of Queen Jade.

He still had time to do as the bitch of a vampire queen had asked and take Ophelia's power. Jade had no right to frighten his sister.

Then he saw something that froze him on the spot. That stunned him to his gut. It would have slammed into his soul, if he'd had one.

His slender, young sister stood on tiptoe and locked her arms around the vampire slayer's neck. Her lips softened, and she cocked her head like a woman accustomed to being kissed. The lad's arms went around her.

Raven could have handled witnessing a sweet kiss, a small peck.

The boy gave Frederica a long, steamy, intimate French kiss.

Raven had one glimpse of their tongues dueling before he staggered back and looked away. Frederica's sigh of delight was like a spike through his heart.

How could his sister have fallen in love with a vampire slayer?

Raven waited in the dark, his heart thumping. He hated that he could not go near her.

He wanted to destroy the man who was now kissing Frederica and caressing her body with his hands. But did he have any right to destroy a man she loved?

The kiss ended on a fluttering feminine sigh and a lusty male groan.

Raven's hands fisted.

"I should go in now," she whispered. "In case I am missed."

"Be careful, my love," the slayer murmured. "Keep your windows locked. Lay the garlic flowers along them and wear them around your neck while you sleep. Do not open your doors or windows for anyone. I am going to hunt that vampire tonight."

They shared a hasty kiss, then Frederica turned and slipped through the shadows toward the house. Raven watched her, to make sure she got inside safely. So did the slayer.

"Who's there?" It was the boy, moving carefully through the dark, searching the stretches of blackness.

Raven knew he hadn't made a sound. The boy was not as much of an idiot as he thought. The lad could sense him. He tried to send thoughts into the slayer's head. Now he found resistance as he tried to break into the young man's mind and plant thoughts. Apparently without Frederica there, the boy had much more control over his wits.

He did not want to battle with Frederica's paramour. He would be too tempted to rip the slayer's head off.

Then the boy's face popped around a shrub and they stared

face-to-face. Familiar blue eyes gaped at him, and Raven's heart lurched as he recognized the boy's features.

Ophelia. The young vampire slayer looked exactly like her, except his hair was a darker gold. The vampire hunter courting his sister must be Ophelia's brother.

Shock made Raven slow, made him stand in place longer than he normally would. Suddenly, the boy's arm arced and the stake plunged toward Raven's heart. He twisted to escape and the wooden point struck his right side. It drove in, tearing his clothing, biting slightly into his chest. With a soundless roar, he jerked back.

Normally he would fight a vampire hunter. One less slayer meant he was safer, after all.

But he couldn't break Frederica's heart.

The slayer had let the stake drop and had pulled out another. "I'm going to destroy you, you blood-drinking plague. Your kind took everything from me. My parents. My oldest brother. My sister."

"What in Hades are you talking about? Vampires killed your parents? She never told me that." Raven paced around the lad as his gut clenched. He thought of Guidon's words. To look back over the men he had assassinated for Jade.

"Who never told you what? Who are you talking about?" In anger and fear, the lad's voice rose to a squeak.

Raven didn't answer.

He'd preyed on mortals, but he had never assassinated one for Jade.

He could not be responsible for the deaths of Ophelia's family. With a lunge forward at vampiric speed, Raven grabbed the lad's wrist. He tried to see inside the boy's thoughts, but what he saw wasn't in the slayer's head. It was a scene from his past, a scene buried deep inside his mind. Ophelia's brother froze, the stake clutched in his hand, and Raven saw the truth flashing through his mind . . .

* * *

It felt real. As if he was reliving it.

Jade drew her fangs from his neck and sat up on top of him. She had forced him down using her strength. Her servants had chained him to her bed. Now she licked his blood from her lips. "I have work for you," she said smoothly.

Her razor-sharp fingernails scratched his chest, adding more wounds to those that already crisscrossed his bare flesh. Jade slicked her pink tongue over the furrows of parted skin, slurping up the blood.

"There is a demon you must kill for me. He is a vampire and warlock crossbreed. Very lethal to our kind and very dangerous. He must be destroyed."

Those had been the days when he had obeyed her every command, but he had needed to know more about his foe.

Jade licked her way down his body toward his cock. It was soft now, and the shaft and head were covered in healing wounds from her fangs and her nails.

"He was sired by a vampire who had studied the dark arts of magic," she purred as she made harsh bites in his flesh. "He has studied witchcraft and is about to acquire an enormous power and could destroy both vampires and mortals. He could have power equivalent to a vampire queen, and we cannot let that happen. You are an assassin. You must do this for me; it is your duty to protect me. But I do want you—" She hesitated. "I want you to take care. I do not want to lose you."

For a moment he'd thought she cared about him.

But she had smiled with cruel pleasure. "None of my other playmates can take as much punishment and pain as you."

With that, she had released him so he could do his duty. As she'd said, he was an assassin. He carried out his task swiftly and efficiently.

To destroy a warlock was difficult. Raven was only a vampire and couldn't combat spells. Jade had helped him by giving him spells to combat some of the magic the warlocks would use to destroy him. With her protective incantations, he could not be destroyed by anything they conjured, like fire, lightning, or vicious beasts. But he could be killed by any demons they summoned.

It had been a hell of a battle. He had destroyed six demons before the vampire-warlock, who had been young and inexperienced with spells, collapsed in exhaustion, unable to summon any more magic.

Raven had gone for his throat. The crossbreed's gaze had fixed on him as he took the last drops of blood. Golden hair. Blue eyes, large blue eyes—

He looked like this man, who was Ophelia's brother.

The man he'd killed must have been her eldest brother.

Raven released his grip on her younger brother, and it broke the spell that held the young man transfixed.

"Ophelia told you!" the slayer shouted. "That's what you mean. You are the monster who killed my sister?"

"Your sister is alive." Raven snapped it out before he had time to think. She was supposed to be hidden.

This time, the brother grabbed him. "Where is she? Take me to her. I'll spare your existence, vampire, if you take me to her."

At any other time he would have laughed. He was in control here.

But this knowledge of what he'd done left him stunned.

This was something she could never forgive him for. She could never love him. This would break her heart.

Without a love given and received, Ophelia would die when he took her power. He could not take her power, which meant he could not satisfy Jade.

He shifted with speed, so he grabbed her brother by the

shoulders. Before the boy could stake him, he threw the lad across the lawn. With a howl, the slayer landed in a lilac bush. Unharmed, but it gave Raven time to turn and run.

He was running for his house, for his sister. He had to get to her to protect her. It would terrify her to discover what he was, but he had to keep her safe from Jade—

A woman's scream split through his skull.

Raven ran toward his house, moving at preternatural speed. Gravel sprayed as he rushed up the drive like a hurricane's wind. He could no longer see the bats in the sky. The damned things were gone.

His heart hammered with fear. "Frederica!" he shouted.

A jolt of pink lightning flew out from the doorway of the house, struck him in the chest, and sent him flying back down the stairs. Gravel bit into his back as he sprawled on the drive. He jumped to his feet.

Jade stood in the front of his former home. She floated a few inches above the foyer floor. Her long gown rippled with the night's breeze, and her hair swayed and danced around her. A seductive smile played on her full lips, which were rouged to a deep scarlet.

"We have taken your sister," she said softly.

Raven ran at her, ready to tear her apart, moving so fast a human would not see him. But it was no match for Jade's speed. She easily danced away from his grasping hands. She laughed lightly. Then she lifted her hand, and a bolt of pink light flew from her hand. It compressed into a thin, powerful beam that shot right through his chest below his heart.

The pain drove him to his knees. The wound began to heal over as he forced his weakened body up from the ground. "Let her go, damn you."

"I no longer trust you," she said smoothly, her voice cold. "You have been stalling and I have waited long enough. I have taken your sister as a hostage. You must take Lady Ophelia's power now, if you wish to free your sister."

"I cannot, damn it," he roared. "There is a chance it would kill Ophelia. I need more time to know for certain."

He knew what he had done to hurt her—he had killed her brother. If she forgave him for that, she could survive . . . hell, how could she forgive him? It was impossible.

"You have until midnight tomorrow night to make your choice," Jade commanded. "Either take her power and kill her, or watch your sister die."

With that, Jade threw bolts of sizzling light and energy at him from both hands, knocking him onto his arse.

When Raven struggled back onto his feet, his chest smouldered where his clothes had burned away, and the vampire queen was gone.

15

Lost

Raven leapt to the side. A crossbow bolt narrowly missed his chest.

Damned Royal Society.

He stood in the shadowy, mucky mews that ran behind the yard of his town house. Fixated on returning to Ophelia, he had not noticed the two men positioned in the mews, until they'd jumped out and starting firing at him with crossbows.

"I don't have time for this," he roared. He shifted shape and flew at them, darting from side to side to avoid the hurtling arrows. Panic made the men clumsy. They messed up their loading, and he had his chance.

But instead of killing them, he transformed back into human form and threw one down the mews. The slayer landed on his arse, scrambled to his feet, and ran away. Raven knocked the other unconscious.

With that, he jumped up onto the tall fence that separated his small yard from the mews and dropped over the side.

Landing softly on the grass, he called in his thoughts to Guidon. *Jade has my sister and will kill her unless I take Ophelia's power. Is there a way I can fool Jade, make her believe I took Ophelia's power when I didn't? Make it look like I have the power to kill people with just my touch?*

You could tell Lady Ophelia the truth, Guidon answered. *About her brother.*

So you know I remembered that. Damn it, are you reading my thoughts?

Of course not, my lord. It is in my records of the vampire world. I knew you would remember it.

I don't want her to know the truth, Raven growled. *She will hate me.*

Her brother was an evil being. Jade only told you part of the truth. If Ophelia knew—

He was her brother, Raven snapped, his tone harsh, filled with anger. *I don't believe she will forgive me. Can't you give me a spell that would make Jade think I took her power?*

You can take her power, Ravenhunt. I have researched through many ancient books, and I believe Ophelia will not be hurt. Since you will have betrayed her love, you will pay the price. Ophelia will not be hurt, but you will die.

Do I have enough time to take the power to Jade, or do I die right away?

You will have enough time.

Ophelia met him in the foyer, wearing the thick robe he'd acquired for her. It hung open, giving a glimpse of her sweetly rounded breasts, her slim waist, the enticingly soft and beautiful golden curls between her legs.

"Where did you go?" she asked. "We only had four orgasms and it wasn't enough. I am ready to try for the fifth."

He grinned. The sweetness of her serious expression touched his heart. He could lie about where he had gone, but he had to prove he loved her by giving the truth. "I went to see my sister. I never let her see me, but I like to know she is safe."

"Is she?"

Now he had to lie—lie by omission. "Yes, she is safe." For now, she was. For now, Frederica would not be harmed, as long as Jade thought he would take Ophelia's power.

Ophelia suddenly gave a soft cry and flung herself against his chest, hugging him tight.

She needed touch. He had to remember that. He had to give her all the touching he could before he was destroyed.

"Guidon spoke to me." She tipped her face up and met his gaze.

"He did?" Why in Hades had Guidon done that?

"He told me that it was still too dangerous to take my power—that I would be safe, but you would be killed. I will not do it. I will not let that happen."

He cupped her chin and lowered to her mouth. It had been years since he'd had love like this—

No, he had never had love like this. Not from his fiancée. Now, he knew what love was.

Ophelia was willing to sacrifice for him. That was love.

But he intended to sacrifice himself for her. Now that he knew she would be safe. He brushed his lips against hers. "I've changed," he said softly. "You've changed me. I can never take another mortal life. But I'm a vampire, and I am one who is cursed to kill. I'm not one of the gentle ones who can drink his blood from crystal glasses and who can behave like a human. I'm a monster. Before, I didn't care. Now I do. Let me take your power and be destroyed, Ophelia."

"I can't do it. I love you too much."

He gripped her arms. "You are in danger if you do not. Let me have this. One chance to make amends for the things I have done as a vampire. Let me make love to you, and save you, then die having done one noble thing in my life. There is a secret in my past, and it is a terrible one. It would make you hate me, so your love cannot save me."

He told her about the passage in Guidon's book. That it

meant their love had to be proven that it could withstand the harshest tests. He did not believe it would. But from what Guidon had told her, Raven alone would pay the price for that.

"I—I would be killing you, and I can't bear to live with that." Tears leapt into her eyes.

He hated himself for doing this to her ... then he saw the answer. "You aren't killing me, angel. This is something I'm going to do to myself."

He pushed her back, forcing her to stumble backward until the foyer wall stopped them. Using the bulk of his body, he pressed against her, pinning her in place. Slanting his mouth over hers, he teased and suckled and played with her mouth, certain he could arouse her, even while he held her captive.

His tongue tangled with hers, and she breathed hard into his mouth.

Then her foot, in a slipper, slammed into his shin.

She was fighting him.

Instead of stopping, he kissed a line of teasing sensation down her neck. She gave a soft gasp of surrender. Down he kissed, pushing aside her robe with his jaw. He licked her nipples, making her sob.

He pushed open her robe completely, pressed his groin heavily against her.

"No!" she gasped. "Stop, please stop. Don't force me to do this."

His cock throbbed, his heart ached, but inside, a voice demanded that he do this. He could save her and save his sister, and he would be saving her heartbreak.

She would hate him for this.

Angrily, he tore open the placket of his trousers. He stroked her quim, even as she tried to escape him. Dexterous caresses of his fingers made her wet, but he knew she didn't want this.

"Let me free you," he growled. He sank inside her, his cock sliding in.

Heat gripped him, making him cry out with pleasure.

"No," she cried. "I can't hurt you. I can't."

"This is all on me," he muttered. He drove his cock into her, slid his finger down to stroke her clit with his every thrust, and he sucked her nipple.

The assault of sensation was too much. He knew she didn't want to come, but she couldn't help it.

"Oh!" she gasped. Her hips suddenly rocked against him wildly. The climax took her, and tears streamed down her face as her body moved with her orgasm.

Did he have to give her five in a row? Or was this one soon enough after the other four? He had to try now. The words to the incantation were hazy in his mind. He couldn't forget them now, damn it. Fighting to bring them back, Raven whispered them softly. They were Latin, and translated to:

I pledge myself forever to you, my heart to your heart, my life with yours,

And as yours, I take from you the burden placed there, the dark power, the pain you have borne,

Give me your power; give it to me through love,

Let me take your black burden from you, let me give you this gift of my deepest love,

Freedom.

Felie lifted her head, and he moved back from her to let her breathe. Raven stared into her wide blue eyes, searching for change.

Her eyes rolled back in her head, and her body slumped back against the wall. Bonelessly she began to fall, and he caught her in his arms. He scooped her up as her body began to shake.

Her skin burned as if flames roared over her body. Something touched her, and Ophelia screamed. Her eyes were wide open, but she could not see.

She reached out, her hands like claws. She had to fight free of this awful pain.

A sudden violent pain exploded in her chest. Her heart must have burst—that was what it felt like. A brilliant white light flashed in front of her eyes. All she could see were whirling silver stars.

"Ophelia?" Someone called to her. Her mother? She had not seen her mother for years. She reached out her hands toward the tall woman who wore white, and whose golden hair tumbled free around her. She wanted to hug Mama . . .

She flew into her mother's embrace. Mama pulled her close, her skin smelling of vanilla, her hair of roses. Ophelia pressed her cheek to her mother's bosom and cried.

Why was she crying?

She had not been able to hold her mother for years. This was her only chance—

"Ophelia."

She forced her eyes open. Raven bent over her, and she lay on the floor.

"I can't touch you," he growled. "I'm so sorry. I want to touch you, but I can't. I could hurt you."

"Oh my God, my power is gone." The awful pain was gone, leaving her numb. "I'm free now," she croaked. "My power is gone. It must be. But you are going to die. Raven—"

"It was my choice," he growled.

Raven hungered to give her one last kiss, but he could not. They no longer shared the power, so if he touched her, he could kill her.

He had done it. He had taken her power, forced her to climax against her will, and she would hate him forever. She didn't know that he had been commanded to kill her brother years ago, but she did not need to. She hated him and his destruction was guaranteed.

214 / *Sharon Page*

Her sobs broke Raven's heart. They hurt so much he felt as if he actually had a soul.

Ophelia had loved finding her pleasure. When they made love, she was so sweet and innocent as she had explored him. Everything she'd done to him had been amazing, and he had ruined it. By forcing her, he'd taken something beautiful for her and made it ugly. She would never forget this. Never forgive him.

Raven wanted to say he was sorry, but it was wrong to spout those words as if they made a difference. It would be a pitiful attempt to plead with her to not hate him so much.

He left her. To go to Jade's home, give up the power, and die.

Lady Ophelia, it is Guidon. I must tell you why Ravenhunt took your power against your will. It was to save his sister. She is a prisoner of Queen Jade, and she will be killed if Ravenhunt does not give Jade your power by midnight tonight. That is why he hurt you.

Ophelia jerked awake.

Footsteps thundered in the hallway, slamming down on the floorboards with a force that spoke of anger. It had to be Raven. He was running back to her?

Rubbing her head, Ophelia pushed up from her bed . . . how had she gotten into bed? Raven had left her in the foyer. What had happened?

Then she remembered. She had come up to her room. She had meant to dress and chase him. But that was the last thing she could recall. She must have collapsed.

Ophelia slid her arms into her thick robe, tied the belt around her waist.

He hadn't reached her room yet, but the slap of boot soles had stopped. He was not running anymore. But he was still coming to her, and she didn't know what to do.

She hurt all over from the way he had pressed her against the wall and had forced her to climax by thrusting in her, stroking her clit, and sucking her nipples. She had struggled against him, and it left her feeling sore everywhere. Losing her power to him had exhausted her.

She hadn't wanted Raven to take her power. She knew he was going to be destroyed—he had told her there was a secret in his past, something that would make her hate him. He had told her about the passage in Guidon's book, about how they must prove their love could withstand the harshest tests. He did not believe it would, so her love couldn't save him.

She had refused to hurt him. He'd forced himself on her.

Tears leaked to her cheeks again, and she brushed them away. She felt dead inside. She'd expected to feel happy when her power was gone. But that hardly mattered now, when she was going to lose Ravenhunt forever.

Logic told her she should not forgive Raven for forcing sex on her, for forcing her to harm him. Since the beginning, when he'd kidnapped her, this had been about what he wanted. But she believed Guidon's words, the ones he had just spoken through her thoughts, were true.

Everything Raven had done was to protect his sister. She remembered the pain in his silvery eyes as he'd told her he had let his sister believe him dead. It hurt him that he could never be with his sister. Obviously he dearly loved the girl.

No matter what Raven had done to her, she didn't hate him. How could she hate a man who was willing to sacrifice himself for a beloved sister? There was no hate in her heart and soul. She loved him deeply.

The footsteps sounded again. "Ophelia? Are you here?"

It wasn't Ravenhunt. For moments she was utterly dazed. Memories flooded to her with the voice . . .

She remembered laughter as two young children ran to the plum orchard at their country home and gorged on tart plums until their chins were sticky with juice. Then playing ring-around-the-rosies until one collapsed and was sick, and the other was the winner, or playing hide-and-seek in the enormous gallery by hiding behind their father's collection of Grecian statues.

"Harry." Her voice was a mere whisper. She was too stunned to speak with force.

"It's your brother, Harry. Ophelia—" His voice broke, the voice she knew so well from her past, that she'd thought she would never hear again. Then Harry shouted, "Are you all right?"

She pushed off the bed, and made her sore legs take her to the door. Her brother was here. It should have been impossible, but it wasn't. Ophelia leaned out the door, and called, "Harry, I'm here."

A tall, broad-shouldered, blond man emerged from a bedchamber into the hall. Moonlight alone lit the space. The fire in her room had died out, and she had snuffed the candles after Raven had left. She had wanted to be in the dark.

Then she saw her brother's face, just as he yelled joyously, "Ophelia!"

His long strides brought him to her in two heartbeats, and his broad, white smile was almost blinding as he grinned with delight. Harry pulled her into his arms. Hugged her so tight, she couldn't breathe as she was pressed into his hard chest.

Years and years had gone by since she had last seen him, before she'd gone to Darkwell's. How much bigger he'd grown. As a boy, he'd been a display of prominent ribs, bony shoulders, and skinny arms. Now he was a man and a powerfully built one.

Her younger brother was just a bit smaller than Ravenhunt.

Tears of happiness choked her as she embraced her brother. She *could* hug him. There was so much the same about him. Dark gold curls fell across his brow and hugged the base of his neck. She could never forget his large blue eyes. Even when he'd been naughty as a child, Harry could use his huge eyes to make anyone forgive him.

Her heart ached. Harry and she had been high-spirited friends, until her power had come and she had been locked away. Harry was almost all she had left. She had lost her parents and her eldest brother, Simon. Simon had been devilish, but not like Harry. Mean-spirited and cruel, her other brother had always been filled with anger.

But they were all gone. After she had gone to Mrs. Dark-well's, Mama and Father had been attacked by thieves on the street and killed. Then, a few years later, the same thing had happened to Simon. Harry had suddenly become the head of the family, taking care of their youngest sister, Lydia. She knew Lydia was now a healthy fifteen.

But she knew what had *really* happened. She had touched all of them, and her power must have eventually caused them to die. The other stories were probably lies to hide the truth. She had stolen her family away from Harry and Lydia.

"You're alive, Ophelia. I couldn't believe it was true." Harry's eyes were no longer the twinkling, naughty eyes of a carefree boy. They were a man's eyes, older, more shadowed, and they were filled with tears. "I didn't dare hope—" Harry laughed hoarsely. "I did, I guess. I ran in here to find you. Praying it would be true."

She didn't have to pull away from him.

"They told us that you were killed by a vampire," Harry mumbled.

Ophelia lifted from his chest. "That was what they told you? I knew you had been told I had died, but never how."

Now he stared at her with troubled blue eyes. "Who told you this? That damned vampire? Has he kept you with him all this time?" Harry stepped back, his eyes filled with horror. "Did he turn you? Is that why he's kept you for all these years?"

"He? Goodness, do you mean Ravenhunt?"

"I mean a black-haired man with black eyes and no soul. He was there, at Ravenhunt House."

Her brother had encountered Raven. But she must reassure him. "I am not a vampire. I am perfectly—" Her voice broke, but she managed to say it. "Normal." She could only say that word because of Raven.

Then she thought of more questions. "Why were you at Ravenhunt's home? How did you know to find me here?"

"I followed him here. He walked through the streets of London, as confident as you please. I waited until I saw him leave—this place is like a fortress, and it took me hours to find a way in." Harry put his hands on her shoulders and peered deeply into her eyes. "*Have* you been with the monster all these years?"

She flinched. *She* had been a monster. "I haven't been with him, but I was a prisoner. I went to live with a woman who kept me locked up so I could not hurt anyone. I had a power that—" Her brother knew nothing about this. How could he believe her? He would think her completely mad.

"I am a vampire slayer, Ophelia." Harry's gaze held hers, filled with concern. "I have seen the monsters that really live in London. There is nothing you can tell me that would stun me."

"A vampire slayer? Oh goodness, are you a member of the Royal Society?"

Her brother frowned. "You know of them?"

"From Ravenhunt. He's been protecting me from them." There was so much to explain, and she didn't have time. Raven had not come back. He was going to hand over her power and let himself be destroyed. "The power I had—the Royal Society was going to kill me to try to get it from me. Please, Harry, tell me you are not one of them."

Her brother hugged her. She heard a sob catch in his throat. "Dear God, I would never hurt you. I am a member of the Society, but work with good men. Some are vampires—the Earl of Brookshire is one. These are vampires who live among mortals without hurting them. Have learned to control how they take blood and harm no one. The Society hunts the rogue vampires, the dangerous ones."

He spoke with such pride. "The Society is not all good," she insisted. "There are members of the Royal Society who are not noble."

Ophelia quickly blurted out what she'd learned while a prisoner: some men of the Society did not trust the vampires in their ranks and wanted to destroy them. She told her brother in a speedy, garbled rush of words about her power and what those men had tried to do to her. Breathlessly, she finished, "They are still out there. They are the truly dangerous ones."

Her brother looked down at his hands, where they touched her. She knew what he feared.

"My power is gone. Ravenhunt took it from me." She blushed fiercely. She couldn't tell her brother how that had happened. "But if Raven turns the power over to the vampire queen, he will die. I have to go to him and somehow save him."

"Why will he die, if you did not?"

"I was protected." Love had protected her. Was there any way her love could protect Raven? Any way she could save him now?

She didn't care what he'd done in his past. She forgave him for forcing her into sex, for taking her power against her will— he'd done it to save his sister. He had thought she would hate him. She could *never* hate him. "We have to hurry."

Harry clasped her hand. "That vampire you were with—I heard him talking with a female vampire outside this house. The way he spoke . . . he's the brother of the woman I love. She believes him dead, and she is under the guardianship of the new marquis. But her brother is not dead, he is a vampire—"

"You love Ravenhunt's sister?" she broke in, astonished.

"Yes, his sister, Frederica. A vampire queen has taken her prisoner."

"I know," she said, hurriedly. "It is to force him to give up the power he took from me. We must find them both. But how?"

There was so much Ophelia wanted to know. Why had her brother become a vampire slayer? How had he found her? There was no time for questions. Nor to find out about her brother's life for the years she had not been there.

Harry groaned. "I don't know where to find the vampire queens. I don't even know them all. There are several, all representing different clans of vampires, and they either work together, or they war with each other. This is one I do not know, but I did hear the vampire Ravenhunt use the name Jade. We have to go to men I know. Men I work with."

He tried to pull her to get her moving. She resisted.

"I am sorry," her brother said quickly. "You are in your nightgown. But we do not have time for you to dress. We'll put a cloak over you, get you to Lady Brookshire's, and she will look after you."

"Lady Brookshire?"

"She is also a member of the Royal Society. She is a vampire, like her husband, but she is one who can be trusted."

Ophelia felt like Ravenhunt: racing to the rescue without wearing clothes. Harry thought she wore a nightgown, but that wasn't true. She was naked beneath the robe.

"I had my carriage follow behind me when I followed this Ravenhunt from Frederica's house." Harry frowned. "The Earl of Brookshire is a vampire. Does this mean—hell, would this mean Ravenhunt could pretend he was still alive and reclaim the title? Could he be head of Frederica's home? I tried to slay him—"

"Harry, we can worry about this later." Then she grasped his arm. "You didn't hurt him, did you?"

"No."

A shiver went down her back. He'd said that ruefully.

"Come on, we must rescue them." But would her brother, a vampire slayer, rescue Ravenhunt? Or would he want to kill Ravenhunt?

No, Harry couldn't kill the brother of the woman he loved. No man would do such a terrible thing.

Ophelia followed Harry into the foyer of the Earl of Brookshire's residence. Over her belted robe, she had on her black cloak, the one borrowed from Ravenhunt. She had stuck her feet into light shoes so she did not have to waste time with boots.

Her brother insisted she had nothing to fear from Brookshire. After all, he was a vampire.

Still, she was ready to run—or defend herself—as two men emerged from one of the gilt-trimmed doors that led to the foyer. Her time with Raven had given her courage.

She had explained everything to Harry: about Ravenhunt kidnapping her, protecting her, saving her life, then being willing to die to take her power and give her a normal life.

The Earl of Brookshire stalked toward her, accompanied by another blond gentleman who looked so much like him, they had to be brothers. An elegant auburn-haired lady hurried down the stairs, holding up the hem of her green silk gown. A young girl pursued her, waist-length golden-red curls bouncing.

Lady Brookshire stopped midway down, staring at Ophelia with wide green eyes. Her gaze went to Harry, lingering there for moments. A dazzling smile illuminated her face. She reached out with a pale, elegant hand, and drew the child to her side, stroking the girl's small shoulder.

"Goodness, Darlington, you have found your sister. This is remarkable. And wonderful!"

Ophelia had seen female vampires at Mrs. Darkwell's house. Lady Brookshire was one of the most beautiful ones she'd ever seen. Her pale skin glowed, almost like starlight. Her lips were full and red, her hair a rich auburn that gleamed like flame. She looked so friendly Ophelia felt instantly she could trust Lady Brookshire.

"I just rescued Ophelia from the house of a vampire—" Harry broke off and his cheeks went red. "My apologies, Lady Brookshire, I meant a vampire who is not part of the Royal Society. He is a dangerous predator. It turns out that my fiancée did not lose her brother in battle. He was turned by Queen Jade."

"This sounds complicated." Lady Brookshire came down the stairs and approached Ophelia. She clasped Ophelia's hand. "I believe I see a robe underneath your cloak, and I suspect you have run away from somewhere in your nightclothes."

"Well . . ." Her cheeks heated as swiftly as her brother's. "That is sort of what happened. I don't have any clothes."

"I have to rescue my fiancée," Harry declared. "Will you allow Ophelia to stay here, where she will be safe? There are men of the Royal Society who have tried to hurt her."

"What is this?" Brookshire demanded. "Men of the Royal Society?"

"I don't have time to explain, Brookshire. I have to get to Frederica. Queen Jade has taken Ravenhunt's sister prisoner. They are threatening to kill her."

"This is an attack on you?" Brookshire demanded of Harry.

"No," Ophelia cried. "It is all because of me. I had a power—a wretched power that kills people—and others want it. A vampire queen wants it. Someone hired Mr. Ravenhunt to kidnap me to take my power for them. I don't know who, but I think it was men of your Royal Society. But now the queen has taken Ravenhunt's sister as a hostage to ensure she gets the power."

She looked at them all. They must think her mad. "There's so much to explain, but there isn't time. I need to dress. Ravenhunt is going to sacrifice himself for his sister. He wants to do it, but I don't want to let him. I want to save him, but I need to have clothes. I need to go with you, Harry, to the vampire queens."

"Which queen is it?" the second blond man asked.

"That is my husband's brother, Mr. Sebastian de Wynter," Lady Brookshire explained. "Now we must move quickly. You come with me, Lady Ophelia, and I will find you clothing. The men can determine which queen this is and how to carry out a rescue."

Lady Brookshire spoke soothingly, and she put her hand on Ophelia's back and guided her toward the stairs. But Ophelia balked. There was one logical reason they were leaving the men to discuss things—to arrange for her to be left behind.

"I must go, too," Ophelia cried. "No one else would try to save Ravenhunt." And Ravenhunt would be the least likely to try to save himself.

"Of course, you will go." Lady Brookshire looked up and locked gazes with her husband.

"It's too dangerous," Harry insisted.

"It would be wiser for her to stay here," Brookshire began.

"You know what women are like, my dear husband," her ladyship said softly. "We will go, so there is no point trying to sneak away. You will all be in grave danger if you do."

"From Jade?" Harry asked, frowning.

"No, from your sister and me. You men will need weapons, and you will need to plan. That will take several minutes. In that time, Ophelia, you can dress. Let us not waste more time."

A few minutes. Ophelia did not know how long she had.

Raven had left with the vampire queen just before her brother had found her. It had taken them less than half an hour to reach Brookshire's house.

But what if she was already too late?

His sister was so lovely, so innocent, and she had fainted dead away the moment she saw him.

Raven paced in his cell, in the basement of the house used by Queen Jade. Rats scampered through the dark. He hissed at them, baring his fangs to scare them away.

He had let Jade lock him in here. He had followed Jade docilely down the stairs with his hands tied behind his back, though both knew he could have broken the bonds easily. With Frederica's life in danger, he could not disobey. He could not try to escape.

Until he rid himself of the power, he couldn't even touch Frederica.

Raven gripped the iron bars that fronted his cage. He had demanded of Jade one small favor—he had wanted to give up the power and rescue his sister, but he had not wanted his sister to see him after. Frederica was to be taken home, and he would ensure she never set eyes on him again. After all, once he turned the power over to Jade, he would be destroyed.

It was like a punch in the gut to be so close to his sister, and to know he had to turn his back on her forever. But she had been shocked so badly to discover he was alive. He could not break her heart completely to let her discover he was a vampire.

This was for her sake.

Jade was to tell his sister that she had imagined seeing him. That it had been a hallucination, brought on by fear, or by opium, or whatever lie Jade could concoct. Frederica was to be left to believe he was dead.

It would bring her peace. And he would be—finally—actually dead.

"You are troubled, my beautiful one."

The sultry voice belonged to Jade. Deep in thought, he had not sensed her approach. The basement was pitch dark, but he saw her, of course. Jade wore a loose black gown made entirely of lace. She moved as if she heard an imaginary waltz, like a feather floating upon a breeze. When she wanted, she could make her every step sexually arousing. Using the walk Raven remembered, she approached his cell.

He wasn't aroused. He hated this woman who had turned him.

When he'd been bleeding to death in the dirt in Ceylon, she had come to him. "You are too beautiful to die," she'd said. As he lay there, feeling damned cold, and wondering why he'd ever thought hunting for battles was a solution, she'd drained his blood, taking him to the point of unconsciousness. Then she'd ripped a gash in her wrist and put it to his mouth.

The blood had slicked over his lips. He'd thought he wanted death. If he'd died then, he would have died honorably, and his soul would have gone to heaven.

But when Jade had told him he could live if he took her blood, he'd drunk it. He'd grasped at life. The joke was that he wasn't alive, he was undead.

"What is wrong, Ravenhunt?" Jade demanded. "Don't ignore me. Answer me."

"Take this damned power now, so my sister can go free."

"When I do that, you will die, my love."

"I am not your love. I'm ready for destruction. I'm finally willing to do what I should have done years ago—die for someone I love."

Jade ran her long-fingered hand suggestively up and down the bar of his cell. "It would be a shame to let you die. I could fall in love with you, but that would not spare you. Alas, it has to be her. Lady Ophelia, the frightened virgin."

"She was anything but that," he growled. "Ophelia has remarkable strength and courage. She was a virgin, but she is a sensual, beautiful, desirable woman."

"You are in love with her. I spared your life and you never loved me. You were my lover, but I never touched your heart once. Yet this inexperienced girl has captivated you."

"She is worthy of love. She's also worthy of someone better than me."

Jade smirked. "If she declares her love for you, you could be spared."

"She won't, so there's no point in waiting."

"Why won't she? You have been making love to her for days now. Surely a handsome and virile gentleman such as you could capture her heart."

"She doesn't know the entire truth. I discovered it. You had me assassinate her older brother."

Jade leaned closer to the bars. "Yes," she purred. "Why do you think she has this power? The eldest brother and Ophelia were not children of the woman they believed was their mother. Their father, the earl, was in the thrall of a dangerous demon. He was obsessed with her, utterly in her power. This demon had him impregnate her, then she used her powers to transfer the babies to his wife, who bore them not knowing they were a demon's children. Lady Ophelia's brother was a demon who was developing the powers of a warlock. Soon, he turned to the dark arts. He had to be killed."

"You had him killed because he was a threat to you?"

Jade inclined her head, her black hair rippling like water. "Of course. But he was also a threat to them. Had he been allowed to live, he would have destroyed his entire family. Evil was rich in his heart. He had attacked his younger brother once. Young Harold was spared only because the older brother's powers were not strong then. He would have killed your beloved, Ophelia, but her power protected her. It was not just that he could not touch her. His magic could not work on her. Lady Ophelia should not hate you for what you had to do."

"She will anyway," Raven snarled. "She's been alone for so long and has longed for love and family. I refuse to let her ever know that her eldest brother was evil. I don't want her to know any of this. I want her to have happiness."

"You think she will if you are dead?"

"She will," he said. "She will fall in love with someone else. I'm ready, my queen." Raven spat that out with sarcasm. "Take the power from me. It's time I pay the price for my sins."

16

The Throne Room

"How will we find Jade?" Ophelia turned to Lady Brookshire. Three maids were also in the elegant dressing room off Lady Brookshire's bedchamber, waiting to help Ophelia hurriedly into clothing. The gown she was to borrow was simple and beautiful, but still, she protested, "Why do we not wear trousers and shirts and boots? It would make everything much easier."

Lady Brookshire tapped her chin. "An excellent idea. Much better for an attack on a dangerous vampire queen." Her ladyship commanded gently to the two young maids, "Raid the wardrobes of my husband and Mr. de Wynter and bring us some of their clothes." To her lady's maid, she said, "Robbins, you will stay and will undress me."

Ophelia felt a spurt of panic. "My lady, I was just joking. We shouldn't—"

"It will not take me long." Indeed, Lady Brookshire had her dress undone and removed in moments. The other maids bustled in with trousers and white shirts draped over their arms.

Ophelia hated every moment it took to dress, but at least it was quick to pull on a shirt and trousers. At first she tried to wear her shift for modesty, then abandoned the idea, and pulled off her muslin underclothes. Her breasts were free beneath the shirt, jiggling as she moved, and there was nothing between her trousers and her privates.

But she felt ready for adventure. Even her feminine clothes, she realized, had felt like a prison.

Lady Brookshire opened the door. "Good, you are ready. We must go."

"Where are we going to go?" Ravenhunt told her nothing, probably to ensure she couldn't stop him. There was so much pain in him. Did he want to be destroyed to escape that pain?

"I know where the queens reside," Lady Brookshire said. "The places they go and the houses they use. As do my husbands—I mean, as does my *husband*. Sebastian knows these things, too. He is my brother by marriage."

Lady Brookshire appeared flustered, but she took a composing breath and said more clearly, "We know about the vampire queens. There are three houses used by Queen Jade. We will find Ravenhunt and his sister at one of them."

She hugged Ophelia. "Don't worry. We will save him. I have gone up against the vampire queens before. There is always a way to give them what they want, while you get what you want."

It was good to be embraced, but Ophelia couldn't take much comfort from it. "I do not see how, my lady. Ravenhunt assured me I would despise him for what he did and that our love would never survive it. I want to believe it would. My love is the only thing that can save him. What if there truly is something so awful in his past that I can no longer love him?"

"We will cope with that when it happens." Lady Brookshire faced her. "When the time comes, I will be able to help you."

"How? How could you help me love Ravenhunt?"

"I have learned how love is the most precious thing. I think I could help you learn that, too."

"I know it is precious," Ophelia protested. "But it is not easy to love someone."

"No." A soft smile. "It definitely is not. But you understand that, and that is most of the battle."

Ophelia did not argue. She had no time to dispute or debate love. What she must do was believe in it, believe in Ravenhunt, and save him.

Lady Brookshire strode to a wardrobe in the corner. "To go, we will need weapons. This could be a mission of combat, after all." She swung open the doors.

Ophelia gaped at the contents. Crossbows. Stakes. Lethal daggers. Swords in scabbards. "These are yours?"

"For times when discussion will not work. They usually work better on gentlemen than on ladies. Men are much more enthralled by a woman carrying a weapon."

"Enthralled? Not frightened? It sounded as if you mean men find it . . . arousing."

"Exactly. Now, let us go."

Ophelia was amazed at how comfortable the countess appeared in her husband's clothing. As they walked down the stairs, Lady Brookshire explained, "Queen Jade is the queen of a smaller clan. We have learned that the very ancient vampires divided themselves into houses at one time, and a queen ran each house. As time went on, after many betrayals, murders, and slayings, the houses dissolved. Vampires became more independent in many ways. But the queens still have great power, and they wield it. Queen Jade is originally from the Himalayan Mountains, north of China. She has lived in England for hundreds of years."

Ophelia nodded, drinking in every detail.

"She is queen of a lesser house," Lady Brookshire continued. "If she demanded your power, it is probably because she wants to be stronger."

"I can't let her get it from Ravenhunt. The woman is ruthless—" She hesitated. "If vampire slayers know about the queens and their power, why do you not destroy them?"

"There is a long history of vampire slayers making deals with the queens."

"Isn't that wrong?"

"Not all slayers believed vampires should be completely eradicated. We can live together."

"Is that really possible?" Ophelia stopped. "I am so sorry. I forgot that you and your husband are vampires. I did not mean any offense."

Lady Brookshire smiled. "I am accustomed to it. Your doubt is quite understandable. But remember, any mortal can choose to be a threat to other mortals. Any human can become a murderer. In the same way, a vampire can choose not to be a predator and respect human life."

"Ravenhunt didn't." She bit her lip. Did that not say he should be destroyed? Yet in her heart she didn't want to believe that.

"I believe he has changed. Slayers watch the vampires. Ravenhunt has been changing his ways, and he has only chosen the worst of human society to feed upon. He drinks from men who prey on weaker people such as women and children. And he has ensured he left them alive. I suspect he has changed for you."

"But why?" she asked.

"Perhaps love?"

Ophelia jerked in shock. She had thought a lot about whether she loved Ravenhunt. She had not really thought about whether he loved her. What was wrong with her? Most women in love thought of nothing else.

Did he care for her? He hadn't wanted her to die when he took her power.

But that wasn't quite a declaration of undying love.

"You think we can bargain with this woman, Jade, for Ravenhunt's life," she said to Lady Brookshire.

"You must show her all the respect you would show England's royalty. They require it, and when they are angry there is always hell to pay. But yes, I believe we can. I also believe love can spare him. I know so many it has saved. He was the Marquis of Ravenhunt, was he not?"

Ophelia nodded. "He must have kept the name when he became a vampire, instead of his actual surname."

"It is Rollingsworth. For his Christian name, we do have a Burke's Peerage."

Most young ladies knew the surnames of English peers, but once she had been cloistered away from the world, she had no longer been treated as normal. Why would she have to know it, as she would never be out in Society and would never marry?

Ravenhunt hadn't told her his true name. He had required her love, but he had not even been willing to give her his name. Had he intended to embrace destruction all along?

As they reached a set of white double doors, one opened. Mr. Sebastian de Wynter stepped out, a crossbow held casually at his hip. His golden hair was loose, and fell to his shoulders. "Our evil queen Jade has acquired three buildings," he drawled. "She resides in a new town house on the outskirts of Mayfair, owns a lavish estate in the country, and operates a brothel in the stews. As you know, my dear sister-by-marriage, many brothels are owned by the vampire queens."

Lady Brookshire did not even blush. "Indeed, I do know that. Now, which one will she use? Do you have any clues, Ophelia?"

She remembered everything Ravenhunt had said about Jade.

At first she kept me with her at all times, like a pet. "He lived in a house on the fringe of Mayfair with Jade. It was only blocks from his sister, but he was not allowed to go to her. If Jade is proud, would she use one of her more elaborate homes, such as the estate or the Mayfair house?"

"Very logical," Mr. de Wynter praised.

"She would want somewhere she could quickly transport a mortal," Lady Brookshire said.

Ophelia knew quite a lot about prisons. She had been kept prisoner in her house for years, then as one at Mrs. Darkwell's. "I think Jade would take him back to the prison he had once lived in," she said. "To teach him a lesson. I think she would have taken him to—"

She and Lady Brookshire said, at the exact moment, "The Mayfair house."

"We think she will be using the Mayfair house." Panting, Harry ran out into the hall, from the same door as Sebastian de Wynter.

Harry had a crossbow, held in a more ready position. Lord Brookshire followed Harry.

"The ladies have already figured that out," de Wynter said respectfully.

But Ophelia felt a pang of doubt. She had never led anyone anywhere. "I know each second counts. What if I am wrong, Lady Brookshire?"

Lady Brookshire took her hand. "Believe in yourself, my dear. I suspect that is hard for you to do. It took me time to do so, and I was trained as a vampire slayer. I had to learn where I belonged. You told me you were kept a prisoner. Unfortunately, all along, you've believed you deserved such treatment. You do not. Look to your heart and your soul, and you will know what to do."

How could she know from her heart and soul? Anything would be only a guess—

No, from what Raven had told her, she was convinced it was right. She believed in herself.

Lady Brookshire's eyes twinkled. "You must call me Althea. All my very good friends do."

"Thank you, Althea. And you are right. I do feel certain about this," she said firmly.

"If you believe you are correct, that is enough for me," Lord Brookshire said.

A footman ran up to them, breathing hard, his wig askew. "My lord, your carriage is waiting."

"Come." Sebastian de Wynter put his arm across Ophelia's shoulders and gently turned her in the direction of the foyer. "Let us rescue Ravenhunt and his sister."

But Harry grasped her hand. "Ophelia, do you care for Ravenhunt? Even though he took you prisoner?"

She nodded. "I love him." She touched her brother's arm. "You mustn't destroy him. He is not bad. He's changed. You don't have to take just my word for it. Lady Brookshire is convinced he has."

"He was bitter and angry," Harry said. "He assassinated vampires, preying on them as he did on mortals. For that, the Royal Society let him live. It was advantageous to them to. But Frederica—his sister—believed he had changed after his fiancée died."

"He was engaged?"

"Before he became a soldier. According to Frederica, he was madly in love with Lady Margaret Primworth, but she died, and he went off searching for battles."

Heavens. That was why he had become a soldier. That was what he'd wanted to forget: losing the woman he loved.

Was that why he was willing to be destroyed now? Was he still in love with Lady Margaret? Jade had kept him from ever reuniting with his lost love, even in the afterlife, by giving him immortality.

* * *

Ravenhunt had been kept here as a prisoner. He had been forced to do this woman's bidding. He had been forced to kill for her.

Ophelia's heart clenched as she alighted from the carriage. They had stopped at the end of the street on which Queen Jade had her house. As they gathered in the shadows—Althea, Brookshire, de Wynter, her brother, and her—Ophelia peered down the block. The block consisted of a row of new town-homes. The fronts were of white stone, the windows clean, the railings freshly painted black.

Lord Brookshire, tall and blond, rested his crossbow on his broad shoulder. His black greatcoat snapped around his legs, lifted by the breeze. "This is how we will get into the house. Jade will have it heavily guarded and her servants will be both mortal and vampire. She no longer needs anything from you, Ophelia, which puts you in danger when you go in."

Althea shook her head. Moonlight glinted on her large eyes. "I do not think that is true, my husband," she whispered. "Why was Ravenhunt sent to take her power?"

"Jade wants it."

"True," Althea answered. "And she has forced Ravenhunt to return to her. I have conversed with Guidon, and he has explained the rules of this transfer of power. Ravenhunt needs love to survive when he gives the power to Jade. I think Jade was in love with Ravenhunt."

Ophelia gasped, but it made sense. They had been lovers once. "You mean Jade wants him back. Could *her* love save him?"

"Not if he does not return it," Althea said. "He needs true, unconditional love. Both received and given. That is why she cannot hurt you."

"Because he would hate her if she did, do you mean?" Ophelia asked.

236 / *Sharon Page*

Suddenly she saw the truth. She had survived giving up her power. What a fool she had been. The very fact she survived must mean he loved her.

"She may need you to save him," Althea answered softly.

Ophelia suddenly understood. "Then she will take him for herself. But until he gives the power and survives it, she does need me."

"That is exactly what I am thinking," Sebastian de Wynter said. "She will not hurt you."

But she had no idea how to attack a vampire queen or how to break into a house. Though she had experience in breaking out. "I could be a distraction," she said. "I could demand to see Ravenhunt. Just knock on the door and say I have come for him. They might let me in and they might take me to him."

"It is very dangerous," Althea warned.

"The risk is too high," Harry said gruffly. "I won't allow it."

De Wynter looked to Althea. "What do you think, my dear? *Too* dangerous?"

Althea let out a fierce breath. "I think it would work. I would go with you. They would not see me as a threat. I could easily convince a queen that we females decided to do this alone, and we snuck away from the men to come."

"No, as head of my household, I forbid this—"

"I promise you, Darlington, I will not let your sister be hurt," de Wynter vowed. "And it would give us a good opportunity to get in. If Lady Ophelia, Ravenhunt's beloved, is on Jade's doorstep, I guarantee she will be distracted."

Ravenhunt's beloved. She had realized she might truly be loved by him. Althea had been right. She didn't believe in herself, and she must.

"I think it will work," Althea declared.

"I am not happy about it, either," Brookshire protested. "I know, however, my worries won't stop my wife. All right."

Althea linked her arm. "Have courage." Together they hurried down the street. It didn't matter if they were seen, since they wanted to be a distraction. Ophelia was first up the steps and she put out her hand to halt Althea. "Wait at the bottom, please. I don't want you to be in danger."

"No, we are in this together."

She had never had a friend. It was a heart-warming, wonderful thing. Ophelia grasped the knocker, and slammed it hard against the door. She would believe in herself. Believe there could be a happy ending and she would make it happen.

The door slowly creaked open. Yet she didn't lose her nerve. Ravenhunt was in there and she must get to him.

She expected a footman, not a young blond man with long hair tied back with a velvet ribbon—hair that reached his hips. He wore no shirt, but he was dressed in black trousers and boots. Straps of leather wrapped around his bare biceps.

"I think," Althea whispered, "we can guess exactly what sort of woman Jade is."

Ophelia could not comment. Her mouth gaped open. Another young man stood inside the foyer, in the stance of a servant, and he was equally scantily dressed.

"We wish an audience with the queen," Althea said.

"Yes." Ophelia found her voice. After going to that naughty club with Ravenhunt, she couldn't be shocked. Certainly not at the very moment she had to be brave.

"Her Highness is not receiving," the young man said. The door began to close.

Ophelia stuck her booted foot in it. No, she was not going to be beaten by a shirtless footman and a door. "She will see me. I am the *only* woman who can save Ravenhunt. Tell her that and I know she will insist I am brought to her at once."

His eyes seemed to roll back into his head. The blue irises vanished, replaced by whites. He jerked and trembled. Then he stopped twitching, and his eyes became normal again. He bowed briefly to her and Althea. "You may come with me."

Eight doors led off the octagon-shaped foyer. The servant strode to the one directly opposite the front door. She and Althea went through the door, held open by the blond, and Ophelia gave a cry of surprise.

Two men waited in the corridor on the other side. They wore only loincloths slung low on their hips. They were hewn of solid muscle, and their hair flowed long over their shoulders and down their backs. The ends of their hair brushed the firm, rounded shape of their rumps beneath the cloths.

"Take the two ladies to Her Highness," the blond instructed.

Althea clapped her hand to her mouth as they walked down the corridor. It was dimly lit, and other muscular, handsome men stood in a line along its length. Two at the very end, flanking a door of gold, were utterly naked.

Could a woman surrounded by these men, who obviously had her own harem, care so much about Ravenhunt, she would let Ophelia carry out her plan?

The doors opened, and Ophelia rushed through.

Jade's drawing room looked like a Drury Lane stage set. A raised dais ran along the opposite wall of the rectangular room, and it was made of polished ebony. Upon it sat a throne of gilt and red velvet, and a slender woman lounged elegantly on the large chair. She wore a gown of gold lace, and her black hair spilled over her. A heavy gold necklace set with rubies encircled her throat. At her sides, two brawny men in loincloths fanned her with palm fronds. Another young man sat at her bare feet, massaging oil into the sole of her right foot.

She looked like a queen of Egypt, or something fanciful like that. Queen Jade gazed at her and Althea scornfully, then she kicked lightly at the lad at her feet, so he quickly jumped to attention. Jade waved him to the door. Her fingernails were inches long, like talons.

"Bring him," she commanded to the lad.

Ravenhunt was not here. Ophelia whispered to Althea, "If he is not here, and he is still alive, it means she hasn't tried to take his power yet."

"I think she has been afraid to," Althea murmured. "She is afraid to lose him."

Althea must be correct. Queen Jade loved Ravenhunt. It meant her plan would work, but first she had to make sure.

Ophelia stepped forward and curtsied. "I hope this is the correct way to approach a vampire queen. I've never been presented at court, so I am not sure."

Jade's dark, arched brow lifted. "It will do, mortal. You may address me."

"I wish to know, Your Highness, if you love Ravenhunt. I must know this."

"You make demands of me?"

"Is he special to you? Is he the one man who has captured your heart?"

"You are impertinent!"

"I must know," Ophelia insisted. "I cannot surrender him to a woman who does not love him completely."

"Surrender him?"

Now she had the queen's interest.

Jade pushed up from her throne, in a shimmer of gold lace. "You will give him to me."

"I will save his life and then I will give him to you. If you promise that you will not hurt him, and you will give your word his sister will go free, and you will never hurt her again." Ophelia tipped her chin up, facing the gorgeous woman. "But I also will only do it if I know you will not hurt him, and you will not force him to kill for you again."

"You are in no position to bargain. I have everything; you have nothing. You do not even have your magnificent power anymore."

"I love Ravenhunt and I know he loves me."

Hatred flashed in Jade's black, reflective eyes. "I love him also. I loved him long before you were even known to him."

"But he does not love you in return. Not yet. That means you cannot save him. I can. I know you will not let me take him from you, but I cannot leave him if you are going to keep him your prisoner and force him to kill."

"I could destroy you."

"Yes, you could," Ophelia said, yet feeling no fear. "But if you want his love, you cannot force it from him. You cannot keep him a captive and hope he will grow to love you because he has no other hope. You must be worthy of his love."

"Blast and damnation, I'll shoot you both," shouted a male voice.

A door across the room flew open, and Harry was shoved into the room. Ophelia's heart plummeted. Two footmen followed him. They gripped his arms and dragged Harry between them, hauling him to Jade. They were enormous, muscle-bound men, and Harry was no match for them. They had tied his hands behind his back.

One held him by the arms, while the other man stepped forward. "We caught him in the rear of the house. He was attempting to break in by the kitchen doors. He was armed with this—" The brawny servant held up Harry's crossbow. "We lost one man to him, but overpowered him."

"Hold him there," Jade commanded. Then she yelled, "Bring Ravenhunt to me now!"

A raspy voice came to Raven in the damp darkness of his cell. *Listen, my lord. Lady Ophelia has come for you.*

"Guidon? Where the hell are you? Damn well get me out of here." Then his wits took charge. Guidon had spoken through thought. He'd slumped against the wall, and he lurched upright. His heartbeat thundered. "Felie is here? She cannot be."

She has come to rescue you.

"How do you know when you aren't here?"

It was the tea I gave her. It allows me to see her when I must—when she is in danger and she needs help.

In danger? Has Jade taken her prisoner? He barked the question in his thoughts. Panic clawed at his heart. *Damn, why did she come?*

She loves you.

She has no right to risk her life for me. I am not damned worthy.

Close your eyes, Ravenhunt, and I will allow you to watch and listen.

Raven did as the vampire asked. He gripped the bars, and they creaked under the force of his crushing hands. He shut his eyes. He could see the room in which Jade kept her throne and her male court attendants. The queen was on her feet, barely covered by a gown of gold lace.

In his vision, a woman wagged her finger at Jade. A woman with golden curls, but who wore a man's coat, trousers, shirt.

It was Felie. Another woman stood beside her, also wearing men's clothing. He recognized the lady's auburn hair. Lady Brookshire, a vampiress and member of the Royal Society.

Jade glared with rage. Her smug queenly confidence had been eroded by Felie. "I could destroy you," Jade snapped, her usually sultry tones shrill with anger.

Ophelia had never looked more courageous. Then Raven heard her words.

"Yes, you could," she said coolly. "But if you want his love, you cannot force it from him. You cannot keep him a captive and hope he will grow to love you because he has no other hope. You must be *worthy* of his love."

Guilt writhed in him like a serpent in his gut. Everything she had said could apply to him. How could she love him once she knew the truth? As she had said, he couldn't just take her prisoner and hope.

He saw Ophelia's brother hauled into the room, and a servant showed Jade a crossbow while another man held her brother captive.

"Bring Ravenhunt to me now!" Jade screeched.

Everything blurred, and vanished and all he saw was darkness.

He opened his eyes. *Guidon, what in hell is going on?*

Lady Ophelia is trying to rescue you. She has bargained with Queen Jade. She will save you and let Jade have you, if Jade spares your sister and does not keep you as a prisoner.

I have to save Frederica. And Ophelia. But I can't live as a pet to Jade. I would rather be destroyed. That would leave Jade with Ophelia's power. He couldn't let her wield that kind of destructive force. He knew Jade. She would destroy vampires and mortals by the thousands.

Guidon, is there a way I can destroy Jade?

You will be destroyed, too, Guidon warned, his tone nervous.

I know that. But if she gets Ophelia's power, she will kill thousands of innocents. I must stop her.

Heavy footsteps sounded on the stone steps. The servant Jade had left to watch him was an enormous demon. Soon his cage would be opened.

He would see Ophelia for one last time. He knew Lady Brookshire was a member of the Royal Society but one who could be trusted. If she was here, Brookshire must be. And de Wynter, Lord Brookshire's brother. He would ensure they rescued the two women he loved.

Then he would ensure he was destroyed and he would take Jade with him.

Guidon's voice came into his thoughts again. *You can touch Lady Ophelia, Ravenhunt. You won't hurt her.*

He knew what that meant. He could touch her for the last time.

17

Deepest Love

Relief washed over Ophelia as Raven staggered into the room. His clothing was torn and his face was covered in freshly healing bruises. He must have fought with the enormous creature that pushed him into the chamber—the creature looked like a man but horns protruded from its head, the eyes glowed red, and its skin was a shiny silver-gray.

Raven had no boots; his feet were bare. Heavy iron shackles were clamped around his ankles, and thick chains joined them. Chains also connected to iron bands around his wrists. A leather collar buckled around his strong neck, and the monstrous demon held the silver chain leash attached to the leather. The chains that captured Raven looked as if they weighed hundreds of pounds. Yet when he met her gaze, he straightened.

She hated to see him as a prisoner. She admired him so much. She had capitulated to imprisonment until Raven had spurred her to rebel and to finally grasp freedom. She had been a prisoner because she had been afraid; he was a prisoner now because he was courageous and noble, willing to give his existence to save his sister.

His dark gaze remained on her, even as the beast shoved him

forward. Jade's servant held a two-sided ax at Raven's back and prodded him roughly with the edge of the blade.

Ophelia, you should not have come here, Raven said harshly in her thoughts. *This is too dangerous. You should have left me to my fate. Though I have to admit, you in trousers is one of the most enticing things I've ever seen.*

Raven, this is not the time for that! Was she doing the right thing? She did not know how else to get him out and protect her brother. Her distraction would bring time for Brookshire and the other slayers to arrive.

Firmly, she answered, *I want to believe your fate is to survive and to find happiness.*

Love, it is too late for me, he answered stubbornly.

Jade reclined on her huge chair, her legs crossed to reveal their remarkable length, their beautiful shape. The queen stretched sinuously. "Come here, Lady Ophelia. It is time to take the power from Ravenhunt. Time to see if love can save this wretched, beautiful vampire." Jade laughed in an affected, thoroughly evil ripple. "Bring him to me," she snapped.

The horned creature pulled Raven forward by the chains. Raven stumbled, then followed obediently. He kept looking at her, as if he were afraid something would happen to her.

Althea came to her side. Her friend clasped her hand in a gesture of support.

The large demon shoved Raven to his knees in front of the raised dais and Jade's throne, slamming him so hard Ophelia heard the crack of his kneecaps.

"Don't hurt him," she gasped. She jerked forward, but Althea held her back. Perhaps that was why her new friend had taken her hand. To restrain her and keep her from invoking Jade's anger.

Raven remained on his knees, his head bowed, but beneath thick locks of black hair, he glared at Jade.

"Quiet," the queen commanded. She literally floated down

the steps and stopped in front of her prisoner. Smiling down at him, she slowly caressed his grizzled cheek and cupped his chin. Her lashes dipped, her lips softened.

Ophelia's heart stuttered. The queen did love him. She could see it in the woman's caressing touch and her soft smile. Had Raven ever loved Jade? He jerked his face away from the queen's caressing hand.

"Don't, Jade." He grimaced. "I don't want to be touched by you. There is too much cruelty between us in our past. I no longer want your world."

Do not make her angry, please. I don't want to lose you.

I can't pretend, Felie, to care about her.

"You will not speak to her, not by thought," Jade commanded. Then she cooed to him, "You are mine, Ravenhunt. I made you and I never let you go. To take your power, I will touch you. You will find great pleasure when I do."

Jade pressed her hand to Raven's forehead. His eyes shut. He let out a howl of pain and tried to move back, but he could not—not with the demon holding the chain.

"You begged me to take the power and finish you. We are going to do this now. Finally."

The doors of the chamber flew open, and a small figure ran in, moving so quickly, it was just a blur of motion and color. The undressed footmen stormed in pursuit. "Halt!" they shouted together.

"No, this must halt!" shouted a familiar voice.

Jade lifted her hand, her eyes wild with fury. "What is this interruption? Why was he allowed into the house?"

The small figure stopped and dropped to one knee, bowing before Jade. "Queen Jade, your majesty, you cannot do this yet. He will be killed."

Ophelia recognized the tufts of yellowish hair, the gnome-like face. It was Guidon.

The queen did not replace her hand on Ravenhunt's head.

"Why have you come here, librarian?" She sneered at the words as if they were an insult.

Guidon stood, approached Jade and Raven from the side, constantly bowing. "I know how this is to be done. My queen, you do not."

"What must I do?"

"You cannot take the power from him. He must freely give it, and that would be impossible."

"Why is it impossible?" Raven growled. A red mark marred his forehead where the queen had touched him.

"The pain will be so great he will be unable to do it. There is only one way to stop the pain. That is where true love comes in. If true love saves him, he will be able to release the power. Otherwise, he is destroyed and the power destroyed with him." Guidon stopped, panting.

"How can I know this is truth?" Jade snapped.

"I always speak the truth. That is *my* curse. I need knowledge to survive," said Guidon. "I must use the knowledge I obtain, or I will be destroyed by that curse. And I believe Ravenhunt and Lady Ophelia deserve happiness."

"So she simply tells him she loves him," Jade said. "Fine. We shall do that. Now let us begin again—"

"No, no, no!" Guidon jumped up and down. "It is never so simple." He turned to Raven. "My lord, you cannot do this unless Lady Ophelia knows everything. It will not work. You have to bare your soul to Lady Ophelia, my lord. Only if she loves you still when she knows everything, can you be spared."

Queen Jade muttered some words. Incomprehensible words, but she spat them and they must have been curse words. Sweeping around so her gold skirts fluttered, Jade settled on her ridiculously large throne. She waved her hand at Raven. "Go ahead. Hurry up. You must tell her the truth."

"Then I'll die," he said. "She will never love me after this."

Ophelia met the queen's gaze. Jade tapped her chin. A slow

smile curved her voluptuous mouth. "I believe she will. I believe, Ravenhunt, this girl is capable of loving you for eternity. She will love you even when she surrenders you to me. Now tell her everything."

Raven got to his feet. He had subdued his strength, had feigned obedience to protect Felie and his sister. Standing at his full height, ignoring the weight of the chains hanging off him, he declared, "I want to touch her to tell her. It will be the last time she will want me to hold her."

"You may do it," Guidon added. "The power will not hurt you."

Felie ran to him. In trousers, she moved swiftly, slamming against his chest before he expected it. She rocked him on his heels. Ignoring the chains hanging off him, she hugged him.

But then, Ophelia had always done that. Since the very first moment, when he had taken her captive, and she had faced him with awe-inspiring courage.

He cupped her delicate oval face. This would be their last kiss. He wanted to feel her lush mouth rock him to his heart. Not to his soul, of course, since he didn't have one. Raven needed to make this a kiss she would never forget.

Gently, he tipped up her chin, lowered his mouth to hers. Just before his mouth touched hers, he waited, looking at the sultry way her lids lowered and her lashes dipped. It was a breathless moment, his chest so tight he couldn't even draw a slow vampire's breath.

He had always thought what he'd felt for his fiancée, Margaret, was the deepest love. Now he saw it was nothing compared to what he felt for Felie. Loving Felie hurt, it made his heart clench, his gut ache, his throat dry and tight, his head pound, his cock throb with so much need it was as if he'd spent a lifetime without ever quenching desire. He was an immortal being who could heal wounds, and this love was so strong, so intense, it robbed him of all his strength. It robbed him of the anger and bitterness that had driven him to be an assassin. He didn't want that world anymore. Losing Felie's love would mean losing her. It would be a wound he could never heal, not with any amount of strength or power.

If he lost her, he wanted to be destroyed.

Don't think about destruction. Think of this moment. This kiss.

But loving Felie was not just about hurting and pain, he suddenly understood. Her love was about strength, about giving happiness, about having someone to share that happiness with. Margaret had made love about pain, Felie made it about joy.

His mouth touched heavenly softness. Warmth rushed through his lips into his blood and flooded his heart. His lips sizzled. . . .

He pushed her away. "Damnation, I have the power now. I must be able to hurt you." Desperately, he looked to Guidon. "Are you certain I can touch her? The power can take lives later."

"Because the power came from her, Lady Ophelia has immunity to it." Guidon bowed to Felie, in the respectful way he did to ladies. "You will not be injured—or killed—by Lord Ravenhunt's touch."

"I'm not Lord anything." He could kiss her again, but the moment was gone. His lips had sizzled not because of the power, but because of love. It was time to do this. He had run away from the loss of his fiancée to battle. He had run away from the grueling horrors he had seen from each battle by throwing himself into another.

There was nowhere to run anymore. Felie deserved the truth and his courage.

He tenderly stroked his thumb along her lower lip. Her lips parted and she looked so luscious and sweet, his heart broke. "You will not be able to love me after this," he managed to say gruffly. "I want you to find a gentleman worthy of you. I want you to marry him and have children. I want you to have happiness."

She shook her head. "I believe I will love you always."

"Ophelia." God, it was hard to do this, with her large blue eyes fixed on his face, with apprehension reflected in them but also tenderness and caring. She cared for him when he did not deserve it.

He told her what Jade had told him, as gently as he could, about her eldest brother. With every word she drew back from him. He could almost feel the shock and horror exude from her.

"Jade claims he was hurting your family. She told me he had attacked your younger brother. Your oldest brother would have killed you, but your power protected you. But the truth is, I knew none of this at the time. Jade commanded me to kill him, and I did as she asked. I took your brother from you."

Felie's hand clasped over her mouth.

But to his surprise, her brother stepped forward. "It is true, Ophelia. Simon had become a madman."

"He was a grave threat," Jade said.

Jade was speaking in his defense.

"Your brother had turned to the dark arts," Jade continued. "A black warlock, we would call him. He wanted to enslave mankind and demons. He was an apprentice to an evil and powerful man named Valde—a demigod. Valde had been banished for centuries and required your brother to give him a portal into this world. He used your brother's body as a shell in which he could pass from his prison-like place into this world. Valde intended to use your brother's evil nature, then destroy him. We had to kill your brother to drive Valde back to his prison. It protected all of us. But even without Valde's influence, your brother was dark and vicious, and he was a threat to both mortals and vampires."

"You had to do it," Felie said.

Raven yearned to touch her, but he had no right to anymore, did he? "I didn't know that when I took his life. I was a mind-less demon who did nothing but kill."

He wanted her love, but he could only accept it based upon honesty. Ironic, since he had run away from pain and emotion for his entire life and his undead existence.

Ophelia faced him with a grave face. "You were newly made into a vampire and you were a prisoner. Did you truly have a choice?"

"No," said Jade. "He was required to serve me."

"Do not listen to her. She wants me to survive so she can keep me as a pet again. That will never happen. I heard your words, Ophelia. You told Jade if she wanted my love she could not keep me as a captive and hope I would grow to love her be-cause I had no choice. That was what I did to you. You were my prisoner, and I don't believe you can truly love me. How could you when I kept you a captive, when I forced you to do as I demanded? I did want to save you and protect you, I swear that is true. But how can you forgive me?" His voice broke. "You told Jade you must be worthy of my love. How can I be worthy of yours? How can I ask your forgiveness for the evil that I've done?"

"You have changed," she said simply. "That is the reason I forgive you. I love you."

"Guidon," shouted Jade. "The chit loves him. Is that suffi-cient?"

"Yes, I believe it is enough."

"Good." Jade turned with a smug smile on her lips. "Then let us be done with this." She waved her hand and he fell again to his knees. She had willed it and her power was so strong it made his body submit. Her hand pressed to his head.

But if he lived through this, he went back to Jade. Ophelia

and his sister would go free, but he gave Jade the ability to rule the vampire world—and the mortal world. He refused to give Jade such power and live as her lover.

He would destroy himself.

Hades, it hurt. A river of fire seemed to burn through him,

Guidon, Raven called through his thoughts. *I cannot let her take this power. She will use it to destroy the damned world.*

If you break free, she cannot get your power. You will be destroyed, and the power will end with your death.

His body shook and jerked. He could feel the power rushing through him. His muscles twisted and writhed, out of control.

He fought to pull away from Jade's hand.

Ophelia saw him try to break free of the queen's hold, try to pull away. His muscles rippled, his limbs jerked, his eyes rolled back in his head.

Jade stared at Raven, so Ophelia rushed to Guidon, and she bent so she could whisper into the librarian's ear. "What is he doing?"

He is trying to break the contact so Her Majesty cannot drain the power from him, Guidon answered in her head. *He is afraid of what she will do with such power.*

She projected her thoughts to Guidon. *What will happen to him?*

He will die. But he believes Queen Jade will kill many with this power. I fear he is correct.

Her power was going to cost Ravenhunt's life. Cost hundreds of lives. Maybe thousands. She could not let it happen.

What can I do?

You can take your power back, Guidon answered. *The power will want to come to you. It belongs to you. Touch him now and the power is yours again. But then you will never be able to touch anyone again.*

I won't let him be destroyed. She ran forward and put her hand to Raven's head. A bolt of force raced through her fingers, rushed through her heart, slammed deep into her. She cried out, staggering back. Her fingertips burned, and she shook her fingers, but it did nothing to cool them. A tingling shot up her arms, growing stronger. Her heart raced like mad.

What had she done? She was gulping in air but couldn't breathe.

"Ophelia." It was Althea's firm, lovely voice, filled with concern.

"Don't touch me!" she shouted.

Raven pushed to his feet, his eyes large and wild. He rushed toward her. "Ophelia, what did you do?"

"No!" Jade screeched. "No. That power is mine." The queen lunged at her, grasped her shoulders. She tried to push the woman off, but Jade slapped her and shoved her back. Ophelia lost her balance and fell on her back, slamming onto the wood floor. Her breath flew out and she gasped and coughed. She had to get up—

Jade was on top of her, her knee on Ophelia's chest, and she could not breathe. Raven jumped for Jade, but the queen lifted her hand. Raven flew backward, head over heels, and he smashed against the plaster wall. The queen's demon servant, holding a sword, lunged at him.

No.

But as she struggled to push Jade off, the queen pressed her hand to Ophelia's head. There was pain, then an icy coldness. Her limbs went weak, as if all her blood had drained away.

"Survive, Ophelia. Dear God, I love you so much."

Raven was shouting at her. Shouting that he loved her.

Laughing triumphantly, Jade stood and glared down at her. Ophelia could not force her limbs to move.

"The power is mine. And first I will use it to destroy you—"

The queen jerked, her waist pushing forward, her shoulders

falling back. A shrill scream left her lips and the slender body crumpled to the floor. She lay on her side, her gold lace dress spilling around her long legs.

Ophelia gasped and managed to sit up. The shaft of an arrow protruded from the queen's back. It had gone through her heart.

The Earl of Brookshire swiftly reloaded his crossbow in the moment while everyone stood, stunned. De Wynter trained his weapon on the large demon. Ophelia saw Harry come to her side, and he held a wooden stake in his hand, ready to attack.

"I did not want to have to kill her," the earl said, "but it was necessary."

Warm, strong arms went around Ophelia. She turned, only to be captured by Raven's dark, fierce gaze. He gathered her into his arms, lifted her off the floor, cradling her against his broad chest. "Are you all right? Do you hurt still?"

It felt so good to be cuddled against him. Her head fit in the crook of his shoulder. She breathed in his wonderful, male scent. "No, I am just weak."

With complete seriousness in his eyes, he admonished, "Ophelia, you shouldn't have done that."

She rolled her eyes. "I could not let you die or be destroyed, Raven. If you thought I would do that, you are mad. I love you."

"I know. It's something I can't quite believe."

Althea came up to them. "I think we should have our conversation later. Right now, we should attempt to survive," she pointed out. "We are in enemy territory."

"Indeed, my dear Althea." De Wynter motioned toward the demon with the crossbow. "All of you, on your knees."

None of Jade's servants obeyed. They wore mocking smiles. "You have the weapon, slayer, but you are outnumbered."

It was true and Ophelia's heart lurched. After all this, were they to lose? "How will we get past them?" she whispered to Raven.

He glanced to Brookshire and Mr. de Wynter. "I suspect they would not be so foolhardy as to come with so few men."

Footsteps sounded in the corridor, and many armed men burst into the room. Raven had been right.

At their side, Althea laughed with delight. "It appears my husband sent servants to the Royal Society to bring help, and they came with the Society men."

With so many armed men, and de Wynter barking commands, the queen's servants surrendered completely. They got to their knees, their hands behind their heads.

"Your sister," Ophelia gasped. "We must go to her."

"She is safe," Raven said hoarsely. "Now she needs to be freed."

Her brother ran to Raven's side. "Where is she?"

"Come with me, Darlington. I will take you to her. Unless you want to shoot and destroy me."

"You were willing to die to save Frederica and Ophelia—my beloved and my sister." Harry looked at Raven with genuine admiration. "I would never dream of attacking you. You have my undying gratitude."

Ophelia let Raven hug her closer. "I can take you, Darlington," he said, "but I cannot see her. She's afraid of me."

"No!" Ophelia cried. "She mustn't be. Let me speak to her. I will make her see that you are still the brother she loves."

Raven tenderly, slowly, kissed the top of her head. It was so sweet, so loving a gesture, Ophelia almost burst into tears. To be loved was a dream she had believed would never come true.

18

Tasting Him

"I can walk now," Ophelia insisted as Raven carried her to a heavy oak door. He had gently taken her down the stone cellar steps and along an unlit, stone-walled passage, stopping here at the end of it. Light gleamed through a small gap between the door and the frame, allowing her to see. It was a door to a prison, with large iron hinges, but the thick padlock dangled from a hasp.

"No," he growled. "You went through hell up there. I am trying to make amends."

Her hands held his powerful arms. "You went through just as much. You don't have to do this." She loved being in his arms, but it was strange to be cosseted, treated as if she was broken. She didn't want to act like a fainting ninny with no endurance, no capability of facing risk.

In truth, she had never felt stronger.

"I'm a vampire. To me you are as light as a feather."

"I want you to be ready to embrace your sister," she insisted. "You cannot do that if I am in your arms."

He was sweet, showing her a kindness she hadn't known for

much of her life, but also arrogant. She had saved him by coming after him, but she had overheard him talk with de Wynter
and Lord Brookshire. He would not excuse them for allowing
her to come into danger.

She hadn't yet told him she had agreed to be a distraction so
they could break into the house.

Suddenly she realized she was afraid to tell Raven. He had
been an assassin. What did a man like that do in rage? She owed
their lives to Brookshire, his brother, and Althea. She dare not
say anything that would make him hurt them.

Showing his strength, Ravenhunt shifted her, so he had her
perched on one arm, and he opened the oak door with his free
right hand. In here, torches burned along the walls. Not much
light but enough to blind her eyes.

"God," he muttered. A thud sounded. It had to be his hand
hitting the door.

"What is it? What's wrong?"

Something slightly rough and warm touched her chin. His
fingers, and they tipped up her chin. In a low voice, he said, "I
cannot do this. When she saw I was not dead, she fainted. She
doesn't know yet that I am a demon—a predator and a monster.
Or she does know, because your brother has told her."

"He wouldn't." But he might have. He wouldn't have
thought he would have to hide it. "I will speak to her."

"I can't face it," he growled. "Not her horror, her hatred.
Her rejection."

Footsteps sounded. Ophelia blinked as a dark shadow
emerged from the light. Her eyes focused and she saw it was
Harry.

"I have told her," he said heavily. "I heard footsteps.
Thought it would be you, so I wanted to tell you she knows
you are a vampire. It was a—a bad shock."

Raven kissed the top of her head. Ophelia looked up after he did. His eyes shone, but not because they were a vampire's eyes. It was due to the watery film of tears. "I can't go to her," he muttered. "I told Jade I wanted Frederica released, but it cannot be by me. This is wrong, and it will only hurt her. I can never see her again."

"No," she gasped.

Her brother nodded. "As you wish, Ravenhunt." Harry turned and ran back down the corridor to where Frederica must have been imprisoned.

"You *must* go. I will explain what you did for her."

"No."

"Don't be stubborn and ridiculous. She will accept you, especially once she knows how you heroically risked your existence for her."

"She should never accept me."

He set her on her feet, and though she'd wanted to walk herself, the way he did it made her nervous.

"I am going now."

"Going? Without seeing her?"

"It has to be this way. You do not have to come with me if you don't want to. You are free now, Ophelia. Not my captive anymore."

"I never was your captive. From the beginning, you were protecting me."

His haunted gaze held her. "I was serving myself, Ophelia. I am still a monster, and that is what I will always be." With a swift turn on his heel, he left her, stalking down the corridor with long strides.

She took a step after him, and called, "Stop this. Don't go."

I have to. I can smell my sister's blood from here.

She ran after him. "You can control it. Heavens, you wouldn't attack your sister."

But he was gone. She shouted to him through her thoughts but he didn't answer. Running wildly, she came to the end of the hall, and she could see a rectangle of light ahead, and the stone steps it illuminated. She raced toward the cellar steps.

"Ophelia, what's wrong?"

She almost crashed into Althea, who was hurrying down the hallway in the darkness. She brushed by her new friend and reached the bottom of the stairs. Her chest heaved with shallow breaths. He wasn't there. He'd already gone upstairs. Could she catch him before he left the house?

Althea was there, at her side. Althea's arm slid around her shoulder. "Come home with me tonight. I want you to be my guest. Your brother is obviously very busy with his beloved, and with foolish Ravenhunt stalking off that way, I believe you need some female companionship."

"He refused to see his sister. He ran away. Why would he do that?"

"He is afraid of his sister's rejection. And I think he fears you do not really love him," Althea said. "He fears that you feel in love with him because you were forced to."

"But my love was proven to be real. It was how he survived."

"Everyone says men are much more scientific. I have discovered that they are very emotional. There are things they refuse to believe, even with ample evidence to say it is so."

"He's afraid," Ophelia said. "I know fear. I felt it my whole life. For me, fear kept me *from* running away. But for Ravenhunt, it makes him run away."

"What do you think he fears?"

"He fears hurting his sister." That she knew readily. "And perhaps he does fear I don't really love him . . ."

Althea waited. Ophelia sensed there was something she had to understand. Then it dawned. "He fears love."

"I believe that is so," Althea said. "He is afraid of love, so he seeks to run away from it. Even when it is given to him, he is too afraid to take it. Now, come with me. I will also bring your brother and Ravenhunt's sister. I want to have a physician examine her and ensure she has not been unduly wounded by her ordeal. The poor girl must be ravenous."

Food. Something she had not thought of in forever. "Yes, we must help her right away."

Althea smiled. "And then come home with me, my new friend."

But Ophelia shook her head. "I have to try once more with Ravenhunt."

"You will, I promise. That is what we shall do after dinner. We shall conspire to make Ravenhunt understand he deserves love, and he must stop running away from it."

Ophelia squeezed her friend's hand. "I can't bear to wait. I have to try now."

"Then we will use one of the carriages and I will take you to Ravenhunt."

Ophelia alighted from the carriage and hurried up to the door in her shirt, trousers, and boots. This time she was determined to get *into* his house. Not one light glowed in a window.

The bleakness of his home tugged at Ophelia's heart. She knew the logic of why it was dark. He did not need light. But she now knew there was another reason. Raven had fashioned his own prison. That was why most of the rooms were unused and swathed in covers. He had isolated himself. He chose to retreat from the world. As a vampire, he'd had his soul taken from him, and his loss was revealed in the desolate, isolated way he lived.

He had been a man with a broken heart, and he had run away from pain.

Now he was to be condemned to a prisoner's existence—in a prison of his own making—for eternity. Unless he *changed.*

She had been cursed to be a prisoner, or to be alone forever. The magic of love had changed that. For him, the magic had to rebuild his heart and it had to give him hope. Love and hope were the two keys that would unlock his self-made cell.

Ophelia rapped firmly.

Time ticked with irritating slowness.

Why could he not give up on the past and look to a future?

She slammed her hands against the door, but that hurt. Arcing her foot back, she kicked it over and over.

Fortunately it was late at night and there were few people to see her attack on Ravenhunt's door and likely have her arrested.

She glanced back at Althea. She was about to return to the carriage, think of another plan, when rattling sounded, the knob turned, and the door opened a few inches.

Ophelia almost sobbed with delight at Raven's darkly handsome face. Then she looked down, taking in all of him, and her heart lurched with sorrow. On his lean, powerful frame, he still wore the torn and dirty clothing he had worn as Jade's prisoner. As if he did not deserve to now be free.

"I want something from you," she said throatily.

He jerked back. Her quiet, simple demand had surprised him. "What?" he asked. But he wasn't cool. He gripped the door handle with such force his fingers dented the metal handle. His other hand rested on the door frame, and he gouged his fingers into the wood.

Whatever he was trying to do, he did care about her.

"What do you want?" he asked.

Love forever. But she could not say that yet. "If you are never going to see me again after this night, I want to make love to you one more time."

"Indeed. Why, when you are free to find love?"

Her old doubts crept in for a moment. Perhaps there was no love here to find. She didn't believe that, she believed in herself. Running her tongue in a sensuous circle, Ophelia licked her lips and cocked her head, hoping she was giving him a coy look of wanton promise. "I want you."

"Love, it is probably better if we don't make this harder. You can live a mortal's life. You can fall in love with a good man."

"But Raven, I cannot ask a good man to tie me up."

Wood left the door frame with a splintering *crack*. The knob made a groaning sound as it crushed into a deformed mess.

He pulled open the door. "Come in."

The moment he closed the door behind her and slid the bolts home to secure them, Ophelia grasped the waistband of his trousers and fiddled with the first button.

Raven grasped her delicate, swift-moving hands to stop her, but cool and composed, she said, "I assume you don't want to waste precious time in conversation."

"You will do what I say."

"No. We are equals now. There is a balance of power between us."

"We are not equals and can never be, because I am a vampire. I'm dangerous. You should go home to your brother. That is where you belong. At your home, not mine."

Ophelia got two buttons of his trouser placket open and reached her hand inside.

Raven growled as desire streaked through him. Damn it, why did the woman refuse to listen to logic?

God, the feel of her warm, soft skin sliding over his stomach. The heaven of having her warm, soft palm wrapping around his cock . . .

Gripping his shaft firmly, she put her other hand on his chest and stood on tiptoe. Her hand tugged his cock upward. "Let me kiss you and taste you and suck you," she whispered by his ear, her voice rich and husky.

Her breath was a soft, exotic breeze tickling his skin. Like the caressing heat of India and Ceylon. For moments, her touch pushed away memories of battle and of what he'd done as a vampire, as he imagined her in India, dressed in silk that was damp with her sweat.

"*Houri*," he murmured. "You are an exotic temptress, and you should go home now."

"I've barely begun."

She stuck out her tongue and licked his neck. A long, slow swipe of heat and sensation. He was a vampire, strong, powerful, and he felt his knees almost buckle as his blood surged down, taking his strength with it. His cock swelled against her constricting hand.

Her eyes went innocently wide, sparkling blue. "It pulses. It's grown so huge."

She released his prick. It was what he wanted, but he felt himself groan and start to mutter, "No—" He stopped himself.

Ophelia lifted her palm to her face and took a deep breath. "I love the scent of you," she whispered. "It smells like . . . like how naughty should smell."

She crippled him with her sweet, erotic nature.

Her tongue wantonly licked her palm. "Mmm, rich, sour, and so . . . delicious. I love tasting you like this."

Shivers ran down his back as he watched her. Knowing he was the man who had taken her from naïve innocent to this sultry siren.

"I want to taste you completely. I don't know why. I'm just driven to do it."

Her hands deftly pushed aside the falls of his trousers and his cock pushed heavily forward.

"You're wet," she observed. "I can kiss it, can't I?"

Her words rocked the earth beneath his feet. But he could not indulge himself. It was a mad, delirious fantasy, but this one he could not have. "Ladies don't—"

"What you mean to say is 'of course, you can'," she said firmly, puckering up. Her pink lips made a lush pillow. She brushed their satiny softness over the sensitive head of his cock.

It was one of the most erotic sights he'd ever seen. He rocked back on his heels. But she gripped his shaft again to keep him in place.

She wasn't shy and demure anymore, but she was every inch an adorable woman. A sexual, beautiful woman. He had to let her go.

But he couldn't resist experiencing this.

She pressed a soft kiss to the taut, swollen, aching head. It was like having his every nerve ending struck by lightning. So good. What man didn't love the sensation of a woman's sucking mouth on his cock? He didn't think there was a man alive—or undead—who didn't. But to have an angel like Ophelia offer it . . .

God.

She parted her lips, stopped kissing him, and let the head slide inside her mouth. His leg muscles went rock hard, his ass tightened, and his ballocks pulled up so abruptly at the jolt of pleasure they almost slapped him.

Her gold hair was pinned up, making her look so demure and ladylike as she slowly took more of his cock inside her mouth. Her tongue stroked against him, her lips slid along him. He wanted to cry out. If he grabbed anything, he would crush it.

She sucked, teasing his wildly aroused cock with a light tug. The flat of his hand slammed against the foyer wall. Slowly, she got on her knees in front of him, in that erotic pose where the woman looked to be submissive but was really in charge.

Her tongue ran sumptuously around his cock, wrapping the head in its lush embrace. She sucked lightly at the head, then hard. Her cheeks hollowed as she gave more pressure and took him deep.

He worried for her, putting out his hand so she didn't try to take too much. He gripped the shaft to stop her. Her lips slid wetly over his fingers. He almost came on the spot.

Then she gazed up at him, beneath tumbled gold curls, and it was a shot of sheer ecstasy to look at her.

Her hands explored, finding the thick hilt of his prick, then lightly fondling his balls. She found a rhythm, giving long strokes. In and out of her mouth in a heaven-sent rhythm. Blood flooded to his cock, making it pulse. It was so rigid it felt like it would burst, like it could expand no more but still kept trying.

He was weak with pleasure, hers to command. Anything she asked for, he would promise, just as long as she kept sucking him.

His balls tightened with every slurping sound, his cock lurched in her mouth. Pleasure roared through his head. He couldn't think anymore.

He wanted it for eternity, being sucked, being pleasured. She still had power—the power to enslave him to her for eternity, just by taking his aching cock in her beautiful mouth.

Her hands gently squeezed his ballocks, and he cried out, on the brink of losing control. He could barely hear the words he said, "Felie. Angel. God, yes, squeeze me. Suck me deep."

He shouldn't have been so coarse to her. But he was too weak with pleasure to think. Damn, he couldn't let himself come yet. He didn't want this to end. He was in command here. He had to be in command—

She sucked him hard, and her hand slid along the sensitive bridge between his balls and his arse and he heard a cracking sound. His fist had gone through the wall.

But it didn't stop her. Her gentle fingers were caressing his rump. No, this was too much for a lady to do. He had to stop her.

His eyes widened so fast he felt the tug at his skin. Hell, he never believed she would do *that* . . .

Ophelia loved this so much. His thick, veined shaft filled her mouth and stretched her lips. But she didn't mind. Watching the pleasure, passion, agony in his dark eyes was worth it. This excited her, too, she had to admit.

She'd thought sucking him would be pleasure for him, a gift of love and desire from her.

She'd never dreamed it would be arousing and erotic for her, too.

Her lips savored the satiny feeling of his skin and the sensation of how taut it was, with steel beneath. How could just blood and flesh feel hard as iron? Yet it did. It was another mystical thing about him. He was a mystery because he was a man and a vampire, but a mystery that enthralled her. That she wanted to spend a lifetime solving.

Ooh, her tongue loved the taste of his cock, her nose delighted in the earthy scent. His flavor was rich and tangy and warm, but when his juice flowed, which it kept doing, she tasted a stunning sour scent.

She loved exploring him. Discovering how thick and broad this beast was at its hilt. The wrinkled skin of his ballocks and the way she could feel the egg-shaped testicles within. The intriguing seam and the firm bridge behind, that made him shiver when she caressed it.

Then she'd stroked his bottom. He'd stiffened and his breathing had turned into panting. She could tell he liked it. How warm was the cleft between his hard cheeks. She remembered how erotic it was when he'd touched her there.

Was it the same for him?

Daringly, she slipped her finger to his anus, tight and furled between his hot cheeks. Soft hairs tickled her finger. She stroked him the way he'd caressed her, slow and gently, and she sucked on him hard.

The tight ring of his entrance seemed to relax, and she carefully pushed her index finger inside. Slid in and out.

Raven cried out, shouted her name to the heavens. In her

mouth, his cock swelled to enormous proportions, and she could feel a rushing sensation beneath his skin. She had to slide back for he was so huge—

He grasped her shoulders and tried to pull back, but he couldn't with her finger buried inside him. He was shouting her name. Then his hips jerked wildly, and he spurted into her mouth. The sudden rush startled her and she swallowed quickly, tasting salt and sourness.

His hands caressed her hair, her cheeks, moving over her with great tenderness. She slipped her finger free, then released his cock, which was going soft and sleepy in her mouth.

He dropped to his knees in front of her, and drew her to him. His mouth covered hers, his kiss long and intimate, with a teasing tongue. When he released her, he murmured, "Felie, that was incredible."

She blushed. He looked so awed.

"Come," he said swiftly. He took her into the dining room, then left her. In moments he brought a basin of water and he washed her hands gently. He poured her wine. "I am flattered you tasted me, Felie, but I think this will taste better."

She sipped, but shook her head. "I like your taste."

"I like yours." He grinned.

"I love you," she whispered. "Everything about you. I can't let you go."

But she realized she wanted a lifetime with him. How was that possible? He had a thousand lifetimes ahead of him. An infinite number. She would grow old and he never would. It was one thing to become gray-haired, wrinkled, and stooped together. How could they have a future if she aged and he did not?

Heavens, it was impossible.

Or was it?

* * *

Raven had just climaxed so hard he'd thought his head was going to explode. Yet her words, the amazing thing she'd just done for him, and the sight of her with her hair tousled from his hands in his ecstasy made him hard again.

But this time, his fangs shot out at the same instant his cock shot up. It was happening again. Uncontrollable lust for her blood. It shouldn't be happening.

She swallowed wine, then stared at him. His vampiric hearing detected the soft sound like a shout. The way her throat moved mesmerized him.

Her blood thrummed beneath her soft peach and ivory skin.

His hunger was driving him wild.

And she could tell. She watched him like a rabbit faced with a fox.

He had to send her away before he hurt her. Had to hold on to his control. He jerked out of his seat. "You must go. Now."

"What's wrong?" she gasped.

"You know what's wrong. I can't do this—can't control it." He couldn't speak. It took all his energy to hold on to his restraint. Her lovely feminine, tempting smells wafted up to him.

She smelled of his seed, dewy perspiration, and sweet, pretty skin. And of blood. So much blood.

He turned from her, and called, in his head, for Lady Brookshire. She must have left. *You must come for Ophelia, Lady Brookshire,* he commanded. *You have to rescue her from me. I am going to leave, but you bring your carriage and you take her away at once. Never allow her to return.*

Now he had to run.

Something wrapped around his wrist, something soft but with a strong grip. He looked back.

Her hand clasped his wrist.

"Felie, love, you have to let me go. I can't control it. I crave your blood too much."

"Can you turn me? Can you make me like you? I want to be with you forever. You cannot bite me if I am a vampire, too."

"I can't ask you to give up being mortal. Human. I won't ask it of you."

"I am offering it."

"And I refuse. For your own good. There can be no future for us."

19

Home

The carriage lurched away from Raven's house, the four black horses cantering over cobbles. Ophelia refused to cry. Her days of thinking she was helpless and her situation hopeless were gone. She would fight for what she wanted.

"It did not go well?" Althea asked gently. The lamps burned in the interior of the carriage, bathing the countess's face in warm gold light, revealing the concern in her friend's silvery green eyes.

Ophelia sighed. "It went very well . . . up to the point when I told him I was not going to accept that this is the end. I asked him to transform me. He refused. He said he could not ask me to give up my mortality. I *wanted* to do it. Yet that made no difference. It is like when he took me captive. He was in charge, and I had no say in the matter."

A smile played on Althea's lips. "The men we love are often like that. It makes it a little more difficult for women, but we can find a way to change Ravenhunt's mind." Althea's expression grew serious. "Are you certain you do want to be changed?"

"Of course."

"Listen first, Ophelia. Let me tell you what you will lose as a vampire—and what you will gain."

She did listen as Althea explained to her that she would have to learn to drink blood, that she would experience the day sleep but could go out in daylight if she protected herself from the sun. She could have to struggle at the beginning to fight the natural urge to hunt for human prey. Her brother Harry and her sister, Lydia, might reject her out of fear—though Althea believed Harry would learn to accept. But they might be hurt that she chose that world over their world. She would have to keep her secret from the mortal world, for there was always the risk of frightened mobs armed with torches and weapons.

"You fought very hard to be normal and be part of the world that was denied to you for so long. Are you certain you want to turn your back on that before you have even experienced it? Ophelia, you have not yet even been to a ball—"

"I don't care about those things. They will be empty and meaningless without Raven. I want you to change me into a vampire. Please—this is the only way I can be with him."

But Althea shook her head. "Being turned is an intimate process, and it should be done with someone you wish to spend eternity with. I believe we will be friends for eternity, but I think it must be Ravenhunt who turns you."

"But he won't!" she protested. "If I were a vampire, he would have no guilt over turning me. I know how much guilt hurts him. I fear, if I were to convince him to change me, that eventually he would feel guilty about it. Then he would run away."

"I do not think he would run away from you."

"I fear he *would*. He cannot face guilt." She looked at Althea. "Did your husband change you so you could be with him?"

Althea blushed lightly. "I did it to save him. My story is rather complicated—"

"Please tell it to me. I would love to know . . . unless it is private."

"Not private from a dear friend, and I believe you will be a very dear friend of mine. Though I do have to admit something to you, and I am not sure if you will be too shocked to like me after you know."

Ophelia swallowed hard—her new friend was a vampire, and she suspected the confession must be something to do with that. "I used to kill people by touching them. I would not judge you."

"Not even if I revealed I actually have two husbands?"

She gasped. Then realized she'd misunderstood. "You mean you had a husband before Lord Brookshire—"

"No, I mean that I live in a ménage a trois with Lord Brookshire and his brother, Mr. de Wynter," Althea said, utterly naturally. "I feel in love with both of them, and they were both cursed to die. It was the power of a love shared between three that saved them. I cannot believe love will not prevail between Ravenhunt and you. We must make him see sense."

Her wits still reeled from Althea's explanation. "How?"

"The best method is seduction."

"I think I could seduce him for eternity and never change his mind," Ophelia sighed.

"Nonsense. We just have to find the one delicious fantasy for you to offer him that is so tempting he can't resist it. That will put him in the right frame of mind to understand he has no reason to feel guilty to turn you when it is your choice."

"Do I ask him about his fantasies?"

"No, we must be more subtle. At my house, we will find the solution."

Ophelia hoped so. Raven was stubborn, and he had spent

his life, after his fiancée had died, living in guilt. It was his prison, and it would be much harder than she'd thought to break him free.

"First, though, you should go to Harry," Althea said. "He hasn't seen you for years, and I know he wishes to be with you."

Ophelia found her brother in the portrait gallery of the Brookshire home, wandering back and forth, his fingers pressed against his forehead.

"What is wrong?" Her heart plummeted, and she forced out the question, "Has something happened to Ravenhunt?"

"Ravenhunt?" Harry jerked his head up, making his blond waves tumble over his brow. "Haven't seen him. Got to talk to you, Ophelia. I don't know how to do this."

There was something terribly wrong. Was it about her? Did he not believe she was now normal? If he couldn't accept that, he would never accept her as a vampire.

Was it to be a choice between Raven and her family?

She approached Harry. Her hand hovered near his shoulder. She *could* touch him. It was all right.

But she was afraid to. It had been years since she'd seen him. Her disappearance had wounded him. They had raced to save Frederica and Raven, and she had touched him then, without even thinking about it. But now, in the aftermath, would he want her touch?

"What do you think is wrong?" Harry moaned like a petulant boy. He clasped her hand. Now she had her answer. Now she knew hesitation was foolish. She had to simply do things. Stop holding back and hiding.

She squeezed his hand with reassurance. "What is it you have to do?"

"Propose marriage," Harry muttered. Then he winced.

"How to do it? I know I go down on one knee. I have a ring. I fetched it from home. What do I say to her? Women want something beautiful."

She smiled. Relief and happiness burst in her heart. "Tell her the truth," she urged, her voice filled with delight. "Tell her that you love her. What could be more beautiful?"

But Harry didn't look reassured. Deep lines crossed his brow. "I've known men who have proposed. Was never as simple as that. Half of them were turned down." His face blanched. "What if she says no?"

"She will not say no."

He grinned, and he didn't look quite so ashen. "Sisterly prejudice."

Those words deeply touched her heart. She wanted Raven to have this much happiness.

She looked squarely into her brother's eyes. "I would say yes, if a gentleman I loved told me he felt the same way."

"Does she love me? How does a bloke know?"

"She must love you," Ophelia declared.

"I have to impress her. Should I bring roses? Orchids? What about an orchestra? I should have an orchestra play a waltz. Or I should have a trio of violinists. I should write poetry." He smacked his forehead. "I write execrable poetry."

"She doesn't want any of those things, I assure you."

"Ladies do."

"Not all ladies. Any woman who is not satisfied by a gentleman's honest and humble proposal is not worthy of him." She hugged him. "I *promise* you she will not say no. How could any lady?"

"All right, but what if she does?"

"If she does, then I will eat my bonnet."

Suddenly, his expression was wary. And worried. "You don't. Do you?"

"What?"

"Eat bonnets."

"Of course not." But her earlier buoyant feeling receded like a swift moving tide. "Ask her," she said softly. "Please. I want you to be happy."

He embraced her. "Would you have a word with her first?"

"I would, but you do not need it. You came to her rescue, you saved her. Honestly Harry, you don't need more than that. Any woman loves the man who came to her rescue."

She watched her brother run down the corridor to propose marriage, and her heart soared for him and ached for Raven with her every breath.

"He looks like a very happy man," a deep voice spoke behind her.

She whirled. Mr. de Wynter stood behind her. Apparently he had just come from his bath. He wore breeches and boots, but a loose shirt open at the neck, and his hair was damp, and hung past his shoulders. He gave her a playful bow. "Forgive me for listening in, but I was deeply touched by how you lifted his confidence. Very sage advice, Lady Ophelia."

She blushed. She kept thinking this man was Althea's lover, along with her husband.

He looked stricken. "My most sincere apologies. I've embarrassed you, when I am the one completely in the wrong."

She shook her head. "You are not in the wrong at all. I was just—" She felt the heat leave her cheeks. Strangely, it didn't seem that shocking anymore that Althea should have two husbands. This world of vampires was beginning to feel more natural to her. "You did not embarrass me."

"Actually I came in search of you, Lady Ophelia. Before he left us, Ravenhunt warned us to protect you from rogue members of the Royal Society. I think he did not entirely trust Brookshire and me, because we are long-standing members of the Society, but he does trust your brother. He told us there was rot in our organization, and that members of it want to hurt you. I believe his plan is to hunt them down, make them pay for taking your prisoner."

She could not believe it. In everything that had happened, she'd forgotten that threat. "Hunt them down? Isn't that dangerous?"

"Extremely."

She credited de Wynter with being blunt. "They wanted my power and that was why they kidnapped me. But I don't have any power now. It is over, isn't it?" She could understand he wanted revenge, but he must just forget about it. It was done with.

"They should pay for what they did to you—and what they attempted to do."

"Why? It's done with! Why should he risk his life for that?"

"He should not be tackling them alone," de Wynter said. "If there are such men in the Royal Society, we have to deal with them. Do you feel well enough to tell Brookshire and myself about these rebels? Describe them, tell us what happened. Then we can hunt them. Althea will be there. I know speaking of such things can be emotional and horrific, especially after the ordeal you experienced."

"No, I want this done. I want it to all end," she declared.

De Wynter elegantly offered his arm. With his fair hair, darkly lashed silver-blue eyes, tall and well-built form, he was a most handsome man. But his looks did not affect her. All she could think of was a dark-haired man who had walked away from her. Who believed he could not have her, when all she wanted to do was give herself to him.

A wild holler of joy sounded down the corridor. Harry! He sounded as he had when he'd been a young boy. Footsteps raced, and he charged around the corner.

She knew what answer he'd received even before he yelled, "She said yes!"

"Congratulations," de Wynter said warmly.

Harry was so happy, and she was so happy for him. But her heart felt empty without Raven. Her brother had been afraid, but he had faced his fears and captured love.

She had to make Raven see that was possible.

Or was he going to try to throw his life away again?

In a drawing room decorated with turquoise watered silk walls, soaring marble columns, and dainty plasterwork of white, Althea and Brookshire waited. Althea patted the settee at her side, and the earl bowed and handed Ophelia a restorative sherry. De Wynter sprawled elegantly in a wing chair. She told them everything about the attack by the men in the street the night Raven rescued her and the laboratory, the doctor, and the men. She described everything she could remember, and did it quickly, filled with worry about Raven.

The earl seemed aware of her anxiousness. "Sebastian, you and I will convene a meeting of the men we know we can trust." He stood, bowed again. "Do not worry, Lady Ophelia. We will deal with these men."

She stood. "You do not think Ravenhunt would go after these men alone, do you?"

Brookshire exchanged a glance with his brother. "I am afraid he might, Lady Ophelia."

"He would," she said, seeing the answer for herself. "He was a soldier, then he became an assassin. He used fighting and violence to keep his mind occupied so he couldn't think. Now he has vowed not to be an assassin anymore. He's refused to turn me. I see now—he doesn't intend to live alone, existing as a vampire in the world as you do. He needs escape, and he wanted that escape to be destruction. He still wants it."

"Very astute," de Wynter said. "But we will ensure it doesn't happen."

"But he will just try it again." Love for her wasn't enough to stop him. That realization struck like a blow and she sank back on the chair.

Brookshire and de Wynter bowed and left.

She turned to Althea. "What am I going to do?" She quickly told her friend what she had guessed about Raven. "He's hell-bent on destroying himself."

"First, you should go home and see your sister. Then we will decide what to do with Ravenhunt," Althea said firmly.

This was her *home*. A large mansion marched along part of Brook Street. Dozens of paned windows reflected the pink promise of morning.

Ophelia tilted her head back to drink in the stone front with the beautiful carved window details she'd always admired. She had to close her eyes.

Home—when she'd been a prisoner of Mrs. Darkwell, it was all she'd dreamed of. This should be the most wonderful moment of her life. Her dream sat right in front of her. Her dream of returning home. But she felt empty inside.

The door opened and a footman in livery stepped out. He squawked in surprise as a dervish exploded from the shadowy doorway and shot past him. Her sister rushed down the steps. "Ophelia! We thought you were gone, too! I can't believe you're here!"

Tears gathered and fell before she met Lydia halfway across the drive. Lydia had been just a child the last time Ophelia had seen her. Now she was tall, willowy, with her blond hair pinned up. "Lydia, you are so grown-up!" She had no idea what to say—she wanted to be light and happy about this reunion, and not have to tell Lydia about her power or vampires.

Harry had told her he'd kept his vampire slaying a secret from Lydia.

"I'm so sorry you thought I was dead."

Lydia's eyes, a remarkable blue-green, searched hers, glittering with tears. "Harry said you were very ill, and you were taken away so you could not make us sick. He said we were told you'd died because we could never see you again."

She hugged her baby sister tighter. "I'm cured now. I won't hurt you."

"Of course you won't!"

How much loss her family had suffered: their parents and the oldest son. Before that, she had lost Harry and Lydia and they had lost her. Yet despite all the horror and grief, Lydia could hug her tightly and shed tears of happiness. Harry had done an amazing job of ensuring Lydia grew into a normal young woman.

Lydia drew back. "You must come in. There's tea. It won't be long until breakfast. Harry says they didn't look after you well at this place, but you survived in spite of them."

That much was true. "Don't fret, Lydia." She smiled at the young girl's wide turquoise eyes. Lydia looked so much like Mama. "I will be very happy with anything. I'm just so happy to be home and to see you again."

Lydia frowned, looking to the drive, which was now a bluish color as the sun crept higher. "Where are your things?"

"I don't have any things. All I have is what is on my back."

"Why?"

"It doesn't matter, Lydia. Things don't matter." They were at Darkwell's and therefore lost forever. And she didn't care. Her few dresses and vanity items represented her life as a prisoner.

"Come see your bedroom. We didn't touch it at all. Father and Mother wouldn't allow it."

Her parents had died a year after she had been sent to Mrs. Darkwell's. Then Simon had become earl and had run the household until his death. Harry had been only seventeen when he had become earl. It was at the same time he became a vampire slayer.

Harry had been forced to grow up so quickly.

All because of her power. She knew how Simon had really died, but her power *must* have killed their parents. Guilt bit into her. She had robbed Lydia of parents. How could she be happy and normal with her sister knowing that?

How did one fight this horrible guilt? She wanted Raven-hunt to fight it, yet she didn't know how. She could not just forget it. It was real and it was a pain that wouldn't go away.

Guilt made the rest of her morning with Lydia strange and awkward. She tried to behave naturally, but inside self-reproach gnawed away at her stomach.

Finally she begged the need to lie down. She went up to the attics.

Years ago, in the old nursery, she had made a small studio for sculpting. Everything remained in place. Wooden-handled sculpting tools sat on a cloth on a small table. Partly finished carvings sat in the light of the windows. There were her clay pieces. They had never been fired; they had just dried out with time. Some had crumbled.

She picked up one of the tools. She'd spent hours using it. Banished away from people because of her supposed illness (really her power), she had come up here. The sculptures acquired by Father over his Grand Tour days had inspired her.

Father had agreed to provide her with tools and materials, even though this was a shocking occupation for a girl.

Ophelia set down the carving tool. She didn't want to sculpt anything.

Well, what she really wanted to mold and shape was her own future. She wanted to cut away Raven's guilt, exposing a man who could be happy.

She had picked the one sculpting ambition that would be almost impossible.

Changing a man.

She was supposed to spend the night safely in her old bedroom, but she couldn't sleep. Ophelia got out of her old bed, in this room that now felt foreign and strange. For years, when a prisoner at Mrs. Darkwell's, she'd dreamed of being here. Now she felt she didn't belong here—she belonged with Raven.

Stealthily, she got out of bed. Harry had left her and Lydia here and he'd returned to the Royal Society offices. The house was filled with servants, and that would keep her safe. She knew he, along with Lord Brookshire and Mr. de Wynter, had already circulated the truth throughout the Royal Society: that her power was gone.

She had nothing to fear from them anymore.

She crept to her brother's room and quickly dressed in some of his clothes. His trousers were rather snug over her hips.

Ophelia pulled on one of Lydia's velvet cloaks to hide her masculine attire, then had one of the footmen summon her brother's carriage. The servants had been given no instructions to stop her. She guessed Harry had never thought she would try to sneak out.

She rushed down and clambered into the carriage, giving the address of Guidon's shop. With the carriage waiting outside, she banged on the now familiar door.

In minutes, she was inside the parlor with Guidon. But he did not give her tea. This time he gave her sherry.

At least, she thought it was sherry. She took a sip, gasped a bit, for even just a drop burned on the way down. "Strong," she gasped.

Guidon studied her seriously. "It must be, my lady, for it helps you to see everything you wish to know."

Impulsively, she touched Guidon's arm. "I want to know about Ravenhunt. Did you know what happened to him *before* he became a vampire? He was a soldier, I know, but why does he feel such guilt? Why did he run away when his fiancée died? Was it because he loved her so much and then lost her? Does he feel responsible?"

"I should let Ravenhunt tell you, Lady Ophelia. He did reveal the worst to you. The thing that he feared would hurt you. The death of your brother."

"I don't remember very much about my brother. I had no idea Simon was a warlock—until I went to Mrs. Darkwell's, I didn't know what one *was*. But I want to know what torments Ravenhunt so."

Guidon reached out and clasped her hand. Ophelia looked down as he patted her hand, again amazed at how normal it was beginning to feel to touch.

"Lady Ophelia, I must know . . . was Mrs. Darkwell good to you? Did she take care of you?" Guidon's tufty eyebrows were drawn in a frown, his bulgy eyes filled with concern.

"I suppose she did, but she kept me like a prisoner. I know she had to protect everyone else, but it hurt me deeply."

"She must have done it for the best, Lady Ophelia."

"I don't know. I think—I think she was afraid of me." She shrugged, acting as though that had not hurt her. "I suppose I cannot blame her."

"How did Ravenhunt capture you, my lady, when you were under Mrs. Darkwell's protection?" Guidon looked at her intently. "It was for your protection, you must understand that. There was a great fear that you would be destroyed, if anyone found out the truth."

"I understand that. I could kill people. Of course, people would want to kill me."

"That is all behind you now. Would you tell me how he caught you? It is very important, my lady."

"I—I liked to sculpt. So I snuck out of Darkwells' and went to the British Museum to see the statues and the Elgin Marbles. Ravenhunt met me there. I would go close to closing, as I couldn't sneak out earlier. Once when I got there, he had not come, but he'd left a note for me, inviting me to Lady Cresthaven's house. That was where he took me."

Guidon appeared to be jiggling with anxiety on the seat.

"What's wrong?" she asked.

"Mrs. Darkwell's restrictions drove you to sneak out of the house, my lady?"

She nodded.

"Indeed." He rubbed his chin, nodded his head. "It might be enough."

"Enough for what? What are you talking about?"

"You wished to know more about Ravenhunt," he said quickly. "About his past and why he carries such guilt."

She nodded and sipped more of the sherry. It gave her such a jolt, she coughed. Her eyes watered, and she blinked the tears away. Through the film of them, she opened her eyes and saw a tall, blond gentleman across from her.

"Aah!" The cry of shock flew off her lips. But when she blinked again, there was no handsome gentleman. Guidon sat there. He smiled, which for him looked like a grimace. She shook her head. "I am so sorry. My nerves are not as strong as I thought. I'm imagining things."

She took a deep breath and put the sherry glass down on a small table. "What happened in his past?"

Even as she asked the question, the room seemed to dissolve before her eyes. She could see a lying-in in an elegant bedchamber. The birth was underway. In the middle of the bed, amidst bloody and wet sheets, a sweat-soaked woman cried out in pain. The woman fell back, sobbing as if she could endure no more. Someone cried joyfully, "A boy. My lady, you have been blessed with a son." More images flashed in front of her, then she gasped. The woman who had given birth lay on the bed with her eyes open and unseeing, her skin ashen, her lips blue.

No. Oh no. The images disappeared, leaving her on the verge of tears. She gained control. "Ravenhunt's mother died giving birth to him."

"Yes." Guidon studied her gravely. "His father never forgave him and held him responsible for his mother's death. She died of loss of blood after the birth. Internal bleeding that could not be stopped. His sister, Frederica, is his half sister. Yet even though his father remarried, he never stopped hating Ravenhunt for the death."

"That was not his fault. You cannot mean to say he has always felt guilty for that."

"He has, my lady. It made him very protective of Frederica, which led to many arguments between them."

"What of his fiancée?"

"Lady Margaret Calthorne, an earl's daughter. She was very lovely."

"She died of an illness."

"No, Lady Ophelia, that is not the truth. This is very tragic, but you must see it. Close your eyes, then open them and you will be witness to the truth."

She saw a woman with dark brown curls, with a rounded belly beneath a white shift. Fists suddenly rained down on that tiny bump. Sobbing wildly, the woman beat her own tummy.

Ophelia reached out to stop her.

But the woman didn't really exist. She could do nothing. She couldn't stop the savagery with which the blows rained down. Crying with great heaves, the woman stumbled to her writing table and snatched out paper. Then she sat and meticulously wrote a beautiful letter. Ophelia could see the writing, but she could not read it—it was like looking at the image through wavering glass. The young brunette folded it neatly. Tears no longer ran down her face. She wore an aura of calm.

But then the woman stood and she walked gracefully to the open window. Though it was hard for her to move, she managed to put one foot onto the ledge and she grasped the sash—

The image vanished.

"She took her own life," Guidon said in husky tones, "because she was with child."

"Why?" Ophelia gasped, horrified. "If she was to marry Ravenhunt, why would she kill herself over a—" She remembered when he'd spoken of love as being something fraught with problems. And she *knew*. "Oh my, it was not his child, was it?"

"No, the baby was not his. He was furious when he learned. I gather he frightened her a great deal, threatening to call off the wedding and let the world know about her betrayal. In despair, she killed herself."

"He felt guilty afterward. He must—he must have felt like a killer." It made sense now. He was confused—angry, bitter, wounded, guilty. He must have felt as if he was destined to be a killer forever." She looked to Guidon. "Do you think he could understand he is not responsible for these deaths?"

"There are others he did commit as a soldier and then as a vampire. Those haunt him now."

"What can I do?"

"Make him understand he is not a killer. That he can be free."

"I will try." She smiled weakly. "How do you know so much about everyone? You've helped me so very much but I don't know a thing about you."

Guidon looked surprised. "You wish to know about me?"

"Yes," she insisted.

"I am just a cursed vampire. I mean, I truly do carry a curse, one I've had for hundreds of years. Inside, I am a much different man from what you see. And I was in love once. Deeply in love with the woman you know as Mrs. Darkwell."

* * *

It was dawn and the need for the daysleep crippled Raven. He had ensured his house was locked up. Ophelia was safe at her home—where she belonged.

Why did he feel so damned apprehensive? She no longer had her power, so she was safe. He had spread it around the vampire brothels of the stews, knowing the gossip would travel quickly. The slayers—Ophelia's brother, Brookshire, and de Wynter—were putting out the word through the Royal Society.

Ophelia was safe. She could begin to forget about him. She could begin her normal life.

Tonight, he had nothing to hide. In his bedchamber, he pressed a lever, much like the one that controlled the opening in his roof. A section of wall sprang open, revealing a long, shallow opening. A space filled with a simple black coffin, its lid open and inviting for a vampire.

He needed this. He got his best rest in a coffin. With Ophelia in his home, when he'd tried to hide what he was, he'd used a bed. That had weakened him.

What in hell did he want to be strong for? His eternity of solitude?

Hell, he didn't know.

But Raven hopped in the coffin.

When he slept in the coffin, he went dormant. He could see, his mind could function, but he could not move again until his body naturally awoke at dusk. Fortunately when he'd pursued Ophelia at the museum, it had been early spring, when dusk came early . . .

When the lid rose open hours later, he saw it happen, but he couldn't fight. Caught deeply in his daysleep, he couldn't break out of it. Couldn't move. Or even shout. His gaze fixed on the face of a man he didn't know.

How in blazes had someone gotten in?

Why now, damn it?

Raven knew the voice as the man pointed a crossbow at him. "Like shooting fish in a barrel," the man mocked. "I knew you would follow the trail of crumbs I left. You kept her, took her power, destroyed Jade. You were a good boy, Ravenhunt. You did everything I hired you to do, without even knowing it. All the time, you thought you had won. Yet you were my puppet, doing everything I expected you to do."

The man threw back his head and laughed.

It was the client who had hired him to kidnap Ophelia.

20

The Choice

His blood leaked from two wounds—one in his shoulder and one in his lower thigh. Twin red streams moved sluggishly but relentlessly, spilling out onto the dusty floor of the abandoned church.

Though glassy eyes, Raven saw the pool at his side ooze into a larger circle. His cheek lay in it, his lips bathed in the coppery tang.

In his dormant, day sleep state, he couldn't move. Nor could he heal.

He still had no idea of the name of his client—but he had stared at the man through eyes that he could not move. The client was tall, possessed stark white hair beneath his beaver hat, but had the face of a man in his early thirties. The client was not one of the men from the Royal Society who had attacked him, or whom he had fought in the laboratory.

Who in hell was he?

Raven could barely hear slow, measured footsteps moving up and down the wood plank floor. Pacing. His senses grew weak as he lost blood.

The client had fired a crossbow bolt through his shoulder

and one through his lower thigh. Raven couldn't even grit his teeth against the pain. Couldn't move to reach for the two arrows piercing him. Cold crept over him, making his limbs numb and slowing his heart.

With his arms and legs bound, Raven lay on the floor between two pews in the abandoned church they had used for meetings. Guilt ate at him for the way he'd taken Ophelia prisoner at first. She must have been terrified out of her wits. Now he knew what she'd felt like.

Right now he was paying for every evil he'd ever committed. He knew why he was here. Bait for Ophelia.

He was going to keep her away. He would be destroyed if she didn't come, but he didn't care. Sacrificing himself for her was his destiny. It would pay for everything he'd done.

The man was a lunatic. The client knew she had given up her power, but he still wanted her.

But Raven could stop Ophelia from coming here. Dormancy did not mean he couldn't speak through thought. *Ophelia, I've been taken prisoner to use as bait for you—to lure you into a trap.*

In his thoughts, he heard her gasp of horror. *Raven? Raven, where are you?*

I can't tell you. You cannot come here. The man who has me is the client who paid me to kidnap you. No matter what he says, don't come for me.

If I don't, he'll destroy you, won't he?

Angel, this is what I want. To pay the final price, but to know you're safe.

Where are you? I could send Lord Brookshire and Mr. de Wynter. You can still be rescued. You don't have to die.

Felie, I don't trust you. You'll come here. I don't know what he wants from you. I told him your power is gone, but this lunatic doesn't care.

"Talking to her by thought, aren't you?" Boots landed heavily on the floor in front of his face. The words were snarled at him. "That is exactly what I want you to do. Tell her to stay away. Command her to. She won't listen. When my demand arrives at her home, she will go to Brookshire, gather up an army of Royal Society men, and come here."

Felie, do not come here. It's a trap. Let me do one good thing in my damned existence. Let me save you.

But she was gone. He sensed dark emptiness in his head. She wasn't going to answer him.

She was going to come for him. How in hell did he fight the daysleep?

He needed Guidon.

"Ravenhunt, you want her to come here," the client said smugly. His voice vibrated through the room like the notes of an organ. "What you do not understand is that she gave her power to you, but it has not really left her. It is dormant. Waiting. It is growing inside her like a live thing. Eventually it will grow strong enough to control her. The power will force her to use it, and she will become evil as it grows stronger. She is doomed to die anyway. I can take her power, but that still will not free her from it. She must be destroyed. It would be a blessing for her if I kill her before she can hurt anyone else."

Raven's gut clenched. He couldn't let her be consumed by her power and turned into something evil.

In front of him, the client gave a sweeping bow. "You should thank me. The power is a part of her, you see, intrinsically combined within her body. She cannot escape her destiny to be a monster that destroys mortals with her touch, unless she is destroyed. Just as for you, destruction is the only way out. Unfortunately," came the mocking voice, "she has a soul and you do not. You will not even be reunited in an afterlife."

Guidon, damn it, I need to get free of the day sleep. I need to learn about Ophelia. Is it true that her power is still there?

He waited, shouting Guidon's name over and over, until finally the vampire answered, *It is not evening, Ravenhunt. Stop shouting. You've woken me.*

He repeated his question impatiently.

The vampire answered. *It is true. And you cannot escape the dormancy of your day sleep.*

Like hell, I can't. Love was supposed to save her. I intend to make sure it does.

In his head, Raven heard a scream. Not a woman's—a desperate cry in a male voice.

Guidon?

They've come for me . . . a crossbow bolt . . . damnation, I am not going to die now, Guidon sputtered.

Summoning every ounce of strength he had left, Raven tried to turn his head, tried to lift it out of the pool of blood that drenched his cheek. Nothing happened.

He loved Ophelia. He was not going to let her die because he was a bloody vampire who could not move until sunset.

In his thoughts, he roared in fury. Pain screamed through his body. His cheek rose a bit from the floor, then fell back with a splattering squish.

But he fought and finally dragged his legs ahead, forced his arms to move.

Nothing would stop him protecting Ophelia.

Ophelia was traveling in Harry's carriage. Althea, Lord Brookshire, and de Wynter followed, along with two more vehicles filled with slayers from the Royal Society.

Guidon, she called. *I need your help.*

But she heard a weak groan in her head. *I've been shot, Lady Ophelia. But I must tell you this. The man you seek—who holds Ravenhunt and who had me shot—he is a demigod. Powerful and strong. He is—*

The words ceased to flow to her.

A demigod? What power did he have, what could he do to Ravenhunt and to her, what did he want?

Guidon had told her about how he loved the daughter of the goddess Aphrodite, who was Mrs. Darkwell and that Darkwell was herself a prisoner, with the task of finding love for one hundred preternatural females. To defeat a demigod, would Mrs. Darkwell help her? She did not know why Mrs. Darkwell had kept her for years. She assumed her parents had paid the woman well. But how well did one have to pay a woman who had the powers of a vampire and some of the power of a goddess?

She closed her eyes and sent her thoughts to Althea. *Guidon has been shot. He needs help. Can you send some of the men to him?*

We will, Althea promised.

"We must go to Mrs. Darkwell's house," Ophelia announced to a startled Harry. Quickly she told him everything. Then the turmoil in her heart spilled out. "I think she could help me, but will she?"

"We will convince her," her brother vowed.

"It won't be that easy. Guidon told me she is as capricious as a goddess. It was her duty to find true love for the women under her care. That was how she could find freedom from the curse that holds her here."

"Then she will help you, because this will help you find true love."

She prayed it would. Her heart thundered as she recognized the streets. Ophelia pressed her forehead to the window and saw the town house that had been her prison. "There it is." Strangely she was no longer afraid of the place.

But why should she be? She was never going to be a prisoner again.

*   *   *

Minutes later, she stood in Mrs. Darkwell's office with her brother at her side. Terrible memories of loneliness lurked in Ophelia's mind.

But she would not let them weaken her.

She slapped her hands down firmly on Mrs. Darkwell's large desk, leaned over, faced the woman with courage, and said, "You are going to help me save Ravenhunt."

"The man who captured you? You wish me to save him?" Mrs. Darkwell pursed her lips in anger, her thick black lashes lowered as her pale eyes narrowed. Her former keeper looked just as Ophelia remembered—tall, slender, dressed in a gown of black silk and lace, which made a stark contrast with the woman's golden curls.

"Guidon told me everything," Darkwell continued. "This man took you prisoner to kill you, and now you wish to save him. Child, you are completely mad."

"I'm not a child anymore. I haven't been for years—I'm three and twenty! He deserves to be saved! He may have taken me prisoner, but he rescued me. I intend to do the same for him."

Mrs. Darkwell drew back stiffly in surprise. "You have certainly gained courage."

"I'm not a cowering prisoner anymore, not weak and frightened. My power is gone, and I will never hurt anyone again."

"Your power is gone?"

"Yes," Ophelia hissed impatiently, but knew she would have to give the entire tale. She spilled out her story in a mad rush—explaining how she had lost her power, how Ravenhunt had saved her and was now a captive, and how she needed the help of a goddess to rescue him.

She could face Mrs. Darkwell, the woman who had once made her quake, with the confidence of a mature and strong woman.

"I am delighted you are freed from your power, and I am

proud of how you have grown up, Ophelia. Yes, I will help Ravenhunt for you—if you truly love him."

"I do! Of course I do." How could the woman even doubt it?

Through her mind, she spoke to Raven—and lied, of course, to learn where he was. She promised Lord Brookshire and de Wynter would go to him, with Royal Society men. But the moment she ended the conversation, she turned to Mrs. Darkwell. "He is being held in an abandoned church in the stews. He has told me the way, and we must go quickly."

"Here, Ophelia. Time to learn to use a crossbow."

Harry pushed the weapon into her hand. Nodding, she watched her brother's expert, effortless movements as he loaded the bow, drawing back the taut string to place the arrow. She winced as she forced the string back—heavens, it took so much strength.

Harry pointed at a noticeboard, long unused, on the side of the church. "Aim for that."

She lifted the heavy contraption. Sighted.

"Fire," he said.

She released the arrow. It smacked against the wooden door, three feet to the right of her target. She let out a small cry of fury. Her arms ached with the effort.

Harry looked to Mrs. Darkwell. "Perhaps she should have learned a skill or two with you."

Ophelia's eyes widened. She was ready to defend her brother against the goddess's attack, but Darkwell merely inclined her head. "Perhaps you are correct. But I am a goddess, and this is easily rectified."

Mrs. Darkwell lifted her hand. Sizzling streams of white light, like tiny lightning bolts, leapt from her hand. They arced through the night air. Ophelia stumbled back, but they slammed into her chest. Her entire body tingled.

"Try again, Lady Ophelia," Mrs. Darkwell urged with calm.

Ophelia found it was easy to draw back the bowstring. She lifted the crossbow, which now felt weightless. And let fire.

The arrow hurtled, straight and true, and bit into the center of the board. "Heavens," she breathed.

"I have bestowed the strength of a vampire on you for a while," Mrs. Darkwell said, wearing a smug smile. "Now, let us find the man you love." The smile disappeared. "This will be a very dangerous battle, Ophelia. You can go, if you wish. Save yourself. You will be fighting a very powerful being in that church. Not only that, the rebel members of the Royal Society have followed you here. They will attack."

"Now? When I have to save Raven?"

"Of course now, my dear," Mrs. Darkwell said. "They have been waiting for this chance to claim you and your power."

"My power is gone," Ophelia declared. But fear struck even as she spat out the words.

Mrs. Darkwell shook her head. "There is something you must know."

"I don't want to know it. My power is *gone*."

"No, it is dormant, waiting, preparing to be triggered back into existence—and back in control of your body. But not gone." After a sigh, Mrs. Darkwell explained everything.

Ophelia's entire body went numb and cold as she tried to take in what the woman was saying. Her power was indeed not gone at all. Her only choice was destruction.

"No, it is not," Darkwell said, as if she'd read Ophelia's thoughts. "There is another way. I promise."

"What happens to me doesn't matter. I want to help him." With that, with her crossbow loaded, she pulled open the church door and jerked her weapon up to guide her way into the church.

Candles burned, sitting in pools of wax at the ends of the pews. The flickering light made a length of gold, while darkness reigned everywhere else. Candelabra lit the altar. Guidon's body lay on the floor in front of the altar and her heart lurched. For him . . . and for Raven.

Raven stood, half-naked in his trousers, his hands raised in the air, in the position of surrender. A dark-haired man who stood almost seven feet in height trained a crossbow on Raven, the arrow aimed at his heart. It was as if her thoughts were coming to her through fog-filled air. They came in dizzying snatches and snippets.

She had never seen this man before. His face was as white as marble, his features cut as clean as a sculpture's.

What did he want from Raven, from her?

He had a crossbow, the tip of the arrow pressed right against Raven's bare chest, directly over his heart.

The man motioned with the crossbow. "One more step, demon," he barked at her, "and I shoot him. Rip a hole through his chest, take out his heart, and spear it into the wall beyond."

"I won't move," she said quickly. Her voice didn't even shake. She was terrified, but for some reason, her body was calm, her mind worked swiftly.

"My power is gone," she said. "The vampire queen named Jade took it from me, and she was killed as she did, so the power vanished with her. It is gone. I can't give it to you. We have nothing that you want." It was a lie, but she hoped he believed it.

"You still have your power, my lady." He sneered as he spoke her title. "I want two things from you—the damned vampires in the Royal Society attacked us tonight and arrested most of our group. I escaped. But there is no way those soft-hearted blood drinkers would want your death on their hands, Lady Ophelia. You will be my ticket to freedom. Then I will take your power and give you the freedom you want."

"No." Raven reached for the tall man, but the villain ruthlessly pressed the weapon harder against him. It broke his skin and blood dribbled, reminding them both of the threat.

"Don't move," she implored Raven. "He will kill you. I will go with him." She knew Harry was in the shadows near the door. She had no idea if Darkwell had followed her in.

"Over my dead body," Raven growled.

"You are already dead." The man spat to his side. "You are a corpse that walks around, Ravenhunt—a revolting parasite that should be destroyed. Do not worry—you will be dead."

A mocking grin widened the man's mouth. He looked evil and hideous. He took a step back, and his finger jerked with infinite slowness.

Ophelia screamed as she saw the taut cord move, the arrow flying forward, propelled by the pull of the trigger. It shot, straight and true, across the meager two feet separating the Society man from Raven.

It drove into Raven's chest, and protruded out the back.

He collapsed. Ophelia swayed on her feet, then forced herself to run forward. She dropped to her knees at his side.

He wasn't moving. His eyes were open, staring glassily.

"Raven?"

No response. No twitch of his body, no attempt to move, no life in his eyes. Dear God, no.

A rough, harsh laugh echoed in her ears. The man stalked to her, grasped the collar of the shirt, and hauled her to her feet.

The floor tilted beneath her as the man shoved her forward. In the few seconds she had been at Raven's side, this monster had reloaded his crossbow and prodded her back with the arrow to make her move.

Surely Raven would get up and pull the arrow out of him and he would be healed. Her heart poised in its beating, and she strained to hear him groan, or hear him get to his feet.

Nothing. Just cold silence broken only by the horrible fast breathing of her captor.

She couldn't see Harry or Mrs. Darkwell. Had Brookshire and de Wynter brought men?

What did it matter? If Raven was dead, she didn't care if he killed her now. She didn't want to live.

"Why don't you just shoot me?" she spat.

"Think you'll be reunited with him?" The fiend's laugh was harsh. "He's got no soul. Destroyed, he lives in purgatory. Don't know where you'll go. You've got a soul, but it's a witch's one." He pushed her out to the front steps of the church. "Go to that carriage over there," he snapped.

Should she try to run? Fight him? Do something so he would shoot her and this would be done with?

Ophelia, don't try to run, for God's sake. I'm going to come after you. I need to get this arrow out so I can heal . . .

Raven's voice in her head. He wasn't dead. She had to follow his orders, she had to stay alive.

The carriage steps dropped, and her captor pushed her up them. She lost her balance and sprawled on them. She scrambled up. He held the crossbow pointed at her, then he hauled a pistol from his pocket and kept it in his left hand. "Where are you going to take me?"

"To Darkwell's. She will help me," he muttered. "She will have to. I will not allow my mother to ignore her duties to me. Otherwise those damned Society vampires will kill me."

"Your mother? Mrs. Darkwell is your mother? Who are you?"

"My name is Valde. I am part god, spawn of a mother who is a daughter of Aphrodite. I have powers of my own, you know. Powers you cannot comprehend."

He spoke like a sulking boy. "I am sure you do," she said. "But we do not need to go to Mrs. Darkwell. She is here."

No one responded. She had hoped for a dramatic entrance of the demi-goddess. But there was silence, except for the whinnying of the four horses hitched to the carriage.

Her captor laughed. "A good attempt at distraction—"

"She is here, you fool," Ophelia snapped. "But she now seems to have gone away." Which meant she could not rely on Mrs. Darkwell, the demi-goddess, to rescue her.

How could she rescue herself? "Does my touch hurt you?" she demanded.

"No, because I am part god."

So much for that idea.

A twanging sound came from behind her. Valde jerked around as a crossbow bolt slammed into the carriage between them.

It was not Harry, but the older gray-haired man of the Royal Society, Cartwell, along with young, pimply-faced gentlemen carrying a variety of weapons—pistols, blades, a crossbow.

"Stop, Valde," Cartwell shouted. "No one man can claim her power. Your lackeys believed your rubbish and tried to help you, but they were wrong. No one can have such power."

"I can, you bloody fool."

In the shadows, Harry was approaching the Royal Society men from behind. But Valde lifted both his hands. Lightning bolts shot from his hands, like Mrs. Darkwell's, yet much weaker. But they struck the men and knocked them back.

"Stop right there." Harry came forward, pointing his bow.

Lightning flew at him, and she screamed.

The bolt exploded in midair, and the lightning burst against Harry's chest, driving him back.

"Stop!" she cried. "I will give you anything."

Valde lifted his hands, palms pointing toward her. But as the streak of light burst from his hands, it exploded in a brilliant flash in front of Ophelia's eyes. Valde screamed, and when Ophelia could see again, she saw Valde on his knees, wailing with pain, his hands over his eyes.

"You foolish boy." Mrs. Darkwell stepped forward, pain

etched in her beautiful face, making her look much older and haggard.

"Ophelia!"

Ravenhunt's voice! She looked up. He was limping down the stairs, with Guidon's arm flung across his shoulders, and he was carrying the smaller vampire. Thank heavens they were both . . . alive. He set Guidon on his feet and ran to her.

Mrs. Darkwell turned to her. A tear trickled down the smooth, perfect cheek. "I am sorry, Lady Ophelia. My son wanted your power. I foolishly let him learn about it. He has never been content because he is considered to be even less than a half-blood. He resented his lesser place, and that he is not accepted amongst the gods."

"Damnation, Mother, you have blinded me," Valde howled. "How could you do such a thing to your own son? But it doesn't matter—I can see with my senses, with my powers."

Mrs. Darkwell cried out and rushed toward her son. "No, my dear. Stop—"

Lightning shot from his hands. A stream of it shot into Ravenhunt, ripping into his flesh. Ophelia screamed, then a vivid shot of light hit her.

Terror. Agony. Wild, awful screams tore from her lips.

She was burned. Bleeding.

But Ravenhunt was on his knees, and he was—

Oh, it was awful.

She hurt, but he seemed to have been torn apart. It made her sick to look at him. He slumped to the ground.

Dimly, she heard voices—many voices. Brookshire and his men had arrived, but they were too late. As if through a thick fog, Ophelia heard Mrs. Darkwell cry out, "You must carry them inside. They will be destroyed. I will punish my son, but you must take them into the church."

She couldn't let Raven go. She wouldn't.

21

Pleasure Forever

Warm, soft hands caressed his face. His head rested on a place as soft as a silken pillow.

Raven opened his eyes and saw Ophelia's pale, terrified face hovering over him. She was cradling his head on her lap. His blood soaked his trousers and his shirt, and cold seeped into him as fast as his blood leached out. The power that Valde, the demigod, had thrown at him had almost torn him apart.

The bolt of energy had struck Ophelia, too. She needed him—he should be tending to her, not lying in her lap. But his strength seemed to have exploded out of him when the bolt hit him, and he could barely move.

"I can save you if you turn me," she whispered. Her breath was blessedly warm by his icy ear. "Please turn me."

"No," he said weakly.

Mrs. Darkwell got to her knees at his side, her black skirts flowing around her. The woman's pale face looked almost ghostly, her expression as stern as a schoolmistress. "Why won't you change her, Lord Ravenhunt?"

"I—" Raven fought for strength. "I would be condemning her to the hell of being a vampire for eternity."

"Is it truly hell, Ravenhunt?" the woman demanded. "You have seen the vampires of the Royal Society. Do they look as if they are in hell? *You* were in hell, Ravenhunt, because you did not have love. Now you do. Stop being so foolishly noble, and save the woman you love. I will slap you if you do not hurry up."

Felie managed a smile at Mrs. Darkwell's angry order.

"My son told you her power will destroy her, did he not?"

"Yes," he croaked.

Mrs. Darkwell turned to Felie. "You can destroy your power if you have the strength of a vampire. The only way to save her and yourself, Ravenhunt, is to change her."

"All right, woman." He found the strength to snap at her. "Then leave us in peace. I want this to be special between Felie and me."

"Of course, my lord."

Out of his dimming sight, he saw her rise. Gruffly he added, "I owe you my life. Do not call me 'my lord.' I am not one anymore, and I am your servant."

A glowing smile transformed Mrs. Darkwell's face into something extraordinarily beautiful, with skin that shimmered and enormous eyes that were a vivid blue. She inclined her head gracefully, then retreated.

Leaving him to change Felie.

"I'm sorry if this hurts," Raven whispered. "You're going to have to bend down to me so I can bite you."

He brushed hair from her neck, cupped his hand around the slender column. Then he frowned. "You're cold."

Ophelia struggled to give him a weak smile. Sight and sound grew more indistinct as if layers of muslin were being tossed on her head. Her fingers . . . her feet . . . she couldn't feel them anymore.

"I was shot, too," she whispered. "Just after you fell. I didn't want you to know."

"I have to turn you. To save you."

"Don't care if it hurts," she murmured. It was getting hard to speak. "Do it."

Raven's hand stroked her neck. "Oh angel," he muttered, then his hair tickled her neck and her chest as he drew her neck down and his face lifted to her throat. Something cold and sharp touched her skin just below her jaw, and she caught her breath. Stupid to be afraid of pain when death lurked just behind them both, waiting to drag both of them away.

Gently, Raven licked her skin. That brought a weak smile to her lips, and a tingling sensation to her neck. His hand cupped her face, his thumb brushed her mouth. It felt as if sparks had landed on her lips.

"Do not worry." Mrs. Darkwell spoke in firm tones from the gathering darkness surrounding Ophelia. She could not see anything beyond Raven anymore.

"You love her so you cannot hurt her." The goddess's voice broke at the end. Ophelia heard a sob, and it stunned her.

"Now, love," Raven whispered.

A swift, hot pain punctured her neck. The strangest, most frightening sensation of rushing water went through her throat. It was her *blood*.

Weakly, she tried to pull back, afraid of the feeling. He kept caressing her, and a warm, calming sensation washed through her. The rushing feeling was gone. She felt as if she were floating, turning slowly in the air, hovering just a little above the floor.

An aching feeling grew between her legs. She shifted her hips. The sensation between her thighs became a hungry, demanding throb.

She wanted him. *Now*. She was on fire for him.

She didn't care that she was weak. Even that he was. Forcing her numb arms to move, Ophelia caressed him all over—his shoulders, his chest, his bare arms, then lower, to stroke his hips and the bulge in his trousers, while she wriggled madly, on fire with need.

Then she opened her eyes wide and she couldn't see anything. The warmth went away like a candle's flame disappeared when snuffed. Cold attacked her. Remorseless cold.

She slumped back, falling to the floor, but instead of hitting hard, she seemed to land the way a feather would.

Raven got up and moved over her. She couldn't see him, but she would sense him. His warm, hard forearm pressed to her mouth. She knew from the iron-hard feel of it, the ropy veins, the taste of his skin. Another taste touched her almost numb lips. Coppery. Wet. Hot.

He held her so she had to keep her mouth in his blood.

"Drink," he coaxed. "Drink, Felie. It will save you."

Drink his blood. Courage failed her. She couldn't swallow. But it was leaking between her lips, filling her mouth. Finally, reflexively, her mouth moved. Her jaw ached, and her teeth felt strange, as if they were growing larger in her mouth. She felt her teeth bite into his skin and she took his blood in.

She meant to gag. She expected to be sick. But the taste changed as it flowed into her and became something delicious. More intoxicating than wine, sweeter than cream and candy. She craved more.

Her lips worked against his soft, beautiful skin. The motion, the pressure, drew more blood into her mouth. She didn't care that it was strange or should be terrible. This was *joining* them.

He held her closer, fed her his blood, then his hand caressed her. His palm lightly nudged her left breast, bumping it.

An instant climax exploded in her. She cried out against his arm, and her body arched helplessly as pleasure shattered in her head.

He held her so close and so tightly, and he kissed her all over her eyebrows, her eyelids, her forehead, her nose, her cheeks. She'd never felt anyone show love to her like this.

She hadn't died, but now she knew what heaven was. It was the glorious power of love.

"You," Ophelia said quickly. "I have to save you. How do I do it?"

"Your blood," said Mrs. Darkwell from the edge of the room, from the doorway. "Do what he did. Cut your wrist and feed him your blood."

"Cut it—?"

"With your teeth, my dear. You will find you now have fangs."

Blood stained her lips a rich scarlet. The pallor of her skin was gone. Raven knew what that shattering cry meant. The transformation had made her come. In the afterglow of her orgasm, color bloomed in Ophelia's cheeks and her blue eyes glowed like sapphires.

With eyes wide, she looked at him tentatively as her tongue slid around her teeth. When she found the tips of her brand-new fangs, she cried, "Oh!"

She lifted her wrist to her teeth and gently rubbed the tips of her long, curved white fangs over the delicate skin. She grimaced.

"No, Felie," he protested.

"Yes." Shutting her eyes tight, she pushed her teeth into her wrist. She gave a cry of shock and pain, then sliced her fangs along her wrist so a line of blood welled. Her scarlet, sweet-scented blood.

She bravely held out her wrist, with a droplet racing down her arm. "Drink, Raven. Please."

Shifting so he sat on his arse, he pulled her onto his lap and cradled her close to his chest. Raven bent until his lips caressed the top of her hair and he kissed her. God, he wanted to kiss her everywhere.

He couldn't hurt her now by taking her blood. Closing his

eyes, he drank in the perfume of her blood—like heaven flowing through her—and put her wrist to his mouth.

Ambrosia must taste like stewed mutton compared to this. His head soared like a drunken man's. His body was hot in an instant, his cock rigid.

Fight the pleasure of it. Don't take all her blood.

The words thrummed through him as he drank, as her blood flooded into his mouth. His cock pulsed, feeling as if her warm hand stroked it. Up and down in a sensual, erotic rhythm.

His breath came fast. *Don't drink so much. Stop.*

He couldn't stop. Damn, he was going to come. Like usual, once he was rushing to his orgasm, he was out of control.

Don't trust me, Felie. Stop giving me your blood, take your wrist away. I'm an animal. That's what I am. A mindless monster—

No, you aren't. You aren't an animal or a monster. You are the man I love. I trust you.

Her words broke the spell. Raven's heart slowed. Lust stopped driving him. He didn't have to rush to a climax and mindlessly take her blood. He wasn't a slave to his vampiric nature. He damn well wasn't.

He was in control. He could be free. He could be the kind of vampire who could be a husband.

For the first time, Raven knew he wanted a future. He wanted to fight for eternity with Felie.

Panic hit him with that thought. All his bitter thoughts slammed into him. Margaret's tears and desperation. The empty horror when he'd learned she had killed herself and taken her unborn baby with her. All the young men he'd watched die on the battlefield. His victims—

I love you, Ophelia said firmly in his thoughts. *I know I am not wrong to do so.*

He pulled back and released her wrist. Before his eyes, the wound marring her pale skin began to knit. Her skin now glowed like pearl, as if an inner fire burned within and yearned to radiate out. He kissed her cut as it healed before his eyes.

His strength came back with a rush. Knowledge came faster: he owed his very life to her.

"You're alive," she whispered.

"Thanks to you." Words failed him. His throat was so tight he couldn't have made a pretty speech if he tried. "Thank God, you're alive."

"She is undead," Mrs. Darkwell corrected. "She is your mate, to be with you for eternity."

His for eternity. He loved the sound of that. Throughout his mortal life, he'd heard people speak of their hearts swelling. Now Raven knew what it meant. His heart felt larger, filled by love.

He gazed down at Felie, who lay in his lap. "I've made you a vampire, but I promise we will go to the vampires of the Royal Society and learn how to live with mortals so we do not act as predators. I want to change. For you."

"Again, I love you, Raven."

He had never said the words, for he'd believed he had no right to say them. Strange how easily they came now. "I love you, Ophelia."

Gleeful clapping sounded behind them. Raven jerked around to look. Guidon stood beside Mrs. Darkwell in the doorway, and he applauded merrily. Beaming from ear to ear, the gnome-like vampire gazed up at Mrs. Darkwell and clasped her elegant hands. Laughing, Guidon proclaimed, "You have completed your labors, my darling, my beautiful daughter of Aphrodite. You have found love for all of these happy young couples. Now, you can go free."

He lifted her hand and kissed it.

Mrs. Darkwell nodded slowly. "This was my gravest challenge. I was told that her mate was a vampire assassin, and I knew I could not take her power away from her until she found him. It has been a hard journey for you, Ophelia. I wish I could have made it easier, but then, you two might not have found love."

Ophelia sat up from his lap. Despite disheveled hair, torn clothes, and traces of blood on her neck, her cheeks, she looked gorgeous. His heart soared.

"We were destined for each other?" she asked bluntly.

"Yes," said Mrs. Darkwell. "It was my duty to find soul mates for you girls. You are the last of my labors. And now, if you will stay still, I will take your power away. Forever. As a mortal, you would not have survived it. But now that you are a vampire, you are strong."

"But what about your son?" Ophelia asked softly. "What did you have to do to him? Not destroy him—?" She, who had feared she could hurt her family, could not imagine how horrible that would be.

"I had to imprison him again. He is safe and this time I will ensure he does not escape. He will have his freedom if he changes, if he learns to set aside his bitterness and hatred."

"He will," Guidon insisted gently. "We will help him."

"Are they safe?"

Raven recognized the concerned feminine voice. Lady Brookshire. "Yes, my lady," he called out. "We've survived. Ophelia is my soul mate for eternity, and Mrs. Darkwell, a demi-goddess intends to free her, finally and completely, from her power."

He moved to his feet with one swift, strong motion, holding Felie in his arms, and he set her down gently on her feet. She stood strong, but he kept his arm around her waist.

"Very possessive of you, Ravenhunt." Lady Brookshire smiled knowingly. She wore breeches, boots, and a masculine coat, and rested a loaded crossbow by her thigh. Her cheeks were pink; her silver-green eyes sparkled with delight. "I know what happens next. A very private happy ending. Ophelia, do you wish us to leave now?"

Felie hurried to Lady Brookshire and clasped her friend's hands. "Yes, I am transformed now, and I feel so—"

"Strong?" asked Lady Brookshire. "And perhaps"—she lowered her voice—"somewhat aroused?"

Felie blushed. She saw that Guidon and Mrs. Darkwell had moved into the room, and stood together, by the fireplace.

"All right, we will leave now. You and Ravenhunt should be alone. We'll leave a carriage to take you home."

With that, she was gone.

Raven only had eyes for Felie, but he heard Guidon say softly. "It is time, my dear. Touch her and take her power. Then the curse will be at an end and you will be free. I believe Lady Ophelia is the one hundredth young lady who has found love."

Mrs. Darkwell moved across the room like an angel flowing over a cloud. She smiled and laid her hands gently on Felie's shoulders. Felie cried out, and he raced across the floor, ready to catch her, to help her.

But she squealed with joy. "I feel—I feel brighter! I can't explain it, but I do."

She threw her arms around his neck, almost knocking him off his feet. Her lips touched his, and an explosion rocked Raven in a ripple of the ground and a flash of color and light.

Ophelia pulled back.

She looked to Raven, and saw his brows jerk up. "What—what in Hades just happened?" he muttered.

She spun to see what could have startled a vampire, fear gripping her heart. Guidon was gone. In his place was a tall, handsome blond gentleman who had no clothing at all.

"Go," Aphrodite's daughter said, shooing them with very ungoddess-like motions. "You have finally found happiness. I know where I would rush to if I were you."

She smiled wickedly.

Ophelia grasped Ravenhunt's hand. She gazed into his gleaming black eyes. "Bed!" she declared, at the exact moment he said it.

Hand in hand, they left the abandoned church, where a carriage waited. Her brother's. The footman bowed. "His lordship has left us at your service, my lady."

"Where should we go?" she asked.

"Home—I want my home to be yours now."

"All right," she agreed. "But only if I can decorate it."

He laughed, and she loved the rich, delighted sound. As he handed her into the carriage, he admitted, "Before you, I don't think I ever laughed in my life. Even when I was young, I never had any reason to laugh since I knew my father blamed me for my mother's death. You've brought me pleasure and happiness."

"This is what I always dreamed of having," she said softly. "But that's what love brings, doesn't it? Well, perhaps not happiness and laughter for every moment. But it gives us the strength so we can laugh. Even when there are hard times, or pain, or fear, love gives us the strength to endure."

She settled in the seat, and he sat at her side.

"I hated Mrs. Darkwell for keeping me a prisoner," she continued, "but I must thank her, for she found love for me."

"I think she has been well rewarded."

"I am so happy Guidon's curse is ended. I like him very much."

Raven grinned. "I never would have guessed that was what he actually looked like."

"It's not his looks that are important, Raven. Mrs. Darkwell loved him even when he was a little gnome-like man, and that was because he is intelligent, caring, and has a good and noble heart. Those are the important things."

"So if I were cursed to look like Guidon, you would still love me?"

"Always," she said firmly.

The carriage lurched away.

"When we go to bed," Felie said softly, "I want you to tie me up. I—I know I don't need to do it anymore, since I can touch you. But I liked it."

Raven stared in amazement.

"Oh dear, you aren't shocked, are you?"

"When it comes to lovemaking, Felie, I hope you shock me every day of our lives together. For eternity."

Candlelight illuminated Raven's remarkably sculpted derriere. Squinting at the clay in front of her, Ophelia drew her carving tool along the curve she'd formed, trying to match exactly the beautiful muscular shape that defined Raven's delectable rump.

She didn't have much time, as they were due to leave very soon. She set down her tools, got up, and walked to her model. He stood in a pose, naked, holding a bow and arrow.

She had to make certain she got this right. She just had to explore those firm cheeks of his a little more—

His rigid cock jolted as she fondled his rump.

Meeting her eyes, Raven groaned. "I'm in pain, love. I need a break. An erotic break."

"Again?" She gave a teasing pout. "But this will be the fourth one. This sculpture will never be finished at this rate. Every time I make any progress, you insist on stopping."

He gazed at her with ink-black rueful eyes. "Felie, you spend as much time fondling me as you do sculpting. I'm not strong enough to resist getting aroused when you stroke my arse."

"Think of this as building fortitude—"

She broke off as he tossed down his bow, cupped her chin, and drew her to him. A shiver rushed over her. He lifted her gently, so she had to stand on tiptoe, and he slowly let his mouth play over hers.

In a long, smoldering, melting kiss, quivers tumbled down to hit the throbbing pulses of desire in her quim, and she gasped into his mouth. She ached for him. Needed him. Hungered for him.

"I want to be tied up," she whispered, when he let her catch her breath. It was just for fun now, and how she loved it.

He said nothing. He did not have to. She just knew from the hotter light in his eyes exactly what he was going to do.

He lifted her and put her over his shoulder.

He'd built this studio for her in his attic, and it was equipped with a sumptuously appointed daybed: silk sheets, thick rose-scented pillows, and gilt-decorated frame. Downstairs his servants took care of the house. In the month they'd been together, she had helped him change the entire house. True, as vampires, they were creatures of darkness, but she had used her artistic eye to make their nocturnal world beautiful— lush fabrics, many candles, rooms opened.

Raven gently laid her on the bed. Then worry struck. "Do we have time?"

"Very little," he admitted.

"Then you shall have to tie me up quickly," she admonished, and she put her hands above her head, wrists locked.

He looped a black velvet rope—kept conveniently by the daybed—around her wrists.

"Ooooh," she murmured at the soft stroke of velvet on her sensitive skin. How she loved this—this was the only fun way to be a captive, to be mastered by a handsome, black-haired vampire who loved to give her pleasure.

He tied a firm knot, and she played her part of the game, tugging on the rope to prove it was secure and she was his prisoner.

Grinning as she fought the rope, Raven bent and flicked his tongue over her right nipple. It hardened and stood up instantly. She moaned, closing her eyes, and arching her back so he would take her nipple in his mouth and suck her hard.

But he never let her take command so early in the game. He played with the aching tips with his tongue, licking and laving with agonizing leisure.

"The time," she groaned. "We have to begin to dress."

His tongue left her nipple, which was not at all what she'd wanted. Opening her eyes, she saw him holding another length of rope. He eyed the juncture of her thighs beneath her skirts.

"Maybe they'll wait for us," he murmured. Slowly, oh so slowly, he eased her skirts upward.

"They won't," she gasped, as her hems reached her knees.

"Not for late guests," she added, moaning as the fabric glided over her thighs.

"Not at a wedding," she squeaked as her skirts were thrown up, covering her bare breasts. "Not when they are marrying at night just so we can *attend* the ceremony."

"Don't worry, my love. I can bring you to orgasm very quickly."

"We have mere minutes."

"Watch me." A playful grin touched Raven's lips, and her heart melted at the sight. How she loved to see him smile. Even though when they were together his lips always lifted in happiness, she never tired of drinking in a grin, a teasing smirk, a soft, genuine smile. Each one made her heart ache with joy.

Raven slid the rope between her legs, and she cried out as it stroked through her nether lips and rubbed along her clit. He looped it around her hips, which pulled it tighter, until it was sawing her hard clit and was soaked with her juices. She was panting, almost ready to explode in pleasure.

"Not yet, love."

He moved up between her parted legs on his knees. Lifting her hips, he let her bottom rest on his thighs. His erect cock poked her bottom.

"Deep in your ass today, my angel?"

The words robbed her of speech. She squirmed and that tugged the rope, which stroked her clit. *Yes, oh yes, please.*

His hands cupped and firmly massaged her bottom. That alone made her head loll back in delight against the bed. His thumb moved against the strips of rope positioned between her bum cheeks.

He held his iron-hard cock against her entrance.

She was ready for him, so aroused her tight little opening was slack and open in invitation.

His thumb dipped in, teasing the sensitive rim. Then his cock slid in. So huge, yet she loved to be so full.

Panting, she rocked her hips up and down, taking every inch of him up her derriere. He gently thrust his hips, shoving deep. So deep she felt his groin slap her ass.

God, it was so good with the rope rubbing her clit, his rock-hard prick sliding in and out of her rump. So good. Heavenly good.

"Raven!" She screamed his name at the impact of her climax. It showered over her, thrilling her, taking her, commanding her. Just as he commanded her.

"Felie," he gasped. His hips drove against her, making her rump jiggle, as he banged his cock deep. He arched back, and heat and fluid rushed inside.

He rocked against her and he was commanded by his orgasm, by their shared pleasure.

Then his head dropped forward, and he took ragged breaths. "Heaven," he muttered. "Fucking you is like touching heaven."

She giggled. "We must get ready. You are to be the best man, at the groom's side."

"And you are maid of honor. Though not a maid much longer."

"What do you mean?" She frowned.

He winked, then left the daybed. He returned with an ewer of cool water and a cloth, and he cleaned her studiously. But he didn't untie her.

When he finished, he tossed the cloth in the porcelain pitcher but still left her wrists bound.

"Won't you let me go?"

"I'd like to keep you my captive a little longer. To do this—"

Long strides took him to his clothes, lying across the arm of a leather chair. He searched the pocket of his tailcoat. Holding something in his palm, he returned.

He approached the daybed from the side. She wriggled her fingers, now feeling more anxious. Time was ticking past, and she refused to be late for the wedding of Harry and Frederica. "Raven—"

"Ophelia, will you marry me? I am deeply, passionately in love with you, and I want you to be my wife forever."

The words poured out in a rush. Her commanding vampire blushed. Then he held out his hand. Between his index finger and thumb he held a ring bearing a huge, heart-shaped ruby. A bloodred ruby.

Leaning over her, he slipped it on the ring finger of her bound left hand.

"I haven't answered yet," she pointed out.

"I didn't want to give you the chance to say no," he muttered.

"Say no? You truly thought I might? After everything we have been through, you thought there was any chance at all I might refuse you?"

He nodded. "I did take you prisoner, after all, and I—"

"My answer is yes!" she broke in. "Yes, I love you. Yes, I want to be with you forever."

A second later, he kissed her, a lush, long, breathtaking kiss. His hands tore through the cords holding her wrists, and he undid the ones teasing her quim.

"Now, can we go to the wedding?" she breathed. "Though I do have one more surprise for you, Raven."

He looked so surprised, she giggled. "I am *enceinte*, Raven. We are going to have a child."

He closed his eyes and rocked back. Then he grinned. And let out a whoop of joy. He drew her into his arms, lifting her off the bed, and spun her around.

"I never believed I could be so happy," he whispered against her ear.

"Nor I. Now, we must hurry. We have a wedding to attend."

"The next one will be ours. Ophelia, my love, my heart will be bound with yours for eternity."

He kissed her again, and Ophelia knew her dress and hair were going to be done rather hastily for the wedding, for all she wanted to do was make love to her fiancé.

Again and again and again.

Turn the page for a special excerpt of the new book in
Katana Collins's Soul Stripper series:

SOUL SURVIVOR

*With immortality comes a craving that can't be satisfied,
a need never fulfilled . . .*

An Aphrodesia trade paperback on sale now.

1
———————

The neon-colored lights were blinding as they swooped around the club like laser beams. First purple. Then green. Now blue. It felt like I was in the middle of a lava lamp, watching them spin around me. With the little straw stirrer, I sipped my Long Island iced tea and kept dancing. Sweaty men bumped into me from all angles, each attempting to brush my ass or breasts, in the hopes I might look up and give them even the slightest bit of attention. If only they knew just how deadly my attention could be.

Kayce, my best friend, grabbed my elbow and swung me around, our noses almost bumping in the process. Even with immortal hearing, I could barely make out what she was saying over the thumping of the bass. Grabbing the back of my head, she pulled me in closer, her lips on my ear. "I think I found two!" she yelled.

For normal girls on the town, this could mean anything—two seats, two bucks, two drinks. For two succubi on the town? It meant victims. We prey on the local men and women here in Las Vegas to satiate the raging itch between our legs and sustain our immortal souls on Earth.

With her hand still wrapped around the back of my neck, she turned me toward two college-aged guys who were staring at us, transfixed, while their clammy hands clenched plastic cups spilling over with cheap beer.

My head snapped back to Kayce. "They're so *young*," I said, noting their auras, silver and sparkling. These two were Heaven-bound for sure.

"I thought you didn't care anymore?" Her gaze narrowed.

My stomach twisted, guilt trying to gnaw its way out as if some little animal had burrowed into there. I pushed the feeling aside. "I don't," I shouted over the music with a nonchalant shrug. I was bluffing. If Kayce knew I was lying, then she chose to ignore it.

"What do you say we give them a little something to look forward to?" she said as a devious grin crept its way across her face. She nestled her body into mine, pulsing to the beat of the music. Running her hands through my shoulder-length blond curls, she sent a wicked glance to the two guys watching, their mouths hanging agape. "C'mon, girl," she whispered. "It's show time."

I moved to the music with her, running my fingers down her open, bare back. We turned in rhythm so that I was looking directly at the leaner college kid; he had surfer blond hair that flopped to one side and full lips. An itch surged through my core, shooting between my legs and my mouth went dry. A droplet of sweat tickled its way down the side of my face along my hairline and I quickly shapeshifted it away, making sure to settle my makeup, yet again. Drinking was making me sloppy with my appearance—and I had it much easier than most humans. With one hand, I swept Kayce's curtain of jet-black hair to the side and ran my lips ever so gently up her neck to her ear. My eyes stayed on the college kid as I darted out a tongue that barely grazed her earlobe.

Her fingers splayed against my scalp, weaving into my hair

and she tugged my neck back. "Which one do you want?" she whispered. With my eyes closed, nose aimed at the ceiling, I could feel her kisses as they trailed down my throat. When I finally opened my eyes again, I turned around, still on the beat, dropped myself down the ground, and swiveled my hips back to a standing position.

"Surfer boy. We've been staring at each other," I answered as though I were ordering mustard on a sandwich.

"Okay, then," she answered. "That leaves me with the mocha candy."

The crowd on the dance floor had parted, and there was now a group of people circled around us, watching. Men gazed hungrily and women scowled, eyes red and angry. Their jealousy surged a bolt of energy into me. Even though I used to be an angel, that bad-girl side wins out every time. An angel turned succubus—I was a creature no one in the demon or angel realm could explain. The succubus with a soul.

The song ended and Kayce took my hand, leading me to the two guys. "This is Monica," she said, running a fingernail down the length of the other guy's bicep, which bulged beneath his Hollister polo shirt.

Surfer boy took my hand in his. "I'm Paul," he said. His palm was sweaty and after the handshake ended, I wiped my hand on my slinky, sequined dress, not caring if it stained. That's the beauty of shapeshifting. It took a lot of my focus not to slink away, hoping that none of his other body parts were *that* sweaty.

Kayce already had a leg wrapped around the other guy, pressing herself against him to the beat. I grabbed Paul's hand and pulled him off the dance floor. I wasn't quite the exhibitionist Kayce was. The bathroom was an extremely modern design with clear glass walls that fogged over as soon as you locked the door, so that no one could see in. I tugged Paul inside, locking the door behind me. The glass fogged, encasing us, and making it look as if the entire club on the other side of the glass had filled with mist instantaneously. He grabbed me from behind and turned my hips back to him, his hands squeezing my waist in a way that suggested a carnal need. Our lips rushed to find each other's and his hands cupped my jaw. Bright blond hair flopped forward into his face and I brushed it back, my fingernails running through the silk-like strands. My tongue found his and they twisted around each other.

With my eyes closed, it was easy to pretend for a moment the hair belonged to Drew—my human manager at the cafe where I worked during the day. I pretended that those lips were fuller with a tiny scar slicing across the top. Pretended that this college boy's hands were more calloused and weathered from years of hard work as they circled and caressed my body.

An apelike grunt pulled me back to reality. Cool air tickled my puckering nipples and it wasn't until that moment that I realized he had pulled my dress down over my breasts. A raging erection poked through his jeans against my belly and the contact sent a jolt of electricity through my blood. I needed his life to survive—this wasn't about passion or even sex; it was survival. Never mind that I had had sex the night before as well. Never mind that I had chosen Paul because he had a slight resemblance to the man I loved but couldn't have. Never mind I probably could have gone two weeks without another conquest with all the Heaven-bound men I'd been seducing lately. Right now—all that mattered was the life force in front of me. A morality so strong that its power pushed on my gut causing the air to gush out of my lungs, leaving me breathless.

I shoved Paul against the opposite wall, wrapping my legs around his waist. As I propped myself on his hips, the dress slid up above my ass and I shapeshifted my panties away. One of the glorious things about having more sex than I need—I have plenty of power for superfluous shifting.

A finger slid inside me and I tensed my sex around him.

Again, I captured those pretty-boy lips in mine and drank him in. His soul was glistening, shimmering. He was going to be an amazing fix—the high would be electrifying. Much more so than the assholes and Hell-bound men I used to sleep with. And what's a week off their life in order for me to not be condemned to Hell? A week off their life so that I could maintain a human body and not be a drifting soul in the bowels of Hell. And in exchange, they get a night with me—sex extraordinaire. It's an even trade.

Okay, maybe not even, but it's the closest I can get to justifying my actions. Besides, my broken heart is still on the mend. Anonymous sex speeds up the healing process. Not only had I discovered Drew was working things out with Adrienne, but now she was the apprentice to my Julian. My old mentor back when *I* was an angel. I'd lost both the loves of my life to the same woman.

I shook the memory away, concentrating again on the fix that stood before me. I wasn't against falling in love—but I was against getting involved with humans or angels *ever* again. Demon dates only from now on. And the biggest downside to dating demons—they're a bunch of fucking assholes. But Paul was here in front of me. He was hot. And he wanted me. My job is to corrupt souls for Hell and steal their life force. I used to fight my duties . . . but these days, I was becoming friggin' employee of the year.

His arms, which had been holding me up by the ass, released me back to the ground. We both scrambled to get his pants off. I tore the pale blue polo shirt over his head and threw it on the floor. His hands wound through my golden, soft curls and just as I thought he was going to pull me in for another kiss, he grunted and pushed me to my knees.

Under normal circumstances, this sort of overt lack of regard for my sexual needs wouldn't fly. If I was training him to be a consistent lover at my beckoned need, then I would have taken the time to fight it. But for now, fuck it. I flicked a tongue out and ran it along the tip, then up and down the length of his shaft. His fingers still twisted in my hair, tightening their hold on me. He pulled my face closer to his cock. Done with the appetizer, he wanted the entree.

I grabbed his balls, squeezing perhaps a little too tightly, to where pain turned into pleasure. A gust of air whooshed from his lips, the sudden change from gentle to rough proving too much for him. Amateur. I took his entire length into my mouth, wrapping my lips tightly around his girth. My teeth just barely grazed against him as he fucked my mouth. With the skill of an expert, I used my other hand to grip the base of his dick, rotating my head with a swirl as I reached the tip. His head slammed against my throat.

"Fuck me with those stunning sucking lips, gorgeous." He was growing in size; getting bigger against my tongue. There was no way I was letting him get away with not doing any work. I lowered his hands from my hair and placed them on my breasts. His thumbs rolled over my pebbled nipples sending shock waves through my whole body. The ache between my legs grew and I pulled my mouth away before he could finish.

He groaned and tried to pull my head back towards his cock. Slapping his hands away, I stood, bending over the sink. I flipped my dress up past my hips. "Don't you want this instead?"

His eyes grew wide and licked his dry lips before approaching. Two large hands wrapped around my hips and the sides of my ass. The tip of his finger teased my opening, wet and slick and ready for him. The same hand traced around the curve of my ass and spanked me. It wasn't a hard slap, but I gasped in an exaggerated way. Finally, he pushed himself into me. Reaching around front, he flicked at my clit. My knees buckled with the small, but effective motions. The tension was building and I gripped the sink, body trembling, as an orgasm rolled over my body. The itch between my legs was fierce, reminding me that though it was pleasurable, this fuck was a necessity. I could come a hundred times for him, but until he spilled his seed on me, his soul—his energy—was safe.

Thanks to my succubus senses and inhuman reflexes, I saw him unlock the bathroom door before the fogged walls cleared. Within those milliseconds, I shifted my face to look like someone else. Just because Paul was an exhibitionist, didn't mean I had to be. Modesty might seem silly—being that I corrupt souls by fucking countless men each week—but I didn't like my Hellish duties to cross over into my day job. And even though most of these people here in the club were visiting from out of town, I didn't want to be known and recognized as the girl who was publicly getting it from behind. I did the same thing with my night job as a stripper—shift my looks slightly so that most people wouldn't necessarily recognize me during the day.

The walls around us cleared. See-through. "Oh yeah," Paul grunted and slapped my ass, squeezing it hard enough to leave a mark.

Grabbing a fistful of my hair and yanking my head back, he pushed into me with one final thrust. Sliding out just in time, he came all over my ass. It dripped down into my folds and the rush of his life force was like walking into an air-conditioned room after sweating outside on a hot summer's day. It momentarily took my breath away. His life reeled before my eyes, like I was watching an abridged version being projected before me. He'd graduate cum laude; move to Chicago; work in a boutique marketing firm before marrying and settling down in the suburbs. And lastly, he'd die of a heart attack.

Finally, I released the breath I'd been holding, thankful that

I hadn't stripped too much of his life. I pulled my dress back down over my ass and looked into the mirror above me. I was glowing, radiant with the new life force. Paul's life force.

I turned to face him, not bothering to shift back into my original features. He was so drunk on cheap beer, he wouldn't even notice I looked slightly different from before. I glanced quickly out at the line of people formed to watch our little performance, then touched his cheek, running a finger down his jawline. "Thanks, Paul."

His pupils were dilated, eyes wide, ready to party some more. Just a side effect of my poison. He was high on me. "Who says it has to be over?" He grabbed me around the waist, pulling me in for another kiss. The crowd of people watching outside whooped and hollered. I let him kiss me a moment longer before pulling away and handing him his pants.

"I say so," I said quietly, reaching for the door. "Oh, and Paul?" When I looked back over my shoulder, he still had the energy, but a dejected look was etched on his pretty, boyish face.

He straightened as I turned around, eyes wide and expectant. "Yeah?" he said, hopeful, zipping up his pants. Like a puppy, I imagined two floppy ears perking up.

"Never shove a woman's head to your dick without reciprocating the act yourself." His face dropped, all color draining quickly away. On an exhale, my shoulders slumped slightly. I spoke again, a tad more quietly this time. "And lay off the red meat, okay? I mean . . . it's just—it can be bad for your heart."

A writer, a wife, and a mother of two, Sharon Page holds an industrial design degree and also manages a scientific research and development program. She finds writing tales of sexy Regency rakes and seductive vampires is the perfect escape from her technical world. Sharon Page's style is "sharp, sexy, and will seduce you from the first page" (*Just Erotic Romance Reviews*). She can be reached at www.sharonpage.com.

blood fire

Feel the heat...

USA *Today* Bestselling Author

SHARON PAGE

APHRODISIA

INNOCENCE LOST

It was a night of exquisite rapture that changed Lady Octavia Grenville's life forever. Not only did she long for sexual pleasure—but as a succubus she needed it to survive. Now she is intent upon learning to control her powers and searching for the child she was forced to give up, a quest that takes her into the arms of the rake who ruined her . . .

PASSION FOUND

Matthew, the Earl of Sutcliffe, is not the man Octavia once knew. He is now a vampire, but one doomed to die in a fortnight unless he can win a woman's love. The only one he desires is Octavia, but she wants him merely as a sexual plaything, a source of erotic delight. Somehow he must expose his own heart in order to find hers . . .

USA Today Bestselling Author

SHARON PAGE

Dark rapture...

blood secret

GAMES OF PASSION

Lucy Drake is prepared to do all she must to save her family, even if that means giving herself as a sexual plaything to the Duke of Greystone. Desperate to keep her ability to shape-shift into dragon form a secret, she willingly enters an unfamiliar world of carnal ecstasy with the one man who is sworn to destroy all of her kind . . .

The Duke of Greystone will do whatever he must to discover the Drake family secret and uncover the whereabouts of his missing nephew. A vampire highly skilled in the ways of erotic pleasure and adept with games of dark seduction, he will prevail upon his sexual expertise to ensure Lucy's complete surrender . . .

blood
wicked

Hot blood and sweet release...

SHARON PAGE

APHRODISIA

DANGEROUS PLEASURE

Vivienne knows the dark secrets of London's desires. She fulfills them, twisting men's lust for her into the power and status of a courtesan. But she understands little about her own pleasure and the mysteries it commands. Until, that is, she meets Heath, a vampire capable of giving her profound ecstasy—but sworn to let her taste its release only once.

Heath's cravings for Vivienne sharpen into sweet torture as he guides her through erotic lessons, watching her abandon herself to ever-higher peaks of pleasure. As temptation melts away the bonds of his control, how long can either hope to survive?

Silent Night, Sinful Night

Unwrap me...

SHARON PAGE

MELISSA MacNEAL   CHLOE HARRIS

'Tis the season for sweet seduction and passionate pleasure. Let visions of sultry sex sweep away your inhibitions and savor the delights of these three erotic encounters...

WICKED FOR CHRISTMAS

Sharon Page

Every Christmas, Amelia Watson is reminded of the night Lord Dante Worthington asked for her hand in marriage, took her body in passion, then vanished the next day into the snow-covered streets of Regency London. Every Christmas, she wonders if it will ever happen again.

NAUGHTY OR NICE?

Melissa MacNeal

Anxious to escape her memories of Christmas past, Tess Bennett takes a train west to the mountains of Colorado. And when she meets the sexy and seductive Johnny Gazara, she realizes that a naughty night of erotic delights is just what she needs...

STOLEN CHANCES

Chloe Harris

Winston Matthews knows a thief when he sees one, even if she is stunningly beautiful. And so he offers himself as an easy target for a sensually sinful Christmas Eve seduction...